DIAMOND IN THE DARK

SAVAGE JEWELS
BOOK 1

POPPY JACOBSON

Copyright © 2022 Poppy Jacobson

Cover by Stellar Graphics.

This is a work of fiction. Names, characters, places, and incidents are the product of the author's imagination or used fictitiously. Any resemblance to actual persons, living or dead, events, or locales is entirely coincidental.

All rights reserved. No portion of this book may be reproduced in any form without permission from the publisher, except as permitted by U.S. copyright law. For permissions contact: poppyjacobsonbooks@gmail.com.

To Bertrand.

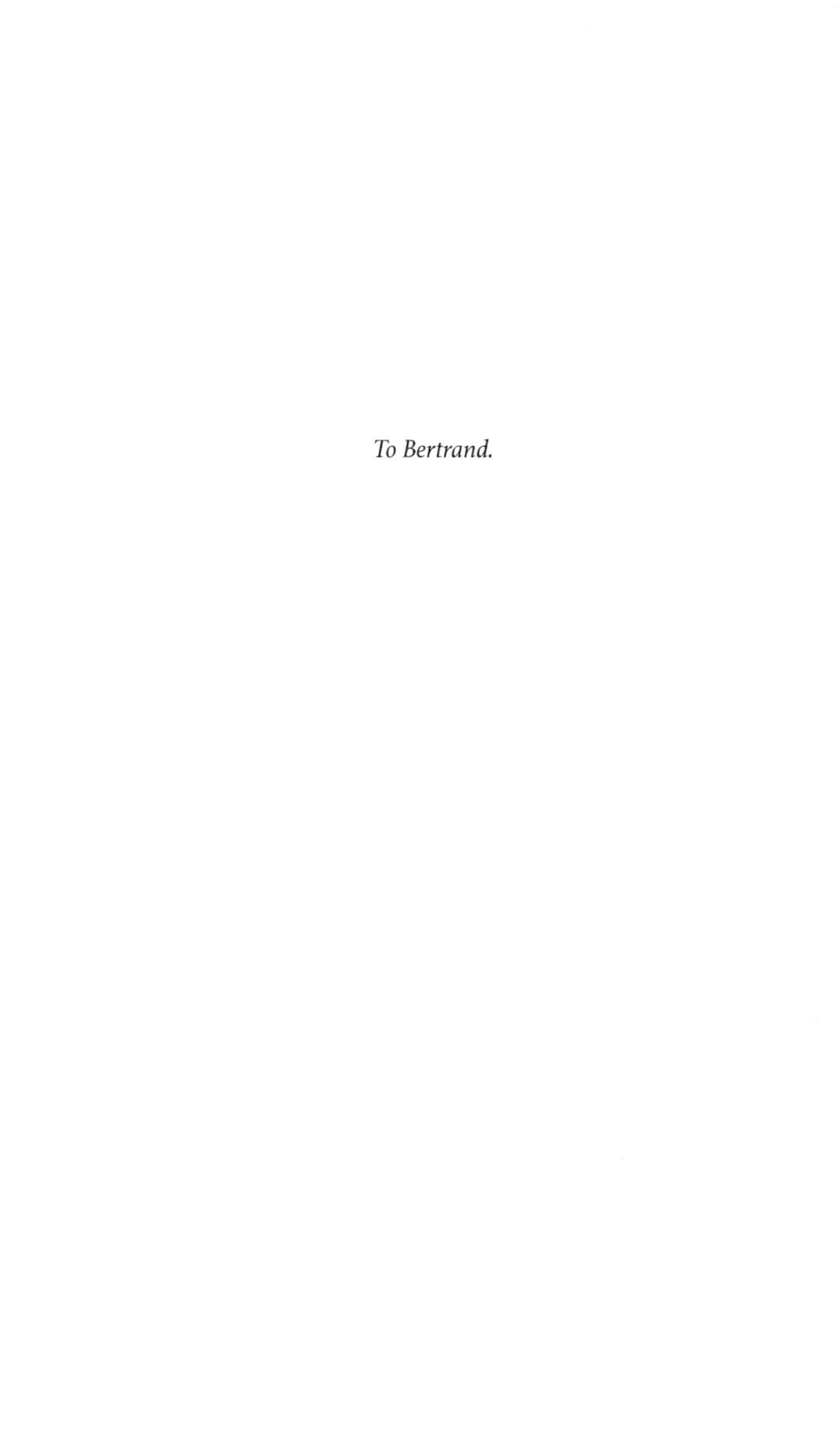

CONTENT NOTE

Diamond in the Dark is a dark and violent reverse harem romance intended for adult readers. Please visit my website at http://poppyjacobsonbooks.com for a content notes and detailed trigger warnings.

1

GINEVRA

"Pregnant," I said to my sister, my voice flat and furious. "You can't fulfill Papà's marriage contract with the Irish because you are fucking pregnant."

Silence weighed heavily on the other end of the line.

Fucking hell. I escaped that world ten years ago, and this fucking idiot was drawing me back in.

I stopped myself. I wasn't being fair. My sister was kind and sweet and compassionate and utterly fucking oblivious to the evil it took for my father to keep her in isolated comfort.

"Does our father know?"

Sofia's despondent sniffle answered my question.

"And our mother?"

"Mamma knows something's wrong, but she doesn't know what," Sofia whispered.

I didn't need to see her to know that tears streamed down her perfect face, turning her nose a delicate shade of pink and making her blue eyes shine. Even as an infant, she was one of those girls who only became more beautiful when she cried.

I pinched the top of my nose in hopes of staving off the oncoming migraine. "Who's the father, sis?"

Sofia was silent.

"Who is the father, Sofia?" I repeated, a tight edge to my voice. I couldn't help her if she didn't give me the information I needed.

"Sergio Accardi," she whimpered.

Fuck. *Fuck*. Accardi was a *capo* from a rival family, a top-level captain, but not an actual family member. My father would gain nothing from marrying her to him. Accardi, on the other hand, had everything to gain from knocking up my sister and trapping her into marriage. Ten years ago, he was a decent man. He treated my sister and me with respect and kindness. Today? I didn't know. I'd been gone too long, and I couldn't be sure of anything.

"Ginevra, Papà invited O'Conner over for dinner. He wants to sign the contracts tomorrow night," my sister wailed over the phone.

"Have you thought about getting an abortion?" I snapped, my temper getting the best of me.

The shocked silence on the other end of the line told me everything I needed to know. Sofia was a Catholic Italian-American raised by a traditional mafia family to be a good wife, an excellent hostess, and to look the other way no matter what her damn husband did.

"Right," I said, exhaling. "I'm sorry. I didn't think before I spoke."

Her voice broke. "I don't live in California, Gin. I live with Mamma and Papà, and I still go to mass every Sunday. I've never known anything else—"

"You don't want to know anything else," I interrupted. Again, I was being unfair. When I took off, our father locked Sofia down. With me out of the picture, she was the only remaining marriageable daughter. She'd graduated high school, but hadn't been allowed to go to college, and my father was arranging her marriage to a stranger.

"Does Luca know?" I asked, wondering if she'd clued in our brother. He was a classic middle child, an attention hound, but also a peacemaker.

"I haven't told him yet," Sofia said, her voice strengthening as she realized I might help. "What are you going to do?"

"I haven't spoken to him in months. He's going to know something's up as soon as I call," I warned her.

"Thank you, big sis," Sofia cried into the phone. "Thank you."

Fuck.

My housemate peered at me over his iPad as I hung up the phone. "You look like you need a drink."

It was nine in the morning, but who the fuck cared anymore? I walked to our fridge and opened the bottle of Cristal I'd been saving for the premiere of my next movie. I poured myself an overfull flute and did the same for Min-joon.

"Cheers," I toasted bitterly, clinking my crystal flute against his.

He watched me in silence, waiting for me to gather my thoughts. Min-joon and I met when we were in college. I'd been studying animation and computer science at UCLA, and he was going to film school. We'd been roommates for eight years, and he still didn't have a fucking clue who my people were and where I came from. It was safer for everyone that way.

"I'm going home," I started.

He shrugged. "You look like you're about to face a firing squad, not visit some assholes you haven't seen in a decade."

"I don't know if I'll be back," I finished.

Min-joon frowned, his brown eyes darkening as he realized I was completely, utterly, and absolutely serious. It was the only way to get my sister out of this mess without any loss of life.

The head of an Irish-American gang wouldn't marry into the mafia for love. He needed something only marriage would give him. And the only reason my father would agree to a wedding was if the situation was so dire he had no choice but to ask the Irish for help. This wasn't a problem I'd be able to solve in a day, or a week, or even a couple of months.

"Okay, bestie," he whispered, standing and taking my hand, pulling me into a hug. "How soon until I can come visit?"

My laugh turned into a sob, and I turned my face into his side, letting ten long years worth of tears finally fall.

Packing up my entire life in Los Angeles was easier than expected. I could theoretically run my company from anywhere, and Min-joon promised not to burn the house down or crash my car in my absence. I had friends, but this was Hollywood. Folks flitting off to see the world on a whim happened all the time.

Perhaps being on the East Coast could expand opportunities for my company in New York City. I shook my head. No, I was going home for Sofia. I was going to stay as long as it took to make sure she and my parents survived the disappointment of her big news, and then I was gone again. I hadn't left everything—fucking *everything*—to move across the country at eighteen just to get sucked back in a decade later because my sister couldn't figure out how to use birth control.

Jesus.

Dwelling on the unfairness of it all wasn't going to help me, and it certainly wasn't going to help Sofia.

It was late afternoon when I arrived in New York. I'd have to get a move on if I planned on arriving at my family's home before dinner.

I ducked into the business class arrivals lounge to freshen my face and change my shirt. The violet silk brought out the deep tan of my sunkissed skin. I yanked my dark brown hair back into a low ponytail and painted my lips a matte red. My mother wouldn't approve of the low-cut blouse or the bright lip color, but I needed to establish up front that I wasn't playing by the same rules as I had as a child. To the mob, appearances were everything.

I hailed a porter to grab my bags, including the hard case I'd checked my gun in, and then picked up my rental car. Yes, it was a giant black Land Rover. No, I wasn't concerned about its emissions. I wanted something I could ram through the locked gate of my parents' compound, if it came to that.

My thoughts were dark. Not for the first time on this trip, I regretted picking up the phone when Sofia called, revealing her pregnancy and pending nuptials. She and I spoke rarely these days. When I first left for school, I'd called her every week, but our lives drifted further and further apart as I separated myself from the family that birthed and raised me.

Too soon, I arrived at my parents' mansion, ostentatiously large in a city where locals couldn't afford rent anymore due to gentrification. A guard scurried over after I flashed my lights at the gate.

"I'm sorry, ma'am. This is a private residence. They're not expecting visitors tonight."

I took pity on him, passing him my driver's license.

The young man gaped at me. "I'm so sorry, miss, I'll let you in right away." He might not recognize my face, but he sure as fuck recognized my name.

I drove up the short driveway and parked by the front door. My eyes closed of their own volition, and I leaned my forehead on the top of the steering wheel, dreading the inevitable. The moment of no return was when I drove through the gate. The guard had already called my father's head of security. Still, it felt that stepping out of my vehicle and onto the gravel driveway was just as momentous a decision.

Before I could collect my thoughts, Alexi stood at my door, opening it and welcoming me home. I stepped out of the SUV into the cool night air.

"*Piccolina*," he exclaimed, enveloping me in a warm hug. "It has been too long."

I stepped back to look at my father's head of security, putting distance between us. Middle age had been kind to the man. His figure was still trim, and his gray hair lent him an air of merry kindness. I knew that air was false. Alexi would cheerfully murder anyone who threatened my family. When I left, he'd threatened to kill me if I spilled my family's secrets.

That's not why I kept my mouth shut, though. Despite the kidnapping and the horrific childhood I'd suffered, I still loved these assholes, and their absence in my life had left a gaping hole in my heart.

Alexi, though, could go fuck himself for threatening a sixteen-year-old who'd just had to execute her kidnapper.

I gestured to the back of the car. "I've got luggage. Would you have it taken to my room?"

He grabbed my wrist. "Tonight is not a good night for antics, Ginevra. They have company."

I scoffed. *He didn't know antics from the hole in his ass.* This wasn't a game, this was going to be a fucking rampage. I twisted away from him, plastering a smile on my face. "Just so there aren't any surprises, I'm packing, Alexi."

He raised his eyebrows. "In your family home?"

I shrugged. "It's been a decade. Would you please ask someone to take my bags up to my room, or any guest room, if mine's not still there?"

Alexi's smile was cruel. "Your mother turned your room into a guest room several years ago."

My answering smile was just as sharp. "Then I guess it's time for me to go say hello."

My mother trained her staff too well for anyone to show surprise as I swept into the house. It was all nods and, "Can I help you with that?" I waved my hand at the maid who tried to shuffle me off to a bedroom and strode into the dining room.

Shocked faces stared at me as I paused in the entryway. My sister, Sofia, gave a choked cry and leapt to her feet, running to embrace me in her delicate arms.

Mamma had updated the colors of the room, painting it, replacing the upholstery on the chairs, but the room still had the same formal air of my childhood. Light from the chandelier glinted off of mahogany wood, and the table was set for a formal dinner.

"Oh, Ginevra, I'm so glad you're here," Sofia said, her voice trembling.

I hadn't told her I was coming so her surprise would be genuine. Sofia couldn't act worth a damn.

"It's good to see you too, love." I stroked her blonde hair as her tears soaked into my silk shirt.

While the men in the room rose to their feet, their manners overtaking their surprise, my mother bustled over, smiling and sniffling and trying to contain the tears that smeared her make-up. I gently kissed each of her cheeks, and then she pulled me into her arms.

"Mamma," I whispered, my lips pressed against her ear. "I missed you too. But I'm interrupting a business dinner! Where are my manners? I'm sorry—I didn't expect you to have company."

My father rose from his seat. I couldn't get a read on him, but his manners were, as always, impeccable. "Nonsense, Ginevra. My eldest daughter is always welcome at my table. Please, let me introduce you."

One of the men at the table caught my eye, amused. Was I so transparent? He was gorgeous—pale skin, black hair, bright blue eyes, and a jawline that could fucking cut glass. Tattoos peeked out of his collar and the cuffs of his shirt.

My father introduced his guests. Beautiful Blue Eyes was Rian O'Conner, the man my father promised my sister to. His companions were Cormac Wallace, a stunning black man who looked at me with ice in his deep brown eyes, and Liam Byrne, a man whose red hair, green eyes, and freckles would have identified him as Irish from miles away, let alone his accent. Their attorney was a black woman named Olivia Gaines. I remembered Pietro Moretti, my father's consigliere, his attorney, and closest advisor.

I exchanged air kisses with my father while my brother Luca pulled out a chair to my father's left hand. My family's well-trained staff rapidly set a place for me while I greeted my father's guests. Luca squeezed my shoulders briefly, whispering, "Welcome back, big sister."

I'd missed the *primo*, the first course, but not the *segondo*, the more substantial course. My mother served veal paired with a Sicilian salad. Los Angeles had world class restaurants, but nothing beat my mother's touch in the kitchen.

My family were excellent hosts. We'd all been raised in a tradition that demanded strict courtesy at all times, and my family's guests were equally willing to make pleasant conversation during a delicious meal. I offered a prayer of thanks.

Dinner should've been a shitshow when I dropped in after a decade of absence. Instead, it was merely awkward as Mamma smoothed over the pauses with small talk.

After we'd finished our food and our wine and our coffee, my father clapped his hands, drawing our attention back to him. "I'd like to suggest we move to my study. Sofia, would you please escort your sister to her room?"

Sofia gasped. She quietly gathered her courage, and took a deep breath before straightening her shoulders. "Father, I'd like Ginevra to join us, if you don't mind."

Rian's eyes flicked to me again, dancing with amusement. *Fuck, I really was transparent.* "I don't mind, Antonio," he said, locking his eyes on mine.

He'd done me a favor and would expect me to pay him back for it. I held his gaze for a second longer than was comfortable and then nodded.

My father glared at Sofia and then at me. He sighed. "I should have known my *piccolina* wouldn't have come home just because she missed us." *Bullshit.* No way Papà hadn't surmised the reason for my presence the moment I walked in the door.

We traipsed to the study, where everyone arranged themselves on couches and armchairs. Like the dining room, my father's study remained untouched, unchanging, as if frozen in time since the moment I left. The deep reds and browns of the wood and leather furniture warmed the room, and books lined the walls. At one end of the room was my father's giant desk. I'd spent hours of my childhood sitting beside him, first alone, and then with Luca, as he'd taught us how to run his empire.

I strolled to my father's bar cart, which also hadn't moved in the decade I'd been gone, and poured a generous serving of whisky. When I looked up, I was staring straight into Cormac's dark brown eyes.

"Pour me one, darling?" he asked.

I handed him the generous pour I'd made for myself and, after a moment of rueful reflection, poured myself a more reasonable serving. As much as I craved the liquid courage, I'd need to keep my wits about me around these devilishly attractive men. Cormac hummed as he sipped, eyeing me over the rim of his glass. "I don't believe it's a coincidence you've come home tonight, Ginevra Russo."

No shit, Sherlock. I gazed up at him through my long lashes. "I guess you'll have to wait and see along with everyone else, won't you?"

He tilted his head and then toasted me with his glass. "Best of luck, then."

I WANDERED over to my father's desk, where a stack of documents waited for signature, in duplicate—a prenup between Rian and Sofia, a marriage contract between the families, and business documents, to sign over shares in each other's companies.

Hm. I couldn't rifle through the stack to see exactly what was on the line here, but I suspected it was more than a simple alliance. A gentle touch warmed the center of my back, and then slid downward until it hit the hard grip of my gun. The scent of sandalwood and leather washed over me.

"Beautiful *and* armed," a low voice murmured in my ear, as its owner rested his hand on my hip, lightly gripping me with his fingers. My heart rate sped up at the possessive touch.

Rian O'Conner stood beside me, staring down at the papers on my father's desk. "What are you up to, princess?"

I met his clear blue eyes and bit my bottom lip. "I don't know what you mean, Rian. I just came home to visit my family."

"After a decade, on the night your father's set to sign your sister's engagement contracts? You've got to be fuckin' kiddin' me."

I saluted him with my glass and pulled away. Hopefully he hadn't heard my sharp intake of breath when he trailed his fingers over the top of my ass, leaving a sensual heat in his wake.

Sofia sat on the couch with my mother. I took my place beside her, a bastion of femininity in the otherwise very masculine study. Her delicate hand trembled in mine as I wrapped my fingers around hers. "It's going to be okay."

My mother must have heard because she gave me a sharp look.

The two lawyers reviewed the contracts in detail. In exchange for my sister's hand in marriage, O'Conner would pay the Russians ten million dollars in my father's name, as well as investing in a number of his legitimate businesses. *What the hell?*

My mouth must have dropped open because Liam winked at me and tapped his chin. I snapped it closed, but couldn't hide the surprise in my eyes. My father's businesses were in bad shape. *What had happened while I was gone?*

When my father gestured for Sofia to stand to sign the prenup, she shook her head violently. "I can't," she whispered.

"What do you mean, you can't, little bird?" Rian asked softly.

"I mean, I can't marry you, Rian."

He narrowed his eyes and focused them on her. I squeezed her hand in reassurance. "You can't, or you won't?"

Sofia took a deep breath and then burst into tears. "I'm pregnant!' she wailed.

My father paled and leaned over his desk, his hand on his heart. My mother rushed to his side while he sat, shaking, sweat beading on his clammy forehead. "No," he whispered in disbelief.

Rian smiled viciously. "Then there's no need for any of this. I'll simply take over your territory and be done with it." I felt the rage radiating off of him from across the room. This was not a man used to being thwarted. Cormac's face was blank, but I could see from his clenched fists that he, too, was furious at the news. Liam was harder to read. He tried to maintain his cheerful visage, but anger peeked through in the tightness around his blazing green eyes.

My mother stroked my father's hair. The tiny woman who'd raised me, who'd turned a blind eye to my father's cheating and abuses, who'd stayed with him as he'd apparently run his empire into the ground, turned to this Irishman and said, "Good luck with that, you upstart. None of the families are willing to do business with you now, and that won't change just because you muscled your way into my husband's territory."

That was the crux of it, wasn't it? These men could own the entire city, but without real legitimacy, they couldn't go straight, and they couldn't do business with the big boys, the politicians that ran the city right alongside the mafia.

"It won't matter to you," Liam drawled, "whether we can do business in this city or not, if you're all dead because you owe the Russians for a bad investment."

That was why my father was so desperate for this deal. The Russians didn't fuck around. Unlike the Italians, they didn't spare women and children when they took out a family.

Well, fuck.

I continued to stroke Sofia's hand while I thought my way through this. Ten million dollars was a lot of cash, more than I could get my hands on quickly, even if I were to use my company as collateral, or sell it.

"We'll take her even though she's knocked up," Rian continued, his voice flat and angry. "She can pop out this baby, then pop out a few of ours, and nobody will fucking care if the first was a few months early."

Sofia drew back into herself, horrified. "No," she whispered, her shoulders hunching as she clutched her arms around her belly.

Ours. Not his. Holy shit, they intended to share her.

Cormac shook his head. "I'm not interested in damaged goods. But one Russo woman is as good as another." He ran his cruel eyes up and down my body, focusing on where I held onto Sofia's trembling hand.

Sofia looked up at him, her eyes brimming with tears. "The agreement was that I marry Rian, not you."

Cormac chuckled, the sound dark and liquid as he winked at us. I shouldn't have found him so attractive. I shouldn't have found any of them attractive. He shrugged. "The terms of the contract were clear. You'll be Rian's to do with as he wills. And he'll share."

My sister gasped, then turned her body into mine, wrapping her arms around my waist, as if to hide in my embrace.

I held out my hand for the contracts, gently pushing Sofia back to a sitting position, studiously avoiding my father's eyes. I couldn't face his guilt, if there was any, and I couldn't face his nonchalance, if there wasn't.

I flipped through the terms, my breath shuddering and my heart racing. My father really had intended to sell my sister not just into marriage, but into a polyamorous relationship involving sex games she'd never even heard of, much less wanted, in exchange for financial support and—my heart dropped—security. Protection from the Russians and the Nigerians.

What the fuck had my father done to piss off so many people?

2

RIAN

The three women in the room could not have been more different. Patti Russo, the matriarch, was slim and elegant, a perfect picture of a mafia wife. She ignored her husband's infidelities, hosted lavish events, and ruled the family with an iron fist. She wasn't blind to her husband's faults. No, she benefited from them. Raised to be the perfect Italian-American queen, she excelled at her role as a mafia wife.

The youngest sister, Sofia, was a photocopy of her mother—blonde, blue eyed, and fucking gorgeous even when she cried. Her parents protected her from the worst of their world right up until the moment her father decided to sell her for his own financial and physical security. When presented with an opportunity to escape her family, she crumbled.

Ginevra, on the other hand, was fucking steel she didn't bother to wrap in velvet. She looked just like her father, from her almost black hair, to her chocolate eyes, to her olive skin, tanned by the California sun. Their eyes were the same too, strangely blank, emotion banked and hidden behind calculating cunning. I couldn't get a read on her.

Cormac eyed her like a predator, itching to snatch up a juicy morsel and devour it. Although he was pissed about the younger sister, I could see the possibilities turning in his head.

"We'll take the older sister instead. Same terms," Liam said, catching the attention of the entire room. Easy for others to forget that behind that carefree attitude, Liam hid a sharp mind.

Ginevra's eyes widened for a fraction of a second before she carefully turned her face blank once again. In that moment, I saw her fear, her fury, and what I hoped was a hint of heated desire.

She let us stew in silence while her younger sister sniveled on her shoulder. Neither of her parents said anything, apparently willing to let her take the hit for their mistakes.

When she squared her shoulders, I couldn't stop my eyes from tracing down the v-neck of her amethyst colored shirt, over the soft curves of her breasts.

"I'll do it," she agreed, her words barely a whisper. She didn't look at her father, but I caught the grim pride in his eyes before his own mask slammed down over his face. In our months of doing business together, I'd never seen him look at Luca or Sofia like that.

"I'll do it," she repeated with more confidence. "But I have my own terms."

I leaned back in my chair, taking back control of the conversation. "I don't think you get to dictate anything, princess. Your father fucking owes us, since the Russo he promised us got herself knocked up."

Ginevra ignored me, while she glared at her father, fury transforming her face. "Sofia goes to college."

Oh. She wanted her pound of flesh from her father, too.

"And you make me a *capo*. Luca remains your heir, but I'm your new right-hand woman."

Antonio raised his hands, about to protest, but she cut him off.

"I made my bones when I was sixteen years old, Papà. Did you forget?" she snarled.

I looked at this fierce woman with new respect as she haggled with her father. She'd killed a man for her family at sixteen and then walked away from it a few years later. *Why?*

She turned toward the three of us. "We don't get married. Instead, we sign legal documents making us a polycule, naming each other as next-of-kin with all the same rights as spouses, and an airtight prenup that keeps your dirty fucking hands off my company."

I raised my eyebrows in surprise. That wasn't nearly as difficult a negotiation as I expected. "Everything else remains the same?"

Ginevra licked her lips, the first sign of nerves she'd shown so far. I admired her giant brass ovaries. "I haven't had enough time to read the entire contract, let alone show it to my lawyer."

"I'm talking about sex, princess."

She looked at me, her stare flat and unimpressed.

"The sex is non-negotiable," Cormac added, his voice equally flat and unimpressed. "Ten million dollars and a long-term security upgrade doesn't come cheap. Your pussy better be made of fucking diamonds."

Patti Russo gasped, her face contorted in disgust at his crude words.

Ginevra chuckled to herself, the sound more sad than amused. She stood, and the room stood with her. When she walked over to shake our hands, she said, "Then we agree in principle. I'll have my lawyer update the contracts and send them to yours."

Her grip was warm and firm. Instead of shaking her hand, I raised it to my mouth, running my lips over her knuckles. She jerked her eyes to mine, then smiled crookedly and nodded.

Cormac pulled her in for a kiss, ignoring the stiffness in her shoulders as he brushed his lips against hers. Her eyes were wide, and her cheeks were flushed when she stepped back from him.

Liam chuckled and accepted her hand to shake, winking at her. His talent was putting folks at ease. It didn't make him any less of a psychopath, but it did help grease the wheels of our relationships.

"Hand me your phone, princess," I said. I added our numbers as everyone else filed out of the room. She held out her hand for my own and quickly entered hers too.

I followed everyone else out through their maze of a house. Patti and Antonio made small talk with us, our lawyers, and their kids. Ginevra hadn't joined us, but after the shock of the last hour, I wasn't surprised. As Cormac and Liam walked out the front door, I turned on my heel.

I wasn't sure where the impulse came from, but I followed it right back to Antonio Russo's study. Warm light peaked through the crack of the open door. I opened it further, just in time to see Ginevra throw a glass of whiskey into the wall, swearing to herself. The glass smashed against the wooden paneling, tinkling as it shattered and fell to the ground.

She dragged her hands over her face, her shoulders

tense and tight. I debated my next step—seduction or control? When she turned and saw me, her eyes large and trembling with unshed tears, her breath hitched.

As she fought to restore her composure, I strode toward her, wrapping one arm around her waist and cupping her jaw with the other. I searched her liquid brown eyes for a hint of her emotional state and found nothing, just a faint curiosity, as if she were waiting to see what I was going to do next. I drew her face to mine, brushing my lips over hers. The kiss turned cruel as I sought to devour her, to conquer her. She tasted like fucking citrus and sin. Our lips battled fiercely for dominance as I pushed her backward across the room.

When the backs of her legs slammed into her father's desk, I reached for her wrists and pulled them behind her back, grasping them together with my left hand. I wrapped my right hand around her throat, my thumb pushing hard against her pulse point.

She froze as I pressed my body against hers, her breasts smashing against my chest as I arched her backward over the desk, forcing my way between her thighs. I smiled, enjoying the fear she couldn't hide when I tightened my fingers around her neck.

I lowered my lips again, brushing them against hers, gentle and careful, a sharp contrast to the tight hold I had on her body. She trembled against me, but didn't struggle as I savored and nipped at her lips. I pressed open-mouthed kisses up her jawline and under her ear.

"Ginevra," I murmured as I stroked my thumb up and down the front of her throat, caressing her soft skin. "I think you're out of your depth."

She gazed at me through eyes cloudy with lust, then pushed forward to capture my lips in hers, testing whether

I'd resist the movement with my hand around her throat. I allowed her sweet exploration, rubbing her tongue against the seam of my mouth until I opened it to let her inside. She delved into me, taking her time, despite the lock I had on her wrists and her neck. To my surprise, I let her.

When she finally slowed the movements of our lips, she looked up at me through her long lashes, amused. "Are you sure about that, Rian?"

I watched her in silence, my hand still clutched around her throat, her lips swollen and bruised from my attentions, her cheeks flushed, and her breathing ragged.

She furrowed her brow. "I'm glad you came back, in any case. We didn't talk about our whirlwind romance, which is going to be necessary if you want to convince the other families this marriage is genuine."

"Let me take you out tomorrow. Somewhere visible."

She nodded. "Somewhere on my father's side of town. Baldino's for brunch? I'll make the reservation."

I released her, unwilling to examine my reluctance to let her go. "I'll pick you up at eleven."

3

GINEVRA

Cheryl picked up her phone on the first ring. "Gin! Love! How are you? How is Yorkfield?" Cheryl's bubbly voice and love of pink hid the sharpest legal mind I knew. We met on opposing sides of a venture capital deal for my first start-up, and had been fast friends ever since.

"Babe, I need your help," I said. "You're never going to believe what I'm about to do."

Cheryl laughed. "Love, my clients are Hollywood starlets and tech entrepreneurs. I promise you can't surprise me."

I took a deep breath. "My father is Antonio Russo. I'm taking my younger sister's place in a poly marriage with Irish gangsters, and I need you to review the marriage contracts and the prenup to make sure that the protections for my business and my family's security are airtight."

My friend was silent on the other end of the line.

"Cheryl?"

"Okay, Ginevra, you win. You did surprise me," she said, a smile in her voice. "Send me what you've got. I'll take a look. But doesn't your dad have a consigliere or something? Isn't that a mafia thing?"

I sighed. "I need someone to look after my interests, not his."

I opened up a group text with my brand new boyfriends.

Ginevra: Send me your attorney's contact information. I'll put mine directly in touch.
Cormac: Say please.

What an asshole.

Ginevra: Please.
Cormac: Good girl.

The contact information popped up in the chat. "I'm sending you their attorney's contact information now."

"Don't worry, love, I've done this before, although it's my first time working with the mob. Now, on to more important things—when can I visit and get eyes on these delicious specimens that have lured you into a committed relationship?"

I closed my eyes. I'd been back at my parents' house for less than three hours and having friends to lean on through the emotional whiplash sounded marvelous. "Come for the wedding," I answered. "We'll set the date soon."

Cheryl agreed, and I dropped into my bed. One more call to make before I could close my eyes and pretend today never happened. I swiped through and opened a video call to Min-joon.

"Bestie!" He exclaimed, looking me up and down through the screen. "I burned down the house and crashed your car, just so you know."

A snort of laughter escaped me, despite my exhaustion. I knew he would take excellent care of my house. "I just wanted to let you know I made it to my parents' okay, and I haven't murdered anyone yet."

"It's only been a few hours. You've still got time," he teased. Min-joon's laughter was infectious, and I let him cajole me out of my dark mood.

"What are you doing at home on a Saturday night, anyway?"

"I'm leaving to pick up my date right now. You should know I'm taking your car so I can impress him."

I laughed. "My car is your car. Do what you need to do."

When I hung up the phone, I felt a million times better. It was getting late, but I still needed to unpack. As I dragged my suitcase onto the bed so I could open it, my mother strode into the room, knocking on the door frame as she entered.

We stared at each other for a moment, taking in the changes that a decade had wrought. She was holding herself back from rushing to me and giving me a hug, but I wasn't inclined to make this easy for her.

"Welcome home, Ginevra," she whispered, her voice raspy after decades of secondhand smoke from my father.

"Mamma," I acknowledged. Taking pity on her, I said, "I could use a hand getting my clothes hung up. I wasn't sure what I'd find here, so I brought a bit of everything."

She snorted. "California informal, no doubt," she said, opening the closet and revealing a couple dozen hangers. "All of your old stuff is in the attic, if you want it."

I shook my head. I didn't want any memories of my childhood intruding upon me here. The room was soothing and elegant, a deep forest green with mahogany furniture and gold accents. Silently, we put away my clothes.

"Turns out, it's a good thing I brought it," I muttered when she didn't bother to hide her amusement at my lingerie.

She lay a hand on my shoulder. "You always were the best of us. Even your father knew that. It's why he let you go."

"I don't want to talk about any of that tonight, Mamma."

She respected my wishes, and began gossiping quietly about the people I'd gone to high school with, the families I hadn't seen in ten years. When we finished putting my clothes away, she eyed the gun I had set on the bedside table. "Do you still sleep with that under your pillow?"

I nodded.

My mother pulled me into a tight hug. "I don't know what to say to you, Ginevra, except that I am, selfishly, so glad you're home."

I hugged her back. "I missed you, Mamma."

Luca knocked on the door, letting himself in just as my mother had. I'd forgotten how little respect for privacy there was in this house growing up. Except for my father, of course.

Mamma smiled at us both. "Mass is at ten tomorrow. Don't stay up too late."

I groaned. "Mamma! I'm jet lagged!"

"Don't undo all the good work you did tonight by skipping out on your obligations." She kissed me on the cheek and wished me goodnight.

"Hey, big sister," Luca said, sitting on my bed. He eyed the gun on the bedside table, but didn't say anything.

"Hey, squirt," I said, elbowing him as I sat down. "Thanks for not letting me know what was going on."

He was the spitting image of our father. "I didn't want

you to get involved," he answered. "You got out, unlike the rest of us."

"You're the heir, Luca. How do you intend to keep Mamma and Sofia safe when the other families, let alone the other gangs, realize what dire straits we're in?"

He leaned his elbows on his knees and buried his face in his hands. "I don't have a good solution, but I still don't like dragging you back into this."

I snorted my derisive laughter. "You were about to sell Sofia! And you're getting bent up about *me*? I have money. I have resources. I have my own fucking lawyer who's reviewing the contracts tomorrow. What capability does she have to look after herself in that pool of sharks?"

Remembering my mother's entreaty about attending mass the next day, I pulled out my phone.

Ginevra: I have to go to mass before brunch tomorrow.
Rian: We'll meet you there.
Ginevra: No need. I'll meet you at Baldino's.
Liam: We'll meet you at mass.

When I looked over at Luca, his eyebrows were sky high. "A group chat already?"

I shrugged. "They're family now, aren't they?"

He wrapped his arm around me and pulled me into his shoulder. "I'm sorry, Ginevra."

"Can't change it now, Luca. We just have to make the best of it, and make sure Mamma and Sofia are safe."

"And you," he added, rubbing the top of my head like we did when we were kids.

"Pretty sure those handsome Irish boys will handle my protection just fine. They strike me as the possessive type." *Whether I like it or not.*

Luca laughed and allowed me to change the subject to less fraught topics.

Alexi stared, fury radiating from his clenched fists, as I stood across from my father in the dawn light. He hadn't accepted my induction into the family at sixteen, and he didn't seem any more amenable to accepting my oath in the backyard twelve years later.

It didn't matter. Bringing me back into the family as a captain, as an authority figure and my father's right-hand woman, was part of the price I'd extracted for selling myself to the Irish. Luca stood to my father's left, Alexi to his right, and then my father's four remaining *capos* in a circle around me.

My father's black suit blended into the dark that surrounded us. He gestured for me to give him my hand. I extended it to him, palm up. He pricked my right index finger with a needle, then smeared the blood on a card with Saint Genevieve painted onto it. I lowered my hand, letting my blood drip onto the ground while he lit the card on fire and passed it to Alexi, on his right. The men passed the card around the circle, as I once again swore an oath of silence to my family.

"As burns this saint, so will burn my soul. I enter alive and I will leave dead. I will take the secrets of our family to my grave."

My father sighed sadly when the card made its way back to him, letting the early morning wind scatter the ashes between us.

He wrapped his fingers around my upper arms and kissed me on each cheek. "You have always been part of this family, and now I am proud to call you my *capo*. We are one until death."

The men standing around me repeated the vow. "One until death."

Twelve years ago, I'd taken the same oath, covered in the blood of the high school kid I'd murdered in cold blood after my father retrieved me from a Russian flesh auction. Ten years ago, I'd graduated high school and packed my bags the next day, escaping to California. Three days ago, my sister called me begging for help, and here I was once again. There would be no escape, no *real* escape, this time. Fine. Whatever it took to keep Sofia safe.

"One until death," I whispered.

Luca was the first to pull me into his arms. "Welcome home, big sister."

One by one, my father's captains welcomed me back into the family. They were less warm about welcoming me as a *capo*, but I'd take my wins where I could get them.

When I would have followed the men into the house, my father held me back.

"Ginevra," he said, his voice gravelly with unspoken emotion. "This is not what I wanted for you."

I repressed the rage that roared through me. Did he think I wanted this? "Papà, you have to tell me what's going on. Why are your finances in such dire straits?"

He shook his head. "I made a bad investment, a luxury high rise, that's been a disaster for the past three years."

I raised an eyebrow. "Ten million dollars of bad investments?"

"More actually, but that's what the Russians are asking for as return on their investment. I sunk our cash reserves—and theirs—into the building."

Shit. Conflict roiled in my belly as I tried to reconcile the hard and uncompromising man who'd raised me with the tired old man who quietly confessed to putting his entire family in danger over fucking real estate. *God, what a mess.*

"And if you don't pay?"

"It's blackmail, *piccolina*. If I don't pay, we die. To them, it's just business. These upstarts don't have the same sense of honor we do."

I snorted. Upstarts or not, the power balance in this city was shifting. My skepticism must have shown on my face because my father laughed.

"Come, Ginevra, let's toast your meteoric rise through the ranks of my men, the Russos' first female *capo*. We have all the time in the world to ruminate over the choices I made while you were off enjoying your freedom."

LATER THAT MORNING, I stood in the kitchen in wide legged black slacks, a tucked-in black turtleneck, and kitten heels. My jewelry was understated, and I'd blown my long hair perfectly straight after washing out the ashes from my reinitiation ceremony.

My Aunt Iris handed me an espresso, looking at me over her cup as she sipped. "Pants? For mass?" she asked. I guess Iris disagreed with my assessment of my outfit.

Sofia walked in wearing a pastel dress and looking like a vision of spring in delicate pink floral and matching pumps. Of course, she was dressed perfectly appropriately. Iris was too, in a floral sheath dress and jacket, her hair perfectly coiffed and styled in an elegant chignon. My family wasn't the trashy Jersey mafia folks saw on TV. No, we were old money, money flowing from Italy to mix with money from the United States over generations, and we looked it.

"*Zia* Iris, surely it's too early in Ginevra's visit to start criticizing her clothes," my sister chided her.

"None of the other *capos* wear dresses to church," Luca added, as he walked into the room, looking quite dapper in his gray suit.

Iris laughed derisively, looking me up and down with skepticism. "Since when is Ginevra a *capo*?"

He looked at her, his eyes serious. "Since dawn."

The surprise on our aunt's face was well worth the news getting out early. I shrugged, sipping my coffee. "It's too early in the season for a granita, isn't it?" I asked my brother, changing the subject.

"What are you, eight?" he laughed.

The traditional Sicilian summer breakfast of espresso and a granita was something I hadn't indulged in while in California.

Iris watched me silently, her eyes critical as she looked me up and down. I ignored her. "So how does this work?" I asked Luca.

He wrapped his arm around me and pulled me into him for a sideways hug. "I drive you to church, we go to church, then we come home, and Mamma and the other women make a giant dinner for us to eat in the late afternoon."

I whispered in his ear, "I have a brunch date."

He looked down at me, smiling with those liquid brown eyes that I'd missed so much in the years I'd been gone. "Rian?"

I nodded.

Iris looked at us with suspicion. "Rian O'Conner? One night back and you've already got a date with the head of an Irish gang?" She continued to mutter to herself about young people and our lack of propriety as Luca drew me out of the kitchen.

4

CORMAC

Our fiancée sat with her family in the front of the church. She didn't quite blend in. Her slacks and dark colors contrasted with the spring aesthetic of the women surrounding her. Even so, it was clear that she belonged, that she was one of them.

We got lucky, exchanging Sofia for Ginevra. We'd have torn that tiny little blonde thing to pieces and sent her back to her family screaming. Sure, Rian would reap the benefits of the Russo name with either sister, but breaking Ginevra would add a great deal of pleasure to the bargain.

I watched Ginevra from the back of the church, where we sat, knelt, and stood, in unison with the other parishioners. This wasn't our neighborhood, but mass was mass, no matter where you found yourself in the world. Her hair was glossy and straight, her make-up perfect, and that bright red lipstick just begged me to smudge it all over her face.

The small of her back bulged slightly, the darkness of her clothing almost hiding it. She was armed. *Good.* The service dragged on interminably, and when it finished, our woman—how easy it was to accept that—made her way down the aisle.

Friend after cousin after passing acquaintance stopped her to say hello, as if she were a celebrity who'd deigned to visit after a decade of absence.

Ginevra's face was friendly, but she'd closed off all other emotions. Whatever she was feeling, I couldn't read it from a distance. After what felt like hours, she finally reached our pew, Luca hovering protectively beside her. "Gentlemen," she said. Her eyes were tight, and she wiped her palms on her pants before nodding to acknowledge us.

Rian held out his arm. "The restaurant is only a few blocks away. Shall we walk?"

She nodded slowly, and curled her fingers around his arm, settling them into the crook of his elbow. Liam elbowed me as my eyes slipped down to her generous ass. My hand itched to smack it, see it turn pink when I turned her over my knee and spanked her, but even a hardened deviant like myself knew this wasn't the moment.

With painstaking slowness, we made our way to the sidewalk, Ginevra on Rian's arm, and Luca on her other side, as Liam and I trailed behind, not at all subtle about enjoying the view of her hips swaying before us. The two siblings whispered furiously, and I pretended to ignore their argument.

She drew back as if slapped. "I did not take on this family's debt as my own so that someone else could begin making decisions for me. I will walk to the fucking restaurant, and that's the end of it."

Ginevra turned around and gazed up at me through her lashes, catching me in the snare of her big brown eyes.

"Surely the heads of the Yorkfield Irish are enough to walk me three blocks in the middle of fucking Russo territory."

Luca was stuck. He couldn't say to our faces that he didn't trust us with his precious sister, and he couldn't admit that his sister wouldn't be safe in the middle of his own family's territory. His eyes roved over us before he nodded and stepped back. "Take care of my sister," he said. "Or the agreement is off."

Rian slipped his arm around Ginevra's waist, gripping her hip tightly and pulling her into him. "She's precious to us, too."

Ginevra rolled her eyes, but allowed Rian to guide her out and onto the sidewalk.

R<small>IAN PLANNED</small> to scare the shit out of Ginevra to give us more leverage as we renegotiated. That was my speciality. As he distracted her with light conversation, we turned down the alley Liam had scouted out yesterday. It was narrow enough that two grown men could block both the passage and the view from the sidewalk.

When she noticed her surroundings, she froze, her eyes darting around to look at each of us, wide and nervous. Rian and Liam blocked the entrance to the alley, and I wrapped my arms around her and walked her back into the brick wall.

"Turn around and put your hands on the wall, sweetheart," I murmured in her ear, giving her cheek an enthusiastic lick for good measure. The sweet taste of her skin, citrus and fresh rain, exploded on my tongue, and I groaned with pleasure.

Ginevra stared at me. "Are you out of your fucking mind?"

Diamond In The Dark

My answering smile was feral. I grabbed her around the waist and yanked her toward me, then spun her around, clasping her wrists behind her back. I didn't quite slam her into the wall, but it was close. The side of her face pressed against the rough brick, and she panted as she realized just how much trouble she was in.

I pressed my whole body against hers, shoving her hard into the wall, my cock pressing into her back, my legs holding her still as I smashed her arms between us. Our princess was beautiful, trembling and scared, totally at our mercy. A powerful urge to take her and possess her, right then and there, shot through me.

"What is this? What do you want from me?" she asked as I dragged her soft turtleneck out of her slacks. I pulled the gun out from where she'd tucked it into the small of her back and handed it to Liam for safekeeping.

When I slid close again, I pressed my torso against her to keep her against the wall. She trembled, her breath uneven and scared. The feel of her round ass jammed into my cock was incredible. I wanted to yank her pants down, bend her over, and fuck her stupid, but that wasn't the purpose of this exercise. No, I needed to remind her she was playing with fire, not three teenagers she could lead around by their dicks.

I slid my hand around her front and fiddled with the buttons on her slacks until they opened.

"No, stop," she whispered, her voice desperate and pleading.

Her olive skin was so fucking inviting. I bit her earlobe hard, drawing a sharp cry of pain from her. "If you keep making noise, you're going to catch the attention of a passerby. Then someone's going to see the princess who swooped in to save her family getting fucking ravaged in a dark and filthy alley. Sure is going to be hard for Rian to sign a contract to protect your family if they decide you're damaged goods." I paused, "Like your sister."

Ginevra froze. I could feel her pulse stuttering under my mouth as I nipped and sucked on her neck.

"Do you understand, darling?" I asked her.

She nodded her head, her cheek scraping against the brick.

"Good girl," I murmured. I stepped back and then slapped her ass hard enough that it'd turn pink under those soft, elegant pants. She closed her eyes, and when she opened them, her face was blank. *That's my girl. Never let 'em see you cry.* Even as I defiled this woman, I admired her backbone.

"Keep your hands on the wall, darling." I let go of her hands, gently raising them to sit on either side of her face against the brick. To my surprise, she held them there, pressing them into the wall as if it could lend her its strength.

I worked my fingers down under the scrap of lace she wore under her pants. When my fingers reached her hot core, I swept them along the seam of her pussy, exploring before I pushed them up and into her, running my finger from her ass to her clit. Ginevra whimpered, but she didn't move away from me. I pulled my fingers up and out of her, then ran them along her mouth.

"Suck," I commanded. "Get them nice and wet."

She opened her lips, and I plunged two fingers into her wet mouth, sweeping them around the inside of her cheeks, claiming her mouth for my own. She licked and sucked my fingers until they were dripping in spit.

When I slid them down her pants this time, I kicked her feet apart, holding her thighs against the wall with my own, and plunged my fingers directly into her. She was tight and dry. Even with the spit, it had to be painful, but she didn't make a sound as a lone tear trickled down her cheek. I lazily pumped my fingers in and out, then ground the meaty part of my palm against her clit.

Her sharp intake of breath at the contact surprised me. *Hm.* I dragged my fingers out of her, then ran them up and down the heat of her pussy, stopping to circle her clit, then repeating the motion. Her breathing sped up. I circled it again, increasing the pressure. Her hips jerked against my hand. When I ran my fingers up and down her pussy again, she was wet.

I played with her clit gently, keeping her trapped against the wall with the weight of my body. Rian and Liam watched us, their eyes hot and hooded with desire. Neither of them realized yet that our little princess was actually a slut for degradation, turned on and wet for my abuse. They'd know soon. I changed the plan in my head.

I stepped back and slapped her ass again, for the pure joy of watching it jiggle and shake under the soft fabric of her slacks. Fuck, she was gorgeous. As I swirled my fingers around that tight bundle of nerves between her legs, I slid my other hand up her stomach. Her abdominal muscles clenched as I traced up to the undersides of her breasts. With a featherlight touch, I explored them, before wrenching one out of her bra and pinching the nipple hard.

She cried out and bucked her hips. *Fuck*, she liked this. I plunged two fingers into her. She was drenched. Now focused on her pleasure rather than her humiliation, I roughly fucked her with my hand, grinding my palm into her clit as I switched between pinching and stroking her nipple.

When I flicked my eyes over to Rian, he nodded. Even if

he hadn't approved, there was no way I was going to miss this opportunity to bring our sweet slut to completion in this filthy alley. This wasn't the original plan, but we could adjust.

I sped up my fingers until she was writhing against me, frantically seeking her release as her ass slid up and down against my hard-on. As I worked her into a frenzy, she mewled and whined with arousal until she came with a shattered cry, clenching around my fingers inside of her. When her knees gave way, I caught her in my arms, resisting the urge to nuzzle my nose in her neck as I balanced her on her feet.

She stood there, her hands still braced against the wall, breathing hard, slumped against me, quivering from the aftershocks of her orgasm.

When I was sure she wouldn't collapse, I spared a glance for Rian and Liam, whose hard-ons matched my own. Liam's gaze was frankly admiring. Rian held his cards closer to his chest, but his breathing was as ragged as mine.

Careful not to scrape her further against the brick, I turned Ginevra around and leaned her against the wall. Her eyes were still vacant, but her breathing evened out. "You're so fucking beautiful, darling."

I stuck my fingers in her mouth. "Clean them," I ordered, and she did. I allowed a moan to escape me as her tongue flicked over my fingers. Her red lipstick was smudged exactly how I'd imagined it earlier, and I was hard pressed not to shove her down to her knees and make her wrap those full lips around my dick in the alleyway.

I slid my hands up her belly again and adjusted her breasts in her bra, resisting the temptation to cup them in my hands and play with them. I pulled a handkerchief out of my suit pocket and gently cleaned up the mess between her legs. After I'd straightened her clothes, I brushed my fingers down her cheeks, wiping away her tears and the debris from the wall.

I hadn't expected her to like it, none of us had. Certainly, *she* seemed surprised by her body's reaction to my attention.

Ginevra stood there, her eyes still vacant, leaning against the wall and shuddering. Uncertainty overwhelmed me. Tentatively, I reached my hand out to cup her cheek. When she didn't respond, I dragged her to me and enveloped her in a hug, holding her tight against me. "You did so well, baby girl. You were so fucking gorgeous when you came all over my fingers while Rian and Liam watched."

She didn't say anything, but slowly relaxed, until she was leaning against me. Her breath evened out and her heartbeat slowed. I couldn't hold back my relief that I hadn't broken her like we'd intended. I shoved the feeling back down, deep inside me, but didn't let her go as I stroked her hair and soothed her until she stopped shivering.

"Fuckin' A, Cormac," Liam rasped.

Rian's answering chuckle was dark. "No, fuckin' *Ginevra*," he said, mirroring Liam's appreciation.

Ginevra straightened. She pulled out of my grasp and held out her hand to Rian. "My bag, please."

He bent down and picked it up from the ground where she'd dropped it. She spent two minutes wiping her tears and fixing her make-up, erasing the mess on her face and replacing it with a blank cipher.

There was a slight scrape on her cheek from where I'd shoved her against the brick. When I reached my hand toward her face to stroke it, she turned away. Her ramrod straight back and trembling hands revealed she wasn't as okay with what happened as she was pretending.

As she swept out of the alley, she slipped her fingers into

the crook of Rian's arm once again, and led us back out to the sidewalk.

5

GINEVRA

Although I clutched my fingers around Rian's arm, I couldn't stop shaking as we walked in a tight diamond to the restaurant, Liam in front, Rian and I in the middle, and Cormac behind us. Cormac had violated me without a second thought, and I not only allowed it, I got off from it! What did that say about me?

Unresolved trauma, is what it said, and this trip home had unearthed a shit ton of it.

When we reached Baldino's, Rian held the door for me, his eyes running up and down my body, warm with appreciation. Cormac and Liam made themselves comfortable at a table on the sidewalk, among the other bodyguards and suits protecting the occupants inside.

In the doorway, Rian reached out and ran a thumb over my scraped cheek. I froze, not sure whether I wanted to lean into the comfort of the caress or jerk back in fear. He chuckled softly, then took my hand and led me into the restaurant.

My uncle, Luciano Baldino, greeted me at the hostess

stand, kissing my cheeks. "It's lovely to see you again, Miss Russo. I'm so glad you're home."

Not *all* of my childhood memories were terrible. I kissed him back, smiling warmly at the man who'd hosted many a dinner for my family while growing up. "I'm happy to be home, *Zio* Baldino."

I stepped back and pulled Rian closer. "This is Rian O'Conner. He's a..." I trailed off, wondering how to play this. Despite my horror at the events of the last few minutes, this all had a purpose. I looked over at the darkly handsome man. "He's a friend," I finished, forcing myself to relax my face and wink at the elderly man.

My uncle winked back at me. "I've reserved a table for you." One of his waitresses stepped up and walked us past crowded tables to a curved booth in a corner, far larger than we needed. I slid in, and Rian followed me, until our knees knocked together under the table. When I pulled back, he spread his legs further, not letting me escape the heat of the physical contact.

Rian furrowed his brow when the waitress walked off without handing us menus. "Wait," I said, when he raised his hand as if to signal her.

Before he could say anything, the young woman returned with two espressos, two granitas, and two piping hot brioche buns. He looked at me skeptically while she set them out on the table before us. "Ice cream for breakfast?"

I shrugged. "We're Sicilian and it's spring. Try it."

Keeping his eyes on mine, he dipped his spoon into the berry granita and raised it to his mouth, wrapping his full lips around the spoon as he swallowed. How could one man make eating breakfast look so sinful? *The same man stood and watched while his friend assaulted me in an alley,* I reminded myself. *The same man stood and watched while his friend gave me one of the best orgasms of my life,* I couldn't help but add as I watched him dip his spoon back into the icy treat.

"It's refreshing," he exclaimed, as if surprised.

Of course it's refreshing, you idiot. "Welcome to Little Sicily," I answered, sipping my espresso.

He narrowed his eyes, perhaps sensing the sarcasm behind my words. "Are you okay?"

I laughed bitterly, surprised at the question. "Am I okay?" I blinked at him, then pointedly glanced around the restaurant, full of couples and families eating breakfast on a Sunday. "My family is safe. That's what's important."

For the first time since I'd met him, Rian looked unsettled. He reached across the table and laid his hand on top of mine, where I was clenching and unclenching my fingers. "Your family is safe," he said, his voice low and certain, as if he were making a vow.

A woman could drown in those deceptive blue eyes. I dug my spoon into my granita, holding back the moan that threatened to escape as its flavor exploded on my tongue. When my tongue darted out to capture a drop about to drip off my lips, Rian's gaze shot to my mouth.

"Let me," he rasped, lifting a thumb to my mouth and tracing the path of the granita, before pushing it inside my lips. Before I could stop to think, I'd captured his thumb in my mouth and sucked on it hard, swirling my tongue around the tip. My breathing grew ragged as he held it there. When he withdrew his thumb with a pop, I shifted in my seat to ease the ache between my thighs before I realized I was broadcasting my desire to him.

Rian gazed at me from hooded eyes, his pupils blown, his breath as ragged as my own. He traced my lips with his wet thumb before sitting back in his seat, seemingly at a loss for words.

We stared at each other for a moment as I struggled to conceal my shock at how quickly that had escalated. I guess I wasn't as freaked out by Cormac's actions on the way here as I'd thought.

"Right," Rian muttered, ripping off a piece of his brioche and leaning back in his chair. "What kind of company do you run, Ginevra?"

Grateful for his turn to less fraught conversation and excited to talk about my babies, I took a deep breath and got my heart rate and pulse back under control. "I'm a serial entrepreneur. I sold my first two, and now I'm building a company that does CGI for Hollywood blockbusters."

"So you're an animator?"

"I'm a software engineer, but yes, I also have an art degree." I tried not to preen under his admiring gaze, but finally gave in to the impulse to grin.

"And now you're here," he murmured.

I shrugged. "I can run my company from here, at least in the short term."

He furrowed his brow. "And in the long term?"

I twisted my lips in frustration. I didn't know. "In the long term, New York City is a hop, skip, and a jump away. Lots of show biz entrepreneurs are bicoastal. What do you do for a living?" I asked.

Rian snorted with laughter. "Real estate," he said. Lord, that man's smile made my heart skip every goddamned time he blessed the world with its presence.

My answering smile was rueful. "Right, real estate."

He tilted his head to the side, the corners of his lips tilted up into a slight smile. "Like your dad."

Like Papà. I wondered if Rian had anything to do with my father's crumbling investment. Had he maneuvered my family into this marriage, these contracts, through blackmail and dishonesty?

I nodded to acknowledge the point, hiding my churning thoughts as I reached for my coffee. The sharp *rat-a-tat-tat* of gunfire and an explosion of glass snatched my attention away from Rian. My heart pounding in terror, I dove to the floor, lying flat on my stomach under the table.

Patrons screamed as the glass shattered. Rian slammed on top of me, driving the air out of my lungs. He caged me in his arms, then immediately lifted his weight off me. I hated how secure I felt with him on top of me, protecting me from whatever danger lay outside of the restaurant.

"Stay down, princess," he whispered in my ear before kissing me hard on the back of my head and moving away. I kept my head down, waiting for more gunfire, but all I could hear were the frightened sniffles and sobs of the restaurant's patrons.

Fuck. *Fuck.*

Less than twenty-four hours after my return, and the violence I'd fought so hard to escape caught back up with me. When another minute passed without a sound, I took a deep breath and popped up to my knees, keeping my head low. Rian glared at me from where he crouched beside me, a gun in hand. "I said, stay down."

I glared at him, drawing my own gun. Did he expect me to trust him to keep me safe?

A few young women sobbed quietly, but the vast majority of Baldino's customers were calm, checking on each other, picking each other up off the ground, making sure nobody was seriously cut. From my vantage point in the corner, damage appeared limited to the giant glass windows in the front of the restaurant. The bullets hadn't hit anyone, thank God.

I blinked, and Cormac stood beside me. He extended his hand to help me up. Mine trembled as I wrapped my fingers around his. I clenched my other hand tightly around the grip of my gun to hide the shaking as terror caught up with me.

Cormac jerked his head toward the back of the restaurant. "Time to go, darling." I followed him to the kitchen at a brisk jog, keeping my head down as he and Rian shielded me from any threats coming from the front of the restaurant.

In the kitchen, Luciano wrung his hands. I stepped toward him, only for Cormac to block my path. While Rian checked the rest of the kitchen for hidden dangers, Cormac ran his fingers over my face, my neck, my hands—every bit of exposed skin. When he finished, he nodded sharply and stepped out of my way.

Oh. *Oh.* He had been checking me for injuries. I hated the tightness his care caused in my chest, as if it fucking meant something, as if he simply didn't want anyone else breaking his property before he did.

"Luciano," I said, grasping his hands in mine. "I'm so sorry."

He shook his head and moaned. "I can't believe it's come to this."

"What do you mean, Luciano?"

When he looked up at me, his brown eyes were clouded and tired. "Talk to your father, Ginevra."

I squeezed the elderly man's hands. "Send the bills to me, okay, *Zio* Luciano?"

He furrowed his brow in confusion. "What's a pretty girl like you going to do with those bills, Ginevra?"

Cormac laughed quietly behind me. I ignored him.

"Send them to me, all right?"

Rian looked up from his phone. "Time to go, princess," he said, echoing Cormac's words from minutes before. He hustled me out of the restaurant, up an alley, and into the back seat of a large black SUV. Rian and Cormac bracketed me in the middle.

Liam was waiting in the front passenger seat. "Where to, boss?"

"Home," I said at the same time Rian said, "My place."

I shook my head in disagreement. "No, we need to go to my father's. If we leave, we'll lose any shot at influencing the next step."

His eyes flicked to my trembling hands. I latched my fingers together in my lap, steeling my spine and meeting his gaze.

Rian's lips pressed into a thin line. He didn't like being challenged, but that was too damn bad. I was right. After a tense moment, Rian nodded to me. "The Russos'," he agreed.

THE DOOR of my father's study loomed before me, a more intimidating gauntlet than it had been the night before. I ducked away when we arrived at the house, excusing myself to freshen up, using the time to calm my shaking hands and aching heart. Entering that fortress of masculinity would mean taking my place at my father's side, and my future husbands', leaping headfirst back into a cruel life of violence and tradition I'd run hard and far to escape.

Ignoring the jack hammering of my heart, I walked in. The men had drinks in their hands and stood in small groups, chattering quietly. Luca smiled when he saw me, walking over and clasping my hands in his. "Are you okay?"

Cognizant of the importance of convincing everyone in

that room that I was not only fine, but an eager and valuable partner, I squeezed his hands back. "I'll be fine. Luciano was really upset when we left. Has someone called him?"

"Papà did," my brother responded. In a low voice, he continued, "He said you told him to send the bills to you."

I glanced around the room, wondering whether my father's captains were aware of his financial situation. "We can talk about it later," I said, pulling my hands away from his.

A warm hand slid around my waist, settling on the side of my hip. The touch was possessive and burned my skin where fingers dug into me, pulling me tightly against Rian's side. I looked up at him with amusement. "No need to mark your territory, Rian."

His laughter was tinged with darkness. "You didn't see the way these men looked at you when you walked into the room, princess."

Luca raised his eyebrows. "They know she's taking Sofia's place."

Rian's answering gaze was hard and angry. "Then they know she's mine—ours—and they should keep their eyes respectful."

I shouldn't find his possessiveness so fucking attractive. Certainly, *he* didn't need to know it was turning me on. I slid out of his grasp and walked away to join my father.

Papà clasped my upper arms, gently pulling me toward him to give me a kiss on each cheek. I returned the gesture, surprised at the crepey texture of his skin. "How are you, Ginevra?" he asked me, sounding like he actually cared.

I tamped down on my innate cynicism and didn't comment on the fact that he'd agreed to sell me to three Irish gangsters the night before. "Why don't we sit down and figure out what's going to happen next?"

My father stood behind his desk, and gradually the room fell silent. Liam scooted over on one of the leather sofas, obviously making space for me. Rian was on his other side, and Cormac stood behind him. There was no way to refuse him without drawing attention to it, so I squeezed in beside him, trying not to think about the heat of his body pressed against mine. When Luca's eyebrows shot up in surprise, I realized how neatly Liam had boxed me into a statement about where my alliances laid.

Damn.

Even if I didn't understand all of the relationships and machinations of the gangs that ruled Yorkfield, I needed to focus and start treating these meetings like the cutthroat corporate boardrooms I was used to.

"Ginevra has been back for less than a day, and the Russians already shot at her," my father began.

Alexi snorted. "Were they shooting at her? Or were they shooting at these upstarts over here who think they have a right to flirt with our *piccolina*? Why are they here, Antonio?" Alexi asked my father, gesturing to the three Irish gangsters, including me in his contempt.

Instead of answering him, my father leaned forward on his desk. "If you have an objection to their presence, Alexi, you can leave. It is, after all, a failure of your security that my daughter was shot at today!" His face turned red as he yelled. Was he furious because it was humiliating for the Russians to have done it on his turf, or was he genuinely incensed that I was in danger? It didn't matter.

Liam rested his arm on the couch behind me, so close, I could feel loose curls from my hair catching on his sleeve as I shifted in my seat. He leaned closer. "Your father's going to ask us to start security now, even though neither of you have signed the contracts yet."

I didn't respond.

Liam continued, the closeness of his lips to my ear driving me mad as he murmured. "We'll do it, but we're going to take it out of your hide."

I turned to him, not bothering to hide the movement. "What does that mean?"

"Give us the pleasure of your company for two days, and we'll make sure your family stays safe while we're negotiating."

The pleasure of my company. What was he asking me to do? "One day," I countered.

"Twenty-four hours. No safeword."

My breath caught in my throat and I turned away from him so that I could collect my thoughts.

Instead of blurting out the panicked objections running through my head, I turned back to him and asked, "When?"

"Tonight," he breathed in my ear, tugging on a strand of my hair behind me.

"I have to work tomorrow," I said, shocked that disappointment colored my voice.

"We'll let you work," he answered, the soft feeling of his fingers tangling in my hair strangely intimate.

My father was grilling his *capos* about their recent interactions with the Russians.

I leaned back over to Liam. "Am I an idiot? Why doesn't someone just pick up the phone and ask the Bratva what the fuck is going on?"

Liam's chuckle was dark. "Admit a weakness? That your intelligence isn't good enough to have predicted it, and your security is too weak to prevent it? This was a test, and your father failed it."

Rian was leaning forward, his eyes intent on my father. "Are you suggesting that we share intelligence and cooperate on security prior to signing the contracts with your daughter?"

Papà raised an eyebrow, and for a moment, he looked like the cruel and powerful *don* I'd grown up with. "You're a damn fool if you don't already realize what a gem Ginevra is, and twice the fool if you haven't already increased protection for her."

Liam whispered in my ear. "We have, if you were wondering."

Rian's laugh was cruel. "This is why your empire is crumbling, Antonio. All bark, no bite."

I stood, tired of the posturing and the dick measuring. "Don't be an ass, Rian. Liam's already negotiated the price with me. Work with Alexi and make it happen. Think of it as a gesture of good faith, on both sides."

Projecting the same tough authority I used when running meetings back home in LA, I walked over to my father's desk and leaned back against it. I speared Rian with my annoyed gaze. "Can we talk about the Russians now?"

6

RIAN

"Fuck this bitch," Cormac said, shoving the laptop away from him. The files Ginevra's lawyer sent were full of red lines where she'd tracked changes to the contracts. "Just marry her the old-fashioned way and leave me out of it, if she doesn't want to play my games."

Liam had stayed behind at the Russos' to coordinate protection details with Alexi, their head of security. Liam's charm would make this work. Our men weren't going to bend over backward for the Italians unless we set the example. Alexi was a real asshole and wouldn't make it easy for us.

I stood behind Cormac, pulling his head back against my stomach and running my hands up and down his front. He leaned on me, sighing as I slid my fingers back up to his shoulders to work the knots, placing a gentle kiss on the top of his head.

"She got rid of all of it!" he muttered, his voice dripping with frustration.

"I told you, you shouldn't have put in that shit about sharing Sofia," I said, smirking at my business partner, sometimes lover, and one of two men in the entire world I wouldn't hesitate to give my life for.

He ran his hands over his closely cropped curls. "She would have signed it, and so would her dick father. Fucking asshole, sacrificing that child for his own security."

We would have broken Sofia in a night or two, sending her screaming in terror back to her parents, and we'd have accrued all the benefits of the marriage without the anchor of a physically present wife around my neck. "Ginevra's made of tougher stuff."

"She's a wildcard," Cormac snapped at me. "And she's smart enough to get in the way of business and our relationships."

He was right. When Liam returned from Ireland eight years ago, we'd just come back to Yorkfield after graduating from college, puffed up and full of ourselves. Eight bloody years of fighting to conquer our tiny corner of the city, peeling it back from the other gangs, making it safe, block by block, so the kids wouldn't have to run drugs and guns like we did. Ginevra was never going to accept the brutality and the violence it took to maintain our empire, let alone grow it.

"Better than giving up the ports to the Russians, though." At least the Italians drew the line at trafficking people. They didn't like drugs either, but the twenty-first century had dragged them kicking and screaming into competition with the cartels. Now they were bringing in heroin from Afghanistan imported through West Africa, the same as the rest of us.

Cormac leaned back and grabbed my hands, holding them to his chest. I leaned my chin on his head, letting him pull me close. "I wish we didn't need the goddamned Russo name."

"The Italians own this town. It doesn't matter how many clubs and casinos we open up or how much real estate we own. Nobody'll do business with us without the Russo seal of approval."

Liam: Security's set up at the Russos'.
Rian: Double check everything yourself. Alexi's lazy.
Ginevra: And a liar.
Liam: Ginevra, show us your tits!

Two seconds later, a photo popped up of Ginevra, fully clothed, giving us the finger.

Cormac: Brats who don't do what they're told get punished, Ginevra.

I snatched his phone out of his hands. "We're supposed to be scaring her so we have more leverage in the negotiations, not flirting."

Cormac grabbed his phone back. "Wait, fool."

Five anxious minutes later, a photo popped up in the group chat. We both scrambled over ourselves to see what the fuck it was. Arranged on a plate were two goddamned raw chicken breasts.

I bit back a startled laugh. "I'm going to enjoy breaking her."

She'd dug deep under my skin already, and I wanted her by my side. And under me. And on her knees in front of me, tears streaming down her face as she sucked my cock. *Fuck.*

My brother-in-arms looked at me from where I loomed over him. "You like her, don't you?"

"She has potential," I said, avoiding the question.

Cormac's teeth flashed bright against his deep brown

skin as he grinned, seeing right through me. "I guess we'll find out tonight, won't we?"

Ginevra stood at the open door, a chic overnight bag slung over her shoulder, waiting for me to invite her in. She'd changed from the all black ensemble she'd worn to church. Instead, she wore a pair of distressed jeans and a chunky sweater. *Gorgeous*, I thought to myself as she fidgeted under my assessing gaze.

I stood aside and gestured for her to come in. She tried to hide her nerves, but her fingers clutched her bag so tightly they'd turned white. The faint scent of citrus wafted from her as she passed by me.

Cormac and Liam sat in my living room, eyeing her like cats playing with a mouse when she stopped in the entranceway.

"Hi," she said, her voice tremulous and uncertain. She cleared her throat. "Hi," she said again, with more confidence and a charming smile.

When I pulled her overnight bag off her shoulder, it was heavier than I expected. "Jesus, woman, what did you pack?"

Her answering look was puzzled. "Laptop, headphones, ring light—everything I need to work tomorrow."

That's right, Liam had promised her she'd be able to work. *Hm.*

Cormac stood, his motions stark and predatory as he paced around her, taking in every detail. Ginevra held herself still, like a mouse hoping to hide in plain sight, if only she could stop herself from shaking.

There's no hiding tonight, princess.

Cormac stopped his pacing directly in front of her. Ginevra wasn't short, but compared to him, compared to any of us, she was tiny. She stared into his chest for a frozen moment before sighing and looking up at him, not bothering to hide her annoyance.

"I would have expected Irish mothers to be more exacting about their sons' manners," she snapped when he looked down at her, saying nothing.

"Whores don't get courtesies," he snapped back.

Ginevra narrowed her eyes. She grew an inch as she straightened her spine and looked straight up into Cormac's eyes. "What's that make you? Just a John then, are you?"

"Fucking slut, trading her body for parents who were relieved to sell her instead of her sister." He yanked her against his body, running his hands down her back and squeezing her ass cruelly. "So desperate for safety, you even negotiated away your safe word."

"I changed my mind," she answered, her hands on his chest, struggling to push him away.

Cormac bent down and took her earlobe in his mouth, dragging his teeth down over it. "Too late, bitch. This isn't a BDSM club. It's not a scene. And this isn't the lifestyle. You're ours, and we're going to treat you like the trash you are."

She shuddered, then murmured, "Tell me how you really feel, Cormac."

He turned her in his arms until he had her back pressed against his torso, wrapping one arm around her hips. When he ran one hand up her bare stomach under the thick knit of her sweater, her breath turned ragged. "I bet if I ran my fingers over your breasts right now, I'd find your nipples tight and hard, begging for my touch. If I slid my fingers down your pants, I'd find your pussy soaking wet, aching for me to run my fingers through your slick arousal and then fuck you hard with them, you filthy fucking slut."

He stepped away from her, abruptly. "But that's not what I'm going to do right now. Strip."

"Are you fucking kidding me?" she asked, looking at Liam and me as if we might step in and save her. Not a chance, but she didn't know that yet.

Liam chuckled and stalked over to her. "Pretty little lamb, thought she could save her sister and didn't realize she was running straight into the wolves' den." He drew a knife out of the sheath he wore on his belt and traced her jawline with the flat of the blade. "Cormac told you to take your clothes off."

When Ginevra didn't move, he angled the blade and traced it downward, leaving a delicate white scratch against her olive skin. Her eyes widened, terrified, perhaps realizing there was a reason we'd been so explicit in our contract with her sister. Liam huffed and puffed when I struck knife play from the original draft, but when Ginevra refused to include any sex at all in our negotiations, I put all our kinks back on the table.

"Okay," she whispered, "okay." When Liam didn't back away, her eyes flashed to his. "You have to let me move, Liam."

She lifted a trembling arm and used one finger to carefully push the knife away from her face. Our brave and pretty Ginevra kept her face utterly blank as she knelt to remove her sneakers and her socks. She set them neatly beside her before standing again.

She took deep, trembling breaths. Her gorgeous brown eyes were watery, but so far, she'd refused to let the tears fall. We'd have to work on that.

"C'mon, little lamb," Liam said. "Don't get shy now."

Ginevra glared at him, but slid her fingers under the hem of her sweater and lifted it up. I fought against the urge to lean closer for a better look as it inched up over her soft stomach and her bra. Liam didn't bother to bite back his hum of appreciation as we got our first look at her magnificent tits. They were glorious, gorgeously framed by her black and teal lace bra, shifting and shaking with every move of her body. She carefully folded the sweater, then bent at the waist to set it on top of her shoes.

"Don't stop there, Ginevra," Cormac said, his voice dark and low.

She exhaled sharply and then undid the button on her jeans. When she slid them over her hips, revealing lacy matching panties, I swore. Our little princess came dressed to seduce us. *Too bad.* Her jeans were tight, and she peeled them down her legs. Every time she bent down, I got a full view of the soft globes of her breasts. Already, I was impossibly hard.

Now, in only her bra and panties, she stood in front of us in my living room, her chest heaving with the force of her uneven breaths.

My turn.

I prowled toward her, lifting my hand to her face. When she flinched, I grabbed her chin, squeezing tight and drawing it toward me as I stared her in the eyes. "He said strip, princess."

A lone tear trickled down her cheek. Finally.

Shaking, she reached around her back and unclasped her bra. I didn't let my eyes drop to the temptation of her naked breasts, just squeezed her chin harder as she dropped the bra and pushed her panties down and over her hips. I released her face with a jerk as they fell to the floor.

"Good girl," I whispered and allowed myself to take in the sight of her as I backed away. Ginevra was stunning, with long wavy hair, a dark brown that was almost black, her heart-shaped face, her luscious breasts and slightly curved belly, and her perfectly round hips and a pussy to die for, shaved bare and open to my gaze.

She was wet.

Sweet Jesus in heaven, this gorgeous creature who we intended to send home crying and whimpering, was fucking wet for us.

Cormac saw it, too. His tongue darted out over his full lips as he took in the pretty sight. Liam was blatant about his appreciation of her, roving his eyes up and down her body and adjusting his hard-on.

"Have you eaten?" I asked her, keeping my voice soft and gentle.

She looked at me, her eyes watery with unshed tears. "What?"

"Have you eaten dinner yet?"

"You told me we'd have dinner here," she answered, her voice tremulous and subdued.

I slid the collar Cormac had left on the end table into my hands and approached her. She shook her head to refuse it, but didn't back away. From behind her, I looped the black leather around her neck and cinched it shut.

She shuddered, sniffling before visibly fighting to calm herself. Once she settled, I jerked my head toward the dining room. "Follow me, princess." I didn't wait to see if she'd follow. I knew she would.

CORMAC HAD PREPARED the dining room well. To the right of my seat at the head of the table laid a soft and luxurious pillow. "Kneel," I instructed our sweet lamb, pointing toward the pillow.

Ginevra gasped. "Are you fucking kidding me?"

"What part of 'ours for twenty-four hours' did you not understand?" Liam asked, sitting down in his place to my left.

Cormac pulled out the chair to my right, sitting without ceremony. "Ginevra, this is going to be a very long evening if you don't learn to obey."

She shook her head, as if she couldn't believe what we were asking her to do. Cormac sighed and swung his hand back, spanking her once, hard. Ginevra jumped and cried out. Cormac and I stood, enjoying the perfect bounce of her ass. We watched it turn red, admiring the outline of his handprint against her olive skin.

"Kneel," he snapped.

She knelt beside me, shuddering and struggling to hold back tears.

I sat and pushed in my chair, ruffling my hand through her long hair and gently scratching along her scalp.

At my request, our chef left finger foods and dishes easy to cut into small bites. The three of us dug in, keeping our chatter to inconsequential subjects, each of us desperate to pretend this meal was normal, like any of the hundreds of meals we'd shared since we met as children on the wrong side of the tracks.

I cut a slice of steak, thin and pink, and held my fork out to Ginevra. She glared at me with disdain in her eyes, pressing her lips into a thin line. "Eat, princess," I commanded, keeping my voice soft.

Cormac tangled his fingers in her hair and yanked it backward. "He said, eat. Open your mouth, slut."

As tears spilled out of her eyes, she opened her mouth. I placed my fork on top of her tongue, and she closed it, chewing the steak and swallowing.

"Good girl," Cormac said, his touch turning gentle as he

took his turn tenderly digging his fingers into her scalp in a soothing massage. "That was perfect," he murmured, keeping his voice low and comforting.

When he held a canapé covered in cheese in front of her, she leaned forward to bite it in half. She chewed and swallowed, then gave the second half a long look before peering up through her lashes at Cormac. Unable to take it without wrapping her lips around his fingers, she took them into her mouth too, then waited. "Oh, fuck yes, that's a good girl," he murmured, when she sucked on his fingers before he pulled them out of her mouth.

Ginevra sat at our feet in silence, trembling, her breath uneven. When I fed her another bite of steak, she accepted it without complaint.

Liam's eyes danced as he watched us tame Ginevra. I wasn't stupid enough to think this was the end of her defiance—I'd be disappointed if it were. She was biding her time, and if she was smart, she'd realize everything in life could be negotiated.

"Russo is losing his hold on his men because his businesses are going under," Liam said. "They're not getting their take, and their loyalty is for sale."

Cormac's lips twisted in disgust. "Like his daughters."

"Keep calling me a whore, Cormac. Think of what that makes the men who are paying for me," Ginevra spat.

Cormac hummed and held a spoonful of mashed potatoes in front of her mouth. She leaned forward and wrapped those lush lips around the spoon. Her eyes flicked to mine, a ghost of amusement reflecting in them as she licked her lips. Our girl knew what she was doing. She wasn't broken yet.

"Alexi's corrupt as shit," Liam continued. "Not sure if he's on the take or just an asshole, but we can't take anything he says at face value. Cormac, you're up tomorrow to look at their information security."

I looked down at our pretty little pet, quiescent on her pillow. "Is that true, princess? You said Alexi's a liar earlier."

She grimaced, fury flashing in her eyes. "That's because he is. His second, Lorenzo, is more reliable. Or was, ten years ago."

The silky feeling of her hair tangling in my fingers was distracting. She leaned into me when I stroked her cheek with my finger, then jerked away.

"Why do you say that?" Liam asked. He could only see the top of her head from his seat, but his smile softened his tone.

"He's a liar," Ginevra repeated, without context. "And a jealous bastard. He won't sacrifice my father, but any of the women? He won't hesitate to put us in danger to set you up."

I frowned. Ginevra wouldn't know that from the day she'd been back. This was an older wound. "What did he do to you, princess?"

"Don't trust him," she repeated firmly.

"Like we can trust anything coming out of your mouth either," Cormac muttered.

Ginevra's face melted into blankness, revealing nothing except that Cormac hit a nerve. She blinked twice, then relaxed her body, letting go of the tension in her shoulders, adjusting her position on the pillow so she could rest her haunches on her feet. She didn't answer him, just stared straight ahead, waiting.

When I slipped her another morsel of food, she accepted it and chewed it mechanically.

7

CORMAC

Ginevra tuned us out as we shot the shit over dinner. While she didn't protest as we alternated feeding her, she hadn't fooled me into thinking that she'd acquiesced. Her lips were soft on my fingers as I gave her morsels of food, making it hard to concentrate on the light conversation Liam seemed determined to keep going.

Finally, our plates were clean, and there was a lull in the conversation. Liam's eyes were bright and hungry.

"Stay," I ordered Ginevra, as the three of us cleared the table. Her eyes danced with amusement when she looked up at me. She was counting on our need to marry her to balance out our desire to break her. Time to disabuse her of that notion.

"Up," I said, yanking roughly on her collar.

She squeaked as she scrambled to her feet before I could choke her. I pushed her forward until her thighs hit the front of the table. "Are you ready for us to treat you like the slut you are?" I whispered in her ear, wrapping one hand around her throat and dragging her up onto her toes.

Ginevra whimpered. Her back arched, thrusting her glorious tits forward as I squeezed her throat and pressed her perfect ass into me. She was stuck between my thighs and the table, with nowhere to go as I slowly cut off her air supply and pushed her head back into my chest.

"Please," she gasped, struggling against me. I slapped her tit with my free hand and she froze.

"Please what?" I snapped, pinching her nipple roughly.

"Please let me breathe," she wheezed.

I jammed my hips into her pelvis, pushing my hard length into the bare crack of her ass. Fuck, she felt good.

"You can still breathe, you spoiled bitch. You just have to work for it."

Liam approached on my left, a questioning look in his eyes. I nodded my agreement. I tweaked her nipple again, hard, and she cried out in pain, a tear streaming down her face.

"Are you sure you're not enjoying this?" he asked. "I bet if I stick my fingers in that cunt of yours, they'll come out slick and wet." When I pinched her nipple again, Liam's tongue followed my fingers, laving the swollen peak of her breast and soothing it after the pain I inflicted.

Ginevra shuddered and raised her hands to her throat, trying to pull my hand off so she could take a full breath. I slapped her tit again. "Stop that," I bit out. "Or I'll fucking bind your hands and then you'll *really* regret misbehaving."

Her fingers loosened from where they clutched at my wrist and my forearm, but they didn't let go.

"Liam!" I snapped.

My best friend peeled our little slut's fingers off me, one by one, looping his long fingers around her wrists and dragging them down. I pushed down and back on her throat, forcing her to keep arching her back and put space between us. Rian handed Liam silk-lined leather cuffs that he quickly strapped around her wrists.

When Ginevra realized what was happening, she struggled in earnest. "Please, stop, let me go," she pleaded, the sound of her begging sweet in my ears.

"Twenty-four hours to do whatever we want," I whispered in her ear. "When I let you go, I want you to stand still."

"And if I don't?" she rasped.

"I'll punish you for it," I snapped right back at her. I loosened my hold on her neck and her breast. Instead of calming down, Ginevra hyperventilated in her panic. "Easy, darling," I said, wrapping a hand around her stomach, more loosely this time. "Breathe with me. In and out. In and out." Once she got her breathing under control, I let her pull her torso away from me, but kept the pressure of my hips on her ass, trapping her against the table. God, her terror was sweet as she quivered against me.

"Good girl," I murmured, rubbing my hands up and down her bound arms, letting the warm heat of them settle her. Ginevra stilled, breathing hard, but no longer fighting. "Now, I want you to lean down and rest on the table."

She tensed all over again, but let me push her downward, until her cheek and breasts smashed against the dining room table, her back rising and falling with her quick, terrified breaths.

I pushed Rian's chair out of the way, then kicked her legs apart, exposing her wet and glistening pussy to the three of us. "Such a wet and needy slut," I said. "Look at you, turned on and horny after we treated you like the filthy whore you are."

She sniffled, but said nothing as we looked our fill. *Good.*

"Now stay," I snapped, backing away. She stood there,

exposed to us, her whole body a delightfully flushed and embarrassed pink.

The three of us gathered behind her, admiring her ass and the swollen folds of her pussy. Ginevra calmed a bit and lay quietly on the table, waiting for my next command.

When I unbuckled my belt, the clank of metal freaked her out. She twisted her body around so she could see what I was doing.

"I told you to stay, bitch," I snapped at her. "Don't test me." Ginevra froze, her eyes taking up her whole face.

"Turn back around, Ginevra," Rian said, more gently than I would have. Slowly, shuddering the entire time, she straightened her torso out, resting her cheek on the table.

I finished pulling my belt out of my pants, unzipped my fly, and pulled out my cock. Rian handed me a foil packet. I was already hard as a rock and dripping pre-cum. Ginevra was hot as fuck, and the thought of plunging into her tight pussy while she struggled and cried had my hands shaking with need.

When I was covered, I stepped up to her and ran my cock along her core. She whimpered and jerked away. "None of that, now," I said, wrapping my hands around her hips and holding her still. "Do you need me to show you what will happen if you don't lie here and take me like the whore you are?"

At that, she fought me in earnest. I held my hand out to Liam, who handed me my belt. "Ginevra, do you really want to fight me?" But she didn't hear me as she twisted and struggled, trying to get away from me as she whimpered.

She cried out as the leather cracked on her ass. For a moment, it seemed to shock the fight out of her. I'd given her a love tap, just enough to leave a reddening stripe, not enough to bruise. I could tell she was unused to corporal punishment. We'd have to change that.

"Do you need another one?" I asked her.

She shook her head frantically.

"Good." I ran my cock up and down her pussy, from her clit to her sweet and beckoning entrance, collecting the evidence of her desire. When I pushed the tip into her, she whimpered, but didn't move. "Easy, darling," I whispered, then grabbed her hips again and plunged all the way in. She cried out in pain as I stretched her, but didn't fight me. God, she was tight. I struggled not to take her with the force I wanted to, the hot snug fit of me inside her sending me careening toward losing control. Whether she wanted to or not, her body would adjust. As she relaxed, her pussy's natural lubrication easing the way, I reared back, then slammed into her, my pelvis slapping against her ass.

I couldn't tell if she whimpered in pain or in pleasure, and I didn't fucking care. Her sweet pussy was tight and hot —absolutely fucking perfect. When her hips jerked back toward me, moving with my rhythm, I fucking lost it, my movements becoming jagged and uneven as I raced toward my climax.

She cried out, "Please." The sound of her sweet begging sent me over the edge, and I exploded inside of her.

She hadn't come yet.

After I pulled out of her dripping pussy, Liam took my place, already sheathed in a condom and furiously fisting his hard cock. He plunged into her, quick and brutal, not bothering to check if she was ready or okay. Ginevra arched her back, meeting him thrust for thrust, her cries of pain turning into mewling whimpers of pleasure and need as he pistoned in and out of her. He yanked a butterfly knife out of his jeans and flicked it open. I watched him warily, not quite ready for him to break our little toy.

Liam winked at me as he plowed hard into Ginevra. She bit back a muffled scream, and he held her hips there, staying deep inside her as he took deep breaths, calming himself and coming back to the present. With a flick of his wrist, he cut into the sides of her back, two shallow cuts down her ribs, deep enough to bleed a little. Ginevra tried to jerk away, but he'd buried his cock deep inside that tight pussy. Jammed up against the table, there wasn't anywhere for her to go. Liam licked his lips, then ran his fingers through the blood, smearing it over her sides and over her ass. As if the sight of her blood released a pressure valve, he slammed into her again. It didn't take long for him to take his pleasure, and she whined in protest when he pulled out before she climaxed.

Rian took his place behind her, his cock in his hand, smiling ruefully as he slid on a condom. Ginevra didn't shift from where she was bent over the table, her cheek smashed into the wood, her used and swollen pussy visible to all three of us. He swiped his fingers up and down her slit, teasing her clit. Her hips twitched, but she didn't move or make a noise.

Poor Ginevra couldn't decide if she wanted to beg for an orgasm or beg for us to stop.

Rian slid his hands around her hips and slammed his cock into her, the same as Liam and I. Ginevra cried out, and again, I couldn't tell if she was moaning from pain or pleasure. As Rian worked her over, pumping in and out of her, I slid a finger around her thigh and circled her clit.

This time, when she cried out, it was with pleasure. "Please," she begged.

"Please, what, you fucking slut?" I asked her as she

whimpered and whined, meeting Rian with her hips on every thrust.

"Please," she begged again.

"Do you think we give whores what they want?" I asked. Rian caught my eye and grinned, smacking her ass over and over again as he plunged into her.

"Fucking let me come!" she cried out.

I let her hover on the edge for a long moment as Rian plundered her, then pinched her clit hard. Ginevra screamed and thrashed as that tiny bit of stimulation drove her off the fucking cliff. She seized, her entire body going taut as her climax ripped through her. Rian continued to pump in and out until his rhythm turned erratic and he came with a shout, collapsing on top of her.

Ginevra lay on the table, shaking and trembling with the aftershocks of her climax.

"Stand up," I ordered her. She didn't move. Her eyes were vacant, and she lay there, shaking violently, tears streaming down her face.

Shit.

We'd planned on making her crawl up to an empty guest room and locking her in for the night, letting her reflect on what a filthy slut she was, but after she'd given herself to us so fucking prettily, none of us wanted to do it.

"Princess, we're going to get you cleaned up, okay?" Rian said softly as he unbuckled her wrists from the cuffs, rubbing them to bring the circulation back. Liam wiped down her back, cleaning the blood off her before applying antiseptic and affixing gauze to protect the wounds from infection. He dumped the wrappers in the trash and returned with a warm, wet towel, carefully running it between her trembling legs.

Through all of this, she lay still, except for the occasional sniffle as her nose dripped.

Shit.

Rian wrapped an arm around her shoulders and gently drew her to a standing position before unbuckling the collar. When her knees gave way, he caught her, sweeping her into his arms, bridal style. She turned her face into his chest, hiding her tears from us.

"You were so beautiful, taking us tonight," he whispered to her. "Such a gorgeous princess. You did so well." Tentatively, she reached an arm around his neck to hold on to, to pull herself into his chest. His fingers tightened on her shoulder and her knee, where he'd wrapped his arms around her. "I've got you, princess. I'm going to put you to bed, okay?"

I grabbed a blanket from the living room and draped it over her, tucking it around her body where Rian held her, careful not to touch the cuts on her sides or the gorgeous red welt from my belt.

When Rian turned to take her to his bedroom, she didn't say a word, just closed her eyes and kept her face buried in his chest. He settled on the left side of the bed with his back against the headboard and gathered Ginevra sideways over his lap, gently stroking her hair and whispering quiet praise in her ear.

I wrapped a second blanket around her shoulders, then dropped into the bed beside Rian, lifting her calves so I could slide beneath them.

Gooseflesh ran up the skin of her legs as she shivered in our laps. Slowly, focus returned to her gaze.

Liam popped into the room with a bottle of water and a bar of chocolate. *Wow.* I didn't even know he knew how to aftercare. He threw himself onto the foot of the bed and unwrapped the chocolate before holding a square to her lips. Ginevra shook her head, refusing it.

"C'mon, little lamb. You were such a good girl down there. Don't ruin it now," he said. The laugh that escaped her was shocked, almost a sob. "It's my turn to feed you, since I didn't get to at dinner." When he didn't take the chocolate away, she parted her lips, accepting his sweet gift.

He alternated feeding her bites of chocolate with sips of water, and we slowly brought her back down to earth. We praised our gorgeous slut of a princess while hydrating her and bringing her blood sugar back up.

Christ, we were so fucked when it came to this woman.

8

GINEVRA

I woke up with a start, thrashing in the bed, my heart pounding out of my chest. By force of habit, I slid my hand under the pillow to check for the gun I kept there.

When I didn't find it, I sat up, pulling against the warm limbs that held me, and slid backward until my back hit the headboard. My breath escaped me in terrified rasps as I remembered where I was and why I was there. Rian's house. Rian's bed. Rian and Cormac sprawled out on the bed, their faces innocent and beautiful in repose. Rian, Cormac, and Liam, who'd fucked me stupid on their goddamned dining room table the night before.

Liam watched me with amused eyes from an armchair across the room, the early morning light highlighting the sharp planes of his face. "You all right, little lamb?" he asked me.

"Nightmare," I muttered, scooting down the bed so I could exit over the foot without waking up Rian and Cormac. He'd seen everything the night before. No need to be shy about my nudity now, I guessed.

"What were you looking for under the pillow?"

Should I tell him? Would he use it against me? "My gun."

Liam blinked, the lids of his green eyes moving slowly, like a lazy predator. He cocked his head and watched me as I practiced the breathing exercises my therapist had given me, exercises I'd been using for a decade now when I woke up terrified in the middle of the night.

"Get cleaned up and meet me downstairs," he said, an edge of command in his voice. He ran his hands through his shock of red hair as he stood. When I didn't move, he looked over my naked body with amusement. "Go take a shower, Ginevra," Liam said, his voice gentler than before. "Then come downstairs and get a cup of coffee."

I wasn't a submissive. I wasn't! And I wasn't ready to accept that these men had the power to command me and my body. But fuck, that shower sounded lovely. After Liam left the room, I hopped off the bed and groaned as pain shot through me. My entire body ached. My *core* ached. I felt like I'd been run over by a tank, then fucked by it. A hot shower sounded fantastic.

My clothes hung on the back of the bathroom door. Someone had unpacked my bag and moved my toiletries to the sink and the shower. The heat of the water pounding down on my sore muscles relaxed the tension from realizing I was alone in that room with three men with no way to defend myself.

Not that I had tried to stop them from doing whatever the fuck they wanted last night. The memory of my utter submission tasted bitter on my tongue as I relived the evening. Shame swept through me, and I let out a choked sob, leaning against the tiles. I couldn't let them know I was ashamed. I couldn't give these men an inch because they would reach in and steal a whole mile from me before I even realized what was going on.

Determination swelled in my chest as I washed the stickiness of the previous night's pleasure and pain off my body. They wanted me as much as I wanted them, more even. I could use that to my advantage. I had to.

When I emerged from the shower, I dressed for work in a simple and elegant navy suit and pulled my hair back into a sharp chignon, heavy and wet against the back of my neck. Although my makeup was mostly subtle, the deep red of my lipstick contrasted with the tan of my skin, drawing the eye to my mouth as I spoke. Clothing was a costume, my armor, and when I slipped my feet into my kitten heels, I looked like the CEO I was, from head to toe.

The greasy smell of frying bacon smacked me in the face as I clattered down the stairs. Liam's smile when he saw me broke a tension I didn't realize I'd been holding in my chest. He slid a plate full of eggs, bacon, sausage, beans, and a grilled tomato onto the table, where a cup of black coffee sat steaming. Beside the plate was my gun.

My breath caught in my throat and my gaze shot to his.

Liam grinned. "You're not a danger to us."

"And if I were?"

Something wild flickered in his green eyes. He licked his full lips and grinned wickedly. "Breaking you would be that much sweeter, wouldn't it then?"

The gun was a trap to get me to the table without reflecting on what I'd let them do to me there, what I'd done on it the night before. It worked. I snatched it up, checked the safety and the clip, then slid it into my waistband, where it sat against the small of my back, comforting me.

Breakfast was delicious. Cormac and Rian eventually

wandered downstairs in their sweatpants. I let my eyes rove over their bare chests despite my resolution to remain cool and distant that morning, unable to resist the appeal of their chiseled muscles clenching and pulling as they pulled up chairs and dug in.

"Like what you see, princess?" Rian asked, grinning as my eyes flicked over his shoulders and chest.

What little I'd eaten turned to stone in my stomach. Confusion and shame about last night, about my wantonness, about what I'd let them do to me, overwhelmed me. I clenched one hand around my coffee mug and hid the other in my lap to hide my violent trembling.

Cormac's smile was predatory as he noticed my unease. "Something bothering you, darling?"

Yes, I was fucking bothered. When I remembered his hands on me, squeezing my hips as he pounded into me, my thighs shifted involuntarily. It would almost have been easier if I hadn't given in, if I hadn't begged them to let me climax. Then I could have pretended that I hadn't been a willing participant in my own humiliation.

"Where can I set up to work? Somewhere the light's good, preferably," I asked, changing the subject.

"We have an office upstairs. Your stuff's already in there," Rian offered.

I pushed my chair back from the table, the legs scraping against the wood floor.

"Stop," Rian snapped. "Finish your food."

My jaw dropped. *Who the fuck does he think he is?*

Cormac's voice was low and angry. "Do as you're told, Ginevra. You won't like the punishment if you don't." His brown eyes bored into mine. "It won't be nearly as sexy as whatever you're thinking right now."

How did he fucking know?

I didn't need to pick fights with them this morning, though. With a sigh, I pulled my chair back to the table and picked up a mouthful of eggs. I ignored their lighthearted banter as I worked my way around my plate. They let me eat in silence.

When I walked to the kitchen and refilled my coffee mug, Cormac caged me against the counter, pressing his hips into my ass, the spicy scent of his cologne surrounding me. I flashed back to the night before, when he'd shoved me into a similar position against the dining room table. Scorching heat suffused every inch of my body, embarrassment and shame mingling with aching need as he pressed his bare chest into my back.

"Put your coffee down," he murmured, his breath hot against my ear. Hot liquid sloshed everywhere as I set the mug on the counter with unsteady hands. "I don't want you to forget whose slut you are while you're working today," he said, reaching around and unbuttoning my slacks. He pushed my pants and my panties halfway down my thighs and kicked my legs apart, baring me to him once again.

I whimpered as the ache in my core intensified, turning into painful need as he pushed my chest down toward the counter. "Rest on your forearms," he said as he ran his hands around my ass, tracing the raised red welt he'd left with his belt, soothing the pain with soft kisses. I didn't know what to make of his gentleness as I stood there, exposed in the fluorescent light of the kitchen.

The sound of a cap popping open startled me, and I jerked around, trying to see what he was doing. Cormac smacked me in the ass. The sharp pain surprised me, making my pussy flood with need.

"None of that," he rasped, dripping warm liquid down the crack of my ass. He reached around to show me what was in his hand—a silicone butt plug, soft and squishy but unnervingly wide. When I felt it enter me, I moaned softly. The stretch felt good until it didn't.

"Easy," Cormac said, running his hands up my back and soothing me before pulling it out and plunging it in just a little bit deeper each time. "Just relax and take it like the filthy whore you are."

My ass burned as it stretched me, pushing and pushing and then it was lodged completely inside me. I couldn't figure out how I felt. Uncomfortable. Full—stuffed, actually, like a fucking Christmas turkey. Turned on. Absolutely fucking dripping with need. With every movement, every shift of my thighs, I felt the plug, distracting me from any semblance of coherent thought.

Cormac wiped the excess lube off of me before pulling up my pants and straightening me out. He handed me my coffee. "Up you go then. Better get to work."

How was I going to concentrate with that monstrosity in my ass? Lord, what would the dry cleaners think when they got my suit pants, soaking wet and stinking of my desire? My body flushed pink with embarrassment. Maybe Rian was right. Maybe I was in over my head.

My phone sat beside my laptop and ring lamp, charging on a desk that faced a window. The laptop was open and plugged into a second monitor. Someone had taken care to find the best lighting in the room and create a space where I could work effectively.

One of the guys had set this up for me while I slept, after

the humiliating sex we'd had the night before. Fuck. I wasn't ready to examine what that might mean, not after Cormac had shoved a plug into my ass and then sent me off to work like the good little slut he thought I was.

Gingerly, I sat in the rolling office chair, biting back a moan as the plug nestled deeper. How was I going to concentrate on anything today? Dozens of notifications displayed on my phone. As I thumbed through them, mentally sorting them into personal, professional, and circular file buckets, I dragged myself back into executive mode.

I had another two hours before the office would open on the West Coast, giving me enough time to quickly take care of personal messages.

Sofia: Are you okay? Tell me you're still alive.
Ginevra: Fine. Will work from their house today and sleep at our parents' tonight. See you at dinner.

Cheryl: They rejected all of your changes to the contracts. I'm worried about you.
Ginevra: I'm not signing a contract that makes me their sex slave. It doesn't have any protections for me! Not even a safeword!
Cheryl: Exactly. Can I call?
Ginevra: Let me speak to them first.

Min-joon: Checking in on my roomie! Blink twice if you need me to fly to NYC right now.
Ginevra: Setting a wedding date this week. Will send info soon.
Min-joon: I want pictures.
Ginevra: You're coming right? To the wedding?

Min-joon: Wouldn't miss it for the world.

I dove into my work messages and emails. Rarely did I go an entire day without checking them. One of the reasons my company had seen such brilliant success was because I kept my finger on the pulse of it. Thankfully, none of the issues that had come up over the weekend required my direct intervention.

Every time I shifted in my seat, the plug in my ass reminded me I'd traded my body to three Irish gangsters for my family's security. I needed to get those contracts signed, and soon, so I wouldn't find myself trapped like this again, making side deals in exchange for my family's physical safety. Instead, I'd be enjoying the security those contracts would bring.

Two hours later, I was about to sign into the morning meeting for senior staff, when a heavy hand landed on my shoulder.

"Take a break," Liam said.

"I'm about to start a meeting," I answered, not even looking up at him.

"Is the plug starting to get uncomfortable?"

I didn't bother to hide my guffaw. "It's been uncomfortable since the moment Cormac put it in."

Liam leaned down to whisper in my ear. "It's very clear to me you're new to ass play. I'd like to add some lube, so it doesn't start to hurt."

Was he fucking kidding me? I spun around in the chair to face him. "I have an hour of meetings and then I'll have a quick break. Can I come find you then?"

He looked at me skeptically. "It's your ass, love."

A familiar dinging sound announced the beginning of the senior staff stand-up. Liam stepped out of the frame as I flicked on my ring light and swung around to face my laptop, my facial expression pleasant but neutral.

"Good morning, folks! Let's get started."

An hour later, I was exhausted from trying to pretend everything was normal with the plug in my ass constantly begging for my attention. Doing so while I checked out code and project milestones? Fine. Doing so while I carried on a conversation and made decisions about the course of my company? Much less so.

I slammed my laptop closed after the call, leaning back into the chair and closing my eyes. The plug really did ache. Liam knocked on the doorframe, a knowing grin on his face. "C'mon, lass, let's get you taken care of."

Every sore muscle from the night before screamed at me as I stood straight and linked my fingers above my head, stretching and clearing out the cobwebs that came from sitting still for so long. He led me through a bedroom to a bathroom and indicated that I should lean over the counter.

"Haven't you made your point? Can I just take it out?" I asked.

He laughed. "Lass, I'm not going to get between you and Cormac. I'm just trying to make you a bit more comfortable."

I wasn't sure what to make of that, so I undid my pants and slid them down to my knees with my panties.

Liam groaned as I bared my ass to him. "Fuckin' gorgeous," he said, running his hands over my naked curves. He ran a well-lubed finger around the edge of the plug where it entered me, then worked it slowly back and forth.

A moan burst out of me at the sensation. It was too much. I was too full. The morning had been too fucking hard with the plug deep in my ass. In a few seconds, I was mewling and whimpering as he fucked me with it.

"God, she's gorgeous when she's whoring for us, isn't she?" Cormac commented from the doorway. I froze. Liam didn't allow me to step away from the counter. My humiliation splashed icy water on the fiery inferno of my rising need.

Liam reached around and circled my clit with his other hand, bringing me higher and higher. My reflection in the mirror was wanton and needy as he expertly played my body. I writhed against him, seeking my climax as pleasure washed through me. He met my eyes in the mirror, then yanked his hands away right before I crashed over the cliff.

"What the fuck?" I snapped, reaching down to finish the job myself, only to find Liam and Cormac each with their fingers wrapped around one of my wrists.

Cormac's laughter echoed cruelly in the tile bathroom. "Only good girls get orgasms."

Was he out of his fucking mind? "What else do you want from me? I have done everything you've asked since the moment I stepped into this house last night."

Cormac hummed and met my eyes in the mirror. "Get on your knees and suck my cock."

"Go fuck yourself."

Cormac leaned in closer, pressing his torso against mine until I felt his hard cock pressing into the crack of my ass. "I told you, darling, only good girls get orgasms." He pushed himself off of me and sauntered out of the bathroom, whistling.

Goddammit.

I hauled up my panties and my pants, adjusting myself in the mirror until once again, I looked like an executive.

Liam wrapped his arms around my middle and pulled me backward into him, nuzzling his nose into the crown of my head. God, I wanted to relax into him and enjoy the hug.

It was a false comfort though, nothing more than trauma-bonding with a man who wanted to buy sex with me in exchange for acceptance by the old money that ran this town.

When I stiffened, he let me go, his easy going grin hiding his thoughts.

9

RIAN

Watching Liam beat the daylights out of some piece-of-shit who sent kids into my clubs to sell drugs didn't cheer me up the way I expected.

Liam stepped back from the chair where he'd taped the dealer into place. I leaned over the bound man, bringing my face close to his, propping myself up with a hand on the back of the chair. "Ikeji, the next time you send a kid into one of my establishments to sell adulterated product, I'm going to slice you up and feed you to the fucking hogs."

The Nigerian laughed. "Do you think my bosses will continue to sell you product, if you murder me?"

When I stuck my hand out for a knife, Liam laughed at me, the fucker. Normally, I left this sort of work to him, but watching Cormac plunge that plug into Ginevra's delicious ass had riled me up. I wanted to take my frustration out on someone, someone like this lowlife who knew where we got our product and seemed to think he could sell at the street level in our territory. *Fuck no.*

"Looks like there's dissent in your ranks, Rian O'Conner," Ikeji said, grinning, his white teeth flashing against the deep brown of his skin.

Liam chuckled, rolling up his shirt sleeves to reveal the tattoos covering his freckled skin. "No, Ikeji, no dissent. Just a good-natured argument about who gets to cut you up first. Rian already knows I'm going to win, so he's going to back the fuck off and let me carve my name in your face."

I fought the urge to pick a stupid fight with my best friend over who got to torture the Nigerian first and stepped out of the way. Liam cut a line down Ikeji's face, forgoing the pleasure of letters in the interest of expediency. "This is to remember me by, friend. Stay the fuck out of our clubs. And tell your bosses the price of arms'll go up if they pull this shit again."

Liam pounded his fist on the door, and his second in command opened it. "Take the trash out, Declan."

Once Ikeji was safely out of reach, Liam rounded on me. I expected a blow, not his wide grin. "Damn, Rian."

I groaned. Was I that obvious? "I need a fucking drink."

Liam laughed and laughed. *Asshole.* "Let's get you one, then." He took his shirt off before washing the blood off his skin, and I flicked my eyes over the clean lines of his taut muscles. He saw the direction my eyes had taken and winked as he buttoned up a clean shirt. He was a fucking animal in bed, but we'd never fallen into easy physical comfort with each other the way that Cormac and I had.

"Less daydreaming, more getting a move on, grumpy pants," Liam said, snapping his fingers in front of my face. Back in his suit, he looked like he'd spent the last half hour in a boardroom and not punishing Ikeji for his insolence. "I've got to get home and relube Ginevra in another hour."

I didn't understand Liam's insistence on caring for her. The previous night had been an aberration for all of us.

Cormac was generally good about taking care of his toys, but Liam happily broke them and left them sobbing. That affable smile hid an emotionless core that terrified even me when he let it loose.

"We want her out of the way, remember?"

Liam shook his head as he slid into the driver's seat of his SUV. "Stop fooling yourself, Rian. None of us want her out of the way."

I looked at him sharply as I buckled my seatbelt. "She's going to insert herself into our business."

Liam shrugged. "We knew things would change when we tied our fates to the Russos."

No, we thought I'd marry Sofia, break her, then send her back to her parents, dragging her out only on special occasions to present a united front to the Yorkfield community. Ginevra wouldn't break so easily, and I didn't want her sticking her nose where it didn't belong. I suspected she'd provide better access to echelons of power in the long run, but at what cost?

"Stop brooding, Rian. It's annoying," Liam snapped, slamming on the brakes and throwing me forward in the seat. "She's smart. She's well connected. She fucking melts when we dominate her, and her pussy is the sweetest I've ever had. What's not to like about her?"

I fucking hated it when he was right.

10

GINEVRA

Cormac poked his head in at five. "Ready to be a good girl?"

I yawned and stretched. With the exception of the humiliating and arousing breaks to relube with Liam, I worked in peace the whole day. Spinning around to face Cormac, I glared at him. "Pretty sure the answer to that question hasn't changed since the first time you asked this morning."

His white teeth flashed bright against umber skin as he smiled, amusement painting his features. "Sluts who sell their bodies don't get to say no to sucking cock."

God, I hated how much those words were a turn on, how wet I got when he used them to describe me. When he noticed me unconsciously pressing my thighs together, he crooked a finger.

I didn't move, so he strolled over to my rolling chair and bent over, wrapping his hands around the armrests and looming over me. "Are you refusing because you don't intend to obey, or because you're not done working for the day?"

Fuck.

How was he so good at making me complicit in my own degradation?

I pursed my lips while he waited patiently for my answer. "I can wrap this up in fifteen minutes or so."

He nodded and slipped out the door. I ruefully turned back to my laptop to close out the day. I'd have to log back on later that night, when I was back at my parents' house. Signing out after eight hours did not a successful entrepreneur make, but I could afford to take a break for a few hours until I got home and ate dinner.

Fifteen minutes later, to the second, all three men walked into the office together. God, they were beautiful. Each wore a suit, perfectly tailored to their trim physiques. Rian, with his black hair and piercing blue eyes, loosened his tie and revealed the tattoos decorating his neck and chest. Cormac's stark white shirt contrasted with his deep brown skin as he slid out of his jacket and rolled his shirtsleeves up, revealing the strength of his forearms. Liam's shock of red hair shined bright against the gray of his suit as he pulled off his belt and snapped it.

My pussy clenched at the sharp noise as it cracked through the suddenly crowded office. Was I looking forward to this? What had these men done to me?

"Strip," Cormac said, his voice raspy as he watched me with hooded eyes.

I stood up from the chair and eased off my jacket. My kitten heels sat under the desk, kicked off hours ago so I could sit comfortably. With trembling fingers, I slid my gun out of the waistband of my pants and set it on the desk. Then I unbuttoned my blouse, shrugging it off my shoulders and dropping it on the floor.

The three men watched me, the heat of their gazes

searing my skin as I unhooked my bra and dropped it to the floor, freeing my breasts. My nipples pebbled as I stood there for a second, my breath turning ragged as desire raged through me. With a sharp exhale and a reminder to myself that this was the price of my family's security, I slid my pants and panties down my legs and kicked them away. Standing before them, flushed with embarrassment, my body on display, the contrast between my nudity and their clothing made me feel particularly vulnerable.

"You're such a perfect little whore for us," Cormac said, one corner of his mouth tilting up into a smile as he admired me. He sat in the seat I'd just vacated and reached beneath it, lowering it several inches with a whoosh. "Kneel."

The clacking sound of the chair as it hit the lowest setting brought me back to the present. I backed away from him. "No. I don't want to do this."

Crack! Liam's belt whipped through the air and slapped my ass. When I cried out, reaching my hands behind me to block my stinging skin from another hit, Cormac just chuckled. "You are mistaken if you think you have a choice, Ginevra."

Shaking and unable to get my breathing under control, I sank to my knees between his splayed legs, my focus on the hard length trapped against his thigh in his pants. Rian and Liam stood behind me. I imagined their gazes raking up and down my naked and glistening pussy, once again on display for them, the red stripe across my ass glowing in the evening light.

Cormac reached down and adjusted himself. "Suck."

As if in a dream, disconnected from my body, I slid my fingers up his thighs and to his fly. Unzipping it, I reached into his boxers and pulled out his cock. He felt like hot velvet under my fingers as I tentatively explored him. It wasn't like I'd never given a blowjob before, but something about this moment felt more significant than the others.

Cormac leaned forward, running his fingers through my hair. "C'mon, my precious little slut, surely this isn't the first time you've seen a man's cock. You can do this."

I could. A bead of pre-cum sat on the tip of him. As if of its own volition, my tongue darted out to lick it. The salty taste in my mouth combined with his musky scent and the spice of his cologne, making me dizzy with need. I groaned, and my pussy clenched on air as I bent my head to take him in my mouth. I fisted the base of his cock, then slid my hand up to meet my mouth. Why wasn't I protesting? Why was I putting up with this bullshit?

"That's right, you filthy little slut, just like that," he murmured, stroking my hair with his fingers, gently, as if to comfort me. God, I hated it. I loved it. I hated that I loved it. I didn't know what the fuck I was feeling. What the hell was wrong with me?

I ran my tongue around the tip of his cock as I held it in my mouth, exploring the feel of him, before hollowing out my cheeks and sucking hard.

He groaned and threw his head back. "Oh yes, that's it, darling. You're so fucking beautiful on your knees like that."

The warmth of his praise shot through me and I reveled in the power I held over this beautiful, dominant man as my mouth moved over him.

God, I'm fucked up.

"Can you take him further, lamb?" Liam asked, his voice hot and tense as I bobbed my head up and down.

I shook my head, taking the opportunity to swirl my tongue around the tip of his cock. Cormac hummed, amused, before wrapping his fingers in my hair, drawing my head closer. "Let me help."

Frantically, I tried to pull away, but a hard hand on my back held me in place as he slammed my face down over his cock, pushing deeper and deeper into my mouth until I was crying and gagging. When I tried to pull back, his grip tightened, dragging hard on my hair.

"Relax your throat," Liam said softly, his voice right behind me. "Breathe through your nose," he rasped. The heat of his body warmed me as he straddled me from behind. I heard him stroking his cock over my back in time with the rhythm of my mouth as tears streamed down my face.

I tried to follow Liam's directions as Cormac's cock cut off my air supply and I panicked, sobbing and struggling. Cormac pulled back, and I sucked in a quick breath before he plunged into my throat again and again. His rhythm turned rough as he yanked on my hair, swearing and praising me.

"Open your mouth all the way," Cormac instructed, jerking me off him and tilting my head back. He spurted hot cum into my mouth, all over my face, dripping down my chest. As I took a shuddering breath, trying to recover from the intense humiliation, I heard two ragged shouts behind me, and felt hot liquid hit my shoulders and back, dripping down my hot, flushed skin.

I couldn't hold back the sob that escaped me. Tears streamed down my face as I knelt on the office carpet, weeping from the humiliation. Warm hands reached out to me, running their hands over my chest and my back, rubbing their cum into my skin, marking me.

Rian hummed his satisfaction. "Good girls get to come, princess."

No. I didn't want to come. I wanted to wash their bullshit off me and run back to California and forget every compassionate instinct that had driven me back to the East Coast to save my sister.

But I didn't move. I just kneeled there and cried, dripping tears into the carpet as I sniveled.

Hands gently soothed my aching, stinging ass, then a wet finger worked its way along the plug still planted deep inside me. One of the men rocked it in and out of me, his motions gentle and careful. I couldn't stop crying, even as the feeling of fullness and friction of the plug pumping in and out of me brought me back to arousal.

"Easy there, princess," Rian said, soothing me as he pulled it out. The empty feeling left me strangely bereft as I waited on the office floor.

Cormac slid down off the chair and pulled me into him, heedless of the sticky cum smearing over his suit as I cried into his chest. He wrapped his arms around me. "You did amazing, darling. Absolutely perfect." Another set of arms wrapped around me from behind, and we kneeled awkwardly on the floor. Nameless hands ran down my hair and tender lips rained kisses over my temple as the men slowly brought me back to earth.

"Good girls get their reward," Cormac murmured in my ear. He took off his jacket, laying it on the floor beside us. "Lie down, darling."

When I didn't move, his voice turned hard. "I don't like repeating myself, particularly not to sluts who aren't smart enough to take a reward when it's offered."

Fingers behind me dug into my ass, pressing on the welts. I whimpered as pain radiated through me. "Okay," I whispered through sniffles and tears. "Okay."

I crawled to his jacket and laid down on my back, my

knees up and together, one arm over my eyes as if I could block their fierce stares from seeing my emotional turmoil. The cold slime of their cum on my back, smooshing against the fine fabric of the jacket, threatened to dislodge another sob from me.

"None of that, darling," Cormac said, pulling my hands from my eyes with infinite care and setting them on the ground by my sides, delicately, as if I were made of glass. He sat behind me and lifted my head until I rested on his crossed legs. Making gentle shushing noises, he stroked my hair and the parts of my face not covered in his cum, as if trying to calm me.

Liam knelt on one knee to my right. He held the belt in front of me. "Do you want me to restrain you for this?"

I whimpered, not wanting to make the decision. If I said yes, I was complicit in my own bondage. If I said no, I wouldn't have an excuse for enjoying this. Another tear trickled down my face. I didn't fucking know what I wanted.

"Too soon, Liam," Cormac snapped.

Liam stroked my cheek. "Easy, sweetheart. At some point, I'm going to expect you to lie still because I tell you to, but that doesn't have to be today. I'm going to bind your wrists above your head, all right?"

I nodded my understanding and lifted my wrists to him. He was gentle, so gentle, as he tightened the belt and raised my wrists above my head, lowering them against Cormac's torso, where they weighed down on the crown of my head.

Liam hummed his approval and walked his fingers down my cheek and then my chest, inconscient of the sticky mess that Cormac had left there. He bent down and licked a nipple, keeping his movements slow and gentle. A soft moan escaped me before I could clamp my mouth shut.

I pressed my lips into a tight line, only for Cormac to

gently run his fingers across the seam. When I tried to hide my face, he tightened his grip in my hair. "I'll let you shut your eyes this time, Ginevra, but don't you dare turn away from me."

At the same time, Rian planted featherlight kisses on my calves, working his way up the tops of my legs to my knees. He pushed them apart, his touch gentle, as if he were asking my permission. Liam chose that moment to take the peak of my breast into his mouth, scraping his teeth against my nipple. I cried out, unsure whether from pleasure or pain or both, relaxing my clenched leg muscles. Rian gently pulled my thighs apart. Cormac slid two fingers into my mouth and I closed my lips around them, sucking on him as if by instinct.

As Liam lavished attention on my breasts, Rian kissed and licked his way up my thighs, leaving tiny love bites on my soft skin. My body grew restless, and the ache in my core intensified. Liam chuckled softly when I shifted my hips against the carpet, seeking relief from the need they were building in me.

When Rian ran his tongue up my folds, my hips jerked as if a current of electricity ran through me. "That's it, princess, take your pleasure," he murmured as he buried his face in my pussy, licking with the enthusiasm of a starving man. I groaned and whined as I tried to push my hips into him. He tapped against my clit with his tongue, circling it, tasting it, exploring my pussy with slow deliberation, hitting every sweet nerve as he figured out what made me tick.

All of it. It all made me tick. In moments, I was writhing and mewling, desperate as the heat of my need drove me higher and higher. "Please, God, please," I begged.

Liam's answering chuckle was wicked. "No God here, sweet Ginevra, just us."

"Rian," I cried out, pleading for release.

My cries and my pleas were to no avail as he continued his implacable assault on my pussy. Liam reached above my head to grip my wrists, holding them in place as I twisted and writhed on the floor.

I felt a finger slide into me, and then two. "Rian, please!" I shouted.

The deep rumble of his chuckle against my clit almost sent me over the edge.

"Look at me, lass," Liam commanded. I looked straight up into his green eyes as he knelt over me, one hand on my wrists, the other stroking my neck.

He wrapped his long fingers around my throat at the same time that Rian sped up the motions of his fingers inside me. As I cried out, Liam tightened his grip, holding my eyes with his as my air supply cut off and terror mingled with intense pleasure.

"Now!" Liam snapped.

Rian bit my clit and shoved a third finger inside me, roughly fucking me as my hips twitched. As the corners of my vision faded to black, stars exploded across my vision and I screamed, my climax crashing into me like a fucking tsunami. Waves of pleasure washed over me as Rian's fingers and tongue drew out my pleasure until I was a whimpering sodden mess, limp on the floor.

Liam leaned back on his haunches. "Damn, if that wasn't the most beautiful thing I've ever seen."

"So fucking beautiful," Cormac agreed, still stroking my hair and my face with his fingertips as I trembled from the aftershocks of my orgasm. I resisted the urge to turn my face into his hand and nuzzle it, to take comfort from his steady presence, to float in a sea of bliss instead of facing the harsh reality of these men.

Rian sat up until he kneeled at my feet and wiped his face on his shirtsleeves. "C'mon, princess, let's get you cleaned up." I didn't have the energy to sit, much less walk myself to the shower. He seemed to understand, scooping his arms under my shoulders and my knees and standing with me pressed against his chest.

Liam carefully unbuckled my wrists, inspecting them closely for bruises, then rubbing the circulation back into them. He and Cormac dropped soft kisses on my forehead before Rian carried me out of the office and into the same bathroom I'd used that morning for my shower.

These men were going to ruin me.

11

GINEVRA

My father sat at the head of the dining room table with his espresso and a stack of newspapers, the same as he had every day during my childhood. When I plopped down beside him in slacks and a blouse, he ignored me until I reached across the table to snag a paper to read. He slapped my hand. Old habits died hard, I guess.

"Good morning, Ginevra."

"Good morning, Papà."

He stared at me over his paper for a long moment, then pushed a disheveled pile of already read newspapers over to me, moving the neat stack I'd touched to his other side.

I skipped the big national papers in favor of our hometown rag. God, it felt good to be home. Hot tears threatened to spill out as I settled back into the habits of my childhood.

Mamma brought me an espresso and a pastry. She hadn't cooked, but scheduled daily delivery from a local bakery before dawn, just as she had since I was a child.

"I'm glad to see you've decided to spend some time with your family," she sniffed.

Was she fucking kidding me? I slammed my cup on the table. My father's eyes were censorious, but he didn't move to stop me. "Mamma, do you know why I spent the night with those gangsters?"

Her face fell before she brought her expression back to neutrality. *Oh*. Picking a fight with me was her way of letting me know she cared. Ten years gone, and we slipped right back into our terrible, dysfunctional habits. I reached across the table and took her hand in mine. "Mamma, it's okay. You're worth it. *Sofia* is worth it."

Papà harrumphed and set his paper down. "We're going to tour the city today, visit the warehouses and the port, maybe some of the other businesses."

Together, Sofia and Luca joined us at the table. "Sofia will be joining us," Luca said, his voice soft and even. Papà harrumphed again, but didn't object. When Sofia reached for my hand under the table, I squeezed it, then leaned over to whisper, "Go put some closed-toe shoes on, okay?"

She looked at me, then darted out of the room. When I looked at Luca, a wide smile took over his face. "Welcome home, big sister."

Our father said nothing, just sighed, and for a moment, I pretended we were a normal family, joking and teasing each other at breakfast. Then Alexi walked into the room, plopped down into the seat beside me, and snatched the newspaper out of my fingers.

"Good morning, *piccolina*," he said, the sharp snap of the paper cracking through the room like a shot.

Luca caught my eye and shook his head. *Right. Pick my damn battles.*

When we made our way to the cars, Rian waited for us, handsome and well dressed, as always. He loomed over the rest of the men, over six feet of gorgeous and well-built male, with eyes only for me.

Relaxing into his embrace, I leaned on him for a second as he dragged me into him, then gently brushed his lips over each of my cheeks. "How are you doing this morning?"

He imbued the question with more meaning than a simple morning greeting. Leaning on his strength, I took stock of my sore muscles and my emotional fragility. "I'll survive," I muttered into his chest.

"Surely we can do better than that," he said, his voice soft and intended for my ears only, as he kissed the top of my head.

I glanced up at him through my lashes, not ready to face the emotions flowing through me. I held on to him, soaking up his strength, as I sorted through my confusion.

When my father cleared his throat, I stepped away, freeing Rian to greet the men in our entourage. Before I realized what had happened, I found myself pushed to the back of the group with Sofia.

Too quickly, Alexi directed Rian, my father, and Luca to join him in the first car, leaving Sofia and I in the follow car with Alexi's second, Lorenzo. *Fuck*. As I debated whether this battle was worth it, my phone pinged.

Rian: How much is it worth to you for me to get you in the car where decisions will be made?

Hot tears threatened to spill, a timely reminder to get my shit together, because mafia dons sure as fuck didn't cry in public. When I inhaled sharply, it caught Sofia's attention. She stood by the second car in her jeans and white tennis shoes looking like goddamned Miss USA, and I didn't have the heart to take this away from her.

I slid into the front seat beside Lorenzo.

"Miss Russo, Miss Russo," he greeted each of us.

"None of that, Lorenzo," I answered with a smile. "You called me Ginevra when I was a child, and the only thing that's changed is that we're both a little bit taller." I filed away the fact that Sofia didn't give him the same license to use her first name.

He scrubbed a hand through his closely cropped hair. "Sure thing, Ginevra. It's good to have you home."

I watched him out of the sides of my eyes as he drove. "Are you giving me the tour?"

"Not sure what you're talking about, Ginevra. My orders are to follow Alexi."

"I was promised a tour of the neighborhood and a rundown of the family businesses."

It was his turn to look at me out of the sides of his eyes. "All of them?"

My laugh rang out sharp and bitter in the confines of the luxury SUV. "Did you forget why I'm here?"

Lorenzo sighed. "No, ma'am, I guess not."

He didn't say a word though, just drove in silence through the city, following the first car.

Rian: Having fun yet?
Ginevra: *middle finger emoji*
Rian: What's it worth to you for me to ask Luca to change places with you?
Liam: Did she get stuck in the follow car?

I swiped into my chat with my brother.

Ginevra: Luca, swap places with me after the first stop.

A cleansing wave of white hot rage washed through me when my brother left me on read. This was ridiculous. "Lorenzo, I'd like to drop by the port first, do you mind?"

"I don't think that's a good idea, ma'am."

"I'd like to do it anyway."

Sighing like I'd just told him I was about to murder an entire litter of puppies, he pulled the car over and called Alexi. Alexi didn't pick up because Alexi was driving.

"No can do, Ginevra."

"When my father gives you an order, do you have to check with Alexi first?"

Lorenzo turned, his face furious, knowing exactly where I was going with this. "No, Ginevra, I don't."

"And did my father make me a *capo* or not?"

He shrugged. "Maybe on paper. But none of the guys are ever going to follow a chick. That's why you were never going to be the heir."

Lorenzo was right, of course. I was never going to be the heir—however progressive my father might have been, the other families would never accept it—but his sharp business sense had prepared me to move out to California and survive on my own. That wasn't the fucking point, though.

"A penis wouldn't have been able to snare the Irish into paying ten million dollars to pay off my father's debt to the Bratva, either."

Sofia choked back startled laughter.

"Forget it, Lorenzo," I said, sighing deeply. "Let's go follow Alexi and the rest of the penises."

I slumped back in my seat.

Ginevra: Fuck you, Rian.
Rian: That's what I'm angling for, to be honest.
Ginevra: What do you want?

Rian: My cock in your mouth.

Ten years of work to get away from this family, to go to school on the other side of the country, to run my own multi-million dollar businesses, and a fucking Irish gangster was texting me to ask if I'd give him a blow job in exchange for not being shut out of my father's business just because I had a vagina.

"The stevedores, the dockworkers, are all union men," my father explained to Rian. "But we own the dry docks and the equipment they use to unload the boats." I trailed behind with my sister, hurt and angry at being shut out of yet another conversation. At the first three stops, I'd tried to shove my way into their conversations, only to find myself on the outside of every meeting, pushed aside with courtesy, but frozen out of every single discussion of substance.

The four men wandered ahead, the love my father had for his business clear in his voice as he explained it to Rian, as Luca and Alexi looked on. Lorenzo waited by the cars, his job to make sure nobody messed with them in case we had to make a quick getaway. In theory, Alexi's presence provided enough security here in the port, deep in my father's territory, where the Russos had an uncomplicated relationship with both the authorities and the unions that staffed it.

Fucking useless, I thought to myself. Not a single one of the men noticed Sofia and me dropping further and further behind.

I took my sister's hand. She was still wide-eyed with wonder, thrilled just to be allowed on the field trip. "I gotta head home, Sofia. The workday for the business that actually makes me money started an hour ago."

Sofia slanted her lips upward in a rueful smile. "You're not getting a lot out of this anyway, are you?"

Ginevra: We're heading back to the car.

Rian didn't look at his phone. He must not have heard it ping, lost in my father's lecture about the history of our presence here. I sighed. Papà's charm and love for the community fascinated me, too. It had grown the Russos from minor players to the force we were today. Too bad I'd allowed myself to be maneuvered out of his orbit today.

Sofia and I wandered back toward the entrance to the port, keeping our conversation quiet as I explained the mechanics of how cargo moved from boats to warehouses. Despite my sister's ignorance about the family business, she was bright and asked smart questions about how we fit into the process.

The first time I heard a clatter above us, clanging against the metal of the rows of containers that surrounded us, I attributed it to the natural noises of the port, or birds jumping from container to container in search of rodents or trash. The second time, I whipped around, shoving Sofia behind me and against a container. I scanned our surroundings, searching for the source of the noise. The third time, heavy footsteps followed us as we continued through the maze of containers, sending my heart drumming in a worried rhythm.

Fuck.

I drew my gun from the small of my back and motioned for Sofia to press herself against a container, ducking into a row of them so we were partially hidden from view of the main path. Holding my gun in front of me, I backed into the metal wall, well aware the layers of steel that made up the container's walls were of limited use for blocking bullets.

Letting whomever followed us lure us into the maze of containers was a death sentence. The offices to the right of us, in containers themselves, were a surer bet in terms of safety.

We only had to cross two hundred yards to reach the safety of the car and Lorenzo, but that two hundred yards was a warren of offices and equipment. It would block the line of sight for any shooters, but would also impede me from seeing where they were. I couldn't see a good way to cover Sofia as we dashed to the car.

Maybe I was overreacting. Maybe I'd imagined the sounds on the containers high above our heads. Maybe I was just looking for the drama and excitement of my youth.

As if God had reached down and pressed the mute button, the port silenced—no birds chirping, no hum of machinery, just dead silence as I realized how fucked we were. No, I wasn't overreacting at all.

Sofia shook in terror as she leaned against the cool metal of the container. I grabbed her hand, hoping to reassure her, to calm her trembling and hide my own fear. My mouth was bone dry and my heart was pounding out of my chest. I slipped off my blazer, wrapped it in a ball, then tossed it out onto the pathway between containers.

The repetitive crack of gunfire filled the air as an automatic weapon blew my designer jacket to pieces.

Whirling, I located the source of the gunfire above us and shot, letting instinct take over my movements. *Bang bang bang!* When I heard a howl of pain, I knew my aim was true. It had been over ten years since I'd shot at a person, but I hadn't neglected my hours on the range.

A spray of gunshots slammed into the corner of the container. Bullets lodged in the layers of steel, interrupting my prayers to a god I didn't believe in that Rian and Luca heard the sound of gunshots. *Fuck.* We needed to get to a place where we could wait for reinforcements.

The next closest solid object was about twenty yards away — a row of concrete planters. "Sofia," I whispered. "When I say go, I want you to dash in a straight line as fast as you can toward the office over there, then hide between the concrete planter and the wall, okay? I'll be right behind you."

Sofia nodded, her eyes wide and terrified. Thank goodness I told her to change her shoes that morning. On my signal, she took off at a dead run. I did my best to lay down suppressing fire as we dashed toward the concrete wall. Pain flashed in my side as I dove for the safety of the planter, tumbling down beside Sofia and wincing as sharp agony burned through me.

Shit, shit, shit. Gasping for breath, Sofia and I crouched as I pressed my hand to my side, trying to assess the damage. It came away bloody.

Tears streaked down Sofia's face as she whimpered in terror, but I couldn't comfort her while bullets slammed into the concrete above us. I'd misjudged where the danger was. I took a deep breath, then popped up, my head and hands peeking above the planter so I could shoot. Silence. I hadn't hit anything. By the time I'd ducked back down, the shooter was firing again.

Concrete shattered and rained down on our heads. The shooter knew exactly where we were. We could crawl further down the planters, but we'd just be trapping ourselves in a blind alley. The only other option to move was back toward the containers.

Fuck.

We were only marginally better off than before, and if they kept shattering the concrete, we'd be sitting ducks when it was gone.

Suddenly, gunfire filled the air from all directions. I dove toward Sofia, pushing her head to the ground and covering her as concrete exploded over us. We listened to the shouts of surprise and pain as we shuddered in fear, followed by the sound of bodies thudding to the ground. Neither of us moved.

"Ginevra?" Rian called out. "It's clear."

I tried to release Sofia, but for some reason, couldn't quite pry my arms away from her. Strong hands reached down to me, pulling me up and into Rian's warm chest. He wrapped his hands around my gun and lowered it before peeling my fingers from the grip, taking it away from me.

"Easy, princess," he murmured as I shook in his arms, taking deep, shuddering breaths as adrenaline surged out of me, leaving me bereft and exhausted. He ran his hands down my back, and I gasped in pain as he grazed my ribs.

"What's this?" he asked, tugging my shirt out of my pants and rolling it up.

I grimaced as he revealed the oozing red streak where a bullet had scraped by me. Even though I knew the searing fury in his gaze wasn't for me, I took a step backward. "Is Sofia okay?"

We both looked over at her, sobbing into Luca's chest.

"She will be," Rian answered, his voice low and angry.

"I've got one," Lorenzo shouted. Together, Rian and I made our way over to him, our hands clasped together like teenage lovers.

When I pulled away, Rian tightened his grip on our interlocked fingers. "Stay with me, princess. I'm about to lose my fucking shit over you getting shot, and the only thing keeping me from murdering this guy right now, is your hand in mine."

An unwelcome warmth suffused me at his protectiveness.

His blue eyes were dark with rage as he stared down at the bruised and bloody body on the ground. Lorenzo made quick work of duct taping the man's hands and feet together, until he lay trussed like a Thanksgiving turkey.

"I'll take him back to the Russos'," Lorenzo told Rian, who nodded his assent. "He's the only one who survived."

"Did anyone escape?" I asked, my voice raspy as I came down from the adrenaline high.

Alexi and Papà jogged toward us. Their swift pursuit of the shooters reminded me of how my father came to be the head of the most powerful mafia family in Yorkfield. Blood was splattered over my father's broad chest and he held a gun in his hands. Although he was breathing hard, his furious energy gave him an air of youth as he shook his head. "Two men on top of the containers got away. A van with run-flat tires was waiting for them as they ran out of the port."

Damn.

Lorenzo and Luca wrestled the struggling body into the trunk of a car, then piled in. Rian dragged me into the backseat of the same SUV, buckling me into the middle seat so he could sling an arm over my shoulders without disturbing the wound in my side. Unwilling to examine why his protectiveness was so comforting, I leaned into him, inhaling sharply at the burning pain as Lorenzo sped to my parents' house.

12

LIAM

Ginevra winced as she climbed out of the SUV before calming her face into neutrality. She was still bleeding. Rage washed over me.

Nobody was allowed to break my toys but me.

Rian walked around from the other side of the car, keeping an eye on her as she walked into her family's home. She refused his help with a curt gesture. Guilt flashed over Rian's face before he slammed down an impassive mask, hiding his thoughts.

Cormac's motorcycle kicked up dust as he slid into the driveway. His eyes flared with fury when he took off his helmet and observed Ginevra's slow walk. Sofia shuddered in her father's arms as he walked her into the house.

Poor kid.

Rian had texted us from the car. Intellectually, we knew Ginevra was going to be fine. The bullet only grazed her, and she just needed antiseptic, gauze, and time. But all three of us were losing our minds over this woman. It didn't bode well for the future—once she realized her power, she'd wrap us around her sexy little fingers.

In the meantime, the instinct to make sure she was okay rode me hard. After he fucked up by letting her out of his sight at the port, I struggled to trust that Rian had it in hand.

Lorenzo and Alexi, two assholes who'd also failed to keep my woman safe, stood behind the vehicle, staring down at the body they'd shoved in there. I joined them.

"Oy there, boys," I drawled, letting my Irish accent shine through. "I hear you had a bit of trouble this morning." They didn't need to know how furious I was about Ginevra.

Lorenzo's eyes were stormy when he looked at me. "More than a bit. You saw Ginevra." He ran his hands through his short, curly hair. "I just don't fucking—" he cut himself off, glancing at Alexi through the side of his eye. "Let's see what this asshole knows."

I reached into the vehicle, but before I could drag the man out by his bound wrists, Lorenzo lay a hand on my arm. I told him to go fuck himself, but he only shook his head.

"Back entrance. We don't drag bodies through the front door because it upsets Patti," Alexi explained, slamming the back door of the SUV shut.

Lorenzo dropped into the front seat and pulled around to the back of the house. This time, I hauled the man out and dropped him on the ground. He was a small white guy, no more than five-eight, and wiry, his head shaved and tattooed. Russian gang symbols covered his visible skin. When I crouched to get a better look at his tats, he spit on me.

Lorenzo crouched down and lifted the Bratva over his shoulder in a fireman's carry. He slid a keycard into the lock on a door partially hidden by bushes. I followed him into the cool basement of the Russo mansion and sighed with envy at the tiled floors and walls, so much easier to wash blood out of than the concrete we had at Rian's.

Note to self, ask Rian if I can renovate.

Lorenzo slammed the man into a metal chair, bolted to the ground. He swiftly sliced through the duct tape before cuffing each ankle to a leg of the chair. When he'd done the same to our captive's arms, we stood back and assessed. Our captive's skin was sallow under the harsh fluorescent light as he sat slumped, his eyes malevolent and angry.

Cormac leaned against the wall, his arms crossed over his chest. "Get a move on, Liam. I can't go up to check on our girl until you've gotten answers out of this asshole."

When I grabbed the man's chin to pull his face up, I asked him, "Are you ready to talk?"

"You haven't asked me any questions yet." His Russian accent was heavy. "Do you think you can break me?" He laughed, a bitter edge to his voice. "You fucking Americans don't know shit about torture."

I grinned. These days, I kept my wildness locked up tight. Rian frowned on torture in general, and especially the painful cruelty I enjoyed inflicting. He'd make an exception for our girl, though. It's not like he'd be able to stuff this guy's intestines back in when I finished, to take him back to the Russians.

"Lucky for you, I wasn't born here either." I slammed his head into the back of the metal chair, and he grunted, but didn't make any other noise.

"Who ordered the hit at the port today?"

The Bratva laughed. "You are a fucking moron."

I walked to the cabinets along the walls of the Russo's basement and rummaged through them until I found the tools I needed. Lorenzo grinned at me, then dragged a metal table across the room so I could drop my armload. He handed me a pair of latex gloves. Perfect.

The scalpel I held in my hand glinted in the light. I pushed it against our captive's cheek, cutting just deep enough to bleed and admiring the dark red that dripped down his face. Twisting my lips at the asymmetry I'd caused, I snapped my wrist and cut his other cheek, too. *Better.*

"Enlighten me."

The Bratva didn't say anything, just stared straight ahead.

Cormac shoved himself off the wall. I guess he was getting bored. "Do you know who you're talking to?"

The Bratva spat blood again, hitting Cormac's shoes. "Who the fuck cares? You're not Tony Russo, and you can't do shit until he gets here."

"Fucking Russians, dumb as bricks," Cormac responded, nudging the Russian's shoe with his own. "My friend's name is Liam Bryne."

The Russian's eyes widened. "The Butcher," he whispered.

"That's right," I said, nodding, unleashing a bit of my crazy as I admired how his grimace stretched the streaks of blood on his face into an artful caricature.

"Why did you try to kill Ginevra today?" I asked.

He spat again. I held out my hand. Cormac handed me a pair of pliers, keeping his eyes on the Russian prisoner the entire time. Lorenzo stepped back, perhaps to watch an artist at work. I jammed the needle nose of the pliers under the prisoner's index finger and yanked. He screamed as I pulled the fingernail out.

"Why did you shoot at the Russo girls today?" I repeated.

The Bratva shook his head, but said nothing. Goddamned Russians.

Cormac muttered something under his breath, but all I caught was his irritation. "Do you have a problem, Cormac?" I snapped at him.

Cormac cut his eyes toward Lorenzo. "Get a fucking move on," he repeated.

Damn. Always ruining my fun. He was right, though. We couldn't trust any answers out of this guy's mouth once Alexi got down here. *Fine.*

I took the pliers and wrenched out a few more fingernails.

The Russian screamed. "They wanted to scare her!"

Without letting him know how surprised I was, I pulled out another nail. "Scare who?" I asked, around his whimpering.

"Scare the Russo bitch!" he shouted.

"Which one?"

"The older one! Bitch never should have come back."

Ginevra? They wanted to scare my Ginevra? Rage overtook my good sense, and I backhanded him, sending his head snapping to the side. "Why?" I growled, leaning close.

"I don't know! But the order came from Yuri!" he sobbed. The number two Bratva was ordering hits on Ginevra? That didn't make a damn bit of sense.

"Think harder. Why would Yuri want to scare a Russo who's been gone for ten years?"

The Russian shook his head. "I don't know," he cried.

I grabbed a knife off the table beside me and stabbed it into his thigh, careful to avoid his artery. Despite the red clouding my vision, I hung onto just enough sanity to know I needed him alive for a few more minutes.

"I need more than that."

"She was here before she left! She was born a fucking

Russo, and she was raised a fucking Russo, and she did fucking Russo shit to the Russians."

Well, fuck. Our little lamb had unplumbed depths. I exchanged a look with Cormac. Before Lorenzo could stop me, I lunged toward the Russian, cut through his belly, then reached in and pulled. He screamed as his intestines spilled out between his legs and onto the floor. After a few moments, I sliced across his neck, sending blood spattering across the room.

"What the fuck!" Lorenzo shouted, looking at the mess I'd made with horror. "You fucking killed him!"

Cormac caught my eye, murder written all over his face. We advanced on Lorenzo together. The Italian-American man stood his ground.

"Do you trust Alexi?" I asked him, my voice soft and sharp.

"I trust him to keep Antonio safe," Lorenzo answered, his face giving nothing away.

"And the girls?"

Lorenzo twisted his mouth in distaste. "You saw what happened today, didn't you?"

His honesty was refreshing. "Something rotten in the kingdom of Denmark?"

But Lorenzo just smiled and said, "My loyalty is to the Russos, all of them."

That would have to be enough. Cormac and I backed off. I grabbed the bloody equipment and walked it over to the sink to rinse it off.

"The cleaners will be by in about an hour," Lorenzo said, laying a hand on my arm. "Go check on your girl. I'll be up in a few minutes."

. . .

Diamond In The Dark

THE GROWL that escaped me as I exited the damp stairwell into the sunny kitchen startled Ginevra. She looked over her shoulder toward me, her warm brown eyes wide and tremulous as a handsome young man taped gauze to her wound.

"Are these scratches new?" he asked, looking at the cuts I'd left on her back two nights before. They were already healing. The medic needed to keep his damn hands to his damn self.

Cormac lay a calming hand on my shoulder as I slowly released the rage pumping through my veins.

Our woman blushed, somehow looking sweet and pretty despite her embarrassment. "The scratches are fine. How do I take care of this?" She gestured to the bandage on her side, changing the subject back to her immediate care.

"Keep it covered and dry for the next day or so, then keep it clean. You'll want to apply anti-bacterial cream and bandage it every time you wash it. Take painkillers as you need them." He handed her an orange bottle with a dozen pills inside.

Ginevra nodded sharply at the medic, then hopped down from the kitchen island where she'd been sitting. When she turned around to face me, her eyes took in my blood splattered clothes and the grim line of my mouth.

"What did he have to say?" she asked me, not bothering with any sort of preamble.

Damn, our woman was cold. I bet if I put a knife in her hand she'd be fucking brutal at interrogations. *Now wasn't that a thought to keep me warm at night?*

"Not much. The Russians are trying to scare you."

She frowned. "Scare me? Do they know about our contract?"

Rian took her hand in his and tugged her out of the kitchen, gently, as if she would shatter at any moment. He hadn't yet realized the immensity of her inner strength. She yanked her hand out of his and strode to her father's study without stopping to see if the rest of us would follow.

The sounds of a furious argument leaked through the walls as we approached. Ginevra strode right in. Antonio's face was red with rage as he tore into Alexi.

"My daughters!" he shouted.

Alexi yelled right back. "I told you they had no business at the port. And now look at them!"

My fists clenched, but before I could call him out on his lack of preparations, Rian was already in his face. "You fucking told us you had it under control!"

"I did! Until this fucking princess," he shouted, pointing at Ginevra, "wandered off on her own!"

Watching Ginevra's fury melt into confused guilt broke something inside of me, and I surged forward, shoving Rian out of the way. Why wasn't he defending her?

"Fuck you, Alexi. How dare you blame her for getting shot?" I poked his chest with my index finger. "You told me I didn't need to provide extra men because you had the whole route covered. How many men were there at the port? Fucking none! You and Antonio are in your goddamned fifties, and you had to go running after the Russians because there was nobody else to fucking do it!"

My voice rose until I was shouting. Rian and Cormac looked at me with surprise. *Fuck*. I never lost my cool. Something about this woman really burrowed under my skin.

Alexi just shook his head and looked at Antonio. "Are you going to let him talk to me like that?"

Antonio sighed and gestured for all of us to sit. Linking his fingers back in Ginevra's, Rian pulled her down on the couch, to sit between him and Cormac. The movement was gentle so as not to disturb her wound, but no less possessive for its care.

Although she didn't object to the press of their thighs against her own, she removed her fingers from his, folding her hands together in her lap as she leaned forward to listen to her father.

"This is unacceptable," Antonio said from where he leaned on his desk, his arms crossed, a flash of the intimidating man he'd been in his youth coming through. "I offered my daughter's hand in marriage in order to protect her, to protect us."

I narrowed my eyes. "I can't protect your daughter if your people lie to me about their readiness to protect her."

Alexi shot back to his feet, ready to get in my face. "I can't protect your girlfriend if she doesn't stay where she's supposed to."

When I stood, I'd shed the affable mask I wore during the day to convince these fucking idiots I was sane and could be trusted. In its place was the Butcher, a man so fucking twisted the Irish sent me to America to get me out of their hair.

Antonio watched me warily as I stalked closer to him. "We're taking responsibility for Ginevra's safety from here on out. I don't want another fucking argument when I say a security measure is necessary."

13

RIAN

Ginevra clutched her hands in her lap, but I could feel her shake as our thighs pressed together.

"Easy, Liam," I murmured, willing him to stand down before he antagonized Antonio Russo so much he called the deal off, or worse, got himself shot.

He turned and pierced me with cold, green eyes. It had been a long time since he'd dropped his charming facade and let the Butcher out to play.

"Our partnership is only good as long as Ginevra's alive. If she doesn't survive until the commitment ceremony, I'll let the Russians pick off every single goddamned Russo," I said.

Liam nodded his agreement and backed off, standing behind us on the couch, one hand on Ginevra's shoulder. To my surprise, she didn't shrug him off, even when her eyes flicked once again to the blood on the cuffs of his shirt.

"Except my sister," Ginevra added, her voice angry, even as she trembled beside me.

"Except Sofia," I agreed, rubbing her knee through her trousers. When she didn't resist, I left my hand there, sweeping my thumb over the inside of her knee, more to reassure myself that she was okay than anything else.

"Great," Ginevra said, closing her eyes and sighing deeply. "Now that the dick waving is finished, would someone please tell me what the fuck happened today?"

As the room erupted again, I almost flew over the same destructive edge as Liam. I was ready to murder Alexi. I'd come a long way since we were kids, running around the wrong side of town, but that rough edge of violence still peeked out from time to time.

Cormac's hands clenched into tight fists. Like Liam, rage wrote itself into every angle of his body. And Ginevra, our beautiful Italian goddess, sat rigid on the couch between us, her face carved into stony fury on her sister's behalf.

"Protecting Sofia was the whole goddamned reason I'm sacrificing everything to be here!" she exploded, leaping to her feet when Alexi offered more mealy-mouthed explanations. "Enough!"

Ginevra took a deep breath, wincing as the movement stretched the wound on her side. "I'm done. And I still have to work today. Papà, tomorrow, I want to sit down with Pietro and your accountant. I want to see everything."

Her father nodded his agreement, slashing a hand toward Alexi to silence the man when he objected.

"And Liam," she continued, "I want you to teach Sofia how to shoot. Tomorrow."

"Anything for you, Ginevra," he promised her.

I FOLLOWED Ginevra out of the office, leaving Liam and Cormac to negotiate the details of security arrangements for the next few days. She paused to lean against the wall on the way to the kitchen and scrubbed tears from her eyes, not realizing I was right at her heels.

When she saw me, she straightened and wiped the misery from her face, replacing it with a pleasant smile, despite her flushed cheeks and red eyes. "What can I do for you, Rian?" she asked.

"I'm your bodyguard for the next few hours. Have you had lunch?" I asked, pretending I hadn't seen her crying. I fought to quash down the intense guilt I felt for her pain, physical and emotional. If I'd paid more attention, kept her with us, neither Ginevra nor her sister would have suffered today.

Ginevra took a deep breath and then smiled. "Let's go make sandwiches."

She led me to the kitchen and then began rooting through the cabinets for fixings. In short order, she'd made ham sandwiches for the two of us. I found potato chips and sodas, and just like that, we were eating in the kitchen while the rest of the family argued over security arrangements.

I wanted the silence to be companionable, but Ginevra was lost in thought, ignoring me as if I really were nothing more than her bodyguard.

"Princess," I said, once we'd both cleared our plates. "We need to get the contracts signed."

With a rueful smile, she nodded her head and chugged the sugary sweet soda. She ran the back of her hand over her mouth to catch stray drops, and my groin tightened. Ginevra was one of the sexiest creatures I'd ever met.

"Lunch tomorrow," she said. "We can go over my changes, then. And set a date for the commitment ceremony."

She hopped off the kitchen stool and raised an eyebrow when I didn't follow. "I'm going to work. You coming?"

Like the lovesick puppy I was, I followed her when she beckoned.

Ginevra had taken over a guest room at her parents' house. The forest green and mahogany furniture suited her somehow, making her seem like an exotic creature stalking through an elegant forest.

She grabbed a clean shirt and bra, then disappeared into her bathroom. When she emerged, she once again looked like the high-powered and successful executive she was, as if the traumatizing events of the morning had never happened.

Ginevra turned and faced me where I sat at the foot of the bed, my elbows propped on my knees. "What happened this morning? That was bullshit."

It took me a moment to realize she wasn't talking about the shooting.

"I have asked for very little over the past few days as I whored myself out to ensure my family's security, and so you can benefit from the Russo name. A little goddamned respect would go a long fucking way, asshole."

"Princess, it was just a game," I said, trying to figure out where this rage was coming from.

A bark of laughter escaped her before she could stop it. "Just a game? Rian, do you speak Italian?"

"No."

"Do Liam or Cormac?"

"No."

"Do any of you three know all the players, their families, and the politics?"

"Do you?" I snapped back at her. "You've been gone for ten years."

Her eyebrows shot up to her hairline. "Was I right about Alexi?"

I nodded, ceding the point.

"What else might I be right about, if you'd let me in? You didn't hold the gun that shot at Sofia and me this morning, but freezing me out of conversations regarding my father's business will have the same effect. I don't want to end up dead because I don't know where the fucking danger is coming from!"

"Princess, calm down—" *Crack!* The bitch slapped me.

For a second, she looked as shocked at the physical manifestation of her fury as I was, then she regained her composure and took a swift step back, as if worried about what I would do next.

As furious as I wanted to be, the fight Ginevra had in her was hot as hell. She was right, of course, but if I ceded ground now, I'd lose an opportunity for leverage later on.

"Are you done?" I asked her, my expression impassive. When she didn't answer, I rose from the bed and stalked toward her, backing her into her desk. I gripped her jaw, my fingers digging into the soft flesh of her cheeks. "You are an imperfect substitute for your sister. We allowed you to take her place because we don't need illegitimate sons, but don't think for a moment that you've earned a place at my side that I wouldn't have granted her."

Ginevra's eyes filled with tears. I shoved down the urge to take her in my arms and tell her I didn't mean it, that she was right, that she deserved better. It wouldn't get us anywhere. All three of us had given away too much when we freaked out this morning, and I needed to gain that ground back. We didn't intend to change our lives to accommodate her, and the sooner she realized it, the better.

A lone teardrop left a wet track down her cheek, dripping onto the fingers that held her face in place.

"Are *you* done?" she asked me.

I dropped my hand, and she jerked away, disappearing into the bathroom, where the sound of her trying to silence her sobs burrowed deep into my chest.

Fuck.

By the time Ginevra reemerged, she had regained her composure and fixed her make-up. I kicked off my shoes, stripped off my jacket, and stretched out on her bed, relishing the opportunity to observe her while she worked. She pretended I didn't exist.

After a few minutes of fussing over the light, she turned on her laptop and angled it so I was out of sight, then logged in as she thumbed her way through dozens of messages on her phone.

Rian: Text us when you're done. We'll come downstairs.
Cormac: Where are you?
Rian: Ginevra's room.
Cormac: *head exploding emoji*
Rian: She's working, asshole.

She frowned at the exchange, but didn't join in. Better that she have no illusions about the type of man I was, even as something in me wanted to do nothing but gather her in my arms and do whatever it took to make her happy.

I watched her cycle through a series of meetings where she checked in with her team, following up on milestones, gently prodding managers, and deftly dealing with myriad personnel problems. Her team liked and respected her, and I could see why she'd been such a successful entrepreneur.

After an hour, she turned around in her chair. "I need

you to be fucking quiet for this next call," she said to me as I lazed on her bed.

"Have I not been quiet this whole time?" I asked, pretending amusement.

"This one's important, Rian," she answered. "Please."

I sat up. "What will you give me for it?"

Ginevra swore. "I should've kept my damn mouth shut."

"You should've," I agreed. "Now, princess, what will you give me for my silence?"

She looked me up and down, her eyes tired. I suppressed the guilt that followed—I didn't want to care that she wasn't in the mood for sex games, or that including her that morning likely would have avoided her injury.

After a pregnant pause, she nodded. "What do you want?"

"Your lips wrapped around my cock as soon as you hang up from that call."

She closed her eyes, but not fast enough to stop a tear from trickling down her cheek. Good. Better that she understand clearly the terms of our relationship. "Yeah, okay," she said, defeated. I tried not to let the disappointment in her eyes hurt.

I lay back down on the bed, with my hands behind my head, and stared at the ceiling.

"Richard," Ginevra said, answering the call, her voice full of fake enthusiasm. "It's so good to hear from you."

Jesus, their conversation was insipid as she sucked up to him, making the man comfortable, coaxing his secrets out. Ginevra was a master at her craft. As I listened, I wondered why she'd never turned that charm on us.

"That's a very flattering offer, but I'm not interested in selling my company. We've discussed this before."

My ears perked up as I escaped from my daydreams to pay attention.

"Ten million," he offered.

Ginevra laughed. "You're hilarious, Richard! So funny! But you know I don't want to sell. What is this really about?"

"You're the best, Ginevra. I saw your work on *Transformations*—Charles had nothing but praise for what you did."

"For what my team did," Ginevra said, a hint of censure in her voice.

"For what your team did," the man acknowledged, amused. "There's no one else I'd rather work with to make my vision happen. Even if you won't sell to me, I can make the partnership worth your while."

"We'd have to build an entirely new animation engine to do what you're asking. I'd have to double my staff and contract out half of the work."

"I'm fine with that. I want you to take the lead on this, Ginevra. You're the best in this town. Ten million," Richard offered. "For the contract, not your company."

Ginevra didn't laugh this time, but I could see the tension in her shoulders. "Richard, I'm flattered that you're so determined to get me to work with you on this film, but it's not what my company does. As always, it was a pleasure speaking with you." She made as if to hang up.

"Wait—" Richard said.

Ginevra waited.

"Fifteen plus costs."

She couldn't hide her gasp. Her shoulders tensed as she sat frozen in front of her screen. "Fifteen plus costs," she agreed.

"Wonderful!" he said. "I'll have my lawyer call Cheryl. I'd like to get this done quickly, and announce it together next Monday."

"I'm on the East Coast for a family emergency. Can you give me another week?"

The man huffed his surprise. "For fifteen million plus costs, Ginevra, make yourself available."

"One week, Richard, please."

Her interlocutor reluctantly agreed.

She slammed the cover of her laptop down and stared at the wall, her breath ragged and uneven. With a soft whimper, she lowered her face into her hands. When her shoulders started to shake, she shoved her chair back and dashed to the bathroom without looking at me.

When she walked out, she stalked straight to the bed and unbuckled my belt. Despite myself, I grasped her wrist, not wanting to cause her more pain. "I'll take a rain check."

Her eyes were full of unshed tears when she looked up at me. "How much will that cost me?" she asked, bitter and angry. She shook free of my grip and pulled my cock out of my pants.

Fuck. I wasn't a goddamn saint. I sat up and swung my legs around the side of the bed. She knelt before me, her chest heaving, her wavy brown hair a halo around her. God, she was gorgeous. She licked her full pink lips, then stuck out her tongue to swipe at the bead of pre-cum that gathered on the tip of my cock.

She hummed before leaning forward and taking me in her mouth, swirling her tongue around me before sucking hard. I groaned and threw my head back, clutching at her blankets, not wanting to ruin the moment by touching her. When she descended on me, taking me to the back of her throat, I stopped caring and threaded my fingers through her hair, struggling not to fist it and fuck her face like her rosy cheeks and plump lips begged me to.

Ginevra ran her tongue up and down my length as she

took me into her mouth. *Fucking heaven on earth.* When she fisted me and started fucking me with her hand in time with her mouth, I moaned out loud, "Fucking hell, Gin, you are so goddamned perfect," as tears streamed down her face.

Murmuring gentle words of praise as she brought me higher and higher, I pumped into her until I was on the cusp of coming. Then I was emptying myself into her mouth as she sucked me dry, swallowing every drop.

I hauled her up to standing and pulled her into me for a kiss. Her mouth was salty with the taste of me as I nibbled on her lips, stroked her tongue with my own. She opened to me for a delicious moment before coming back to herself and shoving me back. "No," she snapped, like I was an errant puppy.

Angry Ginevra was a lot more fun to play with than weepy Ginevra. I let her get back to work without another word.

"Hey, yeah, no video today. I'm working out of my parents' house," she explained on her next call. "But I've got some big news!"

14

GINEVRA

Liam refused to let me sleep at my parents', claiming he couldn't guarantee my safety anymore as he flicked those gorgeous green eyes in Alexi's direction.

Out of energy for fighting, I packed my overnight bag under his watchful gaze.

"I have to work tonight," I murmured.

His eyebrows shot up. "Do you think we're going to get in the way of that?"

I didn't bother to hold back my bark of caustic laughter. "One hundred percent."

Liam tilted his head to the side and looked at me, as if he were trying to stare into my soul. I stared back. Of all three men, I found Liam the hardest to read. He was so affably charming, until he wasn't. I wasn't sure which persona was him and which was the mask.

"What's it worth to you, for a couple of hours to yourself?" he asked, picking up my bag from the bed.

My lips twisted to the side, frustrated I had to bargain

for time to fucking work. "I don't think I should have to trade anything for that."

He frowned. "You're upsetting everyone's routines and we haven't signed the contracts yet."

"Oh, *your* routine's fucked up?" I didn't bother to hide my fury as I gestured to my side. "I was fucking shot at this morning!"

Sofia interrupted what was about to become a heated tirade. I hadn't had a moment to talk to her after the events of the morning, and here I was about to leave again. Not that I'd been present for the last decade anyway, but I owed her my attention while I was here, at least. She enveloped me in a hug.

"Stay safe, okay? Call me before you go to bed?" she asked.

I kissed her on the cheek. "I promise."

The car ride to Rian's house was silent. I was stuck in my thoughts, replaying the scene in the bedroom earlier, upset with myself for giving Rian the blowjob and angry with all of them for their refusal to accept me as an equal partner.

When we arrived, Cormac disappeared upstairs with my bag.

Liam circled me, his eyes thoughtful rather than predatory. "What'll it be, lass? How much are a few quiet hours worth to you?"

I was completely out of fucks to give. "I'm done with this bullshit." Pulling up a ride sharing app on my phone, I ignored them, calling a car to take me back to my parents'.

Rian laid a finger on my wrist to capture my attention, but didn't stop me. "Why don't we have dinner first? We need to talk about a few things, anyway." He cut his eyes to Cormac, who watched the scene with amused interest from the stairs. "Fully clothed, just a regular dinner."

My distrust must have shown on my face, because Rian stepped back, giving me some space.

"Peace, Ginevra. Have dinner with us."

Deep breaths, Ginevra. In and out. In and out. I calmed the frantic beat of my heart as I debated whether his offer was genuine. "Dinner and time to work."

"Dinner and time to work," he agreed, too easily. What was his game? I slid my phone back into my pocket and followed him to the dining room, flushing as I remembered how thoroughly they'd fucked me over the table the last time I spent the night.

With surprise, I noted the table was set for four. Cormac pulled out a seat for me, and I watched with fascination as the three of them served each other, and me, the family style meal.

Once we all had food on our plates, Rian asked, "Ginevra, the Russian said the Bratva is interested in you for something you did ten years ago, before you left. What happened?"

Damn. When Liam mentioned that they were targeting me earlier that day, I knew this moment would come. Ten years of therapy helped, but I still shivered when I remembered those terrifying nights in the cold stone basement, followed by the first and only kill I'd ever made for my family.

"I was a junior in high school, sixteen. I used to walk over to the middle school to pick up Luca before walking home. The schools were in the middle of Italian territory, right on the border between the Espisotos and Russos, and we all thought we were as safe as safe could be."

Until we weren't.

I had been floating on air that day. The boy I'd been crushing on forever had finally asked me out. I thought he'd been scared of my name—I'd been so young and so stupid, I was ready to blame everything on my father. I had been so, so wrong.

On the way to Luca's school, he wanted to show me a shortcut. Ignorant fool that I was, I followed him, right into an ambush by the Bratva. They knocked me out and kidnapped me. I didn't realize he was the bastard son of a minor Russian gangster because he carried his mother's Italian name.

When I came to, I was trussed up and lying on my side on a stone floor, covered in cuts and bruises that stung in the damp cold. The dark was oppressive, terrifying. I screamed myself hoarse, begging for help.

A thin slice of light appeared as a door opened. I scrambled, trying to shove my bound body into a sitting position. A large man chuckled at my predicament and yanked me upright before slicing through the tape that bound my feet together.

"Who are you? Where am I? Let me go!" My pleas fell on deaf ears.

He unscrewed a bottle of water and held it above my lips. I lapped desperately at the cool liquid. He rose without saying anything and slammed the door shut with a clang. The pattern repeated itself. After a few days, I was a starving, disgusting mess, desperate for food, desperate to clean my own filth off of myself. When the man sliced open the duct tape holding my wrists together, I was ready to throw myself into his arms with gratitude. I was sixteen and so stupid.

He ruffled my hair affectionately, then crooked his finger. Thrilled at the opportunity to escape my cell, I followed. He led me into a white room with a shower head installed over a drain and told me to strip.

My eyes flicked to him with fear as I noted his heavy Russian accent.

"I won't tell you again, girl. Time to get clean."

Once again terrified, shivering in the cold fluorescent light of a room I'd recognized as a venue for torture, I dropped my soiled clothes on the floor and stepped into the freezing water. He handed me a bar of soap, the boredom in his eyes strangely reassuring.

"Don't worry, little dove. I don't fuck children," he said.

As soon as I was clean, he handed me a towel, and then simple white garments. "What are you going to do with me?"

His smile was chilling. "Men will pay a lot to get their hands on a virgin Russo." He cuffed my hands together after I dressed and led me down the hall, my hair dripping onto the fabric, making it translucent.

"I'm not a virgin," I whispered, terrified he'd kill me for it, but more terrified of being found out later.

The man only grunted. "It'll lower your price, but they'll still pay for you." He dragged me out onto a stage and locked my cuffs to a T-bar in the middle of it. The bright lights shined on my face, blinding me so I couldn't identify anyone in the audience.

The price went up and up, and I realized what a twisted world my father lived in. These were his peers, the men he did business with, who were bidding on a sixteen-year-old girl. I was young and stupid, but not so stupid that I didn't know what this meant for my future.

A hundred and fifty thousand dollars is what my non-virgin ass was worth, the right to fuck up a Russo good, to stick it to Antonio.

Shadowy figures dragged me off the stage, dropping a cloth bag over my face so quickly I couldn't see the other girls up for sale that night. They threw me into the trunk of a car as I sobbed and begged for them to let me go, promising them anything, swearing my father would catch them and kill them, screaming with despair.

When the car spun out of control, I was sure I was dead. When we came to a crashing halt, I screamed for help, terrified I'd be left in the crumpled trunk to die. Gunshots sounded outside, and I shut the fuck up, as terrified I'd be murdered as I'd been of abandonment seconds before. I needn't have worried. My father extracted justice from my captors.

The day the hospital released me, my father and the head of the Bratva met. Neither of them wanted a violent gang war on the streets of Yorkfield, but the Bratva couldn't dissuade my father from justice for his daughter. He drove me home, dressed me in the same tactical gear his men wore when they were enforcing, and handed me a gun.

I followed him out to the back of our house, where a dozen men waited for my family's retribution. The Russian who'd showered me and locked me on the stage met my eyes from where he knelt, Alexi's gun to his head. His smile was slow. "Little dove, good to see you again." Alexi cuffed him hard, but the man didn't turn his eyes away from me. "Be careful who you trust."

At the end of the line of kneeling men was the boy who'd betrayed me. He had pissed his pants in fear and tears streamed down his face. Papà handed me his own gun. "Justice, Ginevra. Never forget what we do to those who hurt our family." One by one, his enforcers shot the men at their feet. When it was my turn, I hesitated. Papà embraced me from behind, holding my hands around the grip of the gun, but leaving my finger on the trigger. "You are a Russo, and we do not accept betrayal," he said, his voice quiet and reassuring in my ear.

I nodded and squeezed, trying not to flinch as the boy's brains sprayed all over me. That night, my father and his *capos* welcomed me into the family. I was a Made Man at sixteen. I knew then that if I didn't get out of there, surviving would chip away at my soul bit by bit until there wasn't anything left.

"That kid was the illegitimate son of Yuri Semenov, who was, at the time, a junior enforcer," I finished.

"No longer," Rian said, grimacing. "He's now the number two in the Bratva."

Without saying a word, Liam picked up my plate, taking it to the microwave to reheat it. He needn't have bothered. Telling the story had ruined my appetite.

I pushed back from the table. "I need to get a few hours of work in."

Two hours later, Cormac walked into the office without knocking, setting a plate with a sandwich beside me. "Eat."

I spun around in my chair, letting my knees knock into him. "Always have to be in charge," I teased.

He nodded, treating the comment as if I were serious. "Yes, I do. I told you to eat."

"I will." I had to wrap up the plans for this animation contract before I logged off for the night.

He just stared at me until I picked up the sandwich and started nibbling at it. As I ate, he pushed a strand of hair out of my face.

"That's my good girl," he murmured as I finished the sandwich, and I tried not to think too hard about the warmth that shot through me at his gentle praise.

"Are you going to be okay sleeping by yourself tonight?" he asked.

I cocked an eyebrow. "Because I haven't been sleeping alone my entire adult life? I'll be fine."

Strangely enough, with three Irish gangsters down the hall, ready to burn down the city to protect me, and my gun beneath my pillow, I was.

15

GINEVRA

Cormac and I arrived ten minutes late for lunch. We'd decamped to my parents' house, where we spent the morning going over all of my father's companies, both illicit and straight.

Pietro seemed amused at my temerity when I asked questions. My father's accountant, Luis, didn't hesitate to share everything he knew, including the double sets of books that would send me to jail for tax evasion in a heartbeat.

In for a penny, in for a pound.

Rian picked the only Michelin starred restaurant in Yorkfield for lunch. I waved off the maitre d' as Cormac followed me to the table where Rian and Liam waited for us, nestled in an alcove, half hidden by plants. When I leaned over to peck each of them on their cheeks, I got a whiff of their colognes and my knees went weak. Something about the sight of them, three dangerous men in suits, radiating violence, smelling like fucking lust and leather, got me hot and bothered, no matter how furious I was.

As if he could read my thoughts, Rian looked at me

through his lashes and grinned as Cormac pushed my seat in. "You look lovely," Rian said, reaching over to push a strand of hair behind my ear. Damn straight, I did. My olive skin glowed under the emerald of my dress, and the v-neck of a wrap showed more than a hint of cleavage, especially when I leaned over. I needed every weapon in my arsenal when it came to these men.

"Thank you," I said, smiling, feeling his eyes track my chest as I bent to the side to set my briefcase on the ground.

"Is that what she wore to meet with the attorney and the accountant?" Rian asked Cormac.

Cormac pressed his lips into a thin line. "Yes," he said, shortly.

Watching Cormac glare at the old men every time their eyes wandered from my face had added spice to an otherwise bland morning.

"Ginevra knows brats get punished in our household," Cormac continued with a wicked smile.

Rian set his own briefcases on the table and pulled out a stack of well tabbed papers. *Cute.* I pulled out my tablet, quickly swiping to bring up the contract.

"I believe our attorneys have settled on almost everything," I began, persuing the documents on my screen to be sure.

"Almost," Cormac drawled.

"My current company is off-limits. Any other existing companies and property revert back to their original owners if we split, no matter what the reason. Anything new gets split equally among the four of us, unless someone cheats, in which case, they get nothing."

I furrowed my brow. "You provide ten million dollars in cash to my father, who uses it to pay off his debt to the Bratva and infuse much needed cash into his businesses.

And you get a twenty-five percent stake in everything that's legitimate—the restaurants, the real estate, the shipping companies—everything."

I smiled and leaned back in the chair. "And you get me."

Rian nodded. "And we provide security for you and your family as long as you need it."

Cormac narrowed his eyes. "The original contract specified clearly what Rian expected from his wife, in bed and in his household."

I leaned forward, tracing my finger over the swells of my breasts, holding their attention exactly where I wanted it. "I'm not Sofia. I have my own company to run, on the West Coast. A permanent dom/sub relationship doesn't interest me. And neither does being a perfect fucking Italian wife."

Rian leaned over to loop a strand of my hair around his fingers before settling a hand on my shoulder, tracing circles on my neck as I struggled not to let his touch affect me.

Cormac leaned toward me. "Sex is a deal breaker, darling."

I smiled like a Cheshire cat, the tips of my lips curling up with mischief. "Let's negotiate sex separately. On an ad hoc basis."

Rian's eyebrows shot up. "Like we did a few nights ago?"

Would they accept this modification to the contract? I nodded, biting my lip before I realized just how much of my uncertainty it would reveal. "Just like that."

The three of them had been working together for a long time. They exchanged a long glance, but didn't say anything to give away their position. My fingers itched to fidget on the table, so I clasped them in my lap and sat still, waiting for their decision.

Cormac cleared his throat, his lips twisted in frustration.

"We need you to be a perfect fucking Italian wife in public from time to time."

I grinned, understanding they had conceded the negotiating point. "I guess you'd better be ready to pay for that then, hmm?"

Rian nodded sharply. He slid the stack of papers into his briefcase, and I put away my tablet. "My lawyer will be in touch with your lawyer," he said. "I'd like to get these signed as soon as possible. We can do a quick commitment ceremony in a few weeks after we've given the community time to think about our whirlwind romance."

A bubble of laughter escaped me. "Our polyamorous whirlwind romance? Where they all think I'm a whore?"

Cormac yanked me toward him, cupping my jaw in his hand as I bent awkwardly over the corner of the table. "Aren't you, though, darling? Ten million dollars is quite a bit of money."

He ran his thumb along my bottom lip, holding my gaze. I sighed before flicking the tip with my tongue and eliciting a heady groan from him.

When he pushed me back toward my seat, I picked up the menu. "Shall we order?"

AFTER GIVING the waiter my order, I turned back to the table, only to discover Rian had disappeared. Hot hands ran up my calves under the table, but when I reached to twitch the table cloth aside, Cormac's firm fingers caught my wrist. He tugged on my hand until he was close enough to whisper in my ear.

"Not a single noise, Ginevra. We wouldn't want these good people to know what a slut you really are, would we?"

My face heated with embarrassment as I realized what

was going on. Rian pushed my legs apart under the table, careful to stay covered by the long white tablecloth. His fingers walked up the insides of my legs.

"Why are you doing this?" I asked, my voice breathy, giving away more than I'd like. As humiliating as this was, it was fucking hot, too.

Rian's teeth dug into the sensitive skin of my thigh, eliciting a sharp gasp as I struggled to keep my face composed.

Cormac's face was sharp. "Do we need a reason to use our whore however we like?"

I couldn't hide the hurt that shot through me. My face fell for a second before I controlled my expression. Every time I fooled myself into thinking they cared about me as a person, and not a possession, one of them managed to remind me that I was bought and paid for.

On the other hand, one of the most powerful men I'd ever met was on his knees under the table before me, his hands sliding up the bare skin of my thighs, about to offer me illicit pleasure in the middle of a crowded restaurant. So was it really that bad a deal?

As the waiter set the champagne bucket beside our table, Rian pushed the skirt of my dress up, inch by excruciating inch, exposing my legs to his hot breath. He placed gentle butterfly kisses on my skin, and I fought to keep my breath even as Liam and Cormac watched me with amusement.

The waiter poured four glasses of bubbly. When I lifted mine to toast, my hands shook.

"To the future," Cormac murmured.

"To the future," Liam and I agreed. Rian nudged his nose against my panties as our glasses clinked and I bit back a moan. Fuck this was hot. With trembling fingers, I gulped at my champagne. When a few drops escaped my lips, dripping down my throat and my chest, Cormac leaned forward.

"Let me get that for you," he said, kissing his way up my flushed skin, his tongue swirling and capturing the sweet liquid.

"Slut," a voice from another table snapped. Cormac sat up abruptly, rage in his eyes.

When I shook my head. "Let me," I said softly, cupping his cheek with my hand.

Chloe Morelli and her mother, Tina, sat two tables over from us. Tina's eyes were sympathetic. "Don't be rude, Chloe," she admonished her daughter.

"Don't be rude?" I laughed softly. Rian stopped his seduction and instead stroked his hands firmly over my knees, reassuring me rather than leaving me breathless. "Chloe, isn't your father thousands of dollars in debt to my father?" Thank God I'd spent the morning going over the books with Pietro and Luis.

The tables around us quieted, sensing drama about to unfold.

"And yet, he hasn't abandoned your street to the encroaching Russians, continuing to protect your family's businesses, even though you haven't paid him a goddamned cent in months."

"It's not like that," Chloe whispered.

"Really?" I answered, furious once again at our stupid world that worked on handshakes and gentlemen's agreements, but used and discarded women, women like me and my sister, and one day soon, this teenager in front of me, when men didn't feel like paying the consequences of their actions.

"No matter how disloyal your family may be, the Russos will never abandon this city. And this?" I gestured to the two men at the table. "This is the price of that. Be grateful that I am paying it, instead of you and your father."

Chloe's big blue eyes filled with tears. "I'm sorry," she whispered. "I didn't think." I wanted to burst into tears, too. This wasn't the person I wanted to be. This wasn't the future I'd dreamed of. I was selling myself so that she could have that future.

Instead of reassuring Chloe, I looked at her mother, whose face froze in horror at the confrontation between me and her daughter. Tina babysat Sofia and I when we were kids. Was she looking at her daughter and imagining the same dark future for her I'd found? I hoped not.

Exhaling sharply, I returned my gaze to the table. Cormac's gaze was heavy, as if he were assessing me anew. Liam's was warm, not with the heat of desire, but with pride. "I could just gut her for you, Ginevra," he offered.

I choked back a laugh, appreciating the moment of levity. Then I met his eyes and realized he wasn't kidding. "No, Liam, I don't think that's necessary."

In an unexpected gesture of affection, Cormac took my hand in his, running his fingers over my knuckles. "Your enemies are our enemies," he said. "We are the only ones allowed to call you a whore."

I TRIED to push my legs back together, grateful for the long table cloth that hid what was going on beneath. God, after that little outburst, the last thing I wanted was to prove to the room that they were right, that I *was* nothing better than a slut for these beautiful, commanding men.

Underneath the table, Rian held my knees apart, kissing each of them before working his way back up the insides of my thighs, nipping and nibbling until I soaked my panties in anticipation. The rough scrape of his unshaven face sensitized my skin as he approached the apex of my thighs, dragging a gasp out of me as I clenched Cormac's hand where he still held mine on the table.

I flushed, my face turning bright red, and I was grateful my back was to the dining room. As tucked away as we were in this alcove, I was still visible, and this wasn't what I wanted.

Rian shoved my thighs open until I was completely bared to him, my position making me feel wanton and powerful, despite his intention to demean me. I could only imagine what the rest of the dining room thought as I trembled in my chair.

Cormac's grin was wicked. "You okay?"

I shook my head. "I don't want to do this right now."

"We don't care what you want, darling." Cormac lifted one elegant shoulder in a shrug but didn't let go of my hand as I dug my nails into his fingers, struggling not to visibly react to Rian's illicit ministrations.

Fingers danced their way up my inner thigh, sweeping along the seam of my lacy panties before pulling them aside and pressing into the slit of my aching core. I bit back a moan and closed my eyes before tears could leak out, humiliated at how easily my need overcame my good sense as I shifted my pelvis toward the source of my debasement.

"Please," I whispered, not sure what I was asking for.

Despite my plea, a finger slipped through my wetness, proving how turned on I was. Even though my cheeks flushed with painful embarrassment, I didn't move as Rian explored my soaking core with his fingers, running them up and down my folds, teasing my clit and at my entrance.

Our waiter looked at me with worry as he set down our

plates, observing my pink cheeks and the faint sheen of sweat on my forehead. "Are you okay, Miss Russo?"

I nodded, but couldn't formulate a verbal response as Rian thrust a finger inside me.

"She's fine," Liam said with a grin as the waiter arranged our plates on the table. "She's just trying to process some things."

"Exactly that," I breathed as Rian plunged a second finger inside me. I tried to pretend everything was normal, like I wasn't being finger fucked under the table. Rian scissored his fingers as the waiter walked away, stretching me before establishing a punishing rhythm.

Shit. I wasn't able to swallow the whimper that escaped me as I sat, my upper half rigid in my seat. I clutched at Cormac's hand, desperate not to show any sign of the intense pleasure Rian stoked in me from under the table.

When he pulled my panties out of the way, then buried his face in my pussy, licking everywhere his fingers had explored before, I threw my head back, arching my spine before I remembered where I was. *Shit, shit, shit.* I bit my finger, trying to keep silent as he teased and licked my clit at the same time that he slammed his fingers in and out of me.

I fought against the bliss coursing through me. Exhibitionism was not my kink, and I wanted to hide myself in shame as Rian manipulated my body. Yet, I didn't get up and storm out. Instead, I did my best to control my ragged breathing as he drove me higher and higher. I held my hips still despite the instinct to jerk them against his face and force him to give me the friction I needed to dive over the cliff.

"Not eating, sweetness?" Cormac asked me, his eyes fixed on my lips as I bit down on them to avoid the moan threatening to spill out of me.

Frantically, I shook my head. When Rian took my clit into his mouth and sucked hard, ecstasy shot through me. I could no longer hold back the throaty sob that forced its way out of me as my limbs seized and I tumbled into a powerful climax. Rian continued to lap up my juices as I shuddered through the aftershocks of my orgasm. When I finally stilled, I felt a cloth wipe over me before he gently straightened out my panties. He pushed my legs together, dropping kisses on my thighs and my knees as he pulled my dress back down.

Barely holding in my tears of frustration and embarrassment, I set my elbows on the table and buried my face in my hands.

By the time I looked up, Rian had rejoined us in his seat. I expected to find cruelty in the men's eyes, but only saw heat and a deeper, more intense emotion I wasn't ready to examine. I took shuddering breath after shuddering breath, willing my body back under my control.

When I couldn't stop shivering, Cormac took off his jacket and draped it over my shoulders. "Eat, gorgeous," he murmured in my ear. "You're dropping from the adrenaline. Get some carbs in you, okay?"

He stabbed his fork into my gnocchi and lifted it to my mouth. When I didn't open my lips, he whispered, "C'mon, sweet Ginevra. Let me take care of you for a moment."

Nodding at him, still unable to speak, I parted my lips, and he slid a forkful of food into my mouth. I didn't know how to handle these men who swung wildly between wicked degradation and sweetness, alternating stark humiliation with delicious temptation.

16

LIAM

Watching Ginevra fall apart in that restaurant was the sexiest thing I'd ever seen. I loved new toys, and she was proving more resilient than I'd expected that first night in her father's study. She was silent during the ride back to the Russos', curled up in the back seat, still clutching Cormac's jacket around her.

As we pulled into the gates, she sat up and pulled out a compact mirror. She had a role to play, the same as we did, and needed to look perfect when she climbed out of the vehicle.

Sofia waited on the front steps, wearing sneakers and jeans, bouncing up and down with excitement. Ginevra met my eyes through the rearview mirror, her smile quiet and gentle. "Heading to the range?"

I nodded and climbed out of the vehicle, offering Ginevra a hand as she exited. She kept her tiny hand wrapped in mine as she stepped out in her kitten heels and didn't let go of me as we approached her sister.

The two women couldn't have been more different. Sofia was slender, blonde, and looked like she'd stepped right out of a photoshoot. Ginevra was shorter, curvier, her brunette hair always slipping out to frame her heart-shaped face and generous lips. Their eyes met, and they nodded, an understanding passing through them. The identical expressions of resignation on their faces made it clear they were cut from the same strong cloth.

"Are you ready?" Ginevra asked, smiling at her sister.

Sofia grinned. "I can't wait!"

Lorenzo rolled down the window of a black SUV as he pulled up to us. Declan was already in the front seat, his eyes scanning the environment. Thank God, Alexi had finally seen the light about security cooperation and agreed to let me coordinate with Lorenzo. Declan was my second in command when it came to security, and there was no one else I'd trust with Ginevra's sister.

Sofia vibrated with excited energy in the car. How had these two women been raised by the same family? Ginevra was so confident with a weapon, ready to do whatever it took. Her sister had never held a gun before.

As we drove through the city, Lorenzo and Declan updated me on the movements of the Russians in the part of the city controlled by Antonio Russo. They'd chased a gang of teenagers away from the entrance to the port this morning, but couldn't do anything about the free and legal movement of containers imported by the Russians. Sofia listened intently, absorbing everything we said as if her future depended on it. Maybe it did.

The range wasn't officially neutral ground, but a motorcycle club ran it and had little tolerance for the bullshit gangsters typically brought with them. Firebug met us at the garage, his eyebrows shooting into his shaved forehead when he saw Sofia. He was a short man, grizzled, red faced, and barrel chested, his blond beard fading to gray.

"So you really have thrown in with the Russos," he said, his handshake firm.

"Sofia, I'd like you to meet Firebug. He owns this range, and I would trust him with my life. He's going to run you through gun safety today. Then I'm going to teach you how to shoot."

She looked at me out of the corner of her eye, her lips tilting up into a lopsided smile. "Would you trust him with Ginevra's life?"

I laughed at her audacity. "No. The only men I trust Ginevra's life with are Rian, Cormac, and myself."

Sofia laughed to herself as we walked into the range. Firebug made quiet conversation with her, putting her at ease before handing her a small handgun. He ran her through basic gun safety. When he was confident she wasn't going to shoot someone else or herself by accident, he showed her how to load it.

The woman was a quick study. She mimicked Firebug's motions exactly, her movements efficient and careful. The Russos were idiots for not taking advantage of their daughters' brains and charm.

Too soon, Sofia was ready to shoot. I handed her ear protection and a pair of clear goggles. She giggled, but didn't protest. She'd watched the men in her family shoot for decades, so it shouldn't have been a surprise to me when she settled into a comfortable and confident stance in the booth.

After an hour, she hit the target more times than not. She was a bloody natural. When she slid her ear protection off, she was grinning from ear to ear. Twenty-two, surrounded by violence, and she was only now learning to defend herself. Antonio Russo was a fucking idiot.

"Why didn't you learn to shoot as a kid, like Ginevra did?" I asked her as we checked out of the range.

"After what happened to Ginevra, my father wanted to protect me." Sofia's smile was rueful. "He wrapped me in bubble wrap and never let me out."

"Until now," I corrected her.

A perfectly groomed eyebrow shot up. "Do you think that because my father has agreed to let me learn how to shoot a gun that I'm free from my cage?"

It was too easy to underestimate these pretty Russo women. "Not at all. But if you want to expand the size of the cage a little bit, now's the time, before your family freaks out because your belly's getting large."

She nodded, acknowledging the point. "I wish we employed more women as soldiers, like you do."

"Irish women have a long tradition of fighting," I said.

Sofia laughed. "And Italian women don't? My father was ready to change, but we lost our shot when Ginevra left."

"And now that she's back?"

Sofia's smile was sad. "Who knows?"

A PASSERBY ARGUED HEATEDLY with the guard at the Russos' front gate when Sofia and I returned to the house. Lorenzo opened his window, but I shook my head. We needed to get Sofia inside first. Once through the gate, he stopped the car just long enough for me to hop out and stroll to the entrance.

"I am to hand this envelope over to Ginevra Russo personally," the man cried. He was short, swarthy, dressed in slacks and a vest, with a newsboy cap tilted at a jaunty angle on his head.

"What seems to be the matter here?" I asked, nodding at the guard.

"Roberto Morelli told me to hand this to Ginevra Russo

and no one else," the man explained in a huff. "Since when do the Russos turn away members of the community at the gate?"

I looked him up and down. "Since the Russo girls were fired upon yesterday, at the port."

The man's eyes widened. It surprised me the news hadn't spread, but perhaps the Russos' soldiers were more discreet than the Irish.

"But Roberto's wife saw Ginevra eating lunch with her boyfriends today," the man protested. *Boyfriends.* I liked the sound of that.

Lorenzo arrived to smooth the situation over. "Tom," he greeted the man, shaking his hand. "This is Liam," he introduced me. "One of Miss Ginevra's boyfriends."

The man winced. "No disrespect intended, sir."

Lorenzo jerked his head toward the pedestrian entrance, and the guard opened it for us. We walked in together. I stopped before we got close to the house and held out my hand for the envelope.

Tom clutched it to him.

"You may watch me open it, but I will not allow that package into the house without an inspection." My voice was hard, even though I suspected I knew why he was there.

The man handed the manilla envelope to me. I pulled a knife out of my pocket and slit the edge. It was cash. I thumbed through the stacks of hundreds and handed it back to the trembling man. "Let's go."

Liam: Ginevra, someone from the Morellis is here to see you.
Ginevra: Right now?
Cormac: She's busy.
Liam: Right now.

Ginevra met us at the front door, kissing Tom and Lorenzo on the cheeks. I pulled her in for a kiss that left her breathless. The other men looked on with amusement until I pulled my knife out of its sheath, flipping it end to end as I stared at them.

My girlfriend—I decided I liked that word, too—led us to her father's study. She turned to Lorenzo. "Is Luca around?"

Lorenzo shook his head in the negative, then smiled. "You're in charge, Ginevra."

When Cormac would have followed us in, I barred his path with my arm across the door. "She needs to do this on her own."

His eyes flicked to mine, and then he grinned, pulling me in close so he could whisper in my ear. "I'll make you pay for that."

I laughed. "I'm counting on it."

Ginevra charmed Tom. It was a side of her I hadn't seen yet, and I admired the way she gently put him at ease, asking about his family—Roberto Morelli was his cousin—and catching up on the last ten years of harmless gossip.

I brought over two glasses of Antonio's expensive whisky, one for Ginevra, and one for her visitor.

"Miss Ginevra," Tom said, "Roberto wanted me to give this to you."

He handed her the well-worn manilla envelope. Her eyes flicked over the cut I'd made, then up to me. This was a down payment on the money their family should have been paying for protection these last few years. Ginevra had made quite an impression on Tina Morelli at lunch.

She frowned, then set the envelope on her father's desk. "Please offer Roberto my gratitude. Do you have Tina's phone number?"

Tom shook his head. "The boss's wife? Not on my life. I'm just a runner."

Ginevra laughed, the sound genuine, as it tinkled through the room like fucking wind chimes. All of a sudden, I wanted to hear that sound again. She rooted through her father's desk for a pen and paper, and wrote a quick note on a piece of paper, folding it in half. "Please give her mine, then. I'd love to have her over for lunch. And please, save it in your phone too, in case you ever need it."

God, watching her was a masterclass in how to win friends and influence people. In one stroke, she'd earned Tom's loyalty for life, and probably the entire Morelli family's as well. When she stood, we did too. She stopped at the front door and kissed Tom on both cheeks. "Thank you for coming today, Tom Morelli."

As I walked him to the front gate, he turned to me. "I know what you were in Ireland, and I know why they made you leave. You better treat that woman right."

"I will," I promised him, surprised how the weight of my words felt like a vow.

17

RIAN

"Who the hell do you think you are?" Alexi yelled, red in the face, leaning over Ginevra, who sat in her father's study, cool and collected, looking like the fucking queen she was.

She raised an eyebrow and responded, "Ginevra fucking Russo, that's who the fuck I am," and turned to her brother, seated behind her father's desk.

Her audacity got me rock hard. Damn, that woman was hot.

"Luca, Tom Morelli brought by the last couple of months' payments today. I accepted the money, counted it, then handed it straight to Luis. Then, when Gina Caruso stopped by, I did the same. What the fuck is Alexi's problem?"

"You're my problem!" Alexi shouted. When spittle landed on my woman's face, I moved to stand behind her, staring the older man down. Ginevra looked up at me and smiled, affording me a perfect view of her tanned breasts, and fuck, the bright red bra she wore under that damnable green dress. "Why are you inserting yourself in a process that's been working for a decade without you?"

Ginevra laughed. God, the ovaries on this woman. "It obviously hasn't been working, as Luis and Pietro spent the morning going over all the unpaid protection accounts with me instead of going over Papà's business accounts."

She turned to Luca. "Tomorrow, I'd like to walk the territory with you. Lorenzo and Rian can come along for security. It'll get my face out there and start getting folks used to seeing Rian around. Then Sofia, Cormac, and Liam can join us for lunch, somewhere busy and public."

"Absolutely not," Alexi snapped. "I can't guarantee your safety."

"It's a good thing she's not asking you, isn't it?" I asked, my voice quiet, dead serious about cutting him out of tomorrow's excursion. Liam would take point on security, and Ginevra would be as safe as she would be at home, with us.

Luca's eyes flicked between his sister and his father's top soldier, the man Antonio had relied on to keep his family safe since Ginevra was a kid. "Ginevra, you've already brought in fifty grand I never expected to see. I'd like to see what kind of results you could get over the next few days."

Alexi stalked to the desk and leaned over it. "You'll regret this. Your father won't stand for it."

Luca shrugged, looking at Ginevra with warm eyes. "I disagree. But you're a fool if you ask him to choose between you and his children, Alexi."

The older man stood up, pressing his lips together in fury. "You'll regret this, both of you."

I abandoned my position to stand between Alexi and the door, the size difference between us never more apparent.

"Are you threatening Ginevra? The day after she was shot at because you didn't do your damn job?"

Alexi deflated under the force of my gaze. "Never, you asshole. But I can't save these two from their own stupidity." He brushed by me and left.

Luca and Ginevra shared a long look. "Papà's gonna flip," Luca muttered, running his hands through his short hair.

A little laugh escaped Ginevra as Luca's phone rang. He looked at the name and sighed. "Speak of the devil."

She walked over to ruffle her fingers through his hair. "Thanks for sticking up for me."

Luca looked up at her in surprise. "Always, big sister." She kissed the top of his head as he answered his father's call and walked out of the office.

18

CORMAC

"How many men got a peek at that red bra today, Ginevra?" I asked, circling her in the middle of our living room.

Ginevra's lips twisted in frustration. "None, as far as I'm aware."

"Wrong," I whispered in her ear, standing behind her and running my fingers from the nape of her neck down the deep vee of her emerald dress. Her breath turned ragged as I traced the swells of her breasts with the pads of my fingers. "Anyone who saw you from this angle saw that tempting flash of red." I wrapped one fist in her hair and yanked it back until she stared up at me. "And that's unacceptable."

Her eyes flashed with anger and then amusement. "Oh, you think this partnership means you have something to say about my clothing choices?"

My fingers walked down her stomach, then splayed flat, pressing her into me. "I think you were bratting in hopes that I'd notice and punish you."

"I think you're sick and twisted and that you get off on

me struggling." Ginevra tried to jerk away from me, but my hold on her hair was too strong.

"That's absolutely true, darling." I bit her earlobe, hard enough that she winced, then soothed it with my tongue. Running my lips down the sensitive spot right behind her ear, I pressed my hard-on into the small of her back. "Watching you in that dress as you wrapped Pietro and Luis around your cute little finger this morning, as you came so sweetly for Rian at lunch, and then as you charmed your father's people while they paid you over due protection money, all I could think about was flipping up that green skirt, tanning your hide for being such a gorgeous slut, and then fucking you stupid over the dining room table again."

Ginevra's breath turned ragged and uneven. I knew if I looked at her face, her eyes would be glazed over as she struggled to process what she wanted. She was made for submission, I was sure of it. Liam's eyes fixed on mine, but I couldn't interpret the expression on his face. Breaking her wouldn't be hard. She was already on edge, an emotional mess between what we'd done to her and the shooting. I could do it, that night, probably. But I found myself retreating from the thought of destroying this perfect, powerful creature before us.

Wouldn't it be better to turn her into a willing partner in the darkness? This woman would be a perfect fourth to our trio, both in bed and out. She was the whole package—brains, courage, and audacity, rolled up into this perfect, gorgeous woman. She had the potential to be a real partner, instead of just a toy.

I let her go, shoving her away from me. She stumbled, then stood silent and proud, her back ramrod straight, despite her violent trembling.

Liam tilted his head to the side, a question in his eyes,

but he didn't interfere. Rian watched us from the kitchen — he loved seeing her dominated, but kink wasn't really his thing. No, his concern was breaking her sufficiently that she wouldn't get in the way after we'd signed the contracts.

I ran my hands from her shoulders to her hands, lifting them and bringing them behind her. She tried to repress her shudder, to ignore the clench of her thighs, but I saw it all. She couldn't hide from me.

"Ginevra, darling, we'll address your disrespect," I said, holding her wrists loosely in mine as I lay gentle kisses up and down her neck. "But first, I'd like you to strip. Dirty sluts who flash their tits all day have to earn the right to clothes."

She dragged one foot forward after another, until she was free of my grip, then stared at the ground. I waited. She craved this as much as we did, even if she wasn't ready to admit it to herself. Slowly, as if she were moving underwater, she lifted her hands and pulled on the tails of the bow at her waist.

Rian and Liam stared at her, utterly rapt, waiting for the dress to fall to the ground. When Ginevra finally shrugged and pushed it off her shoulders, leaving her nude except for her matching red lingerie, their eyes darkened with lust. They didn't move, trapped, like me, in the enchantment of watching this woman reluctantly bare herself to us.

She waited for a moment before kicking off her shoes, those cute kitten heels that emphasized the sweet roundness of her calves. The lacy red of her bra and thong contrasted with her smooth olive skin, the luscious curves of her ass that begged for me to take a cane and stripe them. God, she was gorgeous.

I dropped my gaze to the gauze taped to her side, covering the wound from the previous day's adventure at the port, and an unreasonably strong wave of fury washed over me. Alexi had a lot to answer for.

Ginevra's deep breath pulled me back to the present as she reached behind her and unclasped her bra. Rian and Liam held their breath as the straps fell down her shoulders, and then it fell to the floor. When Rian licked his lips, she inhaled, the sharp intake of her breath the only sound in the hallway.

She hooked her thumbs under the sides of her thong, then slid it down, bending over and exposing her pussy to me as she pushed the scrap of lace down to her knees. Fuck, she was wet and glistening, evidence that she didn't find this as hateful as she liked to pretend.

And then she was naked, an olive-skinned goddess, bared to us in Rian's hallway. Ginevra sniffled, shocking me as she reached up to her face and wiped away a tear.

Excellent.

"Now bend over, darling," I ordered her.

She stiffened and turned around. "What?"

"I said, bend over, Ginevra. You can hold on to the wall."

"Go fuck yourself," she snapped, wheeling around to look at me, her hands on her hips and her eyes snapping with displeasure.

I caught Liam's eye. He nodded. Before Ginevra could blink, Liam and Rian each grabbed her arms, holding her against the wall as she shouted and struggled. They each kicked out one of her legs until we forced her to bend, her ass gorgeous and inviting as she tried to escape us.

"How many men got a peek down your dress today, Ginevra?"

"Jesus! None, you pervert!"

Liam started counting them. "Pietro and Luis, every man

at that restaurant, Lorenzo and Alexi, Tom Morelli. Who else did you see today, lass?"

Ginevra stilled, her lips pressed into a thin, furious line. "Gentlemen, I appreciate that you all love these games, and that you're looking to inflict some pain on me tonight. As you can see by the fact that I'm fucking *naked*, I'm not entirely opposed. But I'm not going to be punished for looking good in a dress. That's some patriarchal bullshit, and I'm not here for it."

Rian grinned down at her. "Still smarting from yesterday, aren't you?"

"I am," she answered, exhaling in a huff. "I don't want to have a serious conversation pushed up against the wall like this, though."

I slid my fingers from her shoulders to her ass, enjoying the way her soft flesh overflowed into my hands. "I don't want to have a serious conversation at all. How about I punish you because I'm a capricious asshole, and I want to see your ass red and throbbing with pain in Rian's entryway?"

"Fuck you, Cormac," she snapped, and thrashed against Rian and Liam, seeking to escape their firm grip.

"Careful, darling, you'll hurt yourself," I said, running my fingers lightly over her wound. She stilled, trembling, holding back the whimpers that threatened to escape as I ran my fingers up and down her back.

"Stop this," she whispered.

I traced my fingers down her spine, down the curve of her ass, and between her legs, where I found evidence that, as angry and scared as she was, she was turned on as fuck. I rubbed a finger through her folds, gathering the wetness as I explored her.

"Stop, please," she begged as her hips followed the slow

and steady slide of my finger up to her clit and then all the way back to the sweet invitation of her ass.

"No." God, she was such a pretty picture, bent over, her hands pressed into the wall, Liam and Rian each with one of her legs between their thick thighs, holding her still. I plunged a finger into her, and she moaned as I fucked her, careful to give her only enough friction to frustrate her.

"Please," she begged, looking over her shoulder a minute later.

"Please, what?" I asked.

She pressed her lips into a thin line and turned her face back toward the wall.

I pressed a second finger into her, then wrapped an arm around the uninjured side of her waist and yanked her ass into my pelvis, so she could feel the heat of my hard-on as I pushed her into the wall. Liam released her leg and reached down to circle his fingers around her clit. He nuzzled the sensitive spot behind her ear, nipping and sucking at it until she threw her head back toward me and groaned.

Rian bent down to take one of her nipples in his mouth, squeezing her breast in his hands as he sucked hard. Ginevra tried to jerk away, but there was nowhere for her to go between the wall and the three of us. In seconds, she was a whimpering, mewling mess as she sought her pleasure from our fingers and our mouths.

As if we'd coordinated it, we all stepped away at once, leaving her beautiful and wanting, on the edge of her release. Ginevra collapsed against the wall, breathing hard. I waited for her to speak.

When she didn't voice her frustration, I leaned over her and murmured in her ear, "Only good little sluts get to come."

She sobbed once, twice, then dragged her emotions back under control, ignoring the tears dripping down her cheeks.

"I'm going to give you a choice, Ginevra," I told her.

When she turned toward me, I slapped her ass. "Did I say you could move?"

Ginevra didn't respond.

I slapped her ass again. "Did I say you could move?"

"Fuck, Cormac! No! No, you didn't!"

Now we were getting somewhere. "We're going to offer you a choice, Ginevra. Do you want to hear it?"

She hesitated, then whispered, "Yes."

I slid two fingers into her and pushed up hard. She gasped as I forced her up onto her toes.

"We're going to punish you and fuck you no matter what you choose, darling Ginevra. But your choice will give you control over how it happens." I plunged my fingers in and out of her, drawing a whimper from those plump pink lips.

"Option one, we continue on as we are now. You can't stop us from doing whatever we want, no matter how hard you beg. But you can pretend that we've forced you, that you don't love every fucking moment of it."

I continued to fuck her with my fingers, never pumping them fast enough or hard enough to bring her close to the edge. "Option two is a safeword. But you'll have to live with the knowledge that if you don't stop us, you are as willing and complicit as we are. And you better fucking believe we'll test your limits harder than you could possibly imagine. But you can stop it—stop anything—with a word."

When she moaned, I withdrew my fingers, wiping them on her ass.

"What'll it be, Ginevra?"

19

GINEVRA

"I need—could you—fuck." I was too worked up to think. I couldn't even put a goddamned sentence together. "I need a moment," I rasped, as I tried to get my breathing, my body, back under control.

Cormac shifted behind me. "Take as much time as you need," he said, running the palms of his hands up and down my back, as if to soothe me.

His presence was suffocating. "Give me some fucking space," I snapped, pushing back from the wall. I stumbled backward, and as requested, the guys stepped away, letting me catch my balance on my own. I snatched my dress off the ground and wrapped it around me, the silk fabric a protective layer against the jagged emotions that scraped and slid against my heart.

Cormac tilted his head. "You all right, darling?"

Jesus Christ, all of that, and he wanted to know if I was all right? No, I wasn't fucking all right. I was a confused and horny mess. "I need a goddamned moment!" I shouted.

Shit.

Get your shit together, Ginevra Russo.

Liam sighed and reached out for me, tangling his fingers in mine. He pulled me into him and wrapped me up in a warm hug, pushing my head against his chest and rubbing my back. "Take as much time as you need," he said, repeating Cormac's words as he ran his fingers through my hair and soothed the maelstrom of feeling swirling through my chest.

I didn't like either option. Choosing a safe word would mean I could put a stop to it at any time, but I knew these men. They'd use that as an excuse to stretch my boundaries as far as they'd go. I'd have to accept that I liked it when Cormac called me a whore, and when Liam looked at me like he wanted to bathe me in the blood of our enemies before fucking me senseless, and when Rian wanted a public show.

God help me, these men brought something out in me I never knew I had—a submissive streak a mile wide, with some real twisted kinks.

Liam cupped my jaw, dragging my gaze to meet his. I stared into his green eyes, mentally backing away from the deeper emotion in his eyes. He stroked his thumb across my cheek, wiping my tears away.

"Ginevra, I am yours." His voice was raspy and low, meant for me, not the other two men whose fiery gazes burned into my back. "You don't even realize how tightly you've wound me around your adorable little finger. Take back your power."

I hid my face in his chest again. Did he mean what he said? Of course he did. Liam was charming and utterly psycho, but he'd never fucked around with me like Cormac and Rian had. With a sharp exhale, I turned, never leaving the safe cage of Liam's arms.

"I want a safeword." When Cormac inhaled, as if to

speak, I held a finger up to stop him. "And I want this bullshit of treating me like a toy outside the bedroom to stop. We're equal partners, all four of us."

Rian had the grace to flush when I met his eyes. He should feel ashamed for the bullshit he'd pulled at the port, and twice as ashamed for doubling down when I called him on it in my bedroom the day before.

Cormac nodded, decisive. "Done."

I held Rian's gaze. "Well?"

He sighed and looked at Cormac out of the sides of his eyes. "Yeah, okay," he agreed. *Why was he so reluctant?*

Liam nuzzled my ear, sending a shiver of pleasure down my spine. "He wanted the pleasure of breaking you."

My eyes snapped back up to Rian's. "You're a real dick, you know that?"

"You're right. I'm sorry," he murmured, and he stepped toward me, holding out his hands. I took them, and he pulled me into his embrace, careful not to jostle my injured side. Rian's mouth tilted into a half smile before he tucked me into his chest and kissed the top of my head. "I should have taken your frustration seriously. I'm not used to thinking of other people, outside of these two assholes."

Cormac wrapped his arms around me from behind, nestling me between the two men. I hated how fucking safe I felt when I was in any of their arms. "What's your safeword going to be, darling?"

I grinned. "Pineapple."

He laughed quietly behind me, the vibrations rumbling against my back. "Pineapple it is. Let's have dinner, okay? And then I'm going to tie you up and make you scream."

A shiver ran through me. I couldn't wait.

. . .

Dinner was surprisingly pleasant. The table was set for three, with a pillow at Rian's side, but Liam snatched it up as he walked in. Cormac pulled a plate and silverware from cabinets, and by the time I'd reached the empty seat, it was as if they'd planned on all four of us eating at the table together.

As Liam ran down the schedule of events at the clubs and casinos for the next week, I noted the extent of their activities. They had clubs in all the big territories—their own, the Bratva, the Italians, even little China. How the hell had they managed that?

"You're coming, right?" Liam asked me, dragging my thoughts back to the present.

"Coming to what?" I asked, not bothering to hide the fact that my attention had wandered.

"The fight on Saturday," Liam explained.

"Fight?"

He sighed and took my hand. "What are you thinking about, lass?"

I shook my head. "Just musing on how extensive your operations are throughout the city, and wondering how you've managed to integrate yourselves into so many of the different gangs."

Rian's gaze was sharp. "We need to get you smart on our business, but it'll have to wait until after Luca's done getting you smart on the Russos' operation." Unbelievable that after all the turmoil of the last few days, it was that simple.

"Anyway, fight?" I said, shifting in my seat, aware of my nakedness under my dress as all of their gazes fixed on me.

"I host Saturday Fight Nights at one of my clubs," Liam said. "And I'd like you to come with me." His grin was easy, but I could see the undercurrent of anticipatory violence to him. He relished the fights, I realized.

I shrugged. "Sure."

He rubbed his fingers over my knuckles. "Good girl," and I fucking melted right there at the dinner table. These men were going to be the end of me.

Too soon, we finished eating, and the conversation slowly quieted as their attention turned to me. "Funny," Rian said, grinning. "I just ate, but I find myself absolutely fucking famished."

My nipples pebbled, clearly visible under the green silk of my dress. There was probably a puddle between my thighs, too. I didn't know how to act or what would happen next, now that I'd agreed to play their games.

Cormac held out his hand as I stood up. He twined his long fingers in mine, comforting my jangling nerves. We followed him upstairs, and I could feel my thighs slipping against one another as the evidence of my growing desire dripped down my legs.

I didn't know what I was expecting, maybe a stereotypical dungeon, like I'd seen on TV. Cormac's room was nothing like that. It was soothing gray and navy blues, full of well-read books with cracked spines, and dominated by a king-sized bed with four posts and a canopy.

When I paused at the threshold, he pulled me in, his eyes dark and hooded with desire. "C'mon, love. Let go for an evening. Let us show you how pleasurable being our slut can be."

"And painful," Liam added, not at all helpfully.

"Pleasure and pain complement each other," Cormac murmured as he untied my dress, slipping it off my shoulders and folding it neatly over a chair.

Liam cuffed my wrists together in front of me with silk-lined leather, then guided me to the foot of the bed, turning my body to face it. He lifted my arms, hooking the chain between the cuffs onto something above my head, just high enough to raise me up on my toes. When he pushed my feet apart, I felt the stretch in my calves.

I couldn't see any of the men. It wasn't as disorienting as if they'd blindfolded me, but I fought to contain my panic as I listened to fabric rustling behind me, the soft slide of drawers opening and closing, and then the whipping of something through the air behind me.

"Easy," Cormac soothed me. "What's your safeword?"

"Pineapple," I said, my voice breathy as I squirmed in the air, hanging before them, unable to escape the awareness that I'd exposed my ass and my soaked pussy to them.

A breeze whipped behind me and *crack!* A thousand delicate points of sensation lit up the top of my back. It didn't quite sting, but my stomach clenched, knowing it could, that it no doubt soon would. I gasped as I felt the same impact on the other side of my spine, warmth spreading out from the point of contact. The sensations floated up and down my back, to my ass, and the tops of my thighs, until my skin was sensitive and hot, aflame at each stinging touch, and I floated in a euphoric state.

Until *smack!* The tips wrapped around my thigh, and I cried out, pain slamming me back down to earth.

"Don't space out on me, Ginevra," Liam said. Liam? Liam was holding the whip, or whatever it was? I trembled in fear, aware of his penchant for blood. Expertly, he peppered my back and my ass with strokes of the straps lightly, then with more and more strength, bringing me back to euphoria. I moaned and whined at the pain as endorphins flowed through me.

When he paused, I whimpered in protest. As much as it hurt when he hit me with the straps, I could feel a pull in my core. My nipples pebbled, and I whined with need. The heady mixture of pleasure and pain felt so good, I didn't want it to stop.

I needn't have worried. Rian slid in front of me, naked, his blue eyes dark with need as he settled onto the bed, pushing his knees between my thighs. He bent forward and took one of my breasts into his mouth, sucking hard on the nipple, and then releasing it with a pop before doing the same to the other.

Cormac's voice was hot and raspy beside my ear. "You're such a perfect slut, built just for us. Look at you, your pussy clenching around air every time Liam flogs you. You're drenched and dripping, waiting for one of us to fuck you hard."

I moaned at his words as Liam resumed his slow and careful heating of my back. In moments, I was whining and writhing in need, jolted from my floating euphoria by the immediacy of the ache deep in my core.

Rian slid two fingers into my mouth.

"Suck on his fingers, slut," Cormac instructed. He didn't need to. I knew what Rian was looking for. I moaned as Rian moved his fingers in and out of my mouth, the way I ached for him to pump them in and out of my needy pussy. As if he read my thoughts, Rian reached down to circle my clit.

"God, please," I begged, jerking against my bonds, pressing harder against his hand and reaching the limits of how far I could lean toward him with my arms bound above my head and my feet on the ground. Rian grinned at me and ran his fingers through my folds, torturing my aching entrance.

"Please," I begged.

"Liam's going to mark you, so you don't forget whose slut you are," Cormac said, his voice low and soothing, calming me even as my eyes grew wide with worry and I jerked on my bonds.

Once, twice, the flogger lashed into my upper back. I screamed at the pain, then shocked myself by pressing into Rian, searching for friction as the combination of pain and pleasure drove me higher and higher toward bliss.

"Fuckin' perfect," Liam murmured as he pulled my arms up and lifted me off the hook. I collapsed onto Rian, smashing my bound hands into his chest as I leaned on him.

Liam's hands rubbed up and down my back, soothing the heat. His fingers brushed over the cuts, where the sting made me wince, as he rubbed my blood all over me, all over his hands. He reached around to where I was bent over Rian and cupped my breasts, smearing them with red.

"You're going to be a fucking savage, Ginevra," Liam whispered in my ear, "when you finally decide to walk out of that gilded cage you've locked yourself in." He ran his fingers over my bloody shoulders. "Do you remember when I told you I'd ask you to hold your arms still without a binding? Are you ready for that?"

Cormac sat on the bed beside us and reached in between Liam and me, stroking my wrists, ready to release the cuffs. But I wasn't ready for that, not really. Safeword or not, this was too new for me to be comfortable with my own needs. I needed them to control this.

"Good girls use their words," Cormac said, stroking my face.

"No, I'm not ready for that," I whispered.

Cormac and Rian exchanged a long look before Cormac grabbed my wrists and looped them around Rian's neck, still bound in the leather cuffs.

Rian caught my mouth in his own, and pulled me into his lap, bringing my legs up until I kneeled over him on the bed, straddling his lap. He explored my lips with his tongue, then fisted his fingers in my hair, drawing me tight against him. When he nipped my bottom lip, I drew back and then bit him, drawing blood as I sucked on it.

"Fuck, lass, if that isn't the hottest thing I've seen all day," Liam said, pulling me away from Rian so he could kiss him, licking the blood off of his lips.

Fuck if that wasn't the hottest thing *I'd* seen all day.

As their lips clashed, I caught my breath, gasping at the hot sting that spread wherever Liam's torso rubbed against my back. When Liam finally pulled away, Rian's bright blue eyes were hooded and glazed with desire. Rian pulled me in for a kiss as Liam arranged me over the edge of the bed, straddling Rian's lap, leaning on his chest with my arms still around his neck as he propped himself up on his elbows. Rian circled his arms around me, his fingers tracing burning paths into my back.

I twitched my hips, sliding my clit up and down Rian's condom-covered cock. Fuck, that felt good, the sweet bliss of the friction a sharp contrast to my burning, aching back.

"Ah, no, my sweet slut, you're not getting off that easily," Cormac said, pressing down on my stinging shoulders until I was still. "Don't move, love."

Rian's fingers slid down to my hips, digging into the flesh and holding me. *Crack!* Cormac's hand slammed into my ass, delivering a stinging blow.

"What the fuck?" I snapped, unable to jerk my hips away from him as Rian's fingers tightened on my hips.

"I promised punishment, and filthy slut that you are, you're going to enjoy every moment. Count, whore. I'm giving you fifteen."

"One," I gasped, as the sting from the blow radiated out from the point of contact.

"Oh, look at that, you gorgeous slut." Cormac said as he rubbed the sting into my skin, admiration coloring his voice. "Your ass is going to be so fucking beautiful when it's red and stinging."

"I don't need punishment," I snapped. "I need fucking, you asshole."

All three men chuckled. "You'll get that too, love, don't worry," Liam reassured me from somewhere behind me.

Cormac's hand smacked my ass again. I wondered at the ache growing between my thighs, the wetness dripping down my legs and onto Rian's cock as the momentum from the spanking drove me against him.

"Two," I breathed. Did I like pain? Was I into this?

"Stop thinking, Ginevra," Cormac commanded as his hand hit my ass again. "Lose yourself to the pain and the pleasure."

"Three," I whispered, trying to turn off my brain. Why did this feel so good?

"Four." I couldn't get out of my head.

Cormac picked up the pace as he peppered my ass and the tops of my thighs, until I sobbed, not just at the pain, but the utter humiliation of laying here, naked, splayed out over Rian's thighs, my clit aching as I rubbed against his cock, as Cormac spanked me like a child.

"Stop!" I cried out as tears streamed down my face.

"Are you sure, love?" Cormac asked. "Do you need to use your safeword?"

I cried softly, leaning my forehead on Rian's. He gently kissed me on my cheek before stroking his fingers through my hair. "How many do you have left, princess?"

"Just two," I sniffled.

"You can do it," he whispered, wiping my tears away.

"Just two more. Show us how brave you are. Show us what a beautiful slut you are for us. You can do this."

I hiccuped and sniffled. Two warm bodies stood behind me, stroking their fingers down the still burning skin of my back, waiting patiently for my answer. I took a deep breath. "I can do this," I answered.

Rian captured my lips with his as he repositioned me on his lap, the head of his cock pushing against my clit. He gripped my hips and maneuvered me until my center was bared to Cormac and Liam behind me. I felt the breeze of Cormac's hand moving through the air before the sting of the contact blossomed on my ass. I sobbed into Rian's mouth.

"How many, love?" Cormac asked.

"Fourteen," I wailed.

"One more, lass," Liam whispered in my ear, taking a seat beside Rian and pushing my hair out of my tear-stained face, gathering it on my back.

Crack! Cormac's hand impacted my ass, followed immediately by his soothing caress as he ran his hands over my painfully aching skin.

"Fifteen," I whispered against Rian's lips.

"You did so well, darling. You took your punishment so perfectly," Cormac said, his voice filled with pride as he caressed my ass, soothing the sting of the impacts.

I lowered my head and cried softly into Rian's neck, utterly destroyed by their gentleness.

"Are you ready for your reward?" Cormac asked, his voice dark and raspy as his hands dipped into the cleft between my legs. "Our perfect little whore, waiting for us to fuck her."

He didn't wait for an answer, just wrapped one hand around Rian's cock and guided me onto it. I moaned as Rian impaled me, the pain of the stretch mingling with the pleasure of being filled to overflowing. Rian's eyes rolled into the back of his head as he bottomed out inside me. "Fuck, princess, you feel so good."

Warm liquid dropped down my back, into my ass, and a finger invaded me from behind. I gasped and my pussy clenched around Rian.

"Oh fuck," Rian said. "Whatever you just did, Cormac, do it the fuck again."

Cormac chuckled darkly, and set a slow rhythm as he pushed in and out of me, first with one finger, then with two. I couldn't stop my hips from moving as I sought more, faster, harder, and lifted myself, only to slam myself back down on Rian's cock.

"Fuck yes, princess," Rian muttered.

"Fuck, no," Cormac snapped. "Hold her still."

Rian clutched at my hips, groaning with the effort of remaining still, then lowered himself down on the bed until he laid flat and I was on top of him, my breasts crushed against his chest, my wrists locked together above his head.

Liam chuckled and released my wrists from the cuffs, rubbing the circulation back into them. "Up, lass," he said, gesturing to me. I raised myself until I supported myself with my arms, so he and Rian could play with my nipples while Cormac played with my ass.

When Cormac slid another finger inside of me, I tensed, a whisper of pain radiating out from my ass. "Easy, darling. Good little sluts relax when they take it in the ass."

Liam reached between Rian and me and circled a finger around my clit. I groaned and pressed myself against him, desperate for enough friction to reach my climax.

Cormac hummed, and more warm liquid streamed down my ass. He pulled his fingers out and replaced them with his cock. Although I wanted to squirm, Rian held me in place, forcing me to accept Cormac's hot, thick cock as he slowly pushed into me from behind.

The combination of pressure, pain, and pleasure overwhelmed me, and I cried out, only to find my mouth stuffed with Liam's cock. While I focused on my ass, he'd adjusted himself on the bed, kneeling beside Rian's head.

For a moment, all three men remained still, as if they were giving me a moment to adjust. Then Liam tangled his fingers in my hair and shoved his cock down my throat, fucking my face. Tears streamed down my cheeks and I struggled for air. Rian and Cormac pushed and pulled on my hips, moving me up and down their cocks in a shattering rhythm that had me screaming and begging for my release in seconds.

I couldn't move. I couldn't think. I couldn't do anything but let these three men rearrange my insides with brutal efficiency as they pounded in and out of me.

Higher and higher I climbed until I tumbled, screaming over the cliff. My body seized and the edges of my vision turned black as I climaxed. They continued to fuck me, drawing out our pleasure as I shuddered between them, until each of them came to their own powerful release, their rhythms turning ragged as they pounded into me.

I was crying. Why was I crying? I sobbed into Rian's chest as I came down from my orgasm, my entire body trembling with aftershocks. He shushed me, stroking my hair, as each of the three men pulled out of me. I collapsed on top of him, every bit of pent up emotion from the last week pouring out.

One of the men ran a warm cloth up my legs, cleaning me, washing off the fluids. I gasped at the sting as gentle hands smeared cool gel over my shoulders before taping on gauze. Careful fingers ran over the wound on my side, as if making sure we hadn't disturbed it during our vigorous—I shied away from calling it lovemaking. We had fucked, and that was it, I tried to convince myself between hiccups.

Hot, calloused hands pushed and pulled at my body until I was curled up in Cormac's lap, as Liam continued to stroke my hair.

"How're you doing?" Cormac asked me, running his fingers over my cheeks and wiping away my tears.

I shook my head. "I don't know," I whispered as I continued to shake. Liam dropped a blanket over my shoulders, tucking it around me as I cried. "I don't know how I feel. That was the best sex I've ever had, but I can't stop crying."

Cormac nuzzled the top of my head, tucking it under his chin. "It's normal, darling, after an intense scene, or after an intimate one. We've got you, okay? We'll take care of you, I promise."

I nodded into his chest, uncaring that I smeared tears and snot all over him like a child. Served him right for spanking me like one. I tried to laugh, but it just came out as another sob. Cormac's arms tightened around me as I burrowed into his warmth.

"We have you, Ginny-love," Cormac murmured into my hair, continuing to whisper sweet praise to me as I slowly drifted off.

20

GINEVRA

I almost liked it better when they were treating me like their fucking chew toy. I mean, it was nice to be treated like a delicate fucking flower, but Jesus.

"I can pour my own coffee, Cormac," I said, getting up from the kitchen stool, still relaxed from our late start that morning.

Rian pressed down on my shoulders, holding me in place. "Slow down, princess. Let him spoil you for a bit. We can get back to bickering and fucking when we walk out of the house, all right?" He planted a kiss in my hair before pulling up a stool beside me. "Where's my omelet, Cormac?"

Cormac just laughed, the flash of his teeth bright against his deep brown skin. I flushed, remembering how that mouth had woken me up that morning, Liam holding me in place as Cormac's fingers and tongue brought me to glorious frenzied completion.

Both men were already dressed for the day, their suit jackets tossed over the backs of chairs. Cormac had rolled up his sleeves, revealing muscled forearms and dark tattoos.

Rian had unbuttoned the first button of his crisp white shirt, the tattoos on his neck and wrists poking out seductively.

"You're not going to spoil me?" I teased Rian, nudging him with my elbow.

"You don't need me to spoil you, princess. Now that you've submitted to Cormac, he'll fucking pull the moon down from the sky for you. And Liam's a golden retriever, but ready to murder if someone so much blinks at you wrong."

"And how do you fit in?" I asked, an edge in my voice, almost afraid to hear the answer. I didn't like how quickly he'd summed up our relationship.

"I keep the trains running on time. Don't be prickly, princess. They're like that with me too. They were right—you're fucking perfect for us."

"You submit to Cormac?" I raised an eyebrow.

Rian laughed, the sound ringing out clear and bright through the kitchen.

"Princess, we all submit to Cormac," he answered. "Even Liam."

I looked at him with new eyes, lewd images of the men running through my mind. Rian's gaze flicked downward when my thighs clenched involuntarily. He leaned over to run his lips over the delicate shell of my ear and I shuddered as need sparked through me.

"Maybe we'll get back to fucking sooner rather than later," he murmured.

Cormac slammed a plate down in front of Rian. "You won't. She's sore, and I have plans for her tonight after we sign the contracts."

My heart stuttered and my breath caught in my throat as I met Cormac's eyes.

Shit.

Rian jerked back from me, lifting his hands in the air as if he were a kid caught rummaging in the cookie jar.

Liam sauntered into the kitchen, looking good enough to eat. God, he filled out a suit well. They all did. At five foot seven, with my genetic curves, I wasn't a tiny woman, and yet all three of these men made me feel like I was a delicate princess when they held me in their arms.

"Luca and Lorenzo are on their way," Liam said, his lilt strong as he brushed a kiss against my cheek. As he pulled away, he changed his mind, and pulled me into a hard kiss that left me gasping and trembling. "Better," he said, running his fingers over my blushing cheeks and bee-stung lips.

I slid off of the stool, intending to pull him back for more.

"I said, no," Cormac snapped.

I looked at him in surprise. "After the last several days of non-consensual fucking, I'm finally letting you all into my pants, and you're saying no?"

Liam chuckled against me, drawing me in for a hug, rather than the kiss I was hoping for. "Sounds like Cormac's got plans for you, lass."

He stepped away from me and took a long look. I'd dressed appropriately for a day walking around my father's territory—a creamy, short-sleeved sweater tucked into navy slacks and Chelsea boots, with pearls in my ears and a delicate gold chain around my neck. I blushed under Liam's intense scrutiny.

"Gorgeous," Liam whispered reverently.

A woman could get used to these men's admiration. When the doorbell rang, it broke the moment, startling us all into motion. I scooped up the last bites of my breakfast as Liam went to open the door.

The domestic scene in the kitchen would drive home to my brother just what sort of agreement I'd entered into with these men. My heart sped as shame washed through me once again, for what I'd done with them, enjoyed with them.

Rian slid his arm around my waist. "Easy, princess."

I wrung my fingers, listening to footsteps echo on the hardwood floors as Luca and Lorenzo approached the kitchen.

Liam entered first, dropping a kiss on the top of my head as he walked straight to the coffeemaker. "American coffee?" he offered them.

Luca ignored him, wrapping his fingers around my upper arms and leaning in for gentle air kisses. "Are you okay, big sister?" he whispered, drawing me away from Rian, his grip gentle, but insistent.

I wanted to cry with relief. I should have known that Luca would be concerned rather than disgusted. Tentatively, I brought my arms up to bring him into a warm hug.

"I'm fine. I'll be fine," I answered, fierce and once again determined to do whatever it took to protect my family.

I CLIMBED into the backseat of the large SUV, greeting Lorenzo, who was at the wheel. Rian sat up front, and Luca slid in beside me.

Liam pulled out of the driveway ahead of us. His men were already in place along the route, making sure the first several stops were safe.

"Did you have a chance to read the files I sent you last night, on each of the businesses?" Luca asked.

I hadn't even seen the email, I'd been so completely and utterly distracted by getting railed by my men. Swearing to myself, I thumbed through the file on my phone.

"Busy night?" Luca asked, grinning at me.

I swatted at him and laughed. Why did I stay away from this family for so long? My attention strayed back down to the file where I reviewed monies owed for protection. "Protection." What a fucking racket. It was extortion, and I was about to take part in it.

We pulled in front of a café. We'd missed the bustling morning rush hour, so the inside was quiet. Rian was out and opening my door faster than I could blink, helping me out of the vehicle and wrapping a thick arm around my waist before releasing me. Lorenzo held open the door, and I led the way in.

It was adorable—cute white tables, a kitschy atmosphere, and smiling faces behind the counter. "Oh, Ginevra," an older woman said, bustling out as she wiped her hands on her apron. "Welcome back!"

She gave all of us air kisses, then sat us at a table near the back while her staff prepared espressos and plates of pastries for us.

"It's good to see you too, Mrs. Rinaldi," I answered with a wide smile.

Her husband sat down beside Luca. "Ginevra, you've grown so much since we last caught you convincing Francesco to steal pastries for you."

I laughed. Their son, Francesco, and I had been inseparable as children. "I hear he's doing very well these days, with his own construction company." Luca's notes, or rather, Pietro's and Luis's notes, had been thorough.

Mr. Rinaldi nodded. "He is, thanks to your father. Francesco is the prime contractor for a number of Russo projects. But what are you doing back, *piccolina*?"

But he wasn't the prime contractor for the failed building.

"The family needed me," I said, taking Mrs. Rinaldi's hand.

"I hear you've been quite successful yourself," Mr. Rinaldi continued. It shouldn't have surprised me that folks kept tabs on me back here.

This time, my smile was genuine. "I have been. I run a special effects company in Los Angeles."

Luca took over the story. "Ginevra's business sense is one of the reasons we're here today. She's going to be managing the operational side of the family business."

Rian raised his eyebrows. "Is that decided? I'd rather hoped she would do the same for us." My eyes flicked between the two men. Just like that, they'd both elevated me to their equal.

Shit.

Luca's answering smile was sharp. "Should have asked her sooner, then." He turned back to Mr. Rinaldi and explained. "We're signing a contract with the Irish. This is Rian O'Conner."

Mr. Rinaldi narrowed his eyes. "I know who he is. I want to know, what are he and his gangsters doing with our Ginevra?"

My lips twisted in annoyance. I wanted to be charming, but this was some bullshit. "A better question is, why did we need an alliance with the Irish in the first place? If only all the families that my father dragged out of poverty, the families he invested in and funded for decades as he cleaned up his territories and got out of trafficking in people, had continued to support him." I leaned back in my chair. "They didn't, though."

"So you're back for good?" Mr. Rinaldi asked. "And Antonio thought the most useful thing he could do with a smart woman like you is marry you off?"

When Rian stiffened, I reached across the table to lay my hand on his.

Mr. Rinaldi continued, sighing. "All those brains, Ginevra, and you're back here as a pawn in your father's games."

Rian leaned forward, his eyes warm as they stayed on me. He squeezed my hand. "We're lucky to have her."

The Rinaldis knew. Of course they knew. At this point, the whole fucking city knew. My family sold me to three Irish men, and here I was.

When Mr. Rinaldi turned to one of his staff members and asked him to bring his checkbook, I knew we'd won.

I waved him off. "Mr. Rinaldi, *Zio*, that's not why I'm here today. Come by the house this week. Say hello to my father. Then we can talk business."

His answering smile was genuine. "Your family's lucky to have you home."

My answering grin was cheeky. "I think so too."

21

RIAN

Patti Russo sure did set a welcoming table, even if the Italians ate hours after dark. Liam and I raced for the empty seat beside Ginevra, laughing and pushing and shoving as we dashed to the dining room. I won by a nose, sliding into place as Liam dove for the seat. I couldn't stop my eyes from dipping down her neckline to admire the gentle swells of her breasts.

Ginevra gazed up at me through her lashes, grinning at our antics, then followed the path of my eyes. She bit her lip and tilted her head up, and I couldn't resist brushing her lips with my own before turning to the table.

"It's wonderful to hear laughter in the house," Patti said. "It's been a dark couple of days for us."

Liam grumbled as he pulled up a chair beside Luca. "It'd be less dark if I got to sit beside my fiancée."

Luca laughed out loud. "Isn't she Rian's fiancée too?"

Patti passed around the first course, and Antonio poured the wine. "To family," he toasted. Liam, Cormac, and I looked at each other. We'd fought long and hard to come up from poor Irish kids, living six and eight people to one-bedroom apartments, parents strung out or absent, fighting and scrabbling for every inch of territory as we grew up. I wasn't ready to say we'd made it, not yet, but we were getting damn close.

"To family," I agreed, raising my glass.

The Russos were charming, well educated, well read, and erudite in their opinions, even Sofia, who'd never been to college. I looked at Ginevra with new eyes, allowing myself to imagine for a moment, what our family might look like in ten years, if we survived, if we allowed ourselves to relax, if she wanted kids, if Liam and Cormac wanted kids.

I gazed down at her as she teased Sofia about her tennis shoes and her new transition to casual clothes, imagining Ginevra's belly round and her breasts swollen with pregnancy. When she noticed me staring, she looked up at me, nudging me with her shoulder.

"Penny for your thoughts?" she asked me, keeping her voice low.

"Daydreaming about the future," I said.

Her answering smile was curious. "How so?"

When I pulled her knuckles up to my lips for a kiss, her eyes were soft and sweet. I wished I could bottle that look and keep it with me always. She kept her hand in mine as she returned to the larger conversation.

After we'd finished our wine and our espresso, Antonio pushed away from the table. "I'd like to invite you all to join me in my study."

While the Russos filed out, I snagged Ginevra by the wrist, pulling her into me as the room emptied. Liam and Cormac crowded close until we pressed tightly against her. She looked up at me with bright eyes. "Last chance to change your mind," she murmured.

Liam's laugh cracked through the room like a thunderbolt. "We were about to say the same thing to you."

I leaned down to kiss her, nuzzling her jawline and pushing her head back until she was leaning on Liam's chest. "You're right, you know?"

"Right about what?" She asked, her voice breathy and light as my fingers traced up and down her sides. Cormac tangled his fingers in her hair, holding her in place as she arched her back, pushing her perfect breasts into my chest.

"You deserve our respect."

Cormac pulled her hair hard enough that her eyes watered. "Except in bed, where we'll treat you like the slut you are for us."

Her eyes glazed over as her breath turned ragged. "Deal?" I whispered in her ear.

"Deal," she answered.

More than a few minutes later, we filed into Antonio Russo's study, where the lawyers and the Russo family waited for us. A rare smile lit up Antonio's face as Ginevra walked into the room, her hair a little bit mussed, her lips bruised and swollen, my arm around her waist, tugging her into my side. Antonio leaned down to Patti, who sat beside him on the couch, and whispered in her ear.

Patti's eyes flicked to her daughter, and she took Antonio's hand. "You should be proud of her, Tony."

Antonio's smile turned proud. "I am. You know that, right Ginevra? I am so damn proud of what you built in California, and the strength you've brought back to Yorkfield."

Ginevra's eyes widened. "Thank you, Papà. That means a lot." I kissed the top of her head, and released her to join her father at his desk where Olivia, our lawyer, and Pietro, Antonio's lawyer, waited for her. Ginevra propped open her tablet and dialed in Cheryl.

On the desk were three copies of the legal documents that would bind us to the Russos forever. The stacks were tabbed where each of us had to sign, and one by one, we flipped through the pages, initialing at the bottom of each one, signing where the tabs indicated.

Antonio was quick, as were we. We'd been over these documents so many times in the lead up to Sofia's grand revelation, I was confident of their contents. Ginevra less so. She scanned each page with sharp eyes as she signed, making sure her last-minute additions and changes were integrated into the final documents, occasionally conferring with Cheryl.

A third of the way through, she stopped, reading carefully, then rereading. She flipped to the appendices that listed her father's businesses and properties, at least, the ones that we were buying stakes in, then flipped back, and continued to sign. At long last, she finished the stack of papers that required all of our signatures, and we breathed a sigh of relief. We were investors in the Russos' businesses, to the tune of ten million dollars.

Olivia placed two more stacks on the desk. This was our poly marriage agreement—a prenup, a business agreement, and designations of next-of-kin, all in one. As with the contracts with the Russos, Ginevra read through them page by page. She'd seen the contract before, but not the charts of businesses and assets at the end. Her eyes widened slightly when she saw how extensive our operations were, but she didn't share her thoughts, not with the Russos in the room. Ginevra was ours, now, and she knew where her loyalties needed to lie.

When the four of us finished signing, Olivia packed up

all the stacks, including Ginevra's, promising to overnight a copy to Cheryl.

"A toast," Patti proposed. "To our newlyweds."

"Or newly somethings," Luca added, grinning, unable to resist teasing us about our unusual relationship.

She handed each of us a champagne flute, while Antonio popped open the bottle.

"To the future," I proposed, raising my glass. As they echoed my words, I looked down at Ginevra, allowing the rosy tint of optimism about the future to cloud my vision for a moment. Maybe this could work. Maybe we had a shot at a house full of laughter, a house full of family.

I pulled Ginevra to her feet and kissed her gently, brushing my lips over hers, hoping she understood how meaningful this moment was to me. When I pulled back, her eyes were shining with emotion. Maybe she did get it. Liam tugged on her, his kiss much more energetic as he wound his fingers in her hair and plundered her mouth.

Cormac and I angled our bodies to give her some privacy when he wrapped his fingers around that lush ass and pulled her into him. God, Liam could be a real asshole sometimes. By the time Cormac yanked her away, she was flushed and panting.

Ginevra and Cormac smiled at each other, an unusual softness in both of their gazes. "Sweet Ginevra, there's no turning back now."

Her smile turned wicked. "Dear Lord, I hope not."

He bent his head down to hers and brushed his lips over her cheek, before pulling her in for a kiss that was slow and sweet. He'd met his match in her. We all had.

"So when's the wedding?" Sofia asked, grinning widely as she watched the four of us moon over each other.

Ginevra exhaled with a puff of her lips, leaning her face on Cormac's chest. "I don't want to plan a wedding."

Patti raised an eyebrow. "The community is going to need a big visible sign of your commitment to one another if you want them to treat this as anything other than a business arrangement. Which is, I think, what you boys need out of this arrangement more than anything else."

Our wife twisted her lips in frustration, but nodded at her mother, ceding the point. Patti was right, of course. We'd paid a fortune for Ginevra so we could reap the benefits of the Russo name, and that meant continuing to legitimize our relationship.

Sofia laughed, while we guided our wife, our partner, over to a sofa. "Let me handle it for you, big sister."

Ginevra's eyebrows shot up. "You want to plan my wedding?"

"Two weeks from this weekend, I think," Patti said, pulling up a calendar on her phone. "Palm Sunday, then Easter, and then a spring wedding."

"Then it's decided," I interjected before Ginevra could object. "Sofia has two weeks to plan a commitment ceremony for the four of us."

My wife looked up at me, her eyes dancing with mischief. "So high-handed, husband."

Cormac tugged on her hair. "That's how you like it, darling."

Ginevra just laughed. "Let's go home, boys."

GINEVRA DRANK CHAMPAGNE straight from the bottle as she danced with Liam in our living room. Candlelight flickered in the darkness, giving their faces a warm and happy glow.

Cormac dropped onto the couch, pulling me in for a

deep kiss. He was so rarely affectionate. I reveled in the feeling of his soft lips moving over mine, his dark possession as he ran his fingers through my hair, angling my head to allow him to plunder his tongue as deeply as he wished.

I ran my hands up his chest and hooked one around the back of his head, not allowing him to draw away as I took what I needed from him, our teeth and lips clashing, nipping at each other, until we both pulled back. Our chests heaved, and our breath mingled as we rested our foreheads against one another.

His eyes were amused when they met mine. "It's been too long, Rian."

"I've been distracted." I chuckled, cutting my gaze over to the couple swaying in the middle of the room, gazing into each other's eyes like they were the only ones on the planet.

"Yeah, she's something else, isn't she?"

Cormac shook his head as he pushed me back onto the couch. "You good to play tonight?"

I grinned. "With you? Always."

He hummed his pleasure as he kissed his way down my throat and my chest, unbuttoning my shirt as he went, until he was pulling the fabric out of my pants. I knew Cormac well enough to understand that he wasn't going to let me top him tonight, or ever, but I'd enjoy the luxurious feel of him pleasuring me as long as I could.

He rubbed his nose along my abs until he hit the vee that dipped into my pants, then yanked my belt open, unbuttoned my pants, and pulled my throbbing cock out. "Look at you, ready for me already."

I laughed helplessly as he fisted me, smearing pre-cum over the tip of my cock before pumping his hand down once, then twice. When I finally had the wherewithal to look over at Liam and Ginevra, her eyes locked on me as

Liam kissed her neck from behind, running his hands up her top and cupping her breasts with his hands. When she moaned, my cock jerked in Cormac's hands, and he laughed, releasing his firm grip.

Ginevra's eyes drifted shut as Liam's fingers worked their magic, plucking and pinching her nipples through the lacy material of her bra. I stood, dropping my clothes on the floor, and sandwiched her between Liam and me, while Cormac observed us from the couch, his eyes hooded.

Her lips met mine as her hands wandered over my shoulders and chest, sending heat racing through my body wherever our skin touched. With Liam's help, I wriggled her out of her sweater and her bra, then stripped her until we were both entirely naked. I lost myself in her as I plunged my tongue into her mouth, tasting her sweetness, wanting nothing more than to lift her up and bury my cock inside her right at that moment.

As if sensing my growing need, Cormac took Ginevra's hand and pulled her away from us. Her brown eyes glazed over with lust, and her cheeks flushed with need and passion. He kissed her gently, sliding his lips over her mouth without deepening the kiss. "How're you doing, darling?"

She looked up at him with liquid eyes. "Wondering why we're all down here instead of up in your bedroom."

I swore as need bolted through me, but when I would have scooped her in my arms, Cormac held out his hand to stop me. "Have you been a good girl today, sweet Ginevra?"

Naked, her olive skin shimmering in the glowing light of the candles, she laughed warmly. "I tied my life to yours forever. What else do you want from me?"

She tilted her head and met his eyes. Her breathing turned ragged. Gracefully, as if she'd been doing it her entire life, she sank to her knees before him. She closed her eyes as if savoring the moment, then opened them to meet Cormac's heated gaze.

"Good girl," he murmured, and her lips tilted up into a slight smile. "Now crawl to my room like the filthy whore you are, and let all of us admire your pretty pink pussy dripping on the carpet."

Her tongue darted out over her lips as she sank onto all fours. I couldn't believe how completely she submitted to Cormac. It wasn't as if she'd extinguished her natural fire and energy. Instead, she'd redirected them to feed his pleasure. It was the hottest thing I'd ever seen.

He was right, though. Her pussy glistened in the lustrous candlelight as she slowly crawled to the stairs, her hips swaying with every movement of her hands and knees. God, this was torture, watching her take the stairs one at a time, wishing I could wrap my hands around her hips and plunge into her, fucking her until we screamed our pleasure.

Cormac had other plans, though.

When she reached the top of the stairs, she paused and looked back over her shoulder, her eyes sultry with need.

"C'mon, Ginny-darling, you know where to go," Cormac said, his voice raspy, as his need overcame his cool control. "Hop to it."

She grinned at us and waggled her ass in our faces before continuing into his bedroom and sitting on the edge of the bed. Ginevra smiled, mischief lighting up her eyes. She was beautiful no matter what, but with joy shining out of her eyes and her heart, I was a goner, despite my resolution to hold myself separate, aloof from her.

Crawling on top of her, pushing her back on the bed, I kissed her like a starving man, tasting, licking, sucking, working my way down until I nestled between her thighs. I needed her, and even if I wasn't ready to say those words, I could show her.

A sharp sting burned on my ass, and I looked up sharply. Cormac shook his head. I planted a last kiss on the side of her thigh, then pulled away. Ginevra sighed her discontent until Liam distracted her by tying a blindfold over her eyes. She ran her fingers over it, then lay still on the bed, quiescent and waiting for Cormac's next command.

Cormac and Liam exchanged a long gaze, and then they adjusted Ginevra on the bed until her head dangled over the side. "Boys, you sure are taking a long time to get ready for this scene," she said, her voice breathy as she waited for us on the bed, unable to see what we were doing.

Quickly, Cormac and Liam stripped, and Cormac indicated I should once again take my place between her thighs. I didn't wait for further permission, diving in, determined to eat my fill and bring her to pleasure. She tasted like sweet ambrosia, her moans and whimpers driving me wild as I lapped at her growing need.

I wrapped my arms under her legs, pushing her knees over my shoulders. Cormac was right. Ginevra's pussy was fucking pretty. I pressed against her, holding her hips still as I ran my tongue over her, from her fluttering entrance to her swollen and begging clit, and back again.

When I slid a finger into her, she begged for more. As I sucked on her clit, I fucked her roughly with two fingers, pumping in and out of her in time with flicks of my tongue, until she was shouting her release to the goddamned rafters and seizing in my arms. I lapped up the aftermath of her pleasure as she lay there quivering, her entire body flushed with the effects of her climax.

Fucking gorgeous.

Cormac hummed his approval, then shoved at my back

until I knelt between her thighs. I grabbed a foil packet from the bedside table and slid it on. Liam stood at her head, naked, ready to plunge his cock into her whimpering, waiting mouth. I pulled him into a short, hard kiss over her torso. He laughed into my mouth and bit my lip hard enough to draw blood. Liam sucked hard at the wound, drawing a gasp from me, before pulling away and licking at the blood on his lips.

Ginevra shivered under us, and Liam turned his attention to the beautiful woman on the bed. He stroked his hands down her jaw, his pale tattooed hands contrasting against the tanned olive of her skin. He pushed her head down until her face was upside down, hanging over the side of the bed. "Are you ready, Ginevra?"

"Ready for what?" she asked, her voice breathy as I slid my cock up and down her slit.

He ran the tip of his cock around her lips, thrusting it inside of her when she opened her mouth. God, watching her red lips wrap around him only fanned the flames of my own need. I grabbed a pillow and slid it under her hips, then ran my cock up and down her one last time, gathering the slick of her desire, before plunging into her.

Ginevra cried out, "God, yes, please," as I moved in and out. Liam caught my eye, and we found a rhythm as each of us plunged in and out of her. When Cormac kissed my shoulder, I knew what was coming next.

"Are you ready?" he asked.

"For you? Always," I answered, groaning as I slowed my thrusts in and out of Ginevra. He dripped lube down my ass, soon joined by the heat of Cormac's cock. Then he began the slow and intense process of pushing into me.

My groan was guttural, animal, as he pushed into my depths, the combination of pressure behind me and the intense clench of Ginevra's pussy on my cock almost sending me over the edge.

Ginevra hollowed out her cheeks as she sucked on Liam's cock. "So fucking perfect," he murmured as he traced his fingers over her face. "Are you ready to take me deeper?"

She answered by lifting her arms and wrapping them around his hips.

"Fuck yes," he muttered. He met Cormac's eyes behind me and then ripped off her blindfold. "Ginevra, I'm going to come in your mouth, and I want you to swallow every drop." He sped up his thrusts until he was plunging deep into her throat and she was choking on him. He came inside her with a shout, his cum overflowing her lips, dripping out of the side of her mouth as she struggled to swallow it all.

As if that were his signal, Cormac sped up his thrusts. Liam lifted Ginevra until she could lean back on his torso as we fucked her. She moaned when she saw Cormac locked behind me, driving my rhythm, slamming me into her when his hips pushed into mine.

"Please," she whimpered. "I'm so close."

Cormac slid his arms around my sides until they were on top of mine, resting on her hips. "Sweet Ginevra, have you been a good slut for us tonight?"

"God, yes, Cormac. A perfect slut. Please!"

"Whose slut are you, baby?" Liam whispered in her ear.

"Yours! All of yours!"

I could feel Cormac's fierce pride and triumph behind me as he sped up our rhythm. Ginevra's hips pumped in time to mine, to ours, as she cried out, chasing her release as I plunged in and out of her.

When she finally came, her pussy spasming hard around me, I buried myself in her with a shout. Cormac came a moment later, pulling out to spill all over my back.

Liam's eyes were warm as he cradled Ginevra, watching her chest heave as aftershocks rolled through her.

"You were so goddamned beautiful when you fell apart on Rian's dick," he whispered in her ear, and she flushed with embarrassment as he stroked down her arms, bringing her down from the intensity of her climax. She glowed with satisfaction in the soft light of the bedroom. Fucking perfect.

I pulled out of her as Cormac wiped down the mess on my back with a hot towel. He kissed my shoulder and then crawled into the bed, dragging Ginevra up against him. I guess he was the little spoon tonight.

Liam and I slid into the bed on either side of them. Tomorrow, we'd have to face the rest of the world, but for tonight, I snuggled up to Cormac, draping my arm over his waist and dragging Ginevra closer. The pressures and cares of the world melted away against the comforting heat of our —I stopped myself. Against the heat of our *very strong affection*, I thought, laughing at my inability to admit what was going on.

Warm and comfortable, I nodded off in the embrace of my family.

22

GINEVRA

I pushed away from the desk, exhausted from dealing with the time difference between the east and west coasts. At least I didn't have to manage a day of meetings with a plug up my ass this time. Jesus. How fucked up was it that I was grateful that my—I stumbled, still not sure what we were calling each other—grateful my *partners* hadn't forced me to spend all day horny, needy, and humiliated, wishing a cock were stuffed up me instead of the plug?

That's really fucked up, Ginevra.

The office Rian had set up for me sufficed for the time being, but eventually I'd have to figure out how to manage my company from here for extended periods.

A knock interrupted my thoughts. I swirled in my chair to see Cormac's frowning face as he leaned in the doorframe, his T-shirt revealing the sharp cut of his abs. When he caught me ogling him, he tilted his lips into a smirk. I flushed.

"Dinner's ready," he said, straightening.

I closed my laptop and stood, wincing. I was a little bit

sore from last night. And this morning. And Liam's surprise visit at lunch.

Cormac's grin transformed his face, erasing its severity and replacing it with a joy that took my breath away. "How're you feeling?"

"Sore," I answered, my response short.

"Just sore?"

I raised an eyebrow. He snatched at my waist and dragged me to him so he could nuzzle the sensitive skin of my neck.

"I'm horny as fuck from watching you girl-boss your way through that last meeting," he murmured into my skin.

I rolled my eyes. To tell the truth, I was horny as fuck too. Something about these men had broken a dam inside of me, and need poured out all the fucking time. But they didn't need to know that, not right now, not just after we'd found a detente, just as I'd seized some of the power in this relationship back from them.

"I'm hungry," I said as my stomach growled. Cormac kissed the top of my head and nudged me out of the room with a gentle push at the small of my back.

It was just the two of us. Rian and Liam were out making the rounds of their clubs, our clubs, but I desperately needed a night of quiet after the tumultuous events of the week. Cormac volunteered to stay home with me. The guys weren't willing to leave me alone, ostensibly for my safety, but I also suspected they worried I'd run.

Maybe they were right.

"Downstairs," Cormac murmured. I could feel the heat of his gaze on my ass, despite my business attire.

When I arrived at the dining room, my gaze swept over the room. No pillow on the floor, no table settings. Uncertain, I looked over my shoulder at him.

"No pillow tonight, darling."

I blinked.

He grinned and jerked his head toward the kitchen. I slid into a stool at the kitchen island and watched the play of muscles across his back as he plated our dinner.

"Do all three of you cook?" I asked as he dropped my plate in front of me.

Cormac shrugged. "Rian's a fucking master in the kitchen. Liam can't even boil water. We sent the cook away to enjoy a long weekend, so I had to make do tonight."

He'd grilled steak and vegetables. I laughed and made air quotes with my fingers, "Make do." I took a bite and moaned. "It's delicious."

Cormac grinned, his white teeth flashing against the deep brown skin of his face. "I'd burn the world down to get you to make that sound again, darling."

I blushed, but couldn't keep the smile off of my face. "How long have you three known each other?"

"Our whole lives."

My eyebrows shot up. "Didn't Liam emigrate from Ireland?"

He laughed. "If by emigrate, you mean, did the Irish mob work a deal to send him here rather than risk him turning coat in prison? Then yes, he emigrated here ten years ago. But he was here as a kid too. Not as poor as Rian and I were, but still, times were tough."

Hm. I tilted my head, wondering how to word my next question.

He saved me the embarrassment. "My grandparents immigrated to Ireland from Nigeria. My father turned out to be a piece-of-shit, and my mother moved here to escape him when she was pregnant. Then she dated more piece-of-shit assholes until one of them took a beating too far and left her hospitalized."

He didn't take my hand when I reached across the counter. I left it there anyway, waiting for him to finish.

"I murdered the fucker. He'll never beat another woman again."

My breath caught in my throat, sympathy overwhelming me. I didn't want to feel anything, but their stories were as tragic as mine. I leaned further and grabbed his hand. He stared at it for a moment, as if not sure what to do with the affection and comfort I offered.

Stubborn man.

I clambered down off the kitchen stool and walked around to the other side of the island to wrap my arms around him from behind. We stood there together for long moments before he set his utensils down and clasped his hands around mine, accepting the comfort I offered.

"It was a long time ago, darling."

I squeezed him tight, pressing my cheek against his back, before releasing him and returning to my stool to finish my dinner. If Cormac wanted to talk, I needed to take the opportunity to better understand these dark and violent men I'd tied myself to.

"How did you all get involved in the gang, then?"

He gave me a puzzled look. "We *are* the gang, darling. Before Rian, the Irish in Yorkfield were scrappy fighters, nothing organized. He took everything he learned running drugs and guns during his summers in Ireland and brought it back here to build our empire."

I tried to wrap my mind around their history, but came up short. "But you went to school, I thought?"

"Running information security in gangland is as intense an operation as running it for a Fortune 500 company. I studied computer science at MIT while Rian went to business school, and then we came back here and got to work."

That would have been about the same time the Russians kidnapped me, and I made my bones as a Russo for murdering that Russian kid. I shook my head, grateful for the ten-year respite I'd enjoyed, and sorrowful that I'd never have that again.

"And Liam?"

Cormac twisted his lips. "You should ask him yourself."

I raised an eyebrow, but dropped the subject, turning the conversation to lighter topics as we ate. Cormac was companionable, letting me shine a light on him outside of the mind-blowing and stomach twisting sex we'd had for the past few days.

"What do you do for fun, Ginny?" I started at the nickname. He'd used it during sex, but I wasn't sure how I felt about it. I was Ginevra. Something inside me warmed, though, at the sound of it.

I grabbed our now empty plates and walked them to the sink. The guys—no, *we*—had a chef and a maid, but I wasn't quite ready to let go of this moment of domesticity with a man who had, until this point, barely spoken to me outside of sex and business.

"Who has time for fun? I work eighty hours a week. What do you do for fun?"

"Fucking same," he answered. We stared at each other for a moment.

"We have the house to ourselves, right?" I grinned, knowing his mind was going straight toward sex.

"Yes," he answered, drawing out the sound, trying to figure out where I was going with this.

"Do you have a gaming console?"

Fifteen minutes later, we sat on the couch, side by side,

knees knocking together, shouting at each other as we played a racing game for kids.

"You dick!" I shouted as he ran me off the side of the course. "I'll fucking pay you back in spades, you asshole."

"If only you could back up your trash talking with actual winning," he said, laughing as I careened off the track again.

"Right? I'm utter shit at this game."

"Why did you pick it, then?"

I slouched back into the couch, fatigue overwhelming me despite the fun I was having playing a lighthearted video game with this dangerous man. "Because it's been a terrible week, and I needed to do something fun tonight."

He remained silent. When I lifted my gaze to his, his eyes softened with an emotion I wasn't ready to identify, much less accept. He wrapped his arm around my shoulders and dragged me into his side.

"Maybe I'll let you win the next round, since you're so terrible at this game."

I sputtered. "Don't you dare!" I ducked out from under his arm so he could keep playing. Unwilling to examine why touching Cormac provided much needed comfort, I curled my legs underneath me and wiggled on the couch until I'd snuggled up to his side.

Cormac nudged me with his elbow after yet another ignominious defeat. "Keep on losing, darling. I can go all night."

I couldn't, though. Yawns soon overwhelmed me. Cormac pried my fingers off my controller. "Time for bed, sweet Ginny."

He lifted me in his arms and instead of resisting, I burrowed my nose into his chest and wrapped my arms around his neck, seeking his warmth and comfort as exhaustion overcame me.

Cormac brought me to his room. I undressed, half asleep, with his laughing help, then crawled under the covers. Who was this gentle man, and what had he done with the uncompromising and threatening Cormac who drenched my panties so easily? This version of Cormac was attractive too—I loved his smile and his laugh and the possessive way he curled up to me in the bed as I drifted off to sleep.

23

GINEVRA

I woke up to an unbearable pleasure building in my core, my legs thrown up over a man's shoulders, his arms wrapped around my thighs as he explored my pussy with his tongue. Liam's red hair contrasted starkly with the tanned skin of my legs, and I reached my hands down to tangle my fingers in his rowdy curls.

"Fuck yes," I moaned as he flicked my clit, sensation shooting through me.

"Oh good. You're awake," Cormac said from beside me, leaning his head down to capture a nipple in his mouth. "Not that it would make a difference," he added, running his teeth across the sensitive skin of my breast.

Still foggy with sleep and caught up in the ecstasy of their touch, I whimpered, grinding my core into Liam's face as he slid two fingers into me, pumping them in and out. "Please," I whined, not capable of asking for what I needed.

"Are you awake, baby?" he asked, pulling away from my core and nuzzling the inside of my thigh.

"Yes," I answered. "Sort of."

Liam's answering laugh was dark. He yanked on my hips

until I was practically falling off the bed, then flipped me over. I marveled at his strength while he manhandled me until my feet were on the ground and I was bent over the bed, my ass in the air.

"Fucking beautiful," he murmured. He brushed the hot tip of his cock against my throbbing pussy and I groaned. Instead of fucking me, like I hoped, he spanked me hard, twice. When I cried out, he stopped. "Do you want to use your safe word, baby?"

I whimpered, trying to put a coherent thought together. Liam ran his fingers up and down the seam of my core before pinching my clit. I whined, trying to jerk away, but didn't say anything.

"Guess not," he answered himself, then peppered my ass and the tops of my thighs with strikes intended to sting and burn, rather than punish. Soon I was mewling as the pain and pleasure melded together, driving me toward ecstasy.

"Please, Liam," I begged. "I need you."

He swore. "You are so fucking pretty when you beg, baby girl." Liam slammed into me, his groan of pleasure guttural as my pussy clenched around him and his fingers dug into my hips.

"Fuck yes," I whispered.

Cormac slid in front of me until my upper body nestled between his thighs.

"Up, darling," he said, sliding a pillow under my chest when I obeyed. His hard cock bobbed in front of me, a bead of pre-cum glistening in the morning light. I swiped my tongue over it. Before I could take him into my mouth, he slid a finger under my chin and tilted my gaze to meet his. "Can't safeword when your mouth is stuffed with cock, but you can tap my thigh three times."

I nodded and lowered my head to swirl my tongue

around the tip of him. Liam took that as his cue to start moving, and began slowly plunging in and out of me, stretching me, filling me, overwhelming me with pleasure. Cormac tangled his fingers in my hair. "Ready, darling?"

For what?

He yanked my face down onto his cock, the tip plunging into my throat and making me gag. *Shit.* At the same time, Liam sped up his pace, until they were both fucking me roughly, hammering in and out of me without regard to my comfort. A hard edge of pleasure spiraled through me, as tears dripped down my face and I lay there, letting Cormac slam my head up and down on his cock as I sucked on it, swirling my tongue up and down.

"Such a perfect little slut for us," he said as I whined and moaned, unable to move, unable to think, completely lost to sensation as they fucked me together.

Seconds later, I was screaming around Cormac's cock as I came, bliss shattering me, filling the edges of my vision with static. My limbs seized and shook with the strength of my release as they continued to plunder my body, drawing out my pleasure until their own rhythms turned ragged.

The sound of my name on their lips as they came unclenched a tension I'd held tightly inside of me for a long time.

Cormac dropped back onto the bed, breathing hard. Liam collapsed beside me. He snuggled up against my side and ran his hands over my hip and the backs of my thighs, murmuring sweet praise as I slowly returned to earth.

"Glad to see everyone's awake." Rian's dry voice skittered up my spine. I tried to push myself to standing, but found my arms too weak and jelly-like to support my weight. Fuck, these guys destroyed me every damn time.

Warm arms wrapped around my stomach and my shoulders, gently drawing me upward until I could stand on my own. I sank into Rian's warmth as I got my bearings and recovered from the intensity of my early morning orgasm.

"Good morning," I said, my voice still raspy and rough with sleep. Soft light filtered in through Cormac's curtains, smoothing the hard edges of the men I'd tied myself to. I wasn't so foolish to think that fantastic sex conquered all, but it sure was helping to ease the pain of closing the door on the life I'd built before.

His hands settled on my naked hips. "I'm having lunch with Benedict Ford today. I'd like you to join me."

Cormac narrowed his eyes from where he sprawled on the bed, tangling his limbs with Liam's. "Benedict's based out of DC. What's he doing up here?"

"We went to school together," Rian answered.

"That doesn't answer my question," Cormac snapped.

Rian traced shapes on my stomach with his fingers. "Now that we've bought back the Russian's initial investment, I'm looking for a new investor to infuse cash into the business. He wants to take over the construction from Ginevra's father."

I froze. "What does that mean, take over the construction?"

"In exchange for a bigger piece of the pie, he's going to become the prime contractor," Rian explained.

Liam ran a freckled hand through his hair. "Benedict's a scary motherfucker. You should say yes."

I tried to capture Rian's eye over my shoulder. "Am I the decision maker here?"

He kissed the top of my head. "Yup. Get dressed, princess."

. . .

Rian and I stared at the skeleton that would one day be a skyscraper. All construction stopped three months ago, and since then, local graffiti artists had left their mark on the frame. Fences and padlocks meant very little to kids looking for trouble, and all I could think about was the lawsuit waiting to happen when someone got hurt.

He handed me a hardhat, and we strolled through the gate. Liam had sent men ahead to secure the area, but given that we'd already signed the contracts mingling our finances, we were less worried about an attack than earlier in the week.

Rian stared up at the building. "A contractor tried to blame ghosts for the fact that his cement deliveries were always ten percent short. Another one couldn't seem to lift a pane of glass without shattering it. The cost overruns on this building have been enormous."

I sighed, eyeing the debris that littered the lot. "Millions of dollars down the drain," I said, my voice hard with frustration and anger. Luis sent me the file to review, and the waste appalled me. No surprise, the signature on delivery after invoice after mistake was Alexi's. That man was fucking my father over, and now that the immediate and physical threat to my family was taken care of, I was going to get to the bottom of it.

"Easy, princess." Rian wrapped an arm around me, saving me from face planting when I tripped over a pile of cinder blocks barely covered with plastic sheeting. Instead of letting me go, his hand migrated to the small of my back, guiding me through the site as we meandered. I tried not to let his care with my physical person convince me he cared about me in any other way, but it was so damn hard to keep the walls around my heart with all three of them.

We picked our way through the shell of the building,

Rian's sharp eyes calculating potential. I didn't know anything about construction, but the numbers I ran on the materials Luis sent me revealed a dire financial situation. It would be years before we'd break even on rents, let alone turn a profit.

Once back in his sports car, Rian whipped off his dusty T-shirt. My eyes caught on the hard muscles of his chest as he slid his arms into a black button-down shirt. He grinned at me, his dark hair falling across his bright blue eyes as he buttoned his cuffs. No man had the right to be that handsome.

"Don't give him an inch when you negotiate with him," Rian cautioned as I applied make-up at a stoplight. "Wait to hear everything he has to say before making your decision."

I chuckled. Rian so easily forgot that I cut my teeth in corporate boardrooms negotiating with venture capitalists. Benedict Ford didn't have a thing on the last generation of San Francisco tech bros, puffed up on their own importance, appalled that a woman had a brain in her head, much less a profitable app.

"I've already made up my mind," I told him, curious to see his reaction.

He furrowed his brow. "What do you mean?"

"Obviously it's going to depend on the terms, but he's more likely to finish the construction than anyone else." I held up the screen of my phone to him. "Luis assembled a dossier for me this morning. Ford is impressive."

"Nobody rises to that level of success in DC without being corrupt as shit."

I laughed and elbowed him over the console of the car. "Oh, yeah, like you're one to talk."

He cut his eyes to me as he parked. "Exactly, princess."

Ford sat at a table in the corner of the deceptively casual

restaurant. It was a hole in the wall place that had popped up a few months ago—French cuisine, didn't take reservations, full of trust fund hipsters. I couldn't believe they'd seated him by himself while he waited for us. On the other hand, that was the type of power I wielded as a Russo in my own neighborhood, so maybe it wasn't quite so odd.

He stood to greet us. Deep brown hair, long on top and short on the sides, swept down over whisky colored eyes. Like Rian, he wore a button-down shirt over jeans, and like Rian, he filled it out well.

I pasted a perky smile on my face and held out my hand to shake his. "Benedict, nice to meet you. I'm Ginevra Russo."

Ford's smile was lopsided as he shook my hand. "A pleasure. Rian, it's good to see you again."

When Ford would have pulled out a chair for me, Rian jokingly elbowed him aside so he could do it himself. Except I knew it wasn't a joke, not really, and so did Ford. I hated how much I liked the small display of possessiveness, as if he were growling *mine* and marking me as his in front of the world.

Ford waited until I sat, then embraced Rian in that particular way of men, pounding his back with his fist. "It's good to see you."

Rian's smile was easygoing. "It's been a while. Too long."

We ordered, and the men caught up on mutual acquaintances. Slowly, the conversation turned to business. Benedict owned real estate up and down the east coast, as well as a relatively new construction firm. He'd outfitted several luxury buildings in DC and wanted to expand his empire to the north.

"So you want to invest in the building, and then contract out the work to yourself?" I interjected, annoyed with the verbal dance he and Rian had engaged in for the last fifteen minutes. Was this my decision or not?

Ford blinked. "To put it baldly, yes."

Rian followed the first rule of business my father had taught me—never put your own money on the line if you don't have to. With or without this infusion of cash from Ford, we could walk away from the building, now that my father no longer had the threat of Russian violence hanging over his head.

Ford took my measure, and I took his. Like me, it was clear he'd made his decision before we sat down. He trusted Rian, and he liked me. I trusted Rian too, at least as far as business was concerned.

"Are you going to fuck me over, Benedict?"

He blinked again. "I'm not sure I follow, Ginevra."

He said my name like a caress, and Rian bristled beside me. I bent forward and traced my finger down Ford's hand, understanding he was playing a game as much as I was. "My father almost lost everything, including his family, because one of his investors, the Russian mob, thought he should pay out on the risk with his family's lives. Is that the type of business you do?"

I could feel Rian's tension radiating out of him, furious that I touched Ford, but he continued to let me take the lead.

Ford took my hand in his, warm and large. He met my eyes, his gold irises shining in the dim light of the restaurant. "It is, typically."

"But?"

"But Rian took a bullet for me, once upon a time, when we were younger and stupider. Your husband is fiercely loyal, and I intend to repay him for that."

I drew my hand out of his. "Let's do it, then."

Ford frowned, looking at Rian to validate my decision. My husband shrugged. "She's the boss."

Never had I liked Rian more than in that moment. I leaned back in my seat, smiling with satisfaction. Our lawyers would negotiate terms and conditions, but I knew I had him locked in. "A toast then, to new partners."

We raised our glasses and clinked them together. Maybe this could work.

Maybe.

24

CORMAC

Ginevra held up the dress Rian bought for her, wrinkling her nose with disgust. "I'm not going to wear this."

I stalked over to her, pushing her backward until her ass rammed against her door. She didn't seem surprised at my aggression. "You'll wear it. You're going to show everyone at the club what a slut you are."

I couldn't tell what she was thinking, only that the fight in her eyes was calling out for discipline, whether she knew it or not. *Hm.* Carefully, I removed the dress from her hands, doing my best not to snag the sequins on her hair.

"Cormac, I don't have time for this," she said, her eyes growing wide as she divined my intentions.

"Shouldn't have sassed me then, you slut," I whispered. Her whole body shivered as I traced my lips over the shell of her ear. God, she was so fucking responsive.

Ginevra chuckled, pushing at my chest, trying to get me to step back. "Very funny, Cormac. Now let me shower and wear something more appropriate."

"How the fuck do you know what is and isn't appropriate

for Liam's clubs?" I asked, tracing my fingers up her forearms before snatching her wrists in my left hand and yanking them up above her head.

She was right, though. We didn't have time for this, as appealing as I found the thought of her walking through the club with my cum all over her.

"Strip and take your shower," I ordered her, "if you don't want to be walking around the club with stripes from my belt on your thighs."

Ginevra's eyes widened, and she stilled. "Good," I muttered, pushing back from the door and freeing her.

She blew her hair out of her face in a huff. "Can I wear comfortable shoes, at least?"

"Do you want me to micromanage your footwear too?"

Her warm laugh reached something deep inside my chest and yanked on it, drawing me back to her. I kissed her forehead, her cheeks, and finally her lips, capturing them in a sweet kiss that left us both breathless.

"No," she answered, running her fingers over my curls.

"Go get showered, brat."

An hour later she arrived in the living room, a glorious vision in gold sequins. She'd styled her hair so it fell in soft waves down to the middle of her back. And that dress. *Jesus.* It hugged every one of her generous curves, stopping a few inches below the sweet juncture of her thighs. The top sat high in front, arcing just below her collarbones, but in back, dipped all the way down to her ass, the pale gold of the sequins contrasting with her olive skin and brunette hair.

Uncharacteristically, her make-up was bold and vivid, dark smokey eyes and a vampy red lip that begged me to sink my teeth into it.

She fidgeted under our admiring gazes.

"Fuck, Ginevra, you look like a fuckin' queen," Liam

whispered reverently, angling himself out of his armchair to greet her.

"Turn around, Ginevra," I told her, my voice raspier than I expected.

She did, treating us to the sight of the sequined fabric stretched tightly over her perfect ass. "Spread your legs," I whispered.

She did.

I inched the fabric of the dress up until we could see the red ribbon of her thong perfectly centered between the generous curves of her ass.

Smack! Smack! I spanked her twice, for the joy of seeing my palm print bloom on each of her cheeks.

"Perfect," I murmured, straightening her back out and pulling her dress down.

25

LIAM

Excitement rushed through me. I fuckin' loved fight nights—the crowds, the noise, the violence, the women. I looked at Ginevra sitting beside me in the backseat of the vehicle, her knees pushed primly together and her posture regal, like the queen she was. My queen. Our queen. Signed on the dotted line.

I couldn't help the fierce satisfaction that rolled through me at the thought. She belonged to us now. And it was time to introduce her to our people. Just as yesterday's visit to shops and businesses in the Russos' territory had been carefully choreographed, so would be tonight.

The Irish mob was more rough and tumble than the Italians, but no less misogynist. Sure, we had a long tradition of women taking up arms. Women could fuck shit up just as well as any man, but we still expected them to clean up well and serve as eye candy when needed.

Ginevra was definitely eye candy, the expensive kind you got by the gram in high street shops, the kind I couldn't have dreamed of when I was a kid here, or when I was broke and hungry back in Ireland. I eyed the hem of her skirt as it rode up her thighs.

As if she could feel the intensity of my gaze, she swung her head around, a question in her eyes.

"You're fucking beautiful, Ginevra. Inside and out."

Oh fuck, she blushed. Our Ginevra got off on Cormac's degradation, but praise, *praise*, turned her into a puddle of melted goo. This woman deserved all of it, deserved to know how amazing, how worthy she was, how fucking perfectly she fit into our dangerous and bloody lives. I wrapped my fingers around hers, and when she squeezed mine back, my heart stuttered.

Too soon, we arrived at the club. The valet opened Ginevra's door, and she slid out, all grace and smiles as she made her movie star entrance into our world. By the time I'd climbed out behind her, she'd already sauntered past the long line of beautiful people hoping to get in.

Declan manned the door and grinned at her. His smile faltered when I slid my arm around her waist, staring him down for the affront.

"Oh, come on, boss. Your woman is beautiful and charming. I know she's yours," he muttered.

Ginevra elbowed me in the side. *What?* Then she pulled away from me to give Declan those damn Italian air kisses. I kept my fists clenched at my sides. When she pulled back, she stepped into my side and waited. *For what? Oh.* I draped my arm around her shoulders as Declan let us into the club, Cormac and Rian trailing behind us.

The pounding base thumped as we made our way through the crowded dance floor. Ginevra's eyes twinkled as she looked up at me. "Sure we don't have time to dance?"

In that moment, more than anything else in the world, I wanted to wrap my fingers around her hips and move with her in time to the music. I imagined her on the dance floor, her gorgeous curves swaying as the three of us surrounded her, my hands roving over her back then under that sweet dress, palming her perfect breasts as Cormac lifted her leg and pressed her pussy into his cock and Rian shoved his tongue down her throat, listening to her whimpers and moans as partiers and dancers watched us play with her.

But I had to get things ready for the fight. My clubs were successful because I was hands on, not because I delegated. "Another night, baby, I promise."

Another bouncer let us through the double doors at the back of the club. As soon as we hit the dark hallway, I pushed Ginevra face first into the wall. Tracing my fingers along the low back of her dress, I murmured, "This dress should be illegal."

She huffed with amusement. "Take it up with Cormac and Rian," both of whom stood right there, watching me paw her. I slipped my fingers through the deep back, sliding along her silky skin until I reached her stomach, then drew them upward until I cupped her breasts, just as I'd imagined a few moments ago. Her breath turned ragged as she arched her back, pushing her breasts into my hands.

I plucked at her nipples, ignoring the gasp of pain and the deep throated moan of pleasure that followed as I stretched and pulled at them. When I'd hurt her enough that she'd be sore for the evening, I palmed her breasts again, soothing the ache. She pushed back from the wall and leaned against my torso, looping her arms around my neck, soft and sweet, surrendering to me. Her luscious hips ground into me as she writhed in time to the dance music emanating faintly from the club.

"Sure we don't have time to dance, Liam?" Ginevra's voice was throaty and low. It shot straight to my groin.

With a huff of amusement, Cormac untwined her fingers from my neck and pulled her into him. "He doesn't have time, darling."

She grinned. "Worth a try."

Cormac just smiled and tapped her on the ass, pushing her forward down the hall. Was that affection from our broody dominant? *Wonders never cease.*

I yanked our girl back under my arm, wrapping my fingers over her shoulder with possessiveness. She might be ours, but tonight she would sit by *my* side.

Rian and Cormac continued downstairs to confirm security arrangements and greet the fighters, while I pulled Ginevra into my office. Keri, the club's manager, was waiting for me there. She stood when we entered the room.

Keri was dressed in a suit, but didn't appear to be wearing anything under her buttoned blazer. She'd pulled her red hair back in a severe ponytail, and kept her make-up minimal. Keri looked like a doll, but she'd spent years as a professional MMA fighter. She could take on anyone who gave her a hard time.

She and Ginevra eyed each other for half a second, the pause as we entered the room barely noticeable. Keri's eyes flicked over Ginevra, wary about the woman we were bringing into the fold.

I needn't have worried. Ginevra disengaged from my arm and walked forward to clasp Keri's hands in her own. "Keri, I'm so glad to meet you. My name's Ginevra." Ginevra leaned to give her soft air kisses. "Liam tells me he couldn't run this place without you."

Keri's eyes widened almost imperceptibly. "It's nice to meet you too, Mrs.—" She paused and blinked several times. "What are we calling you?"

Ginevra laughed. Sweet and charming Ginevra was far more dangerous than angry and uncertain Ginevra.

"Just Ginevra, I think. We didn't discuss changing my name. Wouldn't that be complicated, with three of them?" Her grin was wide and easy as she dropped into one of the two chairs in front of my desk. "Don't let me get in the way of your fight prep. My job tonight is to be distracting eye candy."

Keri took the seat beside Ginevra, eyeing her up and down. "That you will be, Ginevra." My manager's eyes flicked back to me, seeking cues about how I wanted this conversation to continue.

I shook my head. "Ginevra's a twenty-five percent owner now, same as Rian and Cormac. Go ahead and brief us both."

Ginevra leaned in, listening intently, as we reviewed the night's fighters and the security arrangements. We had VIPs from both the Costa family and the Zhangs, a Chinese-American triad who wanted to establish a presence in Yorkfield.

I was familiar with these details, but Keri ran through them with me anyway, to make sure neither of us forgot anything important.

"Did you say the Costas have a fighter in the octagon tonight?" Ginevra interrupted.

Keri nodded. "Sergio Accardi. He's one of their captains, a strong fighter."

Ginevra couldn't hide the fury that flashed over her face. Keri and I waited patiently. "Sergio's the bastard who knocked my sister up."

Ah. I leaned back in my seat, steepling my fingers. "How do you want to handle this, Ginevra?"

She pressed her lips together in a grim line. "I don't

know."

I laid my hand palm up on the desk. Ginevra wrapped her fingers around mine, and I squeezed her tight. "Trust me to take care of it?"

She nodded.

Keri grinned. "I'll let the guys know. They'll be fuckin' thrilled."

Ginevra furrowed her brow. "What are you going to do?"

"Trust me, baby. You'll see." I winked.

Ginevra and I entered the arena like royalty, my arm around her waist, the cheers and the shouts of the crowd enveloping us. When I clasped Ginevra's hand in mine and raised our linked hands above our heads, the crowd roared. The clamor continued until we reached our seats, comfortable padded chairs at the front of the arena, right up against the ropes, so close to the fighters that we could catch splatters of blood and sweat. Two rows of seats curved up behind us, and beyond that, it was standing room only.

The crowd was well-dressed, as if ready for a cocktail party, not a brutal, bloody underground fight. Waitresses in short skirts and bikini tops circulated, serving drinks and selling cigars to the mostly male crowd.

Cormac and Rian waited for us, two empty seats between them, sprawled out like young gods in their suits, nursing glasses of expensive whisky. Young men in suits sat behind and beside them, double the usual security detail. Normally, I wouldn't be so obvious about it, but I wasn't messing around with our girl's safety.

One of the waitresses made her way to us. She offered me my customary bottle, and one tumbler. I handed it to

Ginevra, and poured her two fingers of the caramel colored liquid before turning back to the girl.

"Where's my glass?" I snarled.

Her eyes widened. Oh, she hadn't meant to insult Ginevra? She just assumed my *wife* was like every other girl in this hall?

My voice was low and mean. "Ginevra Russo is my fucking wife and you will treat her with the same respect you do Cormac, Rian, and I, do you understand?"

Ginevra stepped beside me and ran her finger down my arm, arresting my attention. "Easy there, love," she said, using the same phrase we used to settle her when we were fucking her. "She couldn't have known."

Cormac growled from where he sat, a lion with his eyes focused on prey trembling before him. "Laila did know, though, didn't she?"

The girl, Laila, stood before us in her tiny pleather skirt and black bikini top, looking like a scared rabbit rather than the seductive saleswoman I'd trained her to be.

Ginevra's eyes flashed with fury. She grabbed my arm, and yanked me back from where I towered over the girl. "I said, easy, you asshole."

I didn't think it was possible for Laila's eyes to get bigger. Ginevra had insulted me in front of the whole fucking arena, then she had the ovaries to correct me. And she wasn't done yet.

"The insult was to me, and Russos are made of sterner stuff. We don't need to punish a fucking bottle girl because her boss didn't bother to make my position clear in advance. Fuck you, Liam."

The girl flinched back as if struck when Ginevra dismissed her with a flick of her hand. Ginevra ignored her and slammed down into the empty seat beside Rian who stretched his arm across the back of her chair and grinned up at me, tangling his fingers in the waves of her sable hair.

Fuck.

Cormac growled softly. "Get out of here, Laila. Send Anna Marie down with a glass for Liam."

Laila scurried out of the arena, and I took my seat between Ginevra and Cormac. "Fuck, woman, that wasn't part of the script."

She shrugged. "Beg for my forgiveness, Liam."

I snatched her glass out of her hands and handed it to Cormac, then dragged her over to me, until I could feel the press of her thigh against mine. When she merely raised an eyebrow in challenge, I lifted my hand to cup her jaw, stroking my thumb against her cheekbones. She grinned and her tongue darted out to lick her lips. Unable to resist the invitation, I drew her in for a kiss. She opened her mouth with a sweet sigh, and I slipped my tongue into her mouth, taking my time as I claimed her in front of the entire goddamned arena.

"I'm sorry, lass," I muttered against her lips.

"Is that what you consider begging?" she shot right back, nipping my bottom lip between her teeth as she pulled away.

I tucked the hair I'd mussed behind her ears, then brushed my lips against hers one more time for good measure. "No," I answered, sitting back in my chair, tangling my fingers in hers and holding our twined hands together against my thigh, waiting patiently for her to relax against me.

Our VIPs, Italian and Chinese-American, sat on the opposite side of the ring and watched our exchange with avid interest. Ginevra raised her glass to them in a silent toast, despite her mussed hair and bee-stung lips.

"Good girl," I murmured so only she could hear, and she blushed.

The first rounds of fights passed in a blur. Between each fight, we introduced Ginevra to our crew, to our guests, to the extended family we'd built here. I watched her with pride, confident we'd made the right decision, allowing her to trade places with Sofia.

When Adam Zhang made it over to our side of the arena while I was deep in conversation with one of the Nigerians we sold arms to, Ginevra waylaid him, introducing herself and charming him until I could join them.

"Your wife is a delight," Adam said, smiling at her. "Ginevra was very courteous, distracting me until you finished with Unigwe. She mentioned you and her father are looking for investors in a real estate project."

I underestimated her at my peril. She handled Laila and Adam like she was born to this life. No, Sofia might have been able to tread water in these shark infested waters, but Ginevra? Ginevra was a shark herself.

26

GINEVRA

Sergio Accardi fought next. Liam had disappeared. And I was shaking with anger.

Rian took my hand in his. "Trust him, princess." Easy to say, hard to do. Doubts rushed through me. Would it look like I was condoning Sergio's behavior if I sat here and clapped through his fight? Would he think the Russos approved, that we thought him a fit partner for my sister?

When the arena roared with approval, I looked up. Liam was striding out of the corner entrance shirtless, in loose shorts, his hands and wrists wrapped in white tape. He raised his arms above his head, fists clenched.

I ran my eyes over his bare chest, roaming them over the chiseled lines of his muscles, the tattoos that covered every inch of his pale freckled skin. When he caught my eyes as he strolled to the ring, I couldn't breathe, the emotion welling up in me was so strong, so overwhelming.

Cormac took Liam's seat and threw his arm over the back of my shoulders, pulling me into his side. Rian scooted closer to me, pressing his thigh into mine, stroking his thumb over my fingers as I sat dumbfounded. Their touch grounded me as Liam ducked under the ropes.

Liam was going to fight Sergio. I didn't doubt for a moment who would win.

Sergio's face was blank as they shook hands. He was deeply tanned, his black curly hair cut short. Like Liam, he was covered in tattoos. I could see why Sofia had given him a second glance. He was handsome. Too bad he was also stupid. Once Papà settled his debts to the Russians, he'd turn his focus to getting his second daughter settled. Luca too, probably.

The bell rang, and Sergio and Liam danced toward one another. I couldn't keep my eyes off the ripple of Liam's muscles as he slammed his fists into Sergio's side. Sergio responded with a fist to Liam's face. Liam's head jerked back, a cut blooming on his cheek.

I gasped, my fingers lifting to my mouth to cover the sound. Rian squeezed my other hand.

I needn't have worried. The two fighters danced around each other for a few more moments, before Liam delivered a flurry of kicks and punches, too quick for me to follow, and too quick for Sergio to avoid.

Liam swept Sergio off his feet, then held him to the mat, whispering in his ear. Sergio's face blanched, then he nodded. I'd have given my arm to hear what my lover was saying to my sister's baby daddy. *Welcome to the family, asshole.* I grinned vindictively and shot to my feet with the rest of the crowd when Liam was declared the winner.

Rian pushed me forward until I leaned against the ropes. Liam pulled me in for a deep kiss, to the delight of the arena. When we pulled away from each other, he held me tight, leaning his forehead against mine as we caught our breath.

"Thank you," I whispered.

"Anything you need, Ginevra," he promised. "I'm yours just as much as you're mine."

Liam didn't bother to put a shirt on under the silk robe he wore after the fight. His staff took down the ring and set up a bar, turning the base of the arena into an impromptu club where the rich and violent of Yorkfield could mix and mingle after the excitement of the fights.

With his arm around me, he introduced me to Giovanni Costa, whose fighter he'd so soundly beaten minutes before. The patriarch of the Costa family was older than my father, but no less dangerous. He ruled his family, and his territory, with an iron fist.

"It's a pleasure," Costa said, exchanging air kisses with me before turning to Liam. "I didn't expect you to step into the ring tonight, Liam."

Liam grinned. "The Russos' grudges are my grudges, Gio."

The patriarch nodded. "I heard marriage was in the works, but didn't realize it had already happened—I never received an invitation."

My answering smile was full of teeth. "We'll hold a commitment ceremony in a few weeks, but the contracts are already signed."

Costa's gaze sharpened. "The rumors are true, then. Your father sold you to three men, instead of just one."

I faltered, just for a moment, as I struggled not to internalize his judgment. Diving into a sexual relationship with three men didn't make me a whore. When Liam's fingers tightened around my waist, I knew I had to respond before he made a scene.

"Gio, it's the twenty-first century, and I've spent the last decade in Hollywood. Do you intend to imply there's something wrong with a poly relationship?"

His eyes narrowed. The public challenge to his prejudices was deliberate. I had a hard road to walk, much harder than my men, and the mob wasn't known for their forward thinking when it came to their women.

Gio's smile was sharklike. "It makes you a whore for your family, my dear."

Liam fucking decked the asshole, and the entire arena descended into chaos.

While the bodyguards surrounding Costa pulled the two men apart, the excited crowd pushed me away. I fought against the movement, trying to stay close to the relative safety of Liam. When Alexi appeared, throwing his arm around my shoulders and guiding me out of the arena. I followed him, surprised at his presence, but grateful for his size and his protection.

The hallway was poorly lit. Someone had flicked off the fluorescent lighting, leaving only the dull flicker of the emergency lights. "Alexi, I—"

An arm wrapped around my waist, and a hand slammed down over my mouth. I screamed, but it was futile. Over the echoing noise of the riot, nobody heard my muffled shouts. I struggled and kicked, to no avail. The man who hauled me along was twice my size, and I couldn't seem to get in a blow strong enough to stop him.

A third man waited for us in the dark hallway outside of the arena. Alexi taped my mouth shut while the other taped my wrists together, then my feet.

No. NO!

Memories of being kidnapped as a teenager washed over me, and I panicked. When I screamed again through the tape, Alexi slapped me in the face, shocking me into silence. "Shut the fuck up, Ginevra."

Fuck. *Fuck!* I wanted to scream that he'd pay, that I knew he was as complicit ten years ago as he was in that moment. None of that would be useful in helping me escape though. Did my men know Alexi had betrayed us, had betrayed me? My eyes flicked to the blinking red light of the camera in the corner of the hallway, hoping, praying, they'd see what happened.

With a grunt, one of the men lifted me over his shoulder, my face dangling down his back, and his hand on my thighs to hold me in place as we exited through a fire escape. The fire alarm blared as they dropped me into the trunk of a car, heedless of my ineffectual struggles.

When the trunk slammed shut, leaving me in darkness, a sob escaped me, a guttural, animal sound of terror and despair. The car sped through the city, throwing me against the walls of the trunk as it took turns quickly, the wheels squealing in the quiet of the night.

I held in my whimpers as I tamped down on the terror coursing through me. This wasn't a decade ago. I wasn't sixteen. I was an adult. I'd been in this situation before, and somehow, I would figure out a way out of it.

The car slammed to a stop. Heavy footsteps walked around the car before opening the trunk and dragging me out by my wrists. Before I could get my bearings and figure out where we were, my captor shoved a hood over my face, then threw me over his shoulder again.

Too soon, he threw me to the ground. A door clanged shut, and I lifted my bound hands to tear the hood off of my face, only to find myself still unable to see in the pitch black of wherever I was. My breath sped up, and I hyperventilated, terror overtaking me when I couldn't breathe through the tape covering my mouth.

No. Keep it under control, Ginevra.

This wasn't ten years ago. I was stronger than this, stronger than these captors, stronger than fucking Alexi. Ten years of therapy and independence would get me through this. I breathed through my nose, fighting my instinct to panic.

My men would tear the city apart looking for me.

Hopefully.

I MANEUVERED my body to a sitting position, my feet in front of me, my knees slightly bent, so I could scoot around wherever I was. When I hit a wall, I sighed with relief. My body ached from the tension and the exertion to get here, and I was grateful to lean my bare back on the rough concrete.

Since Alexi had taped my mouth shut and dragged me away from the arena in Liam's club, I'd teetered on the precipice of terror and panic. With no way to tell how much time passed in the silent blackness, I slowly backed away from the brink, taking deep breaths to calm myself.

Why had he grabbed me? Ransom? It would take time for Rian to route the ten million dollars he'd paid for me to the Bratva in a way that wouldn't draw attention to the transaction. No. No way was Alexi in this alone. Revenge? My father pissed off a lot of people when he'd failed to save the other families' investment in his luxury building, and Alexi had borne the brunt of protecting my family from the fallout. But wasn't that the point of the ten million dollar payment to the Russians, to assuage those hurt feelings? Or was Alexi working with Yuri Semenov, finally collecting on the debt I owed for killing Ivan so many years ago?

Were my men really going to search for me? My father had his money and protection, and they were officially shareholders in my father's businesses, legitimate and otherwise. The weight of my father's name now extended to them, with or without me to sweeten the deal as their wife. Sure, they'd be better served by my presence, but as long as my father was willing to go along with it, they didn't fucking need me anymore.

Fuck, I didn't know. Untangling myself from this bullshit was why I'd left ten years ago and built myself a life on the other side of the country. I'd made stupid decision after stupid decision since Sofia had called a week ago, only to find myself in exactly the same situation I'd fled as a teenager.

The door to the room clanged open, slamming into the concrete wall. Fluorescent light from the hallway poured in, creating a halo behind the large man staring at me, his face twisted with disgust.

"Ginevra Russo," he said with a thick Russian accent. "Welcome to my humble abode."

When I didn't respond, he curled an eyebrow up, then strode into the room. With a painful jerk, he ripped the tape off my mouth.

Holding back tears from the sudden burning pain, I inhaled sharply, knowing this might be my only opportunity to get more information about the man who crouched before me. "Who are you?"

"Yuri Semenov, my dear." Semenov's smile didn't meet his eyes as his lips stretched over his teeth. I was so fucked. He reached out a finger and traced it down my cheek. "Memories are long in the underworld, darling Ginevra. I promise you, I never forgot for one moment who murdered my son."

He stepped back and one of his soldiers picked me up with a grunt, dragging me over his shoulder to carry me out of the cell. I tried to ignore the prick of humiliation about being exposed like this, my now filthy dress riding up over my ass. I used my bound fists to push against the back of my captor, lifted my head from where it bounced against him, trying to get my bearings.

We walked through a bland, windowless office space. We'd entered into a warehouse, of that I was certain, but we hadn't walked up or down any stairs. Too soon, we arrived to an open space, well enough lit to see the equipment piled around us.

Without ceremony, the man carrying me dropped me into a metal chair, bolted to the concrete floor. When I realized his intent, I screamed and kicked again, until a harsh blow to the side of my face left me gasping in pain. Before I could recover, he taped my feet to the legs of the chair and my hands behind it. The position was obscene, leaving my red panties bared to Yuri's dispassionate gaze.

When he realized I was trying to press my knees together, he laughed. "Don't worry, Russo. I don't intend to rape you. Although I can't speak for what Alexi and my men will do when I'm finished with you."

I froze. *No.*

Yuri's laugh rang cruelly through the warehouse. He pulled out an ancient digital camera and snapped a photo before one of the men applied tape to my mouth once again. The light snapped off, and once again, I was sitting in the dark.

27

RIAN

My attention snapped to the center of the room just in time to see Liam deck Costa. Just what we fucking needed on top of everything else. The crowd lost their goddamned minds, cheering and pushing closer to get a glimpse of a fight that would, in any other circumstances, be absolutely epic.

Zhang raised an eyebrow. "Is this how you boys typically do business?"

With a deep sigh, I shook my head. "Our business is going to have to wait for another day, I believe."

He laughed, handing me his card. "It will be my pleasure."

I spun on my heel and pushed through the excited and jostling crowd, trying to keep Ginevra in my sights as I shoved my way to the center where Liam and Accardi stood, grappling with each other. By the time I reached them, Cormac and Costa's bodyguards were shoving the two men apart.

Where was she? I spun around, searching for our girl, my eyes wild as I realized she was nowhere to be seen. Fuck.

"Clear this place out," I ordered the closest gang member—a young man with orange hair and tattoos up and down his arms. He looked at me with surprise. "NOW!" I roared, continuing my search for Ginevra.

I pushed and shoved through the crowd, grabbing every brunette in my path and checking to see if it was Ginny.

Where the fuck was she?

The arena wasn't emptying out fast enough. I drew my gun from my shoulder holster, ready to fire in the air, but was interrupted by the harsh ring of fire alarms. The crowd screamed and rushed for the doors, pushing and shoving in their eagerness to escape.

When the arena had cleared out, the three of us stared at each other in shock and horror. "Where the fuck is she, Liam?" I shouted, furious he'd let his goddamned temper put our woman in danger.

Cormac didn't even bother shouting, just drew his fist back and slammed it into Liam's jaw. "You fucking idiot!"

Liam took the hit. His eyes were ice cold. "Gio called her a whore to her fucking face."

I spun on my heel and left the arena, taking the stairs two at a time to get to Liam's office, where he could watch over the security cameras in relative peace, no matter what else was going on in the club. By the time Cormac and Liam joined me a few minutes later, I'd already pulled up the feed from the arena and fast forwarded it to the moment that Liam took a swing at Gio Accardi.

Declan slammed the door open, Keri on his heels. "Call the Fire Department and let them know it was a false alarm," I snapped, sliding out of my seat and allowing Cormac to work his magic.

Keri nodded and got on the phone.

Declan leaned over me. "What's up, boss?"

"They fucking snatched Ginevra," Liam growled, his hold on his temper as tenuous as my own.

Liam ran his hands through his coppery hair. "Declan, search the building while Cormac's going through the security footage, then start interviewing the staff."

Ginevra didn't even blink as Liam defended her honor. She stepped forward as if to break up the fight, and then the crowd swept her backward, eager to get in on the action. I followed the dark brown of her hair as she was jostled to the left and the right, and then hustled out of the arena by a seemingly protective Alexi.

I switched the feed to the hallway and watched two men tape up our girl as she struggled and fought. Her eyes swung up to the camera, wide and terrified, as if begging me to reach back in time and save her. The biggest of the men swung her over his shoulder, exposing her ass to the camera.

Alexi and his two companions jogged out of the arena, using the same service stairs we just did, then pushed out the fire escape, setting off the alarm. We didn't have a camera in the alley where they'd parked. Fuck. We'd talked about installing better security on the outside of the building, but had set it aside for later. Fucking later was now. I swore, furious at myself for telling Liam it wasn't a priority when he'd mentioned it weeks before.

Cormac pushed away from the security system and pulled out his phone, his fingers flying over the touchscreen. "I'll see if there's any CCTV or other footage of the alley or the intersection there. Maybe we can pull plates."

I nodded. "In the meantime, use the footage from the hallway to start running facial recognition on the two men with Alexi."

Liam's bark of laughter was angry and short. "It's the fucking Russians."

"How do you know?"

He squeezed my shoulder, then rewound the scene to where the biggest of them had thrown Ginevra over his shoulder. The tattoos on his hand were clear. Local Bratva.

Fucking hell. What had Alexi done?

I slammed my fist on the desk, sending papers and Liam's office detritus flying.

When Liam looked up at me, his eyes were bleak. "We're going to get her back."

Cormac's deep brown eyes flicked up to Liam and then me. "And then we're going to burn this city to the fucking ground. Nobody will ever hurt her again."

Nikolai's voice was tired on the phone. "I don't have your daughter, Antonio Russo."

"That's what you said twelve years ago," Antonio answered, clenching his fists on his desk as he spoke with the head of the Yorkfield Bratva on speakerphone. "And yet, twelve years ago, I had to storm your father's house to steal my daughter back. Do you remember how many Russians I killed in retribution?"

"Twelve," Nikolai said.

"That's right," Antonio agreed. "Twelve. Two nights ago, I signed contracts binding my family to the Irish so I could pay you back the ten million dollars you invested in a luxury apartment building that hasn't been completed."

"I don't have your daughter!" Nikolai finally roared through the phone.

I stepped up to the desk and held my hand out for Antonio's phone. To my surprise, he handed it to me without question. "Your men do. Alexi Marino and two Russians with Bratva tattoos on their hands took her from Liam's club tonight. Antonio might not be willing to go to war over his daughter, but we sure as fuck will over our goddamned wife."

Nikolai was silent. "This sounds like it's as much a problem within your family as mine. Give me seventy-two hours."

Three days? He wanted us to wait *three days* for news of Ginevra?

"I'll give you twenty-four hours. If you haven't returned her by then, the streets will run red with Russian blood. Do you understand me?" I didn't wait for an answer before hanging up.

Cormac was in his office, doing what he did best, tracking down information on the Internet. Liam was out on the streets with Lorenzo and our combined security teams, his bloodlust on hold only because his desperation to find her outweighed his need to punish those who took her. If Alexi and the Bratva were ready to risk dealing with the Butcher of Cork, then I was going to let Liam off the fucking leash so he could bathe in their blood.

Antonio and I stared at each other over his desk. "Out! Everyone out!" he shouted. The crowd of Russos exited the room. "You promised me you'd protect my daughter," he said to me, pouring me a scotch and sliding it across the desk to me.

"I didn't expect to be protecting her from your goddamned head of security," I snapped right back at him.

Antonio slumped down in his chair. "I should have known."

Yeah, he fucking should have. The Russo operation was a goddamned mess, and Antonio could have prevented all of this if he'd moved with the times, modernized his books, fucking did anything but take Alexi at his word, again and again and again.

When Ginevra's father looked back at me, his face had hardened into determination and fury. "Alexi's a dead man."

Outside of the house, I stared into the Russo's perfectly manicured lawn, resisting the urge to pull out my phone to beg Cormac and Liam for updates. They'd contact me as soon as they had a lead and nagging wouldn't help.

The bastards had grabbed Ginevra just after midnight. Dawn was approaching, and with it, the knowledge that I'd completely and utterly failed her. I ran my hands through my hair, then down my face.

My phone dinged. When I thumbed it open, a photo of Ginevra popped up, still in that gold dress, her hair matted and messy, bound to a chair with her legs spread and those fucking red panties on display.

Cormac's name popped up next. He didn't bother with pleasantries. "The photo taken with a pre-wifi digital camera, looks like a burner number. It's going to take a while to analyze it."

Fuck.

28

LIAM

Lorenzo and I interviewed every goddamn employee at the club last night and we didn't learn a goddamn thing except that the girls were curious about Ginevra, and that my bartender was giving away free drinks when he shouldn't be.

Fuck.

I slammed my fist into the wall of my office, doing my fist more damage than the wall. *Fuck, again.* My worry about Ginevra distracted me from what I did best, scare the shit out of people, torture them, then kill them. Every time I thought of her, scared and alone, murderous rage washed through me.

I was questioning Declan when my phone pinged with that damnable photo. I lost it. He didn't flinch when I held the knife to his throat. He'd let those assholes into my club and he deserved whatever I gave him.

The only thing that saved me from murdering him was Lorenzo, who'd drawn his gun and held it to my head. "This isn't helping Ginevra, Liam," he said, his voice slow and soothing.

As strong as the urge was to bathe in blood, Lorenzo was right. I sheathed my knife. Declan exhaled sharply, and I spun around and decked him in the jaw. "Asshole," I swore at him.

He raised his hands. "I let them in. I'll help get her back."

We'd gone over every second of video, sending as many images to Cormac as we could. We had a photo of the car, a couple of shots of the Russian's faces, and one too many pictures of Ginevra struggling and trying to get free as her captors fucking kidnapped her.

"That doesn't help either," Lorenzo said as I watched them take her again, and again, and again, as if doing so would help me discern enough detail that I could miraculously find her. I tamped down on the itch to kill him for daring to correct me. Like he said, not helpful. Nothing was more important than finding Ginevra and getting her back.

That woman. We'd known her a goddamned week, and she'd wormed her way into my heart. I'd stopped believing in God a long time ago, but at that moment, I prayed for Ginevra.

Bring her home. Please.

My phone dinged.

Rian: Someone set the Russo warehouses on fire.

Fuck.

Cormac: Checking our feeds now.
Cormac: Our buildings are okay.

Lorenzo's phone rang. After a hurried conversation, he looked at me. "I gotta go."

"The warehouses?"

He nodded. It had to be connected. "I'll go with you."

On my way out, I clapped Declan on the back. "You're alive because you're good at your job."

He looked at me with amusement twinkling in his blue eyes. My attempted murder hadn't fazed him at all. That's what I liked about him. "Is that an apology for threatening to cut my throat?"

I frowned. "No. I'm explaining why I didn't kill you. The Russo warehouses are on fire, and they're about to send their men out to investigate. We need to augment the security on their house right now. Patti and Sofia are targets too."

He nodded, his blond hair falling into his face. "I knew what I was getting into when I signed up to work for the Butcher."

"Good. If something happens to those women, your usefulness won't save you. Do you understand?"

Declan's answering nod was sharp. "Got it, boss."

BY THE TIME we arrived at the port, the fire department arrived. The tires of Lorenzo's sports car squealed as he slammed on the brakes and stopped in front of the burning warehouse. Flames licked the roof, but didn't appear to be spreading to neighboring buildings.

We climbed out of the car, both of us breathing a sigh of relief when we straightened our long limbs. Why did he have such a ridiculous vehicle, anyway? *Compensation*, I thought to myself with a bark of laughter. No, that was unfair. Lorenzo was trustworthy, and I liked him.

"Nothing but agricultural products and foodstuffs in there," he said as we leaned on the car, watching the trucks spray the building down. "Wheat from Eastern Europe, liquor from Italy—so much liquor and vinegar. All really fucking flammable."

None of it would be salvageable. Just like that, millions of dollars, literally up in smoke. Lorenzo's men's preliminary inspection revealed no injuries. No way this wasn't related to Ginevra's kidnapping. The timing was too perfect, and Alexi had the means.

A police officer strode to where I stood, watching the spectacle. Lorenzo melted into the pre-dawn light to poke around the port and seek witnesses that might not come forward to the police.

"Sir, I'm Officer Christopher Ramos," he introduced himself, sticking out his hand for me to shake.

I stared at the short black man and let the moment draw out uncomfortably. "I'm Liam Byrne. I represent the owner."

The police officer crooked an eyebrow, his deep brown skin flickering with hints of gold and red in the dying light of the fire. "I know who you are. You're not a Russo."

My answering smile was unkind. "I'm married to one."

"As of when?"

I blinked. Who the hell did this cop think he was? "What do you think happened?" I asked, bringing the conversation back to the immediate problem of the burning warehouse.

"It's too early to tell."

I snorted. "There are two other Russo warehouses on fire in Yorkfield tonight. I'd say we know exactly what happened."

"Yes, sir," the officer agreed with me, his air collegial and friendly. "So far, we haven't found any witnesses. Do you have any idea who might have done this?"

I debated whether to share that Ginevra had been kidnapped hours before. Would it help or hurt? Fuck, this was a Rian decision—my job was piling up the bodies. His job was cleaning up messes.

My phone pinged, giving me a moment's reprieve. It was a photo of Ginevra, trussed up, her face tear streaked but angry and determined. My eyes flicked over her, noting how exposed she was, and how fierce she looked anyway. *That's my girl. Give 'em hell, Ginevra.*

The cop looked at me, a question in his eyes.

"Are you asking if Antonio Russo is likely to retaliate?" I didn't know the answer to that question. The embers of the material inside the warehouse glowed red in the dawn as the sun rose over the port. "Officer Ramos, these warehouses barely even rate in terms of the troubles Tony Russo is facing right now."

Lorenzo meandered back into my field of view, and I waved him over. "Hand the nice police officer your card, Lo."

Officer Ramos nodded sharply. "I'll call if I find anything."

Lorenzo and I slid into his car. I showed him the photo of Ginevra and he swore softly. "Two other warehouses were hit. No way this shit isn't related."

"No witnesses?"

He shook his head. "None that I could find. Cormac might have better luck breaking into the CCTV systems."

Liam: Three warehouses, no witnesses at the port. Cormac, can you check the CCTV?

A few minutes later, Cormac replied.

**Cormac: Bratva again. Fuckers aren't even trying to hide.
Rian: Fuck.**

I roared my fury, the sound echoing loudly in the small sports car. Nikolai swore he didn't know who was behind this, but the hit on the warehouses put paid to that lie. Time to hunt Russians.

29

CORMAC

The photo of Ginevra taunted me, the fury in her eyes cutting at me as I wallowed in my guilt. We hadn't paid attention at the fight, and these assholes had grabbed our woman.

My office was sleek and modern, with giant windows. An array of monitors allowed me, on my good days, to manage our operation's information security. On bad days like this one, I monitored every piece of information I could find that might lead to Ginevra. Our servers in the cloud were running Alexi's and the Russians' faces through recognition software, cross-checking those results with plain white Toyota Corollas. It was a needle in a goddamned haystack.

Liam stormed into my office without knocking. Lorenzo must have dropped him off. "Ready to go hunting?"

I shoved away from my command center. "Let's go." Together, we walked down to the basement, passing the rooms we used for interrogation, and into the vault. I palmed it open.

Liam couldn't hide his mania as he selected his

weapons, guns and knives, throwing ammunition into a duffle bag.

His parents had moved to Yorkfield when he was a kid, so his father could continue his work as an accountant for a local Irish gang. When Liam was sixteen, a gang murdered his parents and young sisters while he was out on a job. He grabbed his guns and went on a rampage. Nothing in this world is more dangerous than a man with nothing to lose, and that night, the rival gang had taken everything from him. After the massacre, Rian's uncle packed him up and sent him back to Ireland to keep him out of jail and out of the hands of gangs seeking revenge.

For another ten years, he earned his name as the Butcher, working for Rian's family in Ireland. When he took a job taking out a corrupt Irish politician on the national stage, he got caught. Liam's knowledge was too valuable to languish in a prison, where he might turn on his masters in exchange for future freedoms. He negotiated a return to the States, to Rian, in exchange for his life.

He now wore the same expression on his face as the day he'd gone after the bastards who murdered his family.

"We're going to find her," I reassured him, as I holstered my own guns. I'd be driving.

He didn't say anything, his eyes empty as he checked his weapons. "That we will," he vowed.

Together, we walked to the garage and loaded up an SUV. Two soldiers met us by the car, Michael and Adrian. They were good kids, reliable, young, and most importantly, had a loose sense of morality that wouldn't be shaken by the damage we were about to do.

Adrian hopped behind the wheel, eyeing me as I climbed into the backseat. "Where to, boss?"

"Corner of 4th and Bruce, South." Arkady Petrov, the

Bratva's money man, would be taking his morning coffee at a tiny cafe, surrounded by mid-level soldiers. I checked the street cameras, and he was just arriving. *Fucking idiot.* Nikolai should have warned his fucking men to stay home today, after he'd snatched our woman.

Our tires squealed as Adrian slammed on the breaks then backed up onto the sidewalk in front of the cafe. Passersby scattered, shouting and screaming. He remained in the car as the rest of us leapt out.

I shot the glass facade of the cafe twice, shattering it, then leapt in, my leather gloves taking the brunt of the shards of glass around the edges.

Pop! Pop! Liam took out two Russian soldiers who should have leapt to their feet and started shooting the moment we parked the vehicle. What were they thinking? Fucking laziness.

Adrian and I trained our guns on the remaining soldiers, and Petrov, while Liam quickly triaged those in the cafe. He grabbed the owner by the collar of his shirt. "Tell fucking Nikolai this will fucking continue until he returns Ginevra," and threw him out the door. The man scrambled to his feet and dashed away, hopefully calling the head of the Bratva as he fled in terror.

Liam stalked toward Petrov. When one of the three remaining soldiers tried to defend the accountant, Liam yanked him up, disarmed him, and then slit his throat from behind, spraying blood everywhere. I sighed. There was a reason we typically unleashed him for interrogations rather than street battles.

Before he could do more damage, I shot the last two soldiers in the head. Liam yanked Petrov to standing by his hair. "Arkady Petrov, good morning."

Petrov trembled as Liam slammed him into a wall, then

traced a bloody knife down his face. "You have something of mine," Liam growled. "Where is she?"

The Russian shook his head. His terror was evident. Perhaps he'd thought his position as the Bratva's accountant protected him. Normally it would. It took days for street wars to percolate up to the leadership of the various gangs in Yorkfield. Not this time. The Bratva shouldn't have gone after our fucking wife.

We bound his hands and feet, then threw him in the trunk of the vehicle before speeding back to our office building. Rian wanted Petrov interrogated without the Russos listening in.

The operation had been remarkably easy. Why? It didn't make any sense, unless Nikolai had been telling the truth last night, that he didn't have Ginevra, and so didn't feel he needed to take precautions.

Cormac: We have Petrov.
Rian: I have Lebedev. Meet you there.

Declan texted separately. His crew hadn't found Yuri Semenov, the Bratva's number two. Fuck. He was the big one—he'd been gunning for Ginevra, and if he wasn't where he was supposed to be, then the odds were, he was involved.

Antonio Russo was on the phone with Nikolai when we pulled into his house. When he saw us, he switched to speakerphone. "Nikolai, you can have them back when I get my daughter back."

"I don't fucking have your daughter, Russo," the head of the Bratva shouted.

"Then I suggest you find out why your people kidnapped her and then burned down my fucking warehouses!"

"I had nothing to do with your warehouses," the Russian growled. "I asked for twenty-four hours. It's not my fucking fault your security is absolute shit. Alexi Marino is your man, not mine."

I snatched the phone out of Antonio's hand. "You expect us to leave Ginevra in whatever hellhole your people have her stashed for twenty-four hours? Fucking find her, Nikolai. Where is Yuri Semenov?"

Nikolai didn't respond.

Liam's grin was feral. "Hide your daughters, Nikolai. They're next."

30

GINEVRA

"I have to fucking pee!" I shouted. Nobody had answered my pleas, and I was about to lose it. Just in time, the light above me flicked on, and a hulking shadow emerged from the darkness. "Hey, help me, please!"

The man was huge and built like a bear. His head was shaved, and his pale skin was covered in tattoos. I eyed him with caution. He wasn't here to help. The tattoos were evidence of time spent in Russian prisons. When he dropped a hood over my head, I screamed and struggled harder against the duct tape that bound me to the chair.

To my surprise, he freed my hands, then retaped them behind my back. When he sliced through the tape holding my feet to the chair, I kicked out. I wasn't about to lose an opportunity to get free. It was like kicking a goddamned tree. The man just grunted, then hauled me up by my hands, yanking them up painfully behind my back.

"Bathroom. Now," he said, pushing me forward. I stumbled, unable to see through the hood covering my face. The path he led me on twisted and turned until he shoved me through a swinging door. I could feel the change in the floor, from the echoing concrete of a warehouse to the tiles of a bathroom. He shoved me backward until I hit the toilet with the backs of my knees, then yanked my skirt up and my panties down. I swore at him and struggled, but he just put his hands on my shoulders and bore down on me until I sat.

"Piss," he instructed.

To my mortification, I did exactly that, desperate to relieve the pressure in my bladder, despite my fury. When the debasing stream finished, he yanked me upwards, pulled my panties back up, then straightened my dress. I was humiliated by how grateful I was that his touch was workmanlike—brusque instead of sexual.

His rough shove forward snapped me out of my thoughts. He led me back to the chair, the fluorescent light over my seat barely visible through the hood. More gently than I expected, he pushed me back down on the chair and retaped me, my legs spread and my hands behind my back.

This time, he didn't take the hood off. He left me sitting in the darkness again, hyperventilating as memories of my captivity a decade ago swept through me.

No. I was tougher than my fear, stronger than my terror.

Deep breaths, I reminded myself, working through the mental exercises I'd developed with my therapist, steadying me over the last decade of panic attacks. Did I ever expect to use them again in an actual kidnapping situation? Fuck no. Were they still useful? Hell yeah. I needed to get my shit under control if I were going to find a way out of here. *Calm down, Ginevra.* As I focused on my breathing, I searched my heart for a peaceful memory, and was shocked to find my happy space had changed from the cool breeze on the beach to the comfort of my men's arms.

I held tight to the memory of their care and their love, steadying myself enough to pay attention to my surroundings, listening to the quiet of traffic outside, the sound of trash cans rattling as the city awoke, and the quiet scrapes and scratches of footsteps against concrete as people walked through the warehouse. *I wasn't alone.*

Men's voices, low and indecipherable, murmured around me. *How many were there?* At least two, possibly three.

The stench of onions and garlic washed over me, and then a man yanked the hood off. Yuri Semenov stared at me, his beady brown eyes boring into mine. Behind him was Alexi Marino, the fucking traitor.

"Beautiful Ginevra," Yuri whispered. "How are you feeling?"

I didn't bother to answer, turning my head away from him.

He slapped me, the hard metal of his rings cutting into my cheekbone. "Don't be disrespectful, Ginevra."

When I glared at him, he smiled. "I'm going to break you, you know. By the time I'm done, you'll be begging me to kill you."

He traced a finger down my face, digging into the bruise blooming where he'd slapped me earlier. "Shall we start?"

I looked around the warehouse. Daylight slipped in through giant skylights on the roof, foggy with dirt and grime. Wooden crates filled the warehouse, stacked in haphazard piles, making it impossible for me to see much further than the corner where they'd placed me.

Yuri stood before me, his scarred face looming heavily as I waited for his next move. The hulking giant who'd taken me to the restroom before stood to his left, and two smaller men to his right. All wore tattoos with sigils of Russian gangs on their hands.

I was so fucked.

"You know they'll pay good money to get me back."

Yuri laughed. "I don't give a shit. Your men will waste days fighting with Nikolai, searching his warehouses and fighting with his soldiers, before they realize this has nothing to do with him. I want you to suffer, Ginevra, and then I want you to die."

Yep, completely fucked.

"After your father interrupted that auction, I paid the price in blood. Nikolai doesn't tolerate failure. I've worked for years to earn my place by his side so I could annihilate him. Your father is going to declare war on him, and they're going to destroy each other while I cut you to ribbons."

Alexi smiled and stepped forward, running a finger down my cheek. "You took off for a goddamned decade, and the moment you showed your face again, you started sticking your nose in shit that's none of your business."

Alexi, too, had paid a heavy price when I was kidnapped —*kidnapped the first time,* I corrected myself. Twice in a lifetime was enough. I was so fucking done with this bullshit. I allowed myself a moment to admire the plan.

While my father was distracted, Alexi and Yuri would exact their revenge. The streets would run with both Italian and Russian blood, costing my father and the Bratva money and loyalty. A gang war in Yorkfield would be bad for everyone, bad for business, and bad for all of the innocent bystanders who'd get caught up in it. It'd allow some of the smaller groups, the Nigerians and the Chinese, to gain a foothold as Papà and Nikolai burned each other to the ground.

Yuri slapped my face again. "No daydreaming, bitch. I want you present for every moment of this." He unrolled a cloth toolholder, revealing knives, pliers, and a number of other devices I recognized from watching interrogations as a child. He rubbed his hands together, maniacal glee rolling off of his shoulders as he contemplated the best way to torture me. "Don't worry, sweet Ginevra. I'll keep you alive for the next few days, at least. I find that sliver of hope, as a prisoner prays for rescue, for escape, makes the pain that much more delicious."

He drew out a slender knife, and I couldn't hold back the visceral fear that shot through me. Interrogations go two ways: the first is brutal, for the weakest prisoners—sharp pain to scare the shit out of them until they're willing to tell you what you want to stop their suffering or save their lives. The second way is slow and drawn out. The pain isn't about extracting information. It's about slowly tearing down the walls we all build around ourselves, carefully removing the bricks in our defenses, until the interrogator holds us in the palm of their hand.

The latter style, that's where Yuri was going. He was going to take this slow and easy, until there was nothing left of me, nothing left of the strong and powerful Ginevra I'd spent the last ten years building. A decade of therapy had built defenses to protect me from the aftermath of kidnapping, but not the defiance and strength to face it again.

Yuri's face was almost kind as he lovingly stroked my face with the dull side of the blade. He traced it down my neck and across my collarbone before pushing the sleeves of my dress down, baring my shoulders and my breasts to his gaze. His eyes roamed over me, thoughtful and reflective. I shivered, terror streaking through me as I imagined what he was about to do to me, along with fierce determination not to let him know I was ready to piss my pants in fear.

I spat at him. "Fuck you, Yuri."

Yuri's eyes widened, and a smile stretched over his yellowed teeth. "Ah, there's the tough bitch I was expecting."

I left this world ten years ago because I didn't want to be tough in all of the ways I'd have to be in order to survive. And yet, here I was once again, terrified and alone in the face of a cruel captor.

"I'll enjoy quenching that fire," Yuri murmured as he sliced a straight cut down the center of my chest, from my collarbone to the bottom of my breasts.

I held back a terrified whimper, but barely. I didn't know how long I'd be able to pretend I was the type of woman who could spit in his face and bravely undergo torture.

"Please, you don't need to do this," I whispered, knowing my words would fall on deaf ears.

Yuri ignored me, running his finger down the stinging cut, smearing the blood. He pulled out the camera and snapped another photo. "Those boys of yours are going to lose their shit."

After what felt like hours, I was a mess. Once the knife dug in deep, I couldn't hold back my tears. Yuri carefully documented every moment of agony, every yelp of pain, as he bruised and sliced my skin, seeking to maximize the visibility of my misery for the photographs he sent my men and my father.

When the giant of a man behind Yuri offered me a sip of water, I jerked my face away, wary of the kindness.

"Drink," Yuri commanded. "You'll eat too, when it's offered. I want you to be alive and awake as I break you into pretty little pieces."

I blanched at the threat, but obediently opened my mouth and allowed him to tilt the bottle against my lips, wetting my parched throat. When the giant man held up a protein bar to my lips, I nibbled at it, gagging as my stomach roiled.

A brutal slap from Yuri stopped the nausea in its tracks. "None of that, bitch. You better keep this food and water down."

The protein bar tasted like sawdust, but I forced myself to swallow, ignoring the urge to puke it up with the water I'd just finished. Satisfied, Yuri and the giant stepped back.

"Now," Yuri said. "We wait."

He flicked off the light bulb that swung above my head, leaving only the thin gray light that filtered through the film of grime on the skylights. I found myself once again alone, with only the sounds of the city to keep me company. The copper smell of dried blood filled my nose, and I finally allowed myself to cry, regretting every choice I'd made since I'd answered Sofia's call a week before.

31

RIAN

I was exhausted. We all were. None of us had slept in over twenty-four hours, but the photos Yuri kept sending of our girl fueled the fire of our determination to get her back. A frisson of guilt wormed its way through my chest. Ginevra would be safe and whole right now if we'd never insisted on this stupid fucking marriage with Sofia in the first place.

Nikolai asked for a meeting in neutral territory. I believed him when he swore he wasn't behind the fires or the kidnapping. It didn't make sense for him to do this, not when we'd already initiated the transfer and laundering of the ten million dollars that Antonio owed him. We hadn't bothered torturing his enforcer or his accountant, just roughed them up enough to make them uncomfortable. They both thought Yuri Semenov was behind the kidnapping.

Fuck.

Yuri had been a wildcard for a long time, a brutal enforcer who'd worked his way up the Bratva through violence and a few brilliant real estate moves that netted the organization millions. We should have known he'd snatch Ginevra when we heard he was out for her blood. God, we should have protected her better.

Adam Zhang watched us with amusement as I strode into the room, Liam and Cormac following behind me. I bet he hadn't expected to find himself so quickly elevated to mediator between the two biggest gangs in the city. Ginevra liked him, though. As sentimental as it was, her opinion counted for a lot right now. He'd arranged a meeting in one of his restaurants, a high end loss leader that he'd emptied for us.

I grasped his hand warmly. "Thank you," I said.

Zhang looked at me, his hooded brown eyes sharp and calculating. "War is terrible for everyone's business." He jerked his head toward the table. "But especially new businesses without strong historic ties to the community, like mine."

That it was, but if that's what it took to bring Ginevra back to us, I'd burn the fucking city down. All three of us would, without hesitation.

Antonio was already there, joined by Lorenzo. We took our seats together, to the left of Lorenzo. Nikolai arrived accompanied by two Bratva captains I knew only by reputation.

"Yuri and a dozen of my soldiers have disappeared," Nikolai began abruptly.

Antonio's eyes shot up to his hairline. "A dozen? How the fuck do you lose a dozen soldiers?"

"More than a dozen," I corrected. "There's no way Yuri's holed up somewhere with Ginevra and lighting fires all over the city with only a dozen men. What the fuck is going on in your house, Nikolai?"

The head of the Bratva narrowed his sky-blue eyes.

"Upstart," he said, dismissing me. I swallowed the fury that burned through me. I'd worked my whole goddamned life to build an empire in this city, and today, my holdings were worth more than his and the Russos' combined. But because I was Irish-American, because we had built our wealth in the twenty-first century, instead of over generations of illicit trade, I was less worthy.

But that fury wasn't going to get our girl back.

Antonio noted my clenched fists, but didn't acknowledge my rage in any other way. "The upstart is my son-in-law, Nikolai."

Nikolai laughed. "Not for long, it seems."

I nodded at Liam, who shoved back from the table, saluted the table with a wild grin on his face, and strode toward the door.

"Where the fuck is he going?" Nikolai asked.

I leaned forward, radiating menace. "Your second in command took my fucking wife. Liam's going to take something of equal value from you."

"Enough, Rian," Antonio snapped. "Liam, sit back down."

Liam waited for me to acquiesce before stationing himself at the door, ready to take off if I changed my mind. For a moment, I regretted every choice in my life that led to this moment where I had to beg this Bratva piece of shit for help getting our sweet Ginevra back. I'd spend the rest of our lives making this up to her.

Nikolai sat back in his seat, his smile satisfied and smug as he lay his hands on his belly. The man was huge. All the Russians made me look small, and I was no slouch at six feet and over two hundred pounds of muscle.

"Nikolai, I am going to unleash these boys on you and

your family unless you help me get my daughter back," Antonio threatened.

The Russian spread his hands. "I don't have her." One of the soldiers who accompanied him pulled a USB key out of his pocket and tossed it into the center of the table. I snatched it. "But this is a list of my properties. Destroy this information when you're done with it." He leaned forward and stared into Antonio's eyes. "I do not want a war with you or these puppies. I cannot help you search for your daughter, and I cannot massacre my own men, but I will not get in your way as you do."

That would have to be enough.

32

CORMAC

I stared at the list of properties Nikolai provided as it scrolled down my screen, shocked at his transparency. He'd given us dangerous insight into the breadth of his operations, all in the name of saving our girl. Or perhaps, in the name of preventing us from snatching his daughters and treating them with the same brutality as Yuri was Ginevra. Would Antonio have done the same, if one of his men had gone after the Bratva girls? I wasn't sure.

"Cross-referencing this will take a couple of hours," I told Rian. We had returned to our office building following the meeting with the Bratva.

He shrugged. "There's no guarantee she's stashed in any of these properties, just a high likelihood."

I twisted my lips. "I ran a search on Yuri. His name's not on any properties in the city databases. Bank accounts are relatively clean. He has one sports car sitting in the garage of his rented apartment. No big red flags. How did he manage to stay clean while he was orchestrating this?"

I turned my head to Dmitri Lebedev, the Bratva's chief

enforcer, where he sat in the corner of my office. "How is Yuri paying for the small army that it's going to take to protect him from us when we find him?"

Lebedev stretched his lean legs out in front of him and propped his arms behind his head. "How do you know the money's coming from the Bratva?"

I blinked. Liam, Rian, and I looked at each other as we put the information together. *The missing money from the Russos' protection payments. Fuck.*

"Go toss Alexi's apartment."

Liam's grin was feral. "Sure thing, boss." He looked at Dmitri. "Want to have some fun?"

Dmitri's answering smile was dark. "Let's go."

Rian watched the two leave my command center with amusement dancing in his eyes. Those two were dangerous enough to begin with, but off their leashes and together? Good thing they were focused on getting Ginevra back.

I returned my attention to the list of properties scrolling on my screen. With a few quick commands, I dumped the list into the database I'd built of sightings of white Corollas in the city, and started cross-checking them against each other. A few more moments, and I added facial recognition software to the mix, outputting all the locations where I'd been able to find those assholes who took her over the last few days. It'd take time for the program to run its course, but when it finished, we'd have a narrower list of properties to check out.

Waiting for the program to run was excruciating. The natural light faded as the day wore on, and all I could think about was the fierce expression on Ginevra's face in that first picture. Despite the smear of mascara down her face from her tears, she'd looked like she was ready to tear Yuri apart. Watching her fall apart over the course of the day, until the last picture, blood dripping down her chest, her body bruised, and her face contorted in pain as she screamed, had broken something inside me.

Ginevra deserved better than this. She'd fucking left this. She'd left the power and privilege that came from being the daughter of one of the most powerful men in this piece-of-shit town, and built her own life. She'd come back to save her goddamned sister from predators, from the violence promised by marrying into our gang. And as payment, she was reliving the very fucking events that sent her running a decade before.

Goddammit.

I rubbed my chest as an unfamiliar ache bloomed. *Fuck.* How had this marvelous woman wormed her way so deeply into my heart in such a short period? She was such a perfect fucking match for us—a brilliant businesswoman, a charming socialite, and a deliciously submissive playmate in the bedroom. We were so fucking bad for her, though, full of violence and pain and broken shards of shared history.

"Penny for your thoughts?" Rian asked.

I shook my head. "She deserves better than us."

His blue eyes shot to mine. "Nobody deserves what she's going through. That has nothing to do with the magnificent woman that is Ginevra Russo, and everything to do with Yuri and Alexi being piece-of-shit human beings." He clasped my hand in his, running his calloused thumb over my knuckles, before moving over to prop his hip on the edge of my desk, letting his knees knock into mine.

I pulled my hand away, frustrated and guilt-ridden.

"Don't," he said.

I looked up, my lips curving into a crooked smile. "Pretty sure you don't give the orders in the bedroom, Rian."

He cupped my jaw with one hand, his face serious as he

searched my gaze. "God, Cormac, love isn't about being deserving enough. It's sliding into each other's jagged cracks and edges and tangling ourselves up in each other, somehow more whole together than apart. I found you, and I held you tight. Liam came back into our lives, and we snatched him up, too. And we're not going to let Ginevra go either. Because she's fucking *perfect*."

He waited for me to nod before releasing my jaw and hopping off my desk.

"Good talk," I shouted over my shoulder as he walked out of my office.

"Love you too, Cormac," he responded, and the ache in my chest subsided for a moment as he walked out the door.

RIAN, Liam, and I had returned to our house to get some sleep after my program had spit out three potential locations for Ginevra—a warehouse, a storefront, and a casino. Lorenzo and Declan were already checking them out.

Antonio placed his trust in us to find his daughter, our fucking wife, while he desperately tried to hold his business together after the devastating fires of the previous day. He was fucked financially, and with twenty-five percent ownership and our cash reserves diminished by the ten million we'd paid for Ginevra, we weren't in great shape either.

Lebedev traced his finger over the map on the monitor, where we'd marked the locations. "The casino doesn't make a lot of sense. Even on a Sunday night, when it's closed to the public, we're accepting liquor deliveries, cleaning, and packaging drugs."

He'd identified three of the men helping Yuri—all low-level soldiers with everything to gain and very little to lose—

but the Russians had lost track of over a dozen. Their house was a fucking mess, and I was pissed that Ginevra was paying the price for Nikolai's negligence.

"The storefront, however, is abandoned. I'm not familiar with the inside, but it's been empty for at least a year."

His lips twisted thoughtfully. "I'd use the warehouse if I were him. It's in a busy district, but security on the building itself is minimal."

Rian's answering gaze was sharp. "What do you store in the warehouse?"

Lebedev hesitated. Rian slammed his hands on the desk. "He's got my fucking wife, Dmitri. The only reason you're not downstairs in one of our interrogation rooms is because Nikolai is acting in good faith. Start fucking around, and you'll find out how I earned my reputation."

The Russian's smile was wintry. He leaned forward and met Rian's gaze unflinchingly. "Arms. The warehouse has a full shipment of small arms—Kalashnikov assault rifles, handguns, and fucking ammunition."

I whistled. "Damn."

Lebedev shrugged. "They would have been well armed, anyway. Nobody takes on two gangs and expects to live without taking precautions."

"Three gangs," Rian corrected.

Lebedev shook his head. "The Russos are irrelevant at this point. They're never going to recover."

He was right. The other four Italian families were no doubt salivating over the decline of the Russos, a decline Antonio had hoped to halt by marrying off one of his daughters. Too fucking bad.

Declan: Storefront is abandoned.

He sent a couple of photos, showing an empty shell, storerooms trashed and covered in graffiti, and no fucking Ginevra.

Lorenzo: They're at the fucking warehouse.

33

GINEVRA

As night fell, and the thin light in the warehouse faded to black, my anxiety ratcheted back up. The large man who'd fed and watered me earlier approached me with caution. He dragged the sleeves of my dress up over my shoulders, offering me the illusion of modesty before dropping a hood over my face and leading me to the toilet once again. I repeated the humiliating exercise of pissing in front of him with my arms duct taped behind my back. Instead of bringing me back to a chair, he led me through a series of twists and turns, then removed my hood.

I stood in the center of the small, dark room with concrete walls. The only light shone in from the doorway, where brilliant fluorescent light framed the hulking man. His lips twisted as we observed each other. He swore in Russian, then slammed the door shut, surprising me with its finality. Okay, then.

Weariness settled in my bones as the misery of a day of abuse and torture caught up with me. Holding back the tears that once again threatened to spill over, I shuffled over to the wall, then slid down to the floor, leaning backward on my arms. As I fought to contain my misery, the door cracked open again. The man who'd brought me here knelt before me.

"Behave," he commanded.

I nodded, angry with myself for my compliance, but unable to resist the temptation of the water bottle he dangled in front of my face. He twisted off the top and let me slake my thirst, heedless of the water that dribbled down my front. When I finished, he unwrapped another protein bar and fed it to me bite by bite. He rocked back on his heels, his sharp eyes observing me as I trembled, determined to present a brave front no matter how scared I was.

He pulled a knife out of his pocket. I flinched back, despite myself, and his lips twisted again, his expression indecipherable. He reached around me and slashed through the tape holding my wrists together. My muscles screamed as he dragged them in front of me and retaped them.

"Behave," he repeated, waving the knife in front of my face.

He had to know I'd spend the night trying to free myself. I nodded anyway, and he stood up, slamming the door behind him on his way out.

The room was small, ten steps in each direction, more of a closet than a room. The walls felt like they were made of cinderblocks. I suspected they were interior walls, as I couldn't hear the noises from traffic and the street that I'd caught while in the warehouse earlier. There was no handle on the interior of the door, no sharp angles for me to rub my wrists on and break the tape.

As exhaustion overtook me, I allowed my tears to fall.

Rian, Cormac, and Liam had promised to keep me safe, and I had to believe they'd find me.

I AWOKE WITH A JOLT, the terror of my nightmare bleeding into the terror of the present. With a whine, I brought my breathing under control, softly counting out loud to ground myself. I struggled to separate my memories of my teenaged captivity from the frightening situation I now found myself in.

Trembling and crying, I sat up from where I'd curled up in the corner and leaned back against the wall. If I got out of here, when I get out of here, I was so fucking done. I swallowed a sob as my heart cracked at the thought of leaving the men who'd wormed their way into my affections over the last week. But even the best sex I'd ever had and our budding love didn't make up for this bullshit.

I looked up at the ceiling and roared my frustration, my fury at the pain, and my sorrow at this fucking life that drove men to capture and abuse women, echoing against the concrete. Fear of nightmares chasing me in my sleep kept me awake and trembling until the door clanged open the next morning.

"Good morning, sweetness," Alexi said, staring at me with dead eyes, his frame illuminated by the light from the hallway. He stalked forward and dragged me to my feet by my hair as I shouted and struggled, trying to get away. By the time I got my feet under me and could follow under my own locomotion, we were halfway out of the room. I tried to kick out at his knee, but missed.

Alexi shoved me to the ground. My bruised and throbbing cheek smacked into the concrete when I failed to catch myself with my bound hands. I cried out at the pain, then clambered back to my feet, cursing his name, his mother's name, and the fucking Bratva.

He just laughed and dragged me by my bound arms into the crate-filled warehouse, not bothering to throw a hood over my head this morning. Fuck. My chances of survival decreased with every moment I stayed here. Surrounded by brutal, ruthless Bratva, I didn't see a way to escape.

Alexi taped my legs to the chair with quick and efficient movements. Yuri watched, his eyes cold and furious. When I tried to slam my bound hands into Alexi's chin, he grabbed them and squeezed until I whimpered in pain, scared he was going to break my fingers. "Don't pull that shit again, *piccolina*."

He sliced through the tape and then roughly bound my hands together behind the chair. My breath caught at his carelessness as I felt the looseness of the connection, but continued to struggle and swear, hoping, praying to a God I didn't believe in, that he wouldn't notice.

Alexi stood up and eyed me with satisfaction, setting up the camera on a tripod. Yuri posed next to me as Alexi snapped photos, tracing my lips with a knife, then pushing the sleeves of my dress down once again, baring my breasts to the lens.

"How does it feel to know that your remaining hours will be nothing but pain, bitch?" Alexi asked, spittle flying out of his mouth as he ran a knife down my chest, blood dripping off the curve of my breast as he grinned madly.

"How does it feel to know you're wasting what few hours you have left on this earth on a goddamned Russo? You might hate me, Alexi, but you're a dead man the moment my men find you."

He laughed wildly, waving the bloody knife in my face. "Do you think your men are going to have time to search for you when your father is burning down the Russian warehouses, murdering the Bratva's daughters?"

My eyes shot to his. Alexi smiled, evil intent in his eyes as he plunged the knife into my thigh. I screamed in pain and terror, and he snapped a photo, capturing my fright. As I sobbed in agony, I cursed myself for not trying to escape earlier. If he fucking stabbed me again, there'd be no walking out of here.

Taking a deep breath, I packed all of my pain and terror into a tiny box and shoved it into the back of my mind. I needed to focus entirely on convincing Yuri that I would do anything, *anything*, for freedom, as my wounds bled out on the concrete floor.

By the time lunch rolled around, Yuri was sloppy and careless. When I refused his offer of water and a protein bar, he slapped me, then walked off to enjoy takeout with his soldiers.

This was my opportunity. As soon as they disappeared into the maze of wooden crates, I began working my wrists loose, wincing as the movement aggravated my injuries. Minute after terrifying minute, I flexed my wrists until I found a rough spot on the chair and began the arduous work of sawing through the tape.

Rat-a-tat-tat! The sound of automatic weapons firing outside spurred me to move faster toward freedom. All of a sudden, the tape gave way, and my hands were free. I ripped them out of the bonds holding them to the chair, then freed my ankles. Oh, thank God, sweet freedom. I pulled my dress up, not that modesty really mattered now.

When I stood, I wobbled, the combination of not eating,

blood loss, and exhaustion making me dizzy. Woozy, I leaned on the back of the chair, searching for balance. Fuck, getting out of here was going to be a problem. Gunshots rang out. Men shouted in Russian and English on the other side of the warehouse. I had no idea where the closest entrance was, but I bet my life that following the sound of gunfire would get me out of there.

Staggering from wooden crate to wooden crate, I stumbled over first one dead body, then another. A bullet whizzed by my head. I slammed my body flat against the nearest crate, swearing angrily. I was too beat up, too tired, and in too much pain for this bullshit.

I waited for a break in the shots, then peeked out from behind the crate. The path seemed clear. I dashed to the next crate, and then the next, praying the entire time that a stray bullet wouldn't find me. When the gunfire started up again, I sank to the ground. I had to be getting closer to the entrance.

"Stupid bitch," Yuri's voice snapped behind me. "Did you think you were going to get away?"

He grabbed my hair and dragged me along the ground. "Next man who shoots, I shoot the Russo woman."

"Hold your fire!" Liam shouted, his voice hoarse with rage.

"That's more like it," Yuri muttered. He held me to his chest as he walked out. Fuck, I'd been so close. Just a handful more turns and I would have been right in front of Liam, walking into the safety of his arms.

Yuri held a gun to my head as he yanked me around. When I met Liam's green eyes, his face was stricken as he looked me up and down, cataloging each wound and injury. Before my eyes, something closed off in him, until all I could see was coldness.

"Let her go, Yuri," Liam ordered.

Behind us, I heard choked screams and grunts, as men swept through the warehouse, killing or capturing every soldier who'd taken part in my captivity.

Yuri's breath was hot on my neck as he laughed. "I think not. I'm going to kill this bitch, just like she killed Ivan a decade ago."

I trembled, not sure how much longer I could stay on my feet.

"Yuri, you won't survive this. Let her go," Rian said, his voice coming from my right side. I cut my eyes to him, the warm comfort of his presence rushing through me, despite the gun he held pointed at Yuri.

Yuri just laughed. "Do you think I didn't plan for this? You fucking idiots." Laser sights centered on my saviors' foreheads from catwalks above the warehouse. I was certain one also aimed at me. Yuri wouldn't leave that to chance.

All this for revenge. All this to make up for one failed auction and the murders that followed. This world—I was so fucking done.

Liam caught my eyes, the warmth back in them. He blinked once, slowly, holding my gaze. He was going to give me a signal. *Shit.* I blinked back, letting my lids drop. When I opened my eyes again, they filled with tears. If I made it out of this, I was going home.

Liam's eyebrow furrowed as he watched a tear streak down my face. "Yuri, let her go," he said.

Yuri dug the gun into my skull. "Never."

Liam never took his eyes off of mine as he straightened his stance. My focus dipped to his hands, his finger tightening on the trigger, then back up to his green eyes. *Shit.* The barrel never wavered as he targeted Yuri's head.

When Liam's chin dipped in a nod, I slammed my foot

into Yuri's instep and dropped to the ground, praying they shot Yuri faster than Yuri's snipers could shoot me. I needn't have worried. His head exploded above me as shots fired from every direction. A warm body covered mine, protecting me from the gunfight that resulted.

"Easy there, darling," Cormac's warm voice whispered in my ear, as I trembled in fear and pain. He stroked the sides of my face as he caged me against the ground with his body. "It'll be over in a minute. You're okay. I've got you."

I nodded, staring at the concrete beneath me, trying to hold it together for just a few more minutes. Even after a day and a half of captivity, I was a fucking Russo. I was *Ginevra fucking Russo,* and I needed to keep my shit together as we walked out of this mess.

As I took comfort in his warmth and strength, I could hear the footsteps of men checking every corner of the warehouse. "Clear!" they shouted, as they checked each room, the catwalks above the warehouse, and the maze of crates.

"All clear," Liam shouted, finally.

Cormac peeled himself up off me, then scooped me up in his arms. "I've got you, Ginny-love, I promise. Stay with me for a few more minutes until we can get you to a hospital, okay?"

Lorenzo shouted from outside, "I've got Alexi."

I placed a hand on Cormac's chest and wiggled, trying to get down. He looked at me with concern, but set me on the ground. I picked my way through the bodies and debris of the firefight until Alexi was before me, on his knees, blood streaming down his face.

Someone had tied his hands behind his back with a cable tie, and Lorenzo held a gun to his head.

Liam strode up to us, his green eyes snapping with fury,

knives in his hands. When he grabbed Alexi's hair and dragged his head up, I stopped him with a look. Understanding exactly what I needed to do, he stepped back, not letting go of Alexi's hair, but making space between their bodies for me to squeeze in. I took a knife from Liam. He wrapped his right hand around my shaking fingers, where they squeezed the hilt. I could barely stand upright, but I was determined to end this.

"Are you sure about this, love?" Liam whispered.

In response, I reached over Alexi's chest and, with Liam's help, dragged the knife across his neck with a cry of anguish. When his heartbeat finally stopped and the blood slowed, Cormac swept me back up into his arms.

I wrapped my arms around his neck and nodded into his chest, telling myself I could hold back my heaving sobs for another minute or two, until Cormac carried me into the SUV. I squeezed my eyes tight, not willing to risk meeting anyone's eyes. All I wanted to do was burrow into the safety of Cormac's arms and fall the fuck apart.

Someone dropped a blanket over me and I whimpered as the fabric slid over my open wounds. "Shit, princess, I'm so sorry," Rian whispered, stroking my hair. I didn't react, just kept my face hidden in Cormac's chest. When he tried to set me down in the car to strap me in, I whimpered and tightened my grip.

"Darling, I have to buckle you in," Cormac said. I shook my head frantically, not wanting to let go. "I'll be right here, okay?"

He peeled my arms off him and set me in the middle of the back seat as tears streamed down my face and I gave into the wracking sobs I'd held back since the moment those fuckers had grabbed me. "Shhhhhh, we've got you now," someone whispered over my head.

When I opened my eyes, Rian and Cormac bracketed me on each side. Liam was in the driver's seat, and to my surprise, my father slid into the passenger seat. Gentle hands stroked my hair and held me as I cried out all the terror and misery of the last two days.

"St. Mary's," my father barked. "They're waiting for her."

34

RIAN

Ginevra looked like hell. Antonio's family doctor had admitting privileges at St. Mary's and promised to meet us at the emergency room doors with a gurney. I wondered how big a donation that would cost us, then dismissed the thought. We'd sign away every penny we owned to make sure she was okay.

"C'mon, stay with us a few more minutes, princess," I whispered into her hair as I stroked her hand, desperate not to let her see my panic that she was passing out. "Sweet Ginevra, brave Ginevra, don't close your eyes, okay? You have to stay awake. We're almost there."

Liam swore at every stoplight and every time we hit traffic.

Cormac met my eyes over her head, worry etched in every line of his face. He ran his fingers over his curls, then resumed stroking her hair and her face, murmuring quiet nonsense, words of reassurance and praise, trying to keep her focused.

Ginevra just cried. Her sobs subsided into silent tears that streamed down her face as she sniffled. I swore softly.

There wasn't a goddamned thing I could do to take away the last two days, to make this better, and it was killing me. It was killing all of us.

We sped into the hospital grounds and pulled up to a door close to the emergency room, where the doc waited with a gurney and small crew, as promised. I unbuckled our girl, wincing when she whimpered at the movement. I pressed my forehead against hers.

"Ginevra, love, we're at the hospital. We need to move you to the gurney, okay? It's going to hurt, and I'm sorry."

She sniffed, then opened up her eyes, her liquid brown gaze full of determination. "Do it," she ordered, and a relief shot through me to hear the command, the strength, in her voice. For the first time since we realized she was gone, I dared to hope she was going to be okay.

I wrapped her arms around my neck and slid an arm under her knees and behind her shoulders. I pulled her out of the SUV and then carried her to the gurney, as if she were made of glass, terrified that the slightest bump would shatter her into a million pieces. Antonio adjusted the blanket that covered her to protect her modesty.

Medical staff strapped her in with efficient movements as Antonio conferred with the doctor. When they rolled her inside, I jerked after them, intending to follow, only for Antonio to lay a hand on my arm. When I growled at him, he cocked an eyebrow.

"They're taking her to the emergency room. You can't go with them," he said.

Fuck that. I followed the staff to the doors and reminded them she was at the hospital because she'd been kidnapped and tortured. She needed someone to keep her safe, and she needed someone familiar by her side. Liam would murder anyone who disagreed with him, and Cormac was a fucking mess over her. We all were, but this situation called for charm and decisiveness, and that meant me.

When the senior nurse nodded, I flipped a quick thumbs up at Cormac and Liam, then followed the medical staff in. Antonio nodded, then herded Cormac and Liam toward the regular emergency entrance, where they'd wait for news.

The hospital staff wheeled Ginevra to the ER. A nurse gestured for me to sit on a short stool near her head. When her hand twitched toward mine, I grabbed it, rubbing my thumb over her knuckle, giving her what scant comfort I could, knowing it wasn't enough, that it'd never be enough.

A nurse asked her a few questions, and Ginevra answered, her breath short and her voice weak, as she described what had happened. I struggled to hold back my rage as she explained how she'd been held, how Yuri had beat her and sliced into her. Instead, I stroked her forehead, pushing her hair out of her face.

She squeezed her eyes shut when they slid the IV into her arm, then bustled out of the room.

"Hey, Ginny, stay awake, okay?" I whispered to her, panicking when she didn't open her eyes again.

Tears leaked out of the corners of her eyes and she squeezed my hand, but she didn't open them.

"Please, princess," I begged her. She didn't let go of my hand, but she turned her face away from me, so I couldn't see her expression, or maybe so she didn't have to see mine.

"I'm here, Rian," she whispered after a long and painful pause.

"Okay, love, just stay with me, okay?"

She squeezed my hand, but didn't answer. When it was time to take her to the OR, the doctor came out to speak to me.

"She needs sewing up in a dozen places. She has a pretty significant blood loss and needs an infusion. It's only luck he missed an artery when he stabbed her thigh. I want to get some x-rays of her bruises to make sure nothing's fractured underneath."

"Fix her, doc," I implored him, my heart breaking as I imagined what she must have lived through to leave this sort of damage.

"I can patch her body up, but she's going to need more help than I can give for the trauma."

My eyes shot to his, and for the first time, I wondered if Ginevra would be better off without the three of us attached to her. If she hadn't come home, hadn't involved herself with us, she'd be safe and whole right now.

I followed them through the hospital until the staff asked me to wait outside while they worked. When they wheeled her out, she was unconscious. I walked with them to the recovery room, where I sat and held her hand until she woke up.

When Ginevra's eyes blinked open, she looked around, her gaze foggy with confusion. "Where—?"

"You're at the hospital, love. Do you remember how you got here?"

She shuddered and turned her face away. "Yeah, I remember."

"You're safe now, love."

"Am I?" she asked, removing her hand from mine and breaking my heart.

I REFUSED to leave Ginevra's side when the nursing techs wheeled her into her own room and transferred her to the bed there. Whatever pain meds they'd given her were effective, because she barely blinked at the movement.

"I want to sleep," she whispered to me, her voice still weak and strained. God, what had they put her through? I stroked her forehead as she nodded off, then pulled out my phone.

Rian: She's asleep, finally.
Cormac: How's she doing?

I didn't know how to answer his question. She was a fucking mess, and I couldn't help but think we'd set all of this in motion when we'd demanded Sofia's hand in marriage as part of the deal to save Antonio.

Rian: She's tough.
Liam: She shouldn't have to be.

He was fucking right.

Antonio explained our unusual situation to the nursing station, and after an hour of discussion and argument, they finally agreed to let Cormac, Liam, and me stay with her at the same time. She was in a room large enough for the three of us to drag in chairs. We sprawled around her bed, each of us resisting the need to curl up and wrap our arms around her, as if we could protect her from the rest of the world.

Selfishly, I refused to abandon my place at her side. I held her hand as she slept, my heart breaking each time she twitched and cried out in her sleep.

Sometime in the middle of the night, Ginevra screamed, her eyes wide, the whites showing around her irises, terrified as she stared into the darkness.

"Fuck," she swore as she swam out of the nightmare and

back to reality. Her eyes focused as they swept around the room, taking in the three of us, the stark white walls of the room, and the IV that pumped her full of pain medication and kept her hydrated.

She pressed her hands to her eyes, as if to hold back tears, then scrubbed her face.

Liam pulled a handgun out from the waistband of his tactical pants, where he'd tucked it under his T-shirt to sneak it into the hospital. He flipped it around and handed it to her, holding onto the barrel so she could wrap her hands around the grip. "Do you want me to slide it under your pillow, baby?"

She nodded, her face forlorn, as she struggled to prop herself up on her elbows. He slid a hand under her back and lifted her, careful not to disturb any of her injuries, then slipped the gun under the hospital issue pillow.

"I'll take it back in the morning, okay?"

She dipped her head in acknowledgment before closing her eyes again, not hiding the tears streaming down her face as she tried to go back to sleep.

"I'm here, baby girl," Liam whispered, one hand wrapped around hers, the other gently stroking her temple. "Go back to sleep, okay?"

Fuck, what had we done?

35

GINEVRA

"Ginevra!" Sofia rushed toward me.

Liam snapped an arm around her waist, halting her forward motion. "Easy there, Sofia." The hospital insisted on limiting the number of people in my room, and Liam was on guard dog duty.

My sister wrenched free of him and strode to the bed, grabbing my hand. "Fuck you, Liam," she snapped, then turned her attention to me. "How are you, big sister?"

I forced myself to smile. "I'm better, Sofia. How're things at home?"

She shrugged and rolled her eyes. "On lockdown, surprise, surprise. It's been super fun puking my guts out every morning and then staring at the walls because Papà wouldn't even let me outside." She grinned. "I'm only talking about how miserable I am, so you don't have to talk about how miserable you are."

This time, my smile was genuine. "Is it that obvious?"

"You mean, other than the fact that you do, in fact, look like a Russian gangster kidnapped you and tortured you for two days?"

Liam cleared his throat and glared at my sister.

"Oh, are we not supposed to be telling her how bad she looks? She lived through it, Liam. She knows exactly what happened to her." Sofia let go of my hand to pull up a chair.

My sister kept the conversation light, talking about the movies she'd watched and the colleges she was researching. We both knew Papà would use my kidnapping as an excuse to renege on his promise to let Sofia get her degree, but hope sprang eternal. She was desperate to get out of that house, and her pregnancy had gotten in the way of that.

The hospital wanted to keep me under observation for a second night. I agreed, only because I wasn't ready to go back to Rian's house and face my men outside the public confines of the hospital. Their guilt was palpable as each of them cared for me in their own way.

Liam never left me to sleep alone. Anytime I nodded off, he was right there, holding my hand, promising me he'd defend my life with his own. Cormac kept me fed and monitored my pain levels. And Rian, Rian quietly took care of all the logistics related to my care and my family, making sure I had anything I needed before I even thought to ask.

When it was time to check out, my whole family assembled outside my room, with balloons and flowers in their hands. It was like we were a normal American family, not the mob, our relationships forged in the fires of violence, rather than love.

Cormac pushed my wheelchair, refusing to let me walk or even steer myself.

"Please, darling, let me do what I can for you," he'd pleaded, his brown eyes filled with guilt and love. I couldn't tell him no.

He wrapped his arms around me and lifted me into the

car, setting me into the backseat beside Rian. He then slid in on the other side of me, gently buckling my belt.

Liam drove, and we made our way back to our shared home in silence.

"What do you mean, you're flying to California tomorrow?" Rian exploded.

"You were in the fucking room when I made the deal, Rian! I had to give you a fucking blow job, so you'd keep your fucking mouth shut while I spoke with Richard." At least he had the grace to flush when I reminded him of that particular cruelty.

He nodded sharply. "One of us will come with you."

"The fuck you will," I exploded, heedless of the pain radiating from my bruised ribs. "It's a one-way ticket."

I never understood the phrase 'deafening silence' until that moment. All three men stared at me. Liam's face was the first to break. He shoved out of his chair and stormed out of the room.

"No," Rian snapped. "You'll come back after the press conference. You signed a fucking contract."

Cormac stood and walked over to where I sat in the rocking chair, a blanket on my lap, looking like a fucking grandma instead of the tough and capable CEO I was. He leaned against the side of the chair and ran his fingers through my hair. "For how long?"

"For good. I can't fucking do this."

"Can't fucking do what, darling?" he asked, his voice gentle as he skimmed his fingers along the sensitive shell of my ear.

I gestured at him, at Rian, and at the goddamned world. "This. I don't want to be part of this world. I don't want to be part of the violence. And I don't want to be looking over my shoulder for the rest of my life wondering if I, or the people I care about most, are going to be snatched off the street and tortured."

"Okay," Cormac said, his voice hoarse and raspy.

"What do you mean, okay?" Rian snapped.

"I mean, I'm not going to lock her in a room and make her a fucking prisoner! We're goddamned better than that. If she doesn't want to stay, then I'm not going to make her!" Cormac shouted back.

I blinked. I'd never heard him raise his voice before.

Rian walked over to me. "Are you leaving us?"

My heart cracked. "Are you willing to give up all of this?" I gestured to the empty chair Liam had left, knowing Rian would understand exactly what I meant—the arms dealing, the protection racket, the violence.

Rian shook his head, his black hair falling over his face, as he met my eyes. "Ginevra, that's not reasonable."

A single tear leaked down my face, and he leaned forward to wipe it off with his thumb. I jerked back out of his grip. "I know that. I'm not asking you to. But I am going to get on that plane tomorrow, and go back to my life in California."

I turned my face away so he wouldn't see the tears gathering in my eyes. Leaving them, leaving my family, was going to hurt so fucking much. But not as much as a day and a half of torture by Yuri, I reminded myself, steeling my heart.

DINNER WAS MISERABLE, all four of us stuck in our heads, each attempt at small talk failing miserably.

"Right," I said, pushing back from the table. Cormac was

by my side before I straightened out. Fuck, I hurt. He handed me my cane, and I stood up, wincing at the sting of the cuts and the deep ache in my thigh from where Yuri stabbed me.

Rian looked up from his phone. "I've booked a private jet for your trip tomorrow. There's no reason for you to navigate a busy airport. We'll leave at ten."

Cormac kept his hand at my elbow as I shuffled up the stairs. God, I was tired. Once he tucked me into my bed, he pulled my suitcases from wherever he'd stashed them and started packing.

I sniffled, unable to conceal my heartache at the care each of them took with me.

He looked up from his task with those liquid brown eyes that I could just fucking drown in, then sat on the bed beside me, his hip pressing into mine as he held my hand. "Why don't you leave some clothes here for when you come to visit?"

I nodded as the enormity of my decision slammed into my heart, grinding the already shattered pieces into dust under the weight of my misery. When a whimper escaped me, I turned my face away from him, hoping he'd have the grace to pretend he didn't see my unhappiness.

Instead, he grabbed my other arm and pulled me up until I sat. The corner of his mouth lifted into a tentative smile as he dragged pillows behind me so I could lean against them. We stared into each other's eyes for a long drawn out moment as I tamped down on the tears. He cupped my jaw in his hand and ran his thumbs over my cheeks, catching the tears that escaped my tenuous control, careful not to press into the bruises Yuri had left on my face.

With tender care, he leaned his forehead against mine, closing his eyes, letting our breath mingle. My eyes shot to his, and he slowly opened them again, before tracing tender kisses along my cheekbones and my nose. He brushed my lips with his, and a strangled whimper caught in my throat.

I dragged my hands up to the back of his head and pulled him to me, kissing him with all the love and sorrow in my breaking heart.

Cormac was gentle, almost careful, as his lips traced over me, sweeping his tongue against mine, worshiping me more than possessing me. When he finally drew back, I searched his eyes for a sign of what he was thinking.

He looked away first and let my hands go. "Let me get you packed, darling."

I must have dozed off because when I next looked up, I was alone in the room. My two suitcases were neatly packed, my carry-on and my purse beside them near the door. The closet was nearly empty. All my small bits and pieces that had migrated over the room to claim it as mine were gone, and once again, I felt like a visitor in this house.

Liam stood in the doorway in sweatpants and a T-shirt that molded to the muscles of his stomach. A gun holster hooked over his broad shoulders, as he waited there with a book in his hands. He grinned as my eyes grazed over the play of his muscles beneath his shirt, then his smile faltered as his gaze roved over my bruised and cut up face.

"How're you doing, babe?"

I shrugged. "I feel like shit."

He nodded, then gestured to the armchair in the corner. "Mind if I sit?"

I shrugged again. He stretched out in the chair and buried his nose in the paperback, ignoring me.

God, he was going to stay with me while I slept. Every time I steeled my heart for my imminent departure, one of my men popped in and showed me just what I'd be leaving behind. Goddamn them for being the men they were, for worming their way into my heart, and for making leaving so fucking difficult.

When I woke, screaming and shivering, Liam held my hand and stroked my back, bringing me back to reality, reminding me that my gun was underneath my pillow, and that most of all, he was never fucking going to let anything hurt me ever again. Wrapped in the heat of his arms, I felt safe. Instead of letting him pull away as my breath calmed, I dragged him closer, intending to burrow into the warm cage of his embrace while I slept.

"Ginevra, please," he said, his voice catching. "Don't ask me to hold you in my arms tonight, and then let you go tomorrow," he rasped, as he pulled away from me and returned to the chair, leaving me aching for the comfort of his arms as I lay in the bed. "I'll be right here, baby."

When I opened my eyes in the morning, he was gone.

36

GINEVRA

Min-joon met me at the airport, his eyes serious as I limped to my car. "Welcome home, roomie," he greeted me with a gentle hug.

"It's good to be home."

"Just kidding on the big poly wedding, huh?" he asked, teasing me, but my eyes filled with tears. "Oh shit, Ginevra, I'm sorry."

I shook my head, dashing the tears away with my finger. "No, it's okay. No wedding, no commitment ceremony, just Ginevra back in California, ready to get back to work after a very exciting week and a half visiting her family."

He kept the conversation light as he drove me home. That seemed to happen to me a lot lately, as if people sensed my emotional fragility and veered away from any subject that could shatter my carefully cultivated calm.

Cheryl: Welcome back! <3 <3 <3 I'm bringing Thai back tonight and you're going to dish on everything that happened.
Ginevra: I don't know if I can.

Cheryl: Did you sign an NDA?
Ginevra: *frowning emoji* Shit, should I have? *laughing emoji*
Cheryl: I'll be there at six.

"Cheryl's joining us for dinner."

Min-joon nodded as he parked the car in front of the house, then jumped out and ran around the car to help me out. "So's Jeff."

"That was quick," I teased.

Min-joon's smile was sweet and sappy. "You'll like him, I think. He's very straight-laced, an accountant."

I blinked. "You're dating an accountant? Like, a numbers guy?"

He sighed. "I *know*. Before you left, I was going to introduce you. I think it's getting serious."

Min-joon left me in the doorway when he returned to the car to grab my bags. I stood there looking at my house, wondering why it didn't feel like home.

"How serious?" I asked my roommate, curiously.

"Serious enough that he's asked me to move in."

Well, damn. "I'm so happy for you!" I hoped my watery smile communicated effectively that I really was happy for him, and that any upset was lingering terror about spending the night in the house by myself.

I'd cross that bridge when I came to it.

I SCREAMED as I woke up, clutching at the gun I'd stashed underneath my pillow. The familiar nightmares of the auction blended seamlessly with the darkness and pain that Yuri left me with. My heart pounded and my hands were clammy as I sat up in my bed, my fingers white where they gripped the gun.

Fuck.

Unable to shake the image of Yuri's grinning, cackling face from my memory, I hobbled to the bathroom and splashed water on my face. My skin was pale and wan, and my eyes were bloodshot. It had taken years before the nightmares had truly faded the first time. Was I doomed to repeat this cycle, over and over?

I lay in bed staring at my ceiling in the dark, unable to close my eyes without memories of the assault and torture overwhelming me. I checked the clock. Three hours ahead, on the East Coast. It'd be almost three in the morning there.

Fuck it.

I thumbed open the phone and called Liam.

"Ginevra? Are you okay?" he asked, opening up the video and letting me see him disheveled and shirtless, dragging himself to a sitting position in his bed. He ran his hand through his red hair. "What's wrong?"

Suddenly, I felt foolish, embarrassed. "It's nothing. Sorry, I didn't mean to wake you up. Go back to sleep." I hung up, only for him to immediately call back.

"What's wrong, Ginevra?" His green eyes filled with an emotion I wasn't ready to accept from him. "Tell me what you need, little lamb."

I sobbed once, twice, and then bottled up the emotion threatening to pour out of me. "Nightmare," I whispered.

"Oh, baby, I'm so sorry."

We stared at each other through our screens. His half smile had me wanting to stroke my fingers over his lips and drag it into a genuine smile. "Would you just—" I didn't know how to ask for what I wanted, for what I needed.

"Want to keep the line open while you sleep?" he offered.

I was crying again. How had I not drowned in all the tears I'd cried over the last two days? "Would you? Please?"

He pressed his fingers to his lips and then touched the screen. "Of course, Ginevra. Anything you need. Just prop the phone up beside you, and I'll be right here, okay?"

I nodded, scrubbing my hands over my face, not caring that he saw me at my weakest. Liam wouldn't hold it against me. I set the phone on my bedside table, leaning it against the book I'd left there when I dashed to Yorkfield almost two weeks before.

"Good girl," he murmured. "You're so fucking brave, you know that? I'll keep an eye on you, I promise."

This time, when I closed my eyes, I saw his face instead of Yuri's and drifted off to sleep.

A ROUND of applause greeted me as I limped into my company's headquarters the next morning, cane in hand. Skillfully applied make-up hid the cuts and bruises Yuri left on my face and visible limbs, but nothing could hide the news articles and social media posts. My celebrity was a flash in the pan, but it'd been enough that everyone in my company knew what had happened to me.

Blinking back tears, I made my way to my office, greeting employees who seemed genuinely happy to see me.

Speak of the devil. My executive assistant poked her head in after I finally settled behind my desk. "Morning, boss! Welcome back!" She set a coffee and pastry in front of me.

"Thanks, Rasmita. Can you catch me up on everything I missed?" I'd kept track of my email until the moment Yuri snatched me out of the club, but had frankly been quite distracted while I was on the other side of the country. I smashed down the ache that bloomed in my chest when I thought about the causes of those distractions. *No.* I was done with that life.

"Richard Huntington would like to speak with you first thing this morning," Rasmita told me, her brown eyes wide with worry.

"What's going on?"

"His lawyer sent over the highlights by email. I forwarded them to Cheryl for review. She's waiting for your call."

An hour later, I was ready to speak with Huntington, that asshole.

"Richard, good morning!" I chirped from my office. "I've taken the liberty of adding my company's general counsel to this call, and I see you've done the same."

"Ginevra, it's so good to see you home, safe and sound. How are you doing?" I clenched my fists under my desk. How had I not realized how fake he was before this? God.

"Good. It's good to be home. It's good to be *safe*," I emphasized.

"You had quite a week, I see."

"I'm glad to be home, though, away from all of that," I answered.

"I'm going to cut right to the chase, Ginevra, dear. You failed to mention that your father was the head of the Italian mafia in Yorkfield, and that you were marrying Irish criminals, when you signed that contract for fifteen million dollars to produce animation with my studio."

Asshole. He was going to use a morality clause to pull out because he'd found a better price elsewhere. I knew the deal had been too good to be true. My staff had spent the last several days frantically pulling in subcontractors, dragging folks back from vacation, and spinning up for this very large last minute contract. I was going to have to eat hundreds of thousands of dollars in immediate costs, not to mention the long-term hit to my reputation.

"You'll need to settle the bills for costs we've already incurred," I answered, pulling up the spreadsheet Rasmita had spent the morning putting together for me. "We can cancel the subcontracts, of course, but we've already paid options for leased space to secure an office."

Huntington narrowed his eyes, and I raised my hand to cut him off before he could say something he'd regret. "I never hid my origins. Don't blame me because you didn't do your due diligence."

He laughed. "Marrying Rian O'Conner has nothing to do with your origins, darling."

I shrugged. Hollywood had been in bed with the mob since its earliest days. I was just taking it literally. "What's this really about, Richard?"

His lawyer interrupted him. "The morality clause, Ms. Russo. We are ending the contract based on your marriage to a known and convicted criminal."

"I'm sorry, Ginevra," Richard said sadly, before we ended the call.

That fucker.

Half a dozen similar inquiries came in over the course of the morning. Hiring my company cost a lot because we were the best, and I refused to allow these assholes to use my marriage to renegotiate and save a few pennies.

Cheryl assured me we could fight them. Marriage to a criminal didn't make me a criminal by association, but the one that stung the most was Richard. Losing his respect and regard fucking hurt. I'd worked my ass off to build this company up to fifty employees from nothing. We'd worked with major studios and the biggest producers, and pivoting from special effects to animation was an opportunity to move up a level in this business.

Those fucking Irish boys. I pressed my palms into my eyes to stop tears from dripping down my face and messing up my make-up.

It was fine. This was fine. We'd make up for the lost contracts in other ways, and this would just be a less profitable quarter than the last.

Fucking fine.

37

RIAN

Two weeks. It had been two goddamned weeks, and the three of us were falling apart. Barely a day went by without a fight, and Liam had to tear Cormac and me apart when we'd come to blows the day before.

I ran my fingers through my hair. "What do you mean, you're cutting out early from dinner with Zhang?" I snapped at Liam. When he'd excused himself from the table, I'd done the same, meeting him outside of the coat closet as he accepted his weapons back.

He shrugged, sliding a handgun back into the shoulder holster he wore under his suit jacket. "I want to be in bed by one. You gotta fuckin' problem with that?"

"Yeah, I gotta fuckin' problem with that." I slammed my hands into the wall on either side of his head, my forehead inches from his. "Zhang is going to give us millions of dollars in exchange for the gun running arm of our gang and you can't fucking stay for drinks?"

Liam turned his head away from me, hiding his green eyes. "I said I have to be home by one. I'm leaving."

I turned on my heel and stormed away. Whatever the fuck was going on with him, I wasn't going to figure it out by slamming his head into the wall, no matter what my instincts were screaming for. With a sharp tug on my jacket to straighten it, I strode back into the backroom of the restaurant where Zhang held court.

"Cormac, Liam's going to need a hand this evening. Would you mind accompanying him to his next stop?" I asked, keeping my smile pleasant.

To his credit, Cormac rose and took his leave without question. I could count on him to find out what the hell was going on with Liam and report back.

"My apologies, Adam," I said to Zhang. "I didn't mean to interrupt."

Adam looked at me through his deep brown eyes. "I was thanking you, Rian, and your spouses."

My bitter smile hid the ache in my heart. I raised my glass in a toast. "To marriage!"

Zhang clinked his glass against mine. "I hear you're also getting out of the import business entirely these days." He referred to drugs we brought in through Southern ports and distributed overland up through the state.

"That's correct."

He tilted his head. "Do you have a buyer?"

I grimaced, cutting my eyes around the backroom, where his staff were in and out, and his second-in-command still lingered. Handing all of our illegal business to Adam Zhang would give him a lot of power, no matter how much he paid for them. Going straight would be worth it, though, if it meant keeping Ginevra safe.

"I'm entertaining offers," I answered. The cash flow from selling off these arms of our business would defray the losses we'd taken from Antonio's warehouse fires.

We toasted each other and continued to drink late into the evening. At 1:05, my phone pinged.

Cormac: You better get the fuck home right now.
Rian: ??
Cormac: Home. Now.

Adam raised an eyebrow. I showed him the texts and shrugged. "I gotta go."

He just laughed. "Your family life seems more complicated than it has to be, my young friend."

I clapped him on the back. "Not that much younger than you, Adam."

Twenty minutes later, I sped into our garage, then barreled up the stairs. The house was dark and empty. "Where the fuck are you?" I bellowed.

"Liam's room," Cormac called.

I slammed Liam's door open. He was in bed, bare chested, his phone propped on his bedside table, with Ginevra's pale face staring back at us. She looked like shit, drawn and exhausted, with deep shadows under her eyes.

"What the hell is going on here?" I snapped.

Ginevra blinked, as if registering my presence in the room for the first time. "You guys are such assholes," she sighed. "Liam, call me back when you're done." And she fucking hung up.

"Call her back right now," I shouted, desperate to see her face again.

"I will not," Liam bit back.

Cormac wrapped an arm around my shoulders and pushed me onto the bed, until he and I sat knee to knee, our hips pressed against Liam's warm body.

Liam pinched his nose. "She still has nightmares. Every fucking night."

I waited, saying nothing.

"She calls me at ten, her time, and I stay on the line with her. When she wakes screaming, I calm her down. It's the only way she gets any sleep."

My heart dropped to the floor. I had been imagining Ginevra happy and carefree, back in California where she'd built her life, with none of the weight of our lives to drag her down.

"How long?" I asked, my voice hoarse with pent up emotion.

"Two weeks. Since she went back."

I slumped on his bed, scrubbing my face with my hands. "Fuck."

"Do you ever talk?" Cormac asked him quietly.

"Not really. She tells me if it was a good day or a bad day or just a long day, but that's it. She's not doing well."

"How could you hide this from us?" I asked Liam, anguished.

Liam stared at me, his green eyes steady, one side of his mouth tilted up in a half-smile. He took my hand in his. "Ginevra would have asked me to share it if she'd wanted me to."

I closed my eyes against the hurt that coursed through me.

"She looked like shit," Cormac said. "One of us needs to go to her." The three of us stared at each other, each of us desperate to be the one who went. When Liam would have spoken, I held up a hand.

"Cormac should go." If there was anyone who could pick up the pieces of Ginevra and somehow glue them back together in a way that made room for us in her life, it was Cormac.

He slid off the bed and strode out the door. "I'll pack a bag."

Liam looked at me with sympathy in his eyes. "Go get changed and come back. You can spend the night here, with us."

With us. With Ginevra.

Ten minutes later, I was curled up beside him in a pair of sweatpants, as he called Ginevra on the smartphone. God, she looked tired.

"How're you doing, princess?" I asked, my voice gentle, holding back the rush of emotion as I got a good look at her for the first time since she'd left.

"I'm okay," she answered, her voice cracking. A lone tear rolled down her face. "Tired," she continued, trying to laugh.

"You never had to pretend for me, baby," Liam interrupted, his voice commanding. "If you're tired, you're tired." I looked at him in surprise. He was so rarely firm. She had wrought changes in all of us.

She nodded. "I'm tired."

"Is it alright if Rian stays with us tonight?"

Ginevra set her phone beside her bed, moving out of view for a moment as she lay down. When her head hit the pillow, she was staring straight into the camera, her dark hair wispy around her face. As she considered the question, my heart broke for at least the third time that week.

"Yeah, that's fine."

"Sweet dreams, baby girl," Liam whispered. He kissed his fingers and pressed them to the screen. She didn't return the gesture, just closed her eyes, and a few minutes later, she was fast asleep.

I flopped down beside Liam, one arm thrown over my face to conceal the parade of emotions I couldn't hide—longing most of all. God, I missed her. We'd had her in our arms for only a few days, and it'd been long enough for her to gouge out a piece of my heart and claim it for her own.

Liam laughed to himself, then reached over and pulled me to him. Go figure that the psychopath was the one among us who'd found a way to make peace with our loss. I burrowed into the warmth of his arms, laying my face on his chest.

"We'll get her back," he promised me, stroking my hair as I drifted to sleep.

38

GINEVRA

Why was there a motorcycle in my driveway? I pushed the front door open, plastering on my fake-for-company smile, getting ready to greet Min-joon's guest, only to see Cormac seated on the living room couch, sharing a drink with my roommate.

My purse fell to the floor with a clatter. I raised a trembling hand to my heart as I stared at him. His deep brown eyes were liquid and warm as he smiled at me. The coppery tint to his skin glowed in the California light. As he walked toward me, his arms out, a strangled, animal sound escaped me, and I threw myself into his arms.

"Oh, sweet darling Ginevra," he sighed, wrapping me in his embrace, and tucking my head under his chin. "I missed you." He stroked my back with a gentle touch.

I squeezed my eyes shut, not quite believing he was there, in my living room. I'd stopped myself from daydreaming about my men dozens of times in the past two weeks. Each time, my broken heart cracked into smaller pieces as I realized the impossibility of my dream. And yet, here he was.

"Min-joon was kind enough to let me in," Cormac murmured into the top of my head, bringing me back to the present.

With a sniffle, I gave my roommate a watery smile.

Min-joon's answering look was dry. "I'm going to pack an overnight bag and crash at Jeff's. I'll be back to host the poolside brunch with you on Saturday, okay?"

Cormac didn't let go of me, just held me and petted me, whispering sweet nothings in my ears, until Min-joon was gone. When we were finally alone in the house, he stepped back, holding my arms so he could look me up and down.

"You look like shit, darling."

I laughed through my tears. "It's been a shit couple of weeks, asshole."

"You've lost weight."

I pursed my lips. It had been all I could do to drag myself to work each day and pretend everything was normal, and he wanted me to take care of myself too? Had I not given enough to this asshole while I was in Yorkfield? And now he thought he could come into my home and tell me I wasn't doing enough in the face of everything that had happened to me?

I took a step back, annoyed. "Fuck you, Cormac."

He dragged me back into his arms. "Darling, I'm so sorry." He nuzzled his nose into the crown of my head, then fisted his hand in my hair, tugging it back so that he could kiss me, brushing his lips against mine once, twice, and then deepening the kiss into one of intense possession.

When he pulled back, my breath was ragged. "I missed you too," I whispered, leaning against his chest.

"Go take a shower," he instructed. "I'll start dinner."

The smell of searing meat drew me downstairs without drying my hair. I pulled it back into a loose braid and dressed for comfort. I didn't want to admit it to myself, but knowing Cormac was in the house was already mending some of the broken, jagged pieces of my heart.

"I'm glad you're here," I said as I leaned on the counter of my kitchen island, admiring the play of his broad shoulders under his snug T-shirt. I dragged my eyes down his body, the muscles of his back, his trim waist, the curves of his ass, and his thick thighs. When I raised my eyes, he was looking at me over his shoulder.

"Like what you see, darling?"

I hummed my assent as he cooked our dinner, watching him move around my kitchen as if it were his own. "I'm glad you're here," I repeated, grabbing wine glasses and a bottle of merlot and walking them to the table. He finished serving the food as I set the table, but once we faced each other over our plates, I didn't know what to do with myself.

"Don't," Cormac said, taking my hand in his. "You don't owe me pleasant conversation. I just—I saw you last night, and my heart broke all over again. Let me take care of you for a little while, okay?"

My phone pinged and saved me from another moment of awkwardness.

Min-joon: Are you okay? Need a rescue?
Ginevra: I'm good. Really good. Enjoy your night with Jeff.

Cormac held his hand out for the phone. With a raised eyebrow, I handed it to him. "Your roommate's a good man," he said.

"We've known each other for a long time."

I played with my food, but the butterflies in my stomach

and my fluttering heart made it impossible for me to swallow.

"Go get a cushion from one of your couches." My eyes flew to his. "Now, Ginevra," he snapped when I didn't move. I scrambled to the living room, looking for something suitable for what I thought he had in mind. I grabbed a wide throw pillow with tassels on the corners and scurried back.

"Set it by my seat," he commanded. "Now, kneel."

Sinking slowly, as if I were moving through honey, I fell to my knees onto the pillow to his left. He bent down and stroked my cheek with one finger. "You're so fucking precious to me, Ginevra. Never doubt that."

When he fed me a slice of steak on his fork, I chewed and swallowed it. The rest of the meal progressed in the same manner, bite by bite, as he fed me, until I was full and leaned my head against his thigh, basking in the warm comfort of his presence.

"Don't move, darling," he commanded as he stood, clearing the table. I waited, fidgeting, but not making a sound. When he returned, he rotated his chair so that I knelt between his thighs. He fed me berries and cream, one spoonful at a time, his eyes darkening with lust each time I licked the sticky liquid off my lips.

"Wait for me on the couch, okay, love?" he said when we finished, offering his hand to help me up. I clung to him.

"Come with me?" I whispered.

Cormac grinned. "Let me do the dishes first."

"I'll wait for you in the kitchen," I answered decisively. His brown eyes flashed with amusement, but he didn't stop me from sliding onto one of the bar stools and watching him as he tidied up my house.

He tucked my hand in his as we walked to the living room together, and I luxuriated in the feeling of not being alone. I knew it wouldn't last. Cormac was here to check on me, and in a few days, he'd have to return to Yorkfield. The business needed him, just like my company needed me.

"Penny for your thoughts?" he asked as we settled into a comfortable couch. I pulled my knees up under me and snuggled into his chest, his arm wrapped around me in a warm hug.

"How long are you staying?"

He sighed. "Rian and Liam will be here in three days, on Saturday." My heart jumped at the sound of their names, at the idea that they'd be here, and then I hardened it once again. "Stop thinking, love, whatever's making you tense up like that."

I raised an eyebrow. "Pretty sure being my dom doesn't mean you get to regulate my thoughts."

He kissed me on the forehead. "We shouldn't have let you go off on your own after what happened. Fucking let me help you get back on your feet again. Please."

They were going to break my heart all over again when they left, but I couldn't bring myself to put a halt to it.

"Okay," I whispered.

"Okay?"

"Yeah, Cormac. Help me put myself back together again. God knows, I'm doing a shit job on my own."

CORMAC TRAILED his fingers up and down my sweatshirt clad arm as we watched some ridiculous action movie. The careful movement was more affectionate than sexual, comforting me, soothing me. My phone beeped from his pocket at 9:45, just as the credits to the movie rolled.

"Time for bed," I whispered into his chest.

Cormac handed me my phone. "I'll close up the house. Go get ready for bed and call Liam."

Fifteen minutes later, I'd washed my face, changed into pajama shorts and a camisole, and tucked myself under my covers. Cormac knocked on the door, his face uncertain. "Can I come in?"

I rolled over from where I was fiddling with my phone set-up, blinking at him. He leaned against the doorframe, looking good enough to eat in a pair of gray sweatpants and nothing else. "I'd assumed you were," I answered with a sleepy smile.

His smile lit up his face, the beauty of his joy absolutely breathtaking. He took the side of the bed closest to the door, sliding his gun out of where he'd tucked it into his waistband and setting it on the bedside table. I hit the call button, and Liam answered right away.

"Hey there, sweetheart," he answered, a ginger eyebrow curling up as Cormac slid in behind me, wrapping an arm around my waist and tucking me against him. My expression was no doubt identical with surprise. Rian lay beside Liam, their limbs tangled together much the same as Cormac and I. Liam held the phone above their faces.

"Hey," I answered, smiling.

"Is that a smile, lass?" Liam asked, his own grin spreading over his face. "About fuckin' time."

"Hey there, princess," Rian said, taking the phone. "How're you doing?"

"She's tired," Cormac said. "And I haven't finished taking care of her yet."

Liam's chuckle shot straight to my core. "Get to it then, but keep the phone on."

My eyes widened. Cormac tugged on my shoulder until I was lying on my back. He propped his head on his hand, leaning over me and dancing his fingers over my collarbone. "What's your safe word, Ginevra?"

"Pineapple," I whispered as my heart raced beneath his hand.

"That's my girl." His voice was raspy as he traced my shoulders, my neck, the contours of my face, with his fingers, as if he were memorizing every inch of me.

Cormac pulled down the blankets, revealing my silk pajamas. He slid his hands down my sides and across my stomach, reverently sliding his fingers over the still healing cuts my ordeal had left. He bent his head to lay featherlight kisses on my stomach, brushing his lips above my skin as he hiked my camisole up higher and higher.

He traced a path up the center of my chest, kissing from my belly to my throat as he pushed the fabric out of his way. When he pushed it up past my face, he trapped my hands together with the silky fabric, looking down at me with satisfaction. "Fucking gorgeous, Ginevra."

No. Terror jerked through me as I realized I couldn't free my hands. I was trapped. My vision tunneled as memories of the warehouse flashed before my eyes. *Shit.* I yanked on my hands, trying to loosen them from their silk binding. My heart raced, pounding out of my chest. "Fucking pineapple, Cormac! Please!" I cried out as I struggled.

He grabbed my wrists and slipped the fabric up and off, freeing my hands. "Hey, hey, hey, of course. You're free, Ginevra. You're home and you're free, and nobody's going to hurt you. Shit, I'm so sorry."

"I'm sorry," I whispered as I cried and shuddered in his arms. "I'm a shit submissive. I'm so sorry."

"Oh no, love, there's nothing to be sorry for. You couldn't have known, and I should have thought to check before getting started."

He held me as I shivered, pressing my body as close to his as I could, seeking comfort in the heat of his skin and the closeness of his heartbeat. After several long minutes, he pulled back an inch. "All right, my little koala bear. I don't want you to do anything but tell me what you do and don't want. Can you do that?"

"Give it a rest, Cormac," Rian rasped through the screen. "She's been through a lot today."

Cormac ignored Rian, gazing down into my eyes. "What do you want to do, darling?"

I took one last shuddering breath, then surged up to meet his lips with my own. "I want to try again. Please."

"Take off your clothes, Ginevra," he ordered, his voice calm and quiet. I wriggled out of my shorts and panties, leaving me bare before him on the bed. I reached up my hand to stroke down his chest. Cormac shook his head. "Keep your hands to yourself, love."

"I thought this was about what I wanted," I sassed back.

"It's about what you need, darling. Can you trust me?"

I nodded.

"Good girl." He lay on his side, facing the phone, stroking his long fingers down my chest to my belly and back up again. When he leaned down to kiss my collarbone, I gasped, then pressed my lips together, trying to hold in the sound.

Cormac moved back up to my face to brush his lips against mine. "Don't, Ginevra. Let them hear how much you love this."

He kissed down my jawbone and my throat, taking a moment to suck on the sensitive spot where my neck met my shoulders. This time, I didn't hold back. I whimpered as electricity sparked in every place he touched.

"That's it love, let me know what you like," he

murmured as he traced lazy circles around my breasts, moving closer and closer to my nipples, until the tight peaks were hard and aching for his touch.

"Please," I whispered.

"Do you want my mouth on you, darling Ginevra?"

"Yes, please," I pleaded. He palmed one breast and brought his lips down to close over the other. I moaned as he sucked my nipple into his mouth, hollowing out his cheeks as he drew it up, then releasing it with a pop. His fingers closed over my other nipple, rolling it between his thumb and forefinger.

"Gorgeous, perfect Ginevra," Cormac murmured as he worshiped my chest. "Look at the phone. See how rapt Liam and Rian are as you squirm for me." My eyes flicked over to the glowing screen where my two men laid enmeshed in each other's arms, their skin luminescent under the light of the phone, their eyes focused entirely on the screen, on me.

Cormac slapped my breast gently, watching reverently as it shook and jiggled. "See that, boys? Fucking perfect." When he slapped the other breast, he grazed my nipple, and the sharp stinging pain coursed through me, straight to my core. I moaned and arched my back. "Do you like that, love?"

"Yes," I answered. His answering smile lit up the damned room.

He bent his head back down to my nipple, taking it in his mouth. He swirled his tongue around the peak, then nipped at it, a sharp bite that took my breath away and left me panting and mewling. He soothed the pain away with his tongue, then repeated the action, until I was a writhing, moaning mess. My hands clutched around his head, digging into his skull as he expertly stoked the fires of my need.

When Cormac kissed his way back up my chest, I

protested, only for him to ignore me as he captured my lips with his.

He softened the kiss, then lifted his head as he stroked my cheek with his thumb. "How are you doing, Ginny-darling?"

I smiled at the nickname. "So fucking good, Cormac."

He shifted his body from where he laid beside me to lie on top of me, spreading my thighs with his own as he slid his tongue against mine in a dark possessive kiss. I wrapped my arms around him, pulling him close, relishing the sensation of our skin pressing together.

Cormac smiled wickedly as he kissed his way down my belly. He gently stroked his hands over the mound at the apex of my thighs, before running his hands down my legs and lifting them over his shoulders, opening me wide. He kissed his way up the sensitive insides of my thighs until I was squirming and breathless with need.

When he spread me open and licked from my entrance to my clit, I moaned, throaty and wanton. "Please, Cormac," I pleaded.

"Anything for you, Ginevra," he answered, reverent as he explored my folds with his tongue, brushing up and down with light flicks, tasting me. He took his sweet time, running his tongue over me, worshiping every exposed inch of skin. I writhed and begged, twitching as he held me still with his strong arms.

"Please," I begged, and finally, he indulged me, circling my clit with his tongue until I thrashed on the bed, begging for release as my need spiraled higher and higher. When he bit down on my clit, the sharp pain sent me over the edge, darkening the edges of my vision, as my limbs seized and I screamed his name.

Cormac didn't stop. He released one of my legs only to

plunge one finger into me, and then two, pumping in and out as he sucked on my clit. "Too much," I whined, the bundle of nerves overly sensitive after my last powerful orgasm, but he didn't stop.

"You can do this, Ginevra," he reassured me as my hips twitched in time with the movement of his fingers, seeking more friction as my need came thundering back. My pussy clenched around him as he fucked me with his fingers and lashed my clit with his talented tongue. He increased his rhythm until I was once again screaming my release, shaking and begging and crying as stars danced across my vision and I trembled with pleasure.

Tears streamed down my face as the pent-up emotions of the last two weeks poured out. Cormac kissed his way back up my body, then gathered me in his arms, rolling us until we were on our sides, our limbs twined together as he pressed my face into his chest.

"Let it all out, darling. I'm here now. I've got you," he said, whispering reassuring nothings to me as I cried.

When my sobs subsided, I was surprised to find that my tears had been cathartic. There was a lightness in my heart that wasn't there before. I met Cormac's gaze with wonder, cupping his cheek with my hand, rubbing my thumb over the stubble on his jaw.

Trailing my fingers down his chest, I slid them under the waistband of his pants. "No, Ginevra," Cormac said, tugging my hands back up. "Not tonight, anyway. Please, I'm here to take care of you." His voice cracked as he held me tightly against him. For the first time, I realized my departure had taken a toll on him, that his presence here was mending his heart as much as it was mending mine.

"Thank you," I said.

He kissed my nose. "Don't be silly. There's nothing to thank me for, darling."

I sniffled one last time, then rotated in his arms until my back was pressed to his torso and I faced the phone again. Liam and Rian peered out of the screen.

"Good night, little lamb."

"Good night, princess."

"Good night, boys," I said, lacing my tone with a hint of the humor that had been missing from my life over the last several weeks.

"Good night, Ginevra," Cormac whispered in my ear, and I drifted off to sleep in the reassuring comfort of his embrace.

39

CORMAC

Ginevra's alarm blared. She blindly swept her arm out to turn it off, knocking it to the ground with a clatter. "Fuck," she muttered as she reached down to grab it off the floor.

I wrapped my hands around her hips so she wouldn't tumble off the bed, and she froze. Her phone forgotten, she rolled over and stared at me, her warm brown eyes cloudy with sleep. She cupped my cheek, running her hand over the rough stubble. "I forgot you'd come." Her voice was raspy and rough.

When I turned my mouth into her palm to kiss it, her breath caught. A lone tear dripped down her face in the early morning light. I wiped it away with my thumb, and she dove into my embrace, tucking her head under my chin as she sobbed into my chest.

"Hey, easy, Ginny-love. It's okay. I'm here. It's okay." I whispered nonsense against the top of her head while she cried, stroking her back, my heart breaking all over again to see her so anguished.

Her tears subsided, and she flung herself on her back,

dropping her arm over my chest, refusing to lose the skin-to-skin contact. I grasped at her hand, holding it tightly to me.

"Hi," she whispered, scrubbing her face with her free hand.

"Go take your shower."

She stared at the ceiling, the barest hint of a smile on her lips. "And if I wanted to call in sick and spend the day wrapped in your arms instead?"

I slid my hand up her chest and wrapped my fingers around her throat, not squeezing, pressing only hard enough so she'd feel my strength. "Don't brat, Ginevra."

Her eyes widened, and she licked her lips. "Maybe I like being punished."

Ah. Ginny wasn't a brat, but she desperately needed me to take control for a few days. "Do you think you deserve to be punished?" I asked, silkily, tightening my hold on her throat enough that she'd have to work a little to draw breath.

She hesitated a beat, and then answered, "No."

I lifted my hand. "Let's keep it that way. Go take a shower, darling."

She swung her legs over the side of the bed. Most of the cuts and bruises from Yuri had healed, but she'd wear the scars for the rest of her life.

I watched the tempting sway of her hips as she disappeared into the bathroom, noting the weight she'd lost, then got up to rifle through her closet and drawers. I pulled out a suit and blouse, then went on the hunt for underclothes. She needed time to put herself back together, and the easiest way to do that was to give her the mental space to do so. Was she still in therapy? I made a note in my phone to ask at breakfast.

I laid out her outfit with a note to get dressed, grabbed a

pair of sweatpants from my suitcase, and ambled downstairs.

Her fridge was full of takeout leftovers. What few vegetables there were, I suspected her roommate had purchased. I made another note to order groceries, healthy groceries. This morning, I'd make do with what she had. In short order, coffee was percolating, I'd whipped up an omelet, and I'd chopped up what little fruit I'd found.

When she came down the stairs, fully dressed, I ran my eyes over her, so fucking glad to be back in her life, even if it was only for a few days. I didn't miss how her eyes lingered on my bare chest and the trail of hair that disappeared into the waistband of my sweatpants. Fuck, I wanted her, but this visit was about her mental health, not sex. I jerked my chin toward the dining room. "Go ahead and wait for me in there."

She raised an eyebrow, but when she would have pulled out a chair to sit down, I snapped out, "No. Kneel."

Ginevra's eyes widened, but she didn't argue. No, to my surprise, she sank down into the pillow I'd left beside the table the night before, graceful in her supplication, as she waited for me to join her. I brought her coffee and an overloaded plate of omelet and fruit.

"Good morning, darling," I said to her, running my fingers over the top of her hair. She just leaned her head against my thigh when I sat, sighing with what I hoped was easy contentment. Bite by bite, I fed her, careful of her work clothes, enjoying the domesticity of taking care of my woman.

After she'd eaten her fill, I reached down to take her hand and hauled her into my lap. She looked at me with surprise as I handed her a mug of steaming coffee. "How're you doing?" I asked her.

She blinked. "I feel like I should be asking you that. You're taking care of me, and—"

I cut her off. "We never should have let you come out here alone after we got you back. I'm so sorry for that, darling. Are you still seeing your therapist?"

She shook her head. "I'm not ready to talk about it."

I stroked her hip and leaned forward to rest my chin on her shoulder. "Would you please make an appointment today?"

She raised an eyebrow. "Are you asking me, or are you telling me?"

Oh, Ginny-love, always looking for trouble. I kissed her cheek, then pulled back so she could sip her coffee. "I'm telling you. Make an appointment with your therapist today."

I kept the rest of the conversation light, until it was time for her to head out to work. "What time do you normally eat lunch?" I asked her.

She tilted her head to the side. "Twelve thirty-ish."

"I'll pick you up then."

"Absolutely not. I don't have time for a long lunch break." I drew her against me.

"What do you have time for, then?"

Her eyes flicked to mine, and for the first time that morning, uncertainty clouded them. She furrowed her brow. "I don't want to impose."

I shifted her from my thigh until she straddled me, so I could look her in the eye. I cupped her face in my palms. "Ginevra, you are not an imposition. You are my fucking wife, and I am going to take care of you. Tell me what you goddamned need." When she flinched, I regretted the force of my words, but not that I'd uttered them.

"Why don't I bring you lunch and we'll eat at your desk, together?"

She looked at me through long lashes. "You're going to bring me something healthy, aren't you?"

I laughed. "Yes, love, I am absolutely going to bring you a healthy lunch. With plenty of nutrients, so you have the energy you need to focus on taking care of yourself."

She dropped against me, wrapping her arms around my neck and settling into a hug. I ignored the pressure of her core against my cock, focusing on the feel of her soft skin against mine and the silk of her hair as it blew across my hands.

"C'mon, let me throw a shirt on. I'll take you to work."

THE RECEPTIONIST I met at the entrance to Ginevra's floor wasn't sure what to do with me. I was out of place in jeans and my leather bike jacket, with my helmet slung over one arm, and a bag full of takeout in my other hand. "Cormac Wallace," I introduced myself. "I'm one of Ginevra Russo's spouses."

The woman's eyes grew large as she took me in. I raised an eyebrow. "Would you let her know I'm here and point me to her office?"

She didn't take her eye off me as she dialed. "Rasmita? Cormac Wallace is here for the boss." She nodded, then hung up. "I'll walk you back."

I followed the petite woman through the open plan office, full of lively people chatting and peeking at each other's screens and laughing, nothing like the image of silently industrious productivity I expected. Their eyes followed me as I made my way to Ginevra's office. The receptionist stopped so abruptly I almost slammed into her.

Through the big glass windows separating her office from the rest of the floor, I watched a man lean over Ginevra, his hand on the back of her chair as he pointed at something on her screen. I reminded myself that I didn't have the same terrifying reputation in LA as I did in Yorkfield. Although, the way the woman behind the desk outside Ginevra's office glowered at me, perhaps I had some cleanup to do on that front.

"Rasmita? This is Cormac Wallace," the tiny receptionist squeaked before fleeing back to her safe desk in front of the elevator bank.

Rasmita was made of sterner stuff. She looked me up and down, unimpressed. "Ginevra's busy. You can wait here, if you like." She gestured to a set of arm chairs against the wall, out of view of the noisy bank of programmers, but where she could keep an eye on me. And where I could keep an eye on the man taking up Ginevra's space like he owned it.

I grinned. "Nice to meet you. I'm happy to wait."

A few minutes later, the man slipped out of the office. "She's back on her game," he murmured to Rasmita. "Wouldn't give me an inch on that deadline."

Rasmita's eyes flicked to me, then back to him. Did I imagine a thaw in her demeanor? Perhaps. "You shouldn't have been pushing the deadline anyway," she answered as she stood, forcing him to step away from her desk.

She nodded to me. "Mr. Wallace, she's expecting you."

Ginevra met my eyes through the glass, and her smile fucking melted the ice I'd been holding inside of me since she left us two weeks ago. She stood to meet me at the door.

"Rasmita, I'd like to introduce my—" She paused.

"We're calling ourselves your brother-husbands these days."

Ginevra burst into laughter. "Are you serious?"

"As death," I answered with a completely straight face. Her laugh floated through the large room, and it was as if every single employee sighed with quiet relief, releasing a tension I didn't realize they'd been holding.

"Rasmita, allow me to introduce Cormac Wallace, one of my three brother-husbands."

Rasmita cracked a smile, then immediately suppressed it. "The pleasure is mine, Mr. Wallace."

Ginevra grabbed my hand and dragged me into the office. "Rasmita makes this entire place work. She's the only reason the lights are still on after the disastrous couple of weeks we've had."

I looked at my wife with concern. *My wife.* God, that thought was satisfying. "What do you mean, disastrous?"

She closed the door behind me and gestured for me to sit on the couch that faced her desk. She leaned over me to close the blinds, and I inhaled her scent. Instantly hard, I ran my fingers up her sides until I settled my hands around her waist.

Ginevra looked down at me with amusement. To my shock, relief coursed through me at the laughter in her eyes. I dragged her down onto my lap and brushed my lips over hers. "I missed you."

Her gaze darkened. "You mean you missed fucking me."

When she tried to pull away, I caged her with my arms, holding her in my lap, making sure she felt the evidence of how much I wanted her against her squirming ass.

"That too," I said. "But I also missed you, Ginevra Russo—your fierce sense of self, and your willingness to wade into danger even when you're terrified, the way you tell Rian to go fuck himself so politely, and how your jagged edges fit so well against those of our odd little trio."

This time, when she met my gaze, her brown eyes softened. "I missed you too." She pushed up from my lap and emptied the white paper bag I'd brought with me. "Tacos? Tacos are healthy?"

"If it gets you eating your vegetables again, I'll count it as a win. Now eat, woman."

Ginevra sat across from me and tentatively took a bite of a taco. When she moaned in delight, I knew I was on the right path. She filled me in on what had happened over the past two weeks at work, as they lost contract after contract over the morality clauses. Rian and Liam had each done time, and there was no getting around that.

When fury overtook me, she held my hand in hers, tracing her fingers over my palm. "In another month, another scandal will take the heat off of me. We're the best at what we do, and I don't expect to be in the red for very long."

I asked her some technical questions about her company's work, and her eyes lit right up. Ginevra loved what she did. She cared deeply about her employees. The engine she'd designed to reduce the costs of CGI and make it more accessible to indie filmmakers was impressive. Just as impressive was how she built her company from scratch using the funds she made from selling her last company instead of seeking venture capital. She was fucking brilliant.

I made her eat one more taco than she wanted to, then stared at her until she drank every drop of the bright green smoothie I brought her. "How're you feeling?"

"Stuffed." Her eyes shot to mine, and I grinned at the unintended pun.

"That'll come tonight, I promise."

Ginevra's eyes darkened with need. She moved from her chair to the couch, where she dropped beside me and wormed her way under my arm. "I'm glad you're here. I needed you."

I wrapped my hand around her shoulder and pulled her into me until we pressed tightly against one another. "I needed you too, darling." When was the last time I enjoyed just sitting with another human being? Even with Rian and Liam, we were always moving, talking, fucking. Ginevra's presence brought me an unfamiliar sense of calm.

A knock at the door interrupted our moment. Rasmita stuck her perfectly coiffed head in the door. "Ginevra, your two o'clock just walked in downstairs."

Ginevra nodded. "Give me a minute, please."

After the door closed, she tugged my face down to hers for a sweet kiss that tugged at my heart. She leaned her forehead against mine. "What now?"

Oh, sweet Ginevra, you are so fucking perfect. "Get back to work. I'll come get you at five."

"Six," she said in an attempt to negotiate. "I won't even be close to finishing my workday at five."

"Five," I repeated. "Did you call your therapist?"

She flushed and shook her head. I captured her chin in my hand, gripping her face firmly. "What happens to bad little sluts who don't do what they're told?"

Ginevra's breath turned ragged as we stared at each other. "They're punished."

"Set up the appointment, darling." She bit her lip. What was getting in the way of her doing this? I drew her into my arms for a hug. "Do you want me to ask Rasmita to do it for you?"

Ginevra swore. "Shit. Yes. I should have just done that as soon as I got back. Yes, would you please?"

I tilted her face up to mine. "Anything, Ginevra. You just have to ask."

40

GINEVRA

Why hadn't the catering arrived yet? It was ten, and they were almost an hour late. Cormac stumbled down the stairs, rubbing the sleep out of his eyes.

"Ginevra, what's going on?"

"Oh, good, you're awake." I admired the play of the muscles on his bare chest. "Put some clothes on. Brunch starts in an hour and we still have a lot of work to do."

He cocked an eyebrow at me. "Are you in charge today, Ginevra?" He had a point. I'd submitted to him entirely over the last two days, letting him take over every aspect of my life outside of my company—what I ate, what I wore, how I relaxed in the evenings.

But today, I had a party to throw. "I am."

God, he was beautiful when he smiled. He trotted down the stairs and pulled me into his arms. "I'm glad you're feeling better, love." He kissed me hard on the lips, then hugged me tight, tucking his chin over the top of my head as he squeezed me. "So fucking glad."

I reveled in the comfort of his embrace. I'd needed the

break, to let him take care of me and spoil me. *Actually*, "Don't think you're done spoiling me. I expect the princess treatment for the rest of my life."

He kissed the crown of my head. "I promise." With a joyous whoop, he dashed up the stairs to get ready. "I'm glad you're back, Ginny!" he shouted from upstairs.

I couldn't wipe the smile off my face. I was happy to be back too. Rian and Liam would arrive around noon. I pushed my worry about my impending heartbreak aside, locking it into the tiny box I hid deep in my heart. Cormac's steady presence over the last few days hadn't convinced me that we had a future together, but I was willing to take it day-by-day.

"Where do you want the booze?" Min-joon asked, pushing the front door open with his foot.

"Out by the pool," I answered, waving him through.

Jeff followed him in, carrying a bouquet of tulips. He was whip thin, and wore a plaid button down over khaki shorts, with white socks pulled up over his calves. He pushed his glasses up on his nose as he peered at me. "These are for you," he said, shoving them at me awkwardly. I set them on the counter and pulled him in for a hug.

"Thanks for taking Min-joon in for the last couple of days."

Jeff's laugh was hearty, breaking the ice. "As a trial run, it worked pretty well. I think he's going to stay, actually." The thought wasn't quite as heartbreaking today as it had been a few weeks ago, or even a few days ago.

An hour later, our guests started to arrive. I'd changed into a bright red sundress, streaked through with gold thread, and liberally applied make-up over my entire body to hide the remnants of my wounds. I'd found that the visible reminders of the violence made folks uncomfortable.

Sure, that annoyed me, but this was a party, and I wanted folks to have fun.

Cheryl and Chana arrived first, on time. Very East Coast of Chana, I liked to tease. Chana grew up in New York, and she'd never shed all of her habits.

"You look great!" Cheryl exclaimed, as if she hadn't seen me every day over the last two weeks to untangle ourselves from contracts with folks who didn't want to be associated with the mob.

We walked over to the outside bar, where I poured them each a flute of Prosecco so we could toast. "To friends!" Cormac wandered over, looking delicious in jeans and a black T-shirt.

"To friends," he murmured in my ear, wrapping his arms around me from behind.

As the patio filled with friends, acquaintances, and business partners, my heart filled too. I was *Ginevra fucking Russo*, and I had built this life with my bare and bloody hands when I left Yorkfield a decade ago. If I had to rebuild parts of it from time to time, I could do it. I would do it. I was going to hold on to these friends with all the strength I had.

A HINT of Irish lilt caught my ear, distracting me from pouring yet another glass of Prosecco for Min-joon, who was tipsily teasing me for my relative sobriety. My eyes caught on Liam's shock of red hair, then met his gaze. He smiled lazily as he made his way over to me. Rian followed, looking good enough to eat in slacks and button-down shirt with the sleeves rolled up to reveal the tattoos on his forearms.

"Whoa there, Ginevra," Min-joon chastised me, as sparkling liquid spilled over the top of the glass. He rescued the glass and the bottle from my distracted hands as I stared.

When Liam reached me, he swept me up in his arms, lifting me against his chest and kissing me. "God, it's good to see you," he said against my lips. When he lowered me back to the ground, I dragged his face back down to mine, kissing him with all of the loneliness and desperation of the last two weeks.

Rian stepped behind me, wrapping his arms around me and leaning his head on my shoulder as I poured out my emotions into my kiss with Liam. When we finally took a breath, I leaned my head back toward Rian. He captured my lips in his, with a gentle, tentative kiss.

"I missed you, princess," he admitted, his voice soft against my ear.

Min-joon cleared his throat from where he stood beside us, watching with avid curiosity. I flushed faintly. Of course. "Min-joon, this is Rian O'Conner and Liam Byrne. May I present my soon-to-be-former roommate, Min-joon Li?"

The men shook hands, sizing each other up. Rian broke the ice. "Thanks for being there for Ginevra, when we weren't. I really appreciate it."

Min-joon grinned and pulled me out of their arms to wrap his own arm around my shoulder. "This woman saved me from myself more times than I can count. She's good people, the best of people." He narrowed his eyes. "Just remember, the Korean mob is as powerful here on the West Coast as you Irish are on the East Coast. And we're meaner sons-of-bitches."

I looked at Min-joon with surprise, and he winked at me. "Go sit with your partners, Ginevra. I'll host while you catch up."

My heart was so fucking full, and I was so fucking scared they were going to shatter it back into a million pieces.

"Hey," Liam began, tilting my face up to his with a gentle finger under my chin. "Stop worrying."

My answering smile was wry. "Easier said than done." I grabbed their hands and led them to empty pool chairs under a bit of shade. Cormac caught my eye from across the pool and acknowledged us with a lift of his beer bottle. He spoke with a producer whom I'd invited on a whim when he reached out to me last week after hearing about my poly family. This was Hollywood, and as puritanical as some were, just as many welcomed me into their world with open arms.

"How are you, baby?" Liam asked as we settled. He lounged in the chaise, drawing me against his leg to sit beside him and resting his hands on my hips. Rian sat across from me, our legs tangled up together. It was as if neither of them could bear a second without touching me.

"I'm surviving. Cormac—" I didn't know how to describe the last few days. "Cormac helped. So much."

I didn't know what to say to them because I didn't know what I wanted. Instead, I wrung my fingers together until they ached. Rian snatched my hands and drew them apart, holding them in his.

"Ginevra, we're going straight," he said.

I blinked, then flicked my eyes between him and Liam, not understanding. Liam rolled his eyes. "No fucking tact, Rian. We're fine, Ginevra. We miss you dearly. The house is empty without you. How is business? How is life?"

I laughed. "No, it's okay, Liam. Our relationship has never been normal. What's one more bizarre conversation?" For a second, I mourned the sense of normalcy I'd lost three weeks ago when I picked up Sofia's call. No matter how far I ran, my life was going to be tangled up with these men until the day I died.

"We're going legitimate," Rian repeated.

"Well, as legitimate as we can," Liam corrected. "It's going to take us years to fully divest, but for now, we've sold off the arms and drugs to Adam Zhang. And we're spinning off the import/exports to a separate corporation that we'll eventually hand back to your father."

I blinked. This was not the conversation I expected to have.

"Ginevra, we want you in our lives," Liam said. "We want you to live with us, to run our businesses with us, to grow old with us. But we can't do that if we can't keep you safe. And we can't keep you safe if we're still fucking trafficking in arms or dealing drugs."

For the umpteenth time that day, I was speechless. I didn't know what to say to these beautiful men who were gazing at me with such earnestness. They'd rearranged their entire lives for me.

As if sensing my discomfort, Liam rubbed warm circles on my back. "You don't have to make any decisions now. Or ever. We just wanted you to know we're going to take care of you, even if you never come home."

The floodgates opened and tears poured out of me until I was leaning forward against Rian and hiccuping as I sobbed into his chest. "I missed you all so fucking much," I whispered, clutching his shirt and holding him tight.

"We're here now, sweet Ginevra," he answered, running his hands up and down my back, comforting me.

Both men wrapped their arms around me and let me quietly cry out my loneliness, my fears, and my uncertainty about the future.

Eventually, my tears dried up, as if I'd pulled from the bottom of the well, and there were no tears left to cry.

Rian looked at my face critically. "You're a mess, princess."

I laughed, aware that my face was blotchy and red, my mascara dripping down my cheeks. "Crying'll do that."

Rian extracted himself from my white knuckled grip and went to get a wet towel from the bar. I cleaned up my face the best I could, then smiled weakly. "Time to introduce you all to the rest of my life."

Liam drew me backward for a quick kiss. "We'd love that."

I SHOULDN'T HAVE BEEN SURPRISED that my husbands slid as smoothly into my life here in Los Angeles as I had into theirs in Yorkfield. They were smart, charming, and handsome, catnip for this star-weary crew. I didn't know how I was going to let them go when they had to fly back at the end of the weekend.

That was a problem for future Ginevra. Right then and there, I was determined to enjoy every moment of their company while they were with me. Sunset found Cheryl, Chana, and I over the fire pit, drinking the dregs of Prosecco straight from the bottle as the guys stacked chairs and took out the trash.

"It's good to see you smiling again," Cheryl said, leaning her head on Chana's shoulder.

"It's good to *be* smiling again." It was. Somehow, over the last few days, I'd found my feet again. The trauma wasn't gone. Just as with the first time I'd been kidnapped, I'd probably be dealing with residual terror and stress for the rest of my life. For today, though, it was tucked into a corner of my mind, sitting in the background rather than coloring every interaction.

When night fell, I found myself alone with my men, dangling my feet in the pool and talking about nothing of import. It wasn't small talk, just the sort of conversation about books and music and how to keep the lawn green that normal families used to fill in the empty spaces between overwhelming feelings of love and fear and heartbreak.

Liam sat beside me, leaning his back on my side as he sipped beer out of the bottle. "This isn't comfortable," I said, my tone dry in the darkness.

"Can't dangle my legs in the pool in jeans, lass."

I scooted to the left, dislodging him. "Take them off." My voice was huskier than I'd intended.

He eyed me up and down. "All right, baby." He stood and slid off his jeans, giving me an eyeful of his powerful thighs. He grasped the neck of his T-shirt and pulled it off, dropping it onto the brick before sliding off his boxer briefs. My breath whooshed out of me as I watched him. He dove into the pool, then popped up a few seconds later, shaking water out of his red hair.

"Coming in?"

In for a penny, in for a pound.

I stood, then pulled my dress over my head, just in time for Rian and Cormac to walk out of the house. They froze, eating me up with their eyes, then looked at each other and set their beers down on the patio before stripping off their clothes.

Rian ran to the pool with a whoop, cannon balling in. Cormac ambled over to me and wrapped an arm around my waist. "You ready for this, darling?"

I nodded. He stepped behind me and unclasped my strapless bra, letting it fall to the ground. He kissed my shoulder, then traced his lips down my spine until he hooked his fingers under my panties and drew them down my hips. In a daze, I stepped out of them, then turned around to kiss him. He held his lips to mine for a moment, then scooped me up and tossed me into the pool.

I shrieked with laughter as I came up for air. "Asshole!"

Rian was right there, waiting for me to pop out of the water. He stepped back until the water was too deep for me to stand, then wrapped me around him like a koala bear, sliding the slit of my hot and aching pussy up his cock before pressing me tight. He wound me up in seconds, and I mewled as I shifted my hips against him, seeking friction on my clit, my breasts, anything to relieve the needy pressure that he'd unfolded in me.

When his lips met mine, we exploded against each other, teeth and tongues clashing as we tried to climb inside each other, desperate for touch, for closeness. I whimpered as he slid a hand between us and circled my clit with his thumb. Higher and higher I spiraled, until hands grabbed me out of Rian's arms and flipped me over, so I was floating belly-down in the water.

I sputtered and flailed, laughing, as Rian grabbed my hips and Cormac wrapped my arms around his neck, lifting my head out of the water and pulling me in for a scorching kiss. I moaned as Rian plunged inside of me. The pain of the stretch quickly turned into intense bliss as he pounded into me. When his rhythm turned erratic, he started to pull out.

No, that's not what I wanted. "Stop," I whispered.

Cormac grabbed my face, concern in his eyes. "What do you need, darling?"

"I'm clean," I gasped. "On birth control."

Cormac looked over my shoulder at Rian, a smile playing at his lips. "We're clean too. Are you sure?"

I pushed against his shoulders to shove myself back into Rian's pelvis, pushing his cock deep inside me, where it fucking belonged. "I'm goddamned sure," I bit out, as Rian took the hint and resumed his brutal pace. Soon, I was screaming my release into Cormac's mouth. God, the sex with these men was always so fucking good.

Cormac stroked my face as I came down from the bliss of my climax. Rian pushed closer, and I reveled in the feeling of being held by these two men. Liam swam over and I dragged him down for a kiss too.

He leaned his forehead against mine. "You're so fucking gorgeous, Ginevra."

"A gorgeous slut who's been spoiled rotten for the past two days," Cormac murmured into my shoulder.

"*Our* gorgeous, spoiled slut," Rian added, and in that moment, all was right with the world. I was going to make this work. We were going to make this work. Somehow.

I hummed my pleasure, then shivered. "This is a lot less sexy when it's cold. Can we go inside?"

Rian pulled me into his arms. "Let's."

41

GINEVRA

Rian carried me out of the pool and enveloped me in a fluffy towel, his motions gentle and careful, like he was wrapping a delicate and precious gift. When I would have walked inside, Liam swept me off my feet. I wrapped my arms around his neck, kissing his chest, determined to enjoy the ride.

"Careful, love, or we won't make it upstairs," he admonished me as I worked my way down his neck and across his shoulder with my lips. I hummed, pulling his face down so that I could kiss his jawline.

By the time we made it to my bedroom, Rian and Cormac were waiting for us, their eyes hot with need as their gazes swept over my flushed body.

Liam set me down and linked our fingers together.

Cormac cocked his head to the side, thinking, as he ran his eyes over my body. I flushed as his gaze caught on my taut nipples, then the curls at the apex of my thighs.

"Ginevra, what's your safe word?" he asked, his voice low and tight with need.

"Pineapple," I breathed.

"I don't want to blindfold you. Can you close your eyes instead?"

I nodded and let my eyelids flutter down.

"Good girl. Don't open them, no matter what happens, okay?"

A warm hand wrapped itself around my free hand and pulled me forward to the bed. I kept the fingers of my other hand linked with Liam's, not willing to let him step away from me.

"Lie down on your back, darling," Cormac said.

I crawled onto the bed. A hint of wicked mischief shot through me. I let Liam go and raised my hands above my head, arching my back, rubbing my legs against each other, and humming with pleasure.

"Fuck, woman," Rian rasped. Two hot mouths captured my nipples and need shot straight to my pussy, putting an end to my short-lived teasing.

"Fuck, yes," I whimpered as I squirmed under their ministrations, bringing my arms down and tangling my fingers in their hair as they sucked and lashed at my aching peaks.

Cormac's voice hummed against my belly. "Can you hold your arms above your head, darling? Hold on to the headboard?"

Could I? Was I ready for restraint, even if I could let go at any time? My heart beating out of my chest, I slid my arms over the shoulders of the men at my chest and back up above my head. I felt around for the slats of the headboard and wrapped my fingers around two of them, holding tight, as my men kissed my sensitive skin.

"Do you need to use your safeword?" Cormac asked me.

Did I? I tugged on the headboard, testing the strength of my grip. When a fission of fear crept up my spine, I squeezed tighter, focusing on the feeling of Rian's and Liam's mouths on my breasts. One of them bit me, hard, and I cried out, the pain distracting me from my fear, before he replaced it with intense pleasure as he soothed the ache with his tongue.

"I'm okay," I whispered, squeezing my eyes closed against the temptation to peek at these glorious men worshiping my body, worshiping me.

"Such a perfect slut for us," Cormac said, his voice vibrating against my inner thigh. He kissed his way down to my knee, then switched legs, working his way back up again. I could feel the men shuffling around, as mouths popped off my breasts, and hands slid up and down my body.

Resisting the urge to open my eyes, to run my hands over their bodies in turn, I lay there, panting, my heart racing, sweat pooling between my breasts.

A hot mouth kissed down my abdomen, the scratch of his five-o'clock shadow, driving me wild as he made his way down between my legs. "I love you, Ginevra," he whispered as he nuzzled his cheek against the sensitive insides of my thighs.

Lips traced their way up and down my neck, stopping to nip and suck at the sensitive juncture between my neck and my shoulders. I cried with need, but strong hands held me down. "Please," I whispered.

"I love you," the voice at my neck whispered.

A third set of lips trailed their way from my ear to my jaw, before brushing against my lips. "I love you."

"Pineapple," I gasped, opening my eyes and grabbing at the bodies around me. "Fucking pineapple."

Cormac's eyes were stricken as he hovered over me. "Darling, what's wrong?" He brushed the tears away from my cheeks as they poured down my face. "Love, God, I'm so sorry. How do I fix this?"

I shook my head as my tears turned into sobs. "I love you too," I whimpered. "I love you all so fucking much, and I don't know how I'm going to wake up tomorrow and know that you're going to be flying back to Yorkfield in the evening."

Rian dragged us up into a sitting position, settling against my headboard, and nestling me between his thighs, my back pressed to his torso. "Shit. Ginevra, princess—" he sighed, and leaned his head on my shoulder.

"I want you back in my life," Liam asserted, rolling himself between my thighs and gazing up at me, his green eyes wide open and brilliant in the soft light. "Whatever it takes."

"We all do," Rian said, kissing my shoulder. "We want to make this work."

"I do too," I whispered, sniffling.

"Then we will," Cormac said, running his thumb over my knuckles, then bringing my hand up to kiss it. "We'll do whatever it takes, and we'll make this work. I want to grow old with you assholes," he said, his white teeth flashing bright against his brown skin as he grinned widely. "All four of us together, grouchy and grumpy, with gray hair, shouting at kids to get off our lawn. I can't wait."

I smiled at the image.

"Good talk?" Liam asked, apparently distracted by the mess between my thighs.

"Good talk," I moaned as his mouth latched onto my clit.

"Slut," Cormac murmured against my ear as he tweaked my nipple, eliciting a gasp.

"Only for you," I gasped.

"Our slut," Rian confirmed, cupping a breast in his hand

as he kissed my neck. I lolled my head back against his shoulder as my men expertly played my body, driving me at breakneck speed toward bliss. Hands lifted me, pushing me forward until I was on my hands and knees, straddling Liam. I rubbed my clit on his cock before sinking onto him.

"Fuck, Ginny," he swore, as I impaled myself on his length. "You feel so fucking good, every fucking time."

Cormac scooted behind me, taking Rian's place. He didn't give me time to adjust to Liam, before pouring lube over me. He breached my ass, the sudden pressure overwhelming me.

"Easy, darling," he said, his fingers clutching at my hips as he pushed into me, too fast and too slow at the same time. I whined, overwhelmed by the feeling of fullness, every thought flying from my head as I floated in the bliss of them.

When Cormac pulled back, then pushed back in until he was fully seated within me, the sound that escaped me was animal, throaty, a primal cry that begged for more.

Rian tangled his fingers in my hair. He kneeled beside Liam, his cock jutting out from his body, begging for my attention. I darted my head forward and licked the pre-cum seeping out from him. His ragged groan poured gasoline on the fire of my need, and I rocked back and forth between Cormac and Liam, seeking the friction that would push me over the cliff of my release.

I opened my mouth, and Rian circled my swollen lips with the head of his cock, teasing me before he plunged into me. As if that were the signal, Cormac and Liam began pumping in and out of me. I could feel their cocks inside of me, rubbing each other through the thin membrane. I could barely breathe, the intensity of being filled with them short-circuiting my brain.

Rian held onto my head, pushing his cock between my

lips as I bobbed up and down between Liam and Cormac. Unable to hold any sort of rhythm, as the two men sandwiched me, I opened up my jaw and drooled as he carefully delved deeper, until he was fucking my mouth deep and rough. Tears streamed down my face as the three of them pounded into me, tension curling tighter and tighter in my center until I was ready to explode. When Cormac reached around me with one hand to pinch a nipple tightly, the pain sent me hurtling out into space, screaming my pleasure as my climax ripped through me, intensifying as they slammed in and out of me, each of them finishing inside of me, until I was a sticky, dripping mess of satisfaction.

Rian cupped my face in his hand as my arms trembled, pushing the stream of cum that dripped down out of my mouth back into me. "Swallow again, love," he commanded. I did, licking my lips and reveling in the salty taste, the sense of being utterly full of these dangerous men who satisfied me so completely.

Cormac drew me down to him as Liam pulled out. I heard water running in the bathroom, and a few seconds later, one of them wiped between my thighs with a warm towel.

Utterly replete and incapable of putting a coherent thought together, I let them maneuver and position me in the bed until I lay snuggled between Rian and Liam.

Cormac bent over Liam and kissed my forehead. "I'm going to lock up. I'll be back in a minute, my loves."

I didn't know what the next day would bring, but for the first time in weeks, I was excited to see what waited for me, what waited for *us*, when we woke up.

. . .

"I'VE SPENT the last three days trying to get her to eat her damn vegetables, and the first thing you do is order junk food for breakfast?"

Cormac leaned against the doorframe, staring into the kitchen. The strip of deep brown abs between his T-shirt and his sweats drew my eye, and he winked at me when he noticed the direction of my gaze.

Liam shrugged, grinning, as he sliced into the waffle and fried chicken in front of us then held a forkful to my mouth. "She says she's been on her knees for every meal since you arrived. I figured she could use a change, just for breakfast."

My eyes flicked to Cormac's, unsure of whether I'd violated the unspoken contract we had between us—my submission in return for his care—by sitting here on the barstool, eating with Rian and Liam.

I needn't have worried.

Cormac kissed the top of my head as he walked past with bare feet. "I don't know very many people who live that lifestyle twenty four-seven, or that either of us would want to. Why don't we just take it day by day until we figure out what works for us in the long term? We should have a conversation about hard and soft limits at some point, too."

"In the meantime, take a look at these." Rian slid a folder across the kitchen island. I flipped through it, my eyes raising at the photos within. It was office space, sun drenched and modern. The plans followed, with conference rooms, a server room, studio space, and a corner office with my name on it.

I looked up at him, only to find his blue eyes watching me, a hint of uncertainty in them. "What is this?"

"Your East Coast office, if you want it. It's two entire floors of our building." He wouldn't meet my eyes, as if worried I wouldn't accept. God, they'd spent the last two weeks rearranging their entire lives so they could keep me safe, to make a space for me to fit into them, and he worried I wasn't going to say yes?

I leaned toward Rian and drew his face to mine, meeting his syrupy sticky lips with my own. "Fucking yes, I want it. I'm coming back with you on Monday."

He leaned his forehead against mine. "We're really gonna do this."

I grinned. "Yeah, yeah, we are."

"We're going to be unstoppable together, you know that?" Liam grinned.

"Damn straight." I tilted my mouth back to Rian's and stole another quick and sticky kiss before dragging Cormac and Liam over for the same.

Thank God, I picked up the phone when Sofia called asking me for help.

EPILOGUE
RIAN

I stared as Ginevra walked up the aisle on her father's arm. She wore a short-sleeved wedding gown of cream, shot through with gold. Her skin glowed in the afternoon light. Step by step, she walked over the white petals one of her cousins had strewn in the grass of her family's backyard. Our girl was so fucking gorgeous. Once again, I marveled at how lucky we were that she'd agreed to swap places with her sister.

Ginevra and Patti had compromised on the commitment ceremony. In every aspect except for the officiant, the location, and the utter lack of mass, it resembled a traditional Catholic wedding. Nobody blinked an eye at our unusual arrangement, possibly because they'd had six months of exhausting back-and-forth flights to get used to the idea. So close to New York, Ginevra hadn't had any problems finding talent on this side of the country, and had opened up her East Coast HQ just two months ago.

Cormac nudged me, amusement in his eyes. "Pick your jaw up off the ground."

I shook my head. "She's fucking stunning."

Antonio lifted her veil, then placed her hand in mine. I took my place to her left, and Cormac took his beside Liam, to her right. The four of us linked hands. We were really going to do this.

Ginevra eschewed the large part of preparations for the ceremony, leaving them in Sofia and my capable hands. The two of us became fast friends, taking delight in driving Ginevra up a wall.

The officiant invoked the ceremony, but kept it short and sweet. When it was my turn to take my vows, I turned to my lovers, my best friends, the people I wanted to spend the rest of my life walking beside.

"I, Rian O'Conner, take you all, Ginevra Russo, Liam Byrne, and Cormac Wallace, to be my family. I promise to be true to you in good times and in bad, in sickness and in health. I will love you and honor you all the days of my life."

We'd kept our vows simple and traditional. Ginevra was the last to say hers, and when she finished, joyful tears streamed down her face.

I pulled four rings out of my pocket, connected with a red ribbon. My brow furrowed with concentration as I untied the bow and slipped them into my palm. The others clustered around me and I slid a ring onto each of their ring fingers until only one remained in my hand.

Ginevra picked it up, grinning. "Last chance to change your mind."

I laughed and brushed a knuckle against her chin. "I would never."

She slid it onto my finger. I wrapped my hand around hers and raised her knuckles to my lips. "Almost done."

Ginevra's tongue darted out to lick her lips and suddenly I couldn't wait for the ceremony and the reception and the endless formalities to be over. Her eyes flicked up to mine, as if she could hear my thoughts. She winked slowly and deliberately.

She reached and pulled my ear down to her lips. "I'm not wearing any panties, Rian."

I swear, my eyes fucking crossed with lust. The officiant must have heard her, because he looked discomfited. He cleared his throat, as if to remind us we needed to finish the ceremony before we could consummate the marriage.

I leaned down to trace my lips over the sensitive shell of her ear, enjoying her shiver. "Such a slutty goddess on her wedding day."

When I pulled back, her eyes were dazed too. The officiant gamely soldiered on, ignoring the two of us. When he pronounced our polycule a family, the guests roared their approval.

Liam bent down to brush her lips, then pulled in Cormac for a gentle kiss. I dragged Ginevra to me and resisted the temptation to slam my lips into hers and ravage her, right then and there. Instead, I gently kissed her lips, her cheeks, her forehead, and her nose until she giggled. "Can't muss your make-up until we get you somewhere private, love."

Liam and Cormac were breathless when they pulled away from each other, but finally, we turned to face the crowd of cheering, excited guests together.

Together.

We'd done it.

Hell yeah, we did. And I was never going to let them go.

***

THANK you for reading Diamond in the Dark. Reviews mean so much to indie authors like me. Please consider leaving one on Amazon, Goodreads, or your favorite social media.

Sofia's story is next! For a sneak peek at the first chapter of Lies like Rubies, sign-up for my newsletter. For exclusive updates on new stories and books, join my reader group on Facebook, or visit my website at http://poppyjacobsonbooks.com.

ACKNOWLEDGMENTS

First, thank you for reading Diamond in the Dark. I'm so glad you took a chance on my debut.

As a new author, I have been delighted to find that writing a story is in no way a solitary experience. I owe a debt of gratitude to my fellow sprinters and critiquers from the Romance Writer's Club Facebook group, the Readers Writing Romance discord, and the Poly/ WhyChoose/ RH Authors group—all amazing and welcoming communities of writers.

Geneva Monroe (the similarity in first names is a coincidence!), you were the first one to read a chapter from this book, and you reassured me that this idea wasn't ridiculous and encouraged me to keep writing it.

Katina J. Rose, you've been a lifesaver in so many ways, from reassuring me I'm on the right track to brainstorming ideas, to critiquing, to checking in when I've had a rough day.

Emma Penny, you advised me early on to treat writing like a job, and it's the best advice I've gotten yet about writing. Hold my beer, I have another ridiculous idea.

Heather E. Andrews, thank you for both your incessant personal encouragement and your amazing and professional editing.

To my amazing alpha, beta, and gamma readers, if a single person enjoys this book, it's because of your frank feedback.

Thank you all for being such amazing and supportive human beings.

And finally, I've been blessed with a spouse who not only understands, but actively supports me as I disappear into my cave (aka a corner of the living room) to churn out words night after night after night. *Merci beaucoup!*

ABOUT POPPY

Poppy Jacobson writes dark, kinky, reverse harem and poly romances where the heroine never has to choose between her love interests. She lives in Virginia with her husband and kids. When she's not dreaming up tales of murder, mayhem, and smut, she loves hiking, crafting, and making soup.

For news and updates about Poppy's writing, subscribe to her newsletter at http://poppyjacobsonbooks.com.

You can also find Poppy here:

Tiktok: https://www.tiktok.com/@poppyjacobsonbooks
Instagram: https://www.instagram.com/poppyjacobsonbooks/
Facebook: https://fb.me/PoppyJacobsonBooks

Printed in Great Britain
by Amazon